For Joan

We'll always have "O'Malley's."

Acknowledgements

I would like to thank the following people for their kind assistance: Asst. Police Chief Kevin McGowan, Dr. Laurette Geldenhuys, Rhea McGarva, Helen MacDonnell, Joan Butcher and Edna Barker. And, as always, Joe A. and PJEC. All characters and plots in the story are fictional, as are some of the locations. Other places are real. Any liberties taken in the interests of fiction, or any errors committed, are mine alone.

March 31, 1991

The old woman knew it all. He was convinced of that. And there she sat, smug and hostile in her flat, in possession of the diaries and other secret records that could explain — and expose — the whole sinister affair. He found entertainment for himself that night in the drinking dens of lower Manhattan. But his mind had homed in on a single point: the collection of papers in the old lady's flat in a rundown house in Brooklyn. He didn't know how he was going to do it, but he was going to walk out of there with the papers in his hands. No more secrets, no more fear of exposure.

He was in a foul mood by the time he arrived at the house the next morning. What were the chances she would give up, or peddle for an extortionate price, the incriminating papers? The day was hot and bright, but she was not to be seen in her regular spot on the stoop, basking lizard-like in the sun. He rapped on her door. No reply. He rapped again, louder. He did not want to make two trips — he never wanted to see her again — so it had to be now. He tried the door knob and pushed. The door swung open. He called her name as he stepped into the hallway. Silence.

When he looked into her living room, he reeled backwards in shock. The room was a shambles of blood and chaos; the smell of death overpowered the stale odour of smoke that hung in the room. He fought down the urge to be sick. His first thought — and it shamed him — was: "What did I touch?" His second thought was to look down at his feet to make sure he had not stepped in anything that would show up in a shoe print. The woman was face down on the floor, blood pooled around her head. There was spatter on the walls and the couch. Resting against the top of her head was a heavy marble ashtray. He didn't have to be a forensic investigator to know it had been used to club her to death. Ashes and cigarette butts littered the floor around her. He remembered some figurines she had displayed in a cabinet; they were nowhere in sight. Books had been yanked from her bookcase in the corner. The scene suggested she had been dead for a while. But not that long: he had been there himself less than twenty-four hours ago. Was that why she had been killed, because he had been there?

Every instinct told him to bolt. But he steeled himself to go through with his plan, to retrieve the papers. To learn the truth himself, and to keep it from the shadowy figures who seemed to be circling around him. He was treading on dangerous ground, interfering with a crime scene and plotting a theft of what would be key evidence for the police investigating her death. But he took a deep breath and told himself to get moving. Then he noticed a pair of worn bedroom slippers sticking out of the hall closet. He removed his shoes and socks, and shoved his bare feet into the slippers. Let those be the footprints they find, if any. As he made his way to the back of the flat, he was relieved to see that the blood and gore were confined to the area immediately around the victim. He peered into the first bedroom. Like the living room, it had been tossed. An old-fashioned jewellery box had been upended on the bed; the mattress was askew as if someone had groped beneath it. On the floor beside the bed was a plastic shopping bag with photographs spilling out of it; he dumped the pictures and wrapped the bag around his right hand before touching any items in the room. No papers. He proceeded to the other bedroom. Here again all the items had been rifled. Two battered leather briefcases had been wrenched open and left empty. He searched every drawer and shelf but found no documents, no diary. He had just entered the kitchen when he heard a sudden creaking sound, and his heart banged in his chest. He stood perfectly still, covered in a sheen of sweat. Nothing happened. After a few tense moments he resumed his quest but again found nothing. How long till someone came to the flat? He grabbed a paper towel from the holder and left the kitchen. He looked ahead through the hallway to the front door and saw a car slowing down in front of the house. He held his breath. It moved on. Probably just on the hunt for a parking space. He searched the front closet, only to confirm what he already knew: the papers were gone.

Had the woman herself destroyed them before falling victim to a murderer's hand? Was this a simple break-in, someone preying on a crippled old lady, taking a few keepsakes to be sold at a flea market? Unlikely. The burglar had one purpose and one purpose alone: the retrieval of the records that had been a threat to somebody's security for forty years. The theft of the woman's trinkets was a cover-up. Was the murder a by-product of the need to get the papers? Or was it a planned execution?

Prologue

Pater noster qui es in coelis sanctificetur nomen tuum
Adveniat regnum tuum
Fiat voluntas tua sicut in coelo et in terra.

Our Father who art in heaven, hallowed be Thy name,
Thy kingdom come,
Thy will be done on earth as it is in heaven.

March 3, 1991

The white-robed priest, murder charges now behind him, lifted his arms, and the building was filled with the music of the spheres. Candlelight illumined the small Gothic church of Saint Bernadette's and flickered against the magnificent stained glass of its windows. My little daughter sat at my side, enthralled with the beauty and the sound. On my other side was my son and his beloved, herself a budding choir director; they too were enraptured. At the end of the row sat the mother of my children, the wife who no longer shared my home. Lost in the music. Lost to me.

We were transported back in time from the Renaissance to the medieval as we heard the famous Gregorian *Pater Noster,* the Our Father. It is said that Mozart, when asked which piece of music he would like to have composed, named this setting of the *Pater Noster.* At times like this, when the music seemed to shimmer between light and sound, between the earthly and the ineffable, I could almost understand how a priest could turn away from the pleasures of the flesh and marry his spirit with the divine. This particular priest had stumbled the odd time, as I well knew. As everyone knew, after the trial. But he had picked himself up, brushed the dust from his robes and carried on. The glory of this night, the first student concert he had put on since coming to the Saint Bernadette's Choir School as music director a year and half ago, would buoy him through the next two days until it was time to leave for New York, for a rendezvous with his former lover, and a probe into the enigmatic past of his redoubtable father. If we had been able to foretell the events of the coming weeks, perhaps we would have remained in the sanctuary, contemplating the infinite and ordering in.

Chapter 1

March 4, 1991

"My old fellow aged ten years when he read this, Monty. See what you make of it."

The choirmaster was in my Halifax law office when I arrived the Monday morning after the concert. In civilian clothes Brennan Burke had the appearance of a military man, one regularly chosen for clandestine, lethal operations. With his hooded black eyes, silver-threaded black hair and austere facial expression, he was a formidable presence. He spoke in a clipped voice reminiscent of Ireland, where he had lived until the age of ten. That is when his family had fled the old country for New York, for reasons that had never been explained. The priest had come to Halifax eighteen months ago, in the fall of 1989, to establish the choir school at Saint Bernadette's. It had been quite a time. He and I had met when he was charged with two counts of first degree murder in the deaths of two young women. I am happy to say I successfully defended him against the charges, and found the real killer, who is now serving a life sentence in prison. All in a day's work for Montague Collins, Barrister, Solicitor and sole criminal lawyer in the corporate law firm of Stratton Sommers.

The priest pulled a piece of paper from the inside pocket of his black leather jacket and slapped it on my desk, and I directed my attention to whatever it was that had taken ten years off the life of Declan Burke. It was an obituary from the *New York Times* dated December 4, 1990. Three months ago.

"My brother Patrick sent it to me. He was visiting our parents. The old fellow was trying to fix something under the sink, and my mother was doing her customary scan of the death notices. 'Declan!' she calls out. 'Do you know a Cathal Murphy? Came over here from Dublin around the same time we did.'

"My father comes in to the living room and takes a look at the obit. The way Patrick tells it, Declan turned white and grew old in the time it took to read it over. 'Da, what is it?' Patrick asks, and tries to get him into a chair. 'Your face has gone the colour of your hair.'

"All Pat gets by way of an answer is: 'I straightened up too fast. You'd be white too if you had your mug parked under a sink all afternoon, then had to stand to attention for another dead Murphy.' And he stalks from the room."

I put up my hand to silence Brennan so I could read the clipping.

CATHAL MURPHY, 73, of Sunnyside, Queens, and formerly of Dublin, Republic of Ireland. He immigrated to the US in 1950 after working in Ireland as a Businessman. What is less well known is that he put in many long and arduous hours doing Volunteer work as well. Here in the US, Cathal quickly made a name for himself in the export business. His loyalty to his Uncle was never in question. He is survived by his devoted wife Maria, and his sons Tom, Brendan, Stanley and Armand. Predeceased by his brother Benedict and stepson Stephen. Those of us who had the privilege of knowing Cathal knew a man who enjoyed a good time, who was never shy about sharing a song or a drink. And if you said no, Cathal would share it with you anyway! He'll be sorely missed. When the members of a generation pass away, the family is often left with little more than its memories; the telling details are locked away in a trunk and never get out of the attic. A better way — Cathal's way — was to celebrate and live the past as if it formed part of the present, as indeed it does. He was fond of saying "nothing ever goes away." You're right, Cathal. Your spirit lives on in our hearts. We'll all be there to see you off, Cathal, dressed to the nines and raising a pint of Lameki Jocuzasem in your honor! Funeral arrangements will be announced when finalized.

Brennan resumed speaking the second my eyes looked up from the clipping. "How often would you say 'Republic of' in something like this?"

"Let me stop you for a second. What is it that has everyone upset? Is this someone your father knew? Someone he had a history with?"

Burke jabbed the paper with his forefinger. "What Patrick thinks, and I'm following him there myself, is that our father read this as —" he cleared his throat "— as an indictment of his own life. And an announcement of his death."

"What?" I exclaimed.

"Volunteer," he said then. "It's capitalized."

"So's 'Businessman.' You should see what gets capitalized here in the office. Lawyer, Adjuster, Report . . ."

He ignored me. "The Irish Volunteers. *Óglaigh na hÉireann*, the IRA. That much is clear. All the more so when the word 'Uncle' is added. My father's father and his uncles were known to have played a role in the 1916 uprising. 'He is survived by his devoted wife Maria.' Maria, a name that could be Spanish like my mother's name, Teresa. As you know, she had a Spanish father, Irish mother. A possibility. We're told he was also survived by his sons Tom, Brendan, Stanley and Armand." He looked at me. "Those four names. Does anything strike you about them?"

"No. Aside from the fact they are all men's names, and one of them sounds like yours — but isn't — I don't see a pattern. They're not even all Irish."

"Right, but Tommy, Bren —" He paused. I waited. "Guns, Collins."

"Brennan, for Christ's sake! This just doesn't sound like you. I can imagine your reaction if someone else came up with this, this —"

"Fantasy, you're thinking. I know, but Patrick and I both think there's something here and he's not a fey kind of man either. And we weren't stocious drunk when we spoke about this on the phone. So bear with me. Tommy gun, Bren gun, Sten gun, Armalite rifle."

"Brennan," I began and put up my hand to fend off an interruption. "Surely it has occurred to you that you may be reading something into this, something that is not really there."

"It has occurred to me. I've dismissed that notion. It's here, I know it." He paused to take out a pack of cigarettes from his jacket pocket. I had given up telling him that Stratton Sommers was a smoke-free office; he found the ashtray I kept for him, lit up a smoke, and returned to his train of thought. "Predeceased by his brother Benedict and by his stepson Stephen. Now, disregard those two names for a moment. I admit they throw me off, because my father did not have a brother who died, and he certainly does not have a stepson."

I shook my head, moved the paper closer with my finger and skimmed the obituary again. "I'm more interested in the pint of 'Lameki Jocuzasem.' What in the hell is that?"

"No idea. Doesn't sound like a local brew, does it? Let's stop by the Midtown Tavern and ask one of the waiters."

"Let's not. I'd like to be able to show my face in there again some day. And the day after that."

What I did not say was that I would like to enjoy the upcoming New York trip my family and I had planned with Brennan Burke. He had been asked to officiate at the wedding of his niece, Katie, and he decided to extend his visit for a few weeks. I hoped his distraction over the death notice would be short-lived. Brennan certainly needed a break, after the year he'd just had. And I could use a rest as well. My holiday was to start the very next day. I had leapt at the chance of a month in New York when a complicated products liability suit had been settled on the courthouse steps, affording me the gift of several weeks with no obligations. I was determined to take advantage of the free time. My wife, Professor Maura MacNeil, had strong-armed someone into taking over her classes at Dalhousie Law School for three weeks, so we could give our kids a trip to New York City.

I mentioned my wife; I should have said "estranged wife." But I'm not one to give up easily. I saw the vacation as an opportunity to put an end to years of squabbling and living in separate houses. After all, if I could oversee the settlement of years of squabbling and costly litigation between the consumers, suppliers and manufacturers of defective concrete, which had caused the foundations of two hundred new houses to sink and crumble, how difficult would it be to charm my own wife back into my loving embrace?

Chapter 2

Doris Day sang "Sentimental Journey"
and the band played "Don't Go Back That Way Again."
— Maynard T. Maitland, "Back That Way Again"

March 5, 1991

I called Brennan the next morning, the day of our departure, to confirm the plans we had made for our first evening in New York. I was catching a later flight with my family but we would be there in plenty of time to meet him in the lobby of the Metropolitan Opera House, where we would be seeing a new production of *Norma*. Our teenage son, Tommy Douglas, and his little sister, Normie, were not at all displeased that they would have the hotel room, with its pay-per-view movies and room service, to themselves while we were at the opera.

"You're bringing the family to the wedding," Brennan said. It was a statement, not a question. "It's at seven o'clock Friday evening."

"Did you inform your brother that four strangers will be showing up at his daughter's wedding and reception?"

"Everyone knows you're coming and, if they didn't, who'd notice you in a crowd of three hundred other people?"

I took that as the gracious invitation it was no doubt meant to be.

"So, Brennan," I asked, "have you issued an invitation to Sandra to join you at the wedding?"

"Hardly."

"Why 'hardly'? She's an old friend of the family, through you, and you gave me to understand you'd be looking her up whenever we made a trip to New York. You're going to see her, right?"

He made a kind of noncommittal noise. He might or he might not; it was of no importance.

He had not seen Sandra Worthington, formerly the love of his life, in the quarter century that had passed since his ordination as a celibate priest. But I had met her; I interviewed her at her posh Manhattan apartment while conducting research for Brennan's trial. Then, after he was exonerated, Sandra showed up unexpectedly at a concert in which he was guest conductor. She had been overseeing repairs at her family's old summer home in Chester, and had driven to Halifax for the concert. Her arrival had rendered Brennan speechless. But once he recovered himself, he, Sandra, Maura and I had spent a couple of hours at the post-concert party, drinking, talking, reminiscing, bickering . . . just like old times for all of us. Sandra had departed early, leaving Brennan to do his best not to look bereft. Now, it seemed, we were back to "Sandra who?"

Well, not quite, as it turned out. "You'll be seeing her tonight."

"I'll be seeing her, Brennan, or you will?"

"We all will. I called her. I ordered four tickets for the opera. Now, I'm busy here and have to sign off." Click.

It would be nice to say the journey to New York went smoothly, that nobody forgot a garment bag at home and had to go back, that we arrived in good time for check-in, that the airline didn't have to delay take-off for us, that the taxi ride from LaGuardia airport into Manhattan was cheap and quick and there was no traffic jam, and that everybody was in a relaxed holiday mood when we got to our hotel near Central Park. But I can't make any of those claims.

Maura and I began sniping at each other as soon as the "fasten seat belts" sign lit up on our departure from Halifax, and it wasn't about the travel snafus. When I arrived at her house on Dresden Row and went inside to help with the family's luggage, what did I hear but her on the phone to the Latin Lothario who had kept her company over the past year. I thought he had dropped out of her life — apparently not. She was giving him her entire travel itinerary. She and the kids — no mention of old Monty — would be arriving in New York at such-and-such a time; tomorrow she was taking the kids on the train to Philadelphia, where she would be participating in a law conference in her role as Professor MacNeil; they would be back in New York early Friday evening in time for a friend's wedding. She gave him the name and address of the hotel in Philly, but not the one in New York.

I quizzed her about this Giacomo. Was she perhaps expecting him at the hotel in Philadelphia? Or was she just hoping for a call? Did she not share my hopes that this vacation would lead to a reconciliation between us? My tone of voice was quiet, reasonable. Her approach, as always, was to treat a marital spat like a debate in her classroom at the Law School: "Collins. Do I understand you to have inferred, based on your shameful and inexcusable skulking around in my house and eavesdropping on a private phone call, that I have procured the services of someone who, according to your overheated fantasies, will fly into Philadelphia where I am sharing a room with our son and daughter, and consort with me in said hotel room without regard for even the most minimal standards of acceptable behaviour, standards so minimal that even you, on a slow night, might be able to live up to them, is that what you're suggesting?" That sort of argument. I've often wondered whether lawyers should be legally prohibited from marrying each other. Anyway, we had ranged far from the original conflict by the time things went nuclear at the hotel. The kids headed downstairs to explore the building and we let 'er rip. Good thing we had reserved a suite with two bedrooms. We were going to need them.

Be that as it may, Maura and I were together in the red-carpeted lobby of the Metropolitan Opera House that Tuesday evening, waiting for Father Burke and his date. I hoped things were going better for them than they were for us. Nonetheless, I had to admit my escort was looking delectable — if hostile — in an elegant black dress and a new hairdo. Maura MacNeil is a woman of unfashionably soft figure and sweet face, a face that belies her astringent personality. Tonight at the opera house her almond-shaped grey eyes were made up and looked enormous, her glossy brown hair was piled casually atop her head, and her generous mouth was stained to give the appearance that she had been gorging on raspberries all day. I was in my best suit and tie, wishing I were one of the stage crew so I could wear a T-shirt, hear the music, and get away from my spouse.

She looked ready to reload and start firing at me again when she raised her eyebrows and stared towards the door. I turned to follow her gaze. Brennan, dressed in a beautifully cut dinner jacket, with his black hair silvering on the sides, his dark eyes and haughty countenance, could have been the maestro for the evening. He cast an appreciative eye towards Maura and said something that escaped my hearing. He looked tense.

"Where's your date?" I asked him.

"Meeting us here."

"So you haven't seen her yet?"

"No. Where are Tommy Douglas and Normie tonight?"

"Watching movies in the hotel room. I had to promise Normie, who after all is named for the opera, that if it's really good, I'll bring her to see it sometime during our stay. Tom's dying to get out and see the city, but . . ."

That's when Sandra swept in. She wore a long black skirt and a watered silk tunic in the palest of blue. A delicate necklace and earrings looked silver but were probably platinum. Her short, light brown hair was brushed back from her sculptured face. Yet even with hundreds of years of cool WASP breeding behind her, she looked less than serene. She and Brennan stood looking at each other, neither of them speaking.

"You look brilliant this evening, Sandra," Maura prompted, in an accent roughly approximating Burke's. Then, higher in pitch: "You're a handsome devil yourself, Brennan. Isn't it marvellous to see each other again?"

Brennan reached out, took Sandra's hand and gave her a chaste kiss on the cheek. "'Tis indeed grand to see you," he said lightly. "It's too bad you didn't have time for dinner beforehand. Perhaps after."

"Perhaps so."

She offered him a fleeting smile and came over to embrace me. In spite of the fact that our friendship had been formed in the stressful months before Brennan's trial, Sandra and I had shared some laughs, and I had heard tales from her past with Brennan, before his thunderbolt call to the priesthood. I had even scribbled a little twelve-bar blues on the subject.

Sandra turned to Maura, whom she had met briefly in Halifax, and the two women greeted each other warmly.

I essayed a bit of conversation. "Who will you be betting on tonight, Brennan? The Celts or the Romans? After all you have a foot in both camps."

"I'll go for whichever side acquits itself best in the vocal department. It will be hard to beat the first *Norma* I heard, though. Thirty-five years ago. Maria Callas in 1956. At the old Met, downtown. It got off to a slow start; I don't know if it was the heat or Callas's nerves. But by Act II it was magical. Sixteen curtain calls."

"You were a little young though, Brennan, to appreciate the story of a Celtic priestess who breaks her holy oath and gives way to her passion for a Roman proconsul," Sandra put in.

If it was a dig, he didn't let on but said evenly: "At sixteen I understood the passion, if not the priestliness."

"And now?"

"Now it's time to face the music." Maura headed in first, followed by Brennan and Sandra. I got the aisle seat. We were in Row A near the back of the auditorium. Five levels of balconies rose above us. We sat, eyes front, until the chandeliers were raised, the massive gold curtain rose and the great drama began. The soprano, a young woman of Greek nationality, had been inevitably and unfairly compared to Callas. But once I got used to the cooler vocal tone and less dramatic persona, I found myself immersed in 50 BC Gaul. The magnificent aria "Casta Diva" comes in Act I, scene i, when the Druid high priestess invokes the moon and prays for peace. Let some of it descend on us:

Casta Diva, che inargenti
queste sacre antiche piante
a noi volgi il bel sembiante
senza nube e senza vel . . .

O chaste Goddess, who silver
these sacred ancient plants,
turn thy beautiful semblance on us
unclouded and unveiled . . .

At intermission, conversation was muted. Brennan did not look like
a man whose homecoming had lived up to his expectations. He was
determined to speak of other things. Apparently his first *Norma*, with
his parents and sister Molly, was memorable in more ways than one.

> *New York City, 1956*
> *Here we are in the lobby of the Metropolitan Opera House. The
> four of us: Da and Mam, Molly and me. I took a bit of slagging from
> the lads about coming out for the opera. Feck 'em! There's more to
> music than the tin whistle. What's this now? Who's this woman who's
> launched herself at Da, roaring and screeching at him? The brogue on
> her — she sounds like something right off the boat from Cobh. The
> woman looks even older than Mam; what did he do, get her up the
> pole? She doesn't look it. I've seen more meat on Good Friday than I'm
> seeing on her.*
> *"I knew I could find you here, Declan Burke! I heard about you
> gettin' the tickets. All fine and good for those that can carry on and go
> to the opera. You won't see my family here — the family you destroyed!
> How can you sleep at night, Mr. Burke? How can you show your face
> at Mass on Sunday?" Ah, here come the ushers to take her away. What's
> that she's giving to Mam? A big envelope of sorts. "Let her read what
> you've done. And may you roast for all eternity in the fires of hell!"
> Jazes! There, they've got her out of here. What was she on about?*
> *Mam is standing there, all speech forsaken. Da's going for the enve-
> lope. Mam won't let go of it. Oh, the look she's giving him. His face
> doesn't have a drop of colour left in it. Is he going to be sick right here
> in the lobby of the Met? Mam has the envelope in her bag. Oul Dec
> will be lucky if she doesn't stuff it down his throat. Time to go and hear
> Maria; she'll have to hit some high Cs to top this.*

"Well?" Maura asked. "Who was she? What was going on?"
"I have no idea. Neither of them would ever speak of it. Next day

I rooted around trying to find the envelope. Couldn't lay my hands on it. Neither could Molly."

"I didn't know you had a sister named Molly," Maura said.

"My older sister, Maire. Nickname Molly."

"Well, I hope she tells the story better than you do. So you never found out who the mystery woman was — that shouldn't get in the way of a hair-raising ending to the tale. Make it up if you have to. I'll never bring you home to Cape Breton if you can't do better than that!"

"Maybe the point is: men by the name of Burke don't seem to make much of a hit with the ladies at the Metropolitan Opera." He directed a quizzical glance at Sandra.

"This evening wasn't my idea, Brennan."

Brennan looked suddenly weary. "I know it wasn't, Sandy. I know it wasn't."

He turned away and started towards the auditorium. Maura caught up with him and put a hand on his arm. Whatever she said to him provoked a quick, impatient shake of the head and he continued on to his seat. I put an arm around Sandra. "What's the matter, Sandy? You've hardly spoken a word."

"Monty, I just don't know what to say to him. I don't understand the life he's chosen. He hasn't asked about my life either: about my children, about my late husband, about any of our old acquaintances. It's as if neither of us wants to acknowledge the last quarter of a century."

"Try not to be too rough on him. He's coming off a very bad year."

"I know, Monty, but he's not facing reality. Let's go inside."

We sat down again. Brennan trained his dark eyes on Sandra for a long, searching look, but said nothing. The curtain went up, the performance resumed, and we found ourselves once again in a world of passion and treachery, prayer and sacrifice.

After the opera we walked up Columbus Avenue to a restaurant called Da Gimignano. We were seated in a large dining room with wall frescoes that depicted the medieval towers of San Gimignano, and other scenes from Tuscany. A waiter appeared immediately to take our orders for drinks. When they arrived, Brennan downed his whiskey and raised his glass for a refill. We all ordered dinner. Maura and I chatted quite companionably about our plans for the next few days. The other two gradually warmed to the conversation and suggested things we should do, or not do, in New York. By the time our orders arrived, the atmosphere had lightened up.

"So, Sandra, what was it like growing up with this guy?"

"Do you mean before he dedicated himself to a life of celibacy? The rationale for which is what again Brennan? Did you ever explain it?"

He raised his glass to his lips, lowered it, opened his mouth as if to speak, shut it. I could almost see the two opposing impulses warring within his soul. The Catholic apologist wanted to give a learned dissertation on the reasons for the Church's insistence on a celibate priestly caste; the regular guy wanted to get the subject off the table, in order to salvage what little chance he still might have of getting lucky at the end of the evening.

"Let's not get into that again," was his reply.

"Again? I didn't realize I was becoming tedious on the subject. After all, this is the first time I've mentioned it in twenty-five years. It's only the second time I've laid eyes on you in all that time." She sipped her wine, then turned to Maura. "But if I go way, way back I seem to remember there was something endearing about him. Everyone certainly noted his arrival at Mrs. Liebenthal's Music School, which is where we met. On the Upper West Side. He had this lovely, lilting brogue — well, you can still hear a rather brusque version of it in his voice now. Black hair, black eyes, a darling smile. He sang like an angel. And I remember our first kiss. It wasn't a success. We were around twelve at the time."

"That's right. She was leaving our house in a taxi and I had worked up the nerve to kiss her goodbye. But I had a fat lip from fighting with my brothers. And the whole crowd of them were lined up in the window staring at us, their eyes out on sticks."

"He tried to kiss me but his lip was bleeding and I said: 'Eeeuuwww, stay away from me!'" She sighed. "If only it had ended then and there."

"You don't mean that, now," he prompted.

"Well?" The edge was back in her voice.

"All the good times we had. You can't regret that." He leaned close and fixed her with his eyes. "Intensely good times."

"Which made the bad times all the more intense for us both, wouldn't you say?" She reached down for her handbag. "Excuse me a moment, would you?"

We turned our attention to the remains of our meal as she walked to the back of the restaurant. Brennan signalled for another whiskey; I decided the wiser course would be coffee; Maura opted for tea.

"And how is your trip to New York, Mr. and Mrs. Collins?"

"This is only your first night, Brennan. She . . . she just has to get used to you," Maura tried.

"Stuff it, MacNeil. I don't want to hear it." Brennan lit up a cigarette and fanned the smoke away from us. We heard an ostentatious cough behind his shoulder. He had fanned the smoke into the face of the returning Sandra. "Shit," he said. "I'm sorry."

"So many bad habits, Brennan, so little time and space in which to indulge them."

Maura sought to redirect the conversation: "What did you make of Brennan's father, Sandra? Brennan seems to think there's a death threat against Declan!"

Sandra stared at Burke. "Really!"

Brennan was silent, so Maura filled the gap. "A death threat disguised as the obituary of someone named Murphy, or so Collins tells me. Do you have it with you, Brennan? I haven't seen it, though the whole thing sounds a little, well, over the top."

"Let's leave that aside for tonight," Brennan replied.

"Well, he was unpopular with somebody," Sandra told us. "Remember that shoving match?" When Burke gave her a blank look, she continued: "Don't you remember a rather bulky man coming to the house and your father nearly slamming the door on your mother's nose, trying to head the guy off? It's funny, I haven't thought of that in decades. It was when we were older, so you may have been passed out drunk at the time." He started to protest but she cut him off. "I was in the living room."

"Go on."

"There was a man at the door, heavyset, taller than your father, and he spoke with a thick accent."

"What kind of an accent? Like my father's, you mean?"

"No, not an Irishman. Just New York, outer boroughs."

"What did they say?"

"I couldn't make it all out, or maybe I've forgotten. But I do remember your father telling him to get the fuck off his property. I had never heard my own father swear, ever, so I was absolutely agog at the scene. The man made a reply to your father about the house. Declan said something like: 'I paid cash for it.' Or I think it was: 'I gave the gougers a great stack of bills for it.' I was picturing a man in a top hat and moustache walking away with a tottering pile of money. So Declan said it was his house and he didn't want this other guy in it.

"There was more arguing, then the guy accused your father of stealing, said he'd seen Declan stuff an envelope into his pocket. Declan told him to F-off or whatever, and gave him a shove. The guy shoved back. They stared at each other and the man walked away."

Sandra sipped her wine, then went on. "Declan could be intimidating, no question. But he had standards. He didn't approve, for instance, of some of Brennan's shenanigans. The company he kept, the carousing, the bimbos, including the one he was with when the rest of us were sitting around the Burkes' dinner table waiting for him — Declan took him by the scruff of the neck when he came in, and delivered some choice words in his direction."

Brennan sat back with his arms across his chest, glowering across the table.

"Let's give him a break, now, Sandra. Monty is no stranger to bimbos, either. One at least, as I witnessed when I walked in unannounced last year and —"

"Tales about you would round things out nicely here, Maura. So keep that in mind before you start in on me."

"Are you suggesting —" my wife whirled on me as if she had only just realized old Monty had been sitting there all night without an unkind word being directed his way "— that I ever dragged home some bit of scruff and —"

"All right, everybody, cool off here," I demanded. "If, on occasion, there's an unsavoury story about us, Sandra, we all come by it honestly. He's a Burke, I'm a Collins, she's a MacNeil. In the *Ulysses* obscenity trial in 1933, here in New York, the judge took judicial notice of our nature when he ruled the book was not obscene. As for sex being a recurring theme in the minds of the characters, the judge said: '— it must always be remembered that his location was Celtic and his season spring.'" Burke and MacNeil joined me in some cathartic laughter; Sandra rolled her eyes and shook her head.

"Sorry I'm late!" We all turned to see a man in his thirties, tie askew, greeting a group of people at the table next to ours. The man was nearly out of breath. "I stopped in at the house to get the music she wants for the funeral. Look at it! A bunch of little squares, and no hint of what note it starts on. How am I supposed to sing that?"

Brennan twisted around in his chair. "Let me see that." The man looked at him for a moment, then handed over a sheet of paper. "Those are called *neumes*. Chant notation," Brennan explained.

"I've been singing at Mass for years, including Gregorian chant, but I've never seen this stuff before. It was something my aunt pulled out of a trunk. I have no idea how to read it, and I have to know it by eleven tomorrow! Jesus."

Brennan got up and dragged his chair over to the other table. He laid the papers out before him. "All right. This little square is called a *punctum*, a single note, and this we call *podatus*, one note above the other with the bottom note sung first. This mark shows where *doh* is, so this *Kyrie* starts on F." Brennan sang it and I recognized the beautiful melody from his work with the choir at Saint Bernadette's.

Sandra leaned over. Her voice was barely above a whisper: "You cannot imagine what a far cry that is from what I used to hear out of him at this time of night."

"Hey, I know that one!" the man exclaimed.

"It's the *Missa de Angelis*. I'm singing it myself, at a wedding later this week."

"So, you sing in church too."

"Yeah. I do."

"I'm Roger Stanton." He held out his hand.

"Father Burke. Brennan Burke." The man eyed his dinner jacket and black tie. "I'm out of costume tonight."

"Or *in* costume," Sandra muttered.

"Thanks, Father," Stanton said. "You've saved my ass here."

Brennan turned back to us and caught Sandra staring at him. He cleared his throat. "Another drink, anyone? A sweet?" The women decided on dessert. Burke brought out a fat cigar and fired it up. He gazed at Sandra through the curls of smoke.

"Where were we?" Maura asked.

"Excuse me," came a timid voice from the mourners' table beside us. "Father?" Brennan turned around. "No, I shouldn't bother you on your night off —" The woman was well dressed but plain of face; her eyes bore evidence of earlier weeping. She was probably in her late thirties.

A man at the table spoke up. "Go ahead, Fiona, ask him. If it's upsetting you this much, get it off your chest before the funeral."

The woman took a deep, steadying breath and went on: "Father, could I speak with you for two minutes, somewhere . . ." Her eyes darted around the room.

"Sure. Let's sit over there." He gestured to an unoccupied table near the entrance. He got up, took the woman gently by the elbow and walked to the table. He pulled the chairs around so they were sitting nearly side by side. Sandra and I could see what was going on. The woman spoke urgently and Burke nodded from time to time. At one point he turned to her, smiled kindly, and wiped tears from her eyes with his thumbs. The confession continued and he listened intently. Then he made a discreet sign of the cross over her and began to speak.

A voice in my ear said: "Don't leave town without calling me. Bring Maura over for dinner." Sandra rose from her chair and mouthed the word "later" to Maura. I tried to restrain her, but she walked out. When she passed by Brennan, he looked at her, without expression and did not miss a beat in his conversation with the penitent.

He returned to our table a few minutes later and tossed back the remainder of his whiskey.

"She was tired," Maura began.

"She was rude to walk out. Teacups would be rattling *chez* Worthington." He shrugged as if to say: "What can you do?" We stayed on for dessert and avoided the subject uppermost in our minds.

✝

The three of us walked to our hotel overlooking Carnegie Hall in midtown Manhattan. Brennan's parents had opened their home to out-of-town guests for the days before and after their granddaughter's wedding on Friday. By the time Brennan had made arrangements to visit, his old room had been spoken for. But no doubt the idea of living it up in a New York hotel appealed to him. I offered him the extra bedroom in our suite for the two nights Maura and the kids would be in Philadelphia; he reserved his own room for the nights he wasn't sharing with me. When Maura and I got to our suite, we saw that Tom and Normie had each claimed a room. I joined my son, and Maura slipped in with our little girl.

†

The next morning, I saw the family off at Penn Station. Normie was as excited about this, her first-ever train journey, as she was about the trip to New York. She kept waving and blowing kisses until the train was out of my sight. I spent the rest of the morning walking around midtown Manhattan, then had a leisurely lunch and took in a movie, enjoying the luxury of having no demands on my time. Late in the afternoon, I took the subway to the Burke residence in the Irish enclave of Sunnyside, Queens. They had half of a large brick house in the leafy area around Skillman Avenue, north of Queens Boulevard. Their corner lot was enclosed by a hedge. It looked as though the white trim on the windows had been recently painted. When I got to the door I could see Brennan inside the doorway with another man.

"Monty, this is my brother Patrick. Pat, meet Montague Collins." We shook hands. Patrick Burke was probably six feet tall, an inch or so shorter than Brennan. He had a stereotypically Irish face, clear blue eyes and sandy blond hair. He wore a soft blue crewneck sweater over a shirt and tie. Patrick was a much more approachable-looking man than his older brother.

"What will you have, Monty? There's cold beer in the fridge."

"That would be fine, Patrick, thanks."

"Brennan?"

"Same."

I followed them into the kitchen, which had a linoleum floor patterned in large blue and grey squares. The table was of grey and white Formica with a strip of chrome around the edge. Six of the chairs matched; two did not. The kitchen had not suffered any upgrades since the 1950s, and was the better for it.

"What brings you to New York, Monty?"

"I had a long trial scheduled and the matter was settled. An unexpected holiday. I've never had a chance to spend more than a few days in New York." I didn't say my last visit was to probe into Brennan's background while Brennan, who was in the city with me, remained oblivious to what I was doing when we weren't together.

"Monty and his family are coming to the wedding," Brennan put in.

"Even though I've never met the bride and groom. The bride is Katie . . ."

"Right. Daughter of our brother Terry and his wife, Sheila. The groom is Niccolo. And you'll be more than welcome. Now, what are your thoughts on this dog-eared obituary, Monty?" he asked, as he set the beer down and pulled up a chair to join us at the table.

"I think you're being very clever in your interpretations, but I'm wondering whether you're being a little creative as well."

"I've pretty well come to that conclusion myself," he said.

"It could be about your father but it could just as easily be what it purports to be, the obituary of Cathal Murphy. Has it been determined whether this Murphy actually existed?"

"The name meant nothing to Teresa or Declan, or so they claimed. I couldn't find any reference to him but my efforts consisted of calling a couple of funeral homes and looking in the Queens phone book. As far as I know the funeral arrangements, which were to follow, never appeared in the paper. But I wasn't very systematic about it."

"Your father's reaction?"

"I thought he was going to drop right then and there. But there could be another explanation for that, an organic one. Physical."

"Do you remember whether he reacted as soon as he began to read, or was it halfway through, near the end, or what?"

Patrick looked thoughtful. "He started to read it aloud. In a stagy brogue, as a matter of fact, with an editorial comment or two thrown in. 'Cathal Murphy, God rest his porr oul soul, flew up to meet his maker at the age of seventy-three —' But he was speaking softly by the time he got to the sons' names and he clammed up entirely after reading about the brother, Benedict. It was then, if my memory is serving me at all well, that he began turning grey in the face. But his behaviour could have been a reaction to the story of this other man's life; it may well have struck a chord with Declan, reminded him of disturbing things in his own past. Whatever it was, Mam was staring up at him in alarm."

"Now, your mother," I said. "Could you tell whether she had any reaction to the article itself, or did her concern just reflect the change in your dad?"

Patrick shook his head. "I don't know. My eyes were on Declan. It was only when he finished reading that I noticed the expression on her face. I took Dec by the arm and tried to sit him down. He was having none of it."

"Why doesn't that surprise me?" Brennan put in.

"What does your mother say about the obit?"

The brothers looked at each other. "She's not saying," answered Brennan shortly, "which speaks volumes in my mind."

"No wonder she kept mum with you grilling her like that."

"Patrick, you've had how many weeks to try to prise some information out of the woman, and haven't made any progress."

"Well, you didn't help matters any. You were brutal!"

"I wasn't brutal. She's my mother!" Brennan snapped. "I was direct, that's all."

Patrick looked at me. "Direct, he calls it. 'Mam, you can't have lived with the old man all these years and remained in —' how did you say it? '— a cloud of unknowing. You're no fool, neither are we. So tell us what you know.'"

"What's wrong with that?" Brennan demanded.

"There are gentler, more oblique ways to bring her around. If only you had the patience —"

"I'm here for a limited time. This write-up, if it pertains to Declan, is not only an allegory of his past, it's also a death announcement. We'd all do well to bear that in mind."

"All right, all right." Patrick raised his hands in a conciliatory gesture. "But this was written three months ago, in December. He's been coming and going as he always does; nobody's touched him or threatened him."

"As far as we know," Brennan said. The brothers fell silent and we all sipped our beer.

"Let's just ease up on our old mam till after the wedding," Patrick suggested. "She's looking forward to it so much. After that, go ahead, haul her into the confession box." He got up and put his empty glass on the counter.

"I hear you, Pat," Brennan said. "We'll leave her in peace till after the wedding, then Monty will put her on the stand and cross-examine her. I've seen him at it. We'll have what we want from her then."

"I notice you two haven't said a word about interrogating Declan himself."

They looked at me in unified astonishment, as if I had just shown unmistakable signs of madness. "Have you met our father?" Patrick asked.

"Oh yeah."

"Well, then. What do you think we'd have to do to him, to get him to talk?"

"Something that would put you in breach of the Geneva Conventions?"

They nodded together, as if to encourage the classroom dunce who had finally put two and two together and come up with something close enough to four that they could all go home. "He'll never talk," they said as one.

When Patrick excused himself to go meet his parents at the home of the bride, Brennan turned to the subject that was uppermost in his mind: a certain female blues singer we had heard in Colly's bar on Queens Boulevard during our brief stay in New York the year before. She had held him spellbound from the instant she opened her mouth. He had found out she was still performing with the house band at Colly's, and these would be her last two nights before moving to Chicago. On our first visit to the bar, we had struck up an acquaintance with two women. Or, more accurately, I struck up an acquaintance with a red-haired, green-eyed woman named

Rosemary, and Brennan had given her friend the brush-off. The friend had then thrown a spanner into my hopes of a night with Rosemary. I wondered whether I had the gall to pick up the phone and call her. I hadn't thought of it till now, given that one of the goals of this trip was a reconciliation with my wife. But when I fastened on the telephone conversation between Maura and Giacomo, I decided to give Rosemary a ring after all. I called her from the Burkes' house, but she could not come out tonight. She might, however, be able to swing it tomorrow.

Burke and I had another beer, then decided to have dinner in Little Italy, at a trattoria called La Mia Suocera. We put away a bottle and a half of Tuscan wine and a magnificent multi-course meal; Burke pulled a portly cigar from his pocket, lit it up and smoked contentedly for a few moments. Then the familiar newspaper clipping emerged and was flattened out on the table.

"Time to get back to the Dead Mick Scrolls, Montague. Brother Patrick seems to be losing his religion on this, but I intend to persevere. Because, of course, I'm right and he's wrong."

"I meant to ask you: what does Patrick do?"

"He's a psychiatrist."

"Really! What's his approach?"

"Common sense. He's a very level-headed sort of fellow and he takes that into his therapy."

"How does religion fit into his world view? I've never had the impression psychiatry and Catholicism were rollicking bedfellows."

Burke looked surprised. "He's more Catholic than I am! Everybody thought he'd be the priest in the family."

"Now he's a priest of the mind."

"Mmmm. Now pay attention here, Collins. I'm wondering why it says Cathal was never shy about sharing a song or a drink and, if you said no, he'd share it with you anyway. That doesn't sound like the old man. He likes a drink and a song, true, but he was never a drinker to the extent you'd note it in his biography. And he was never one of those overbearing party lads who'd hound you into drinking even if you didn't want to. Then it says: 'When the members of a generation pass away, the family is often left with little more than its memories; the telling details are locked away in a trunk and never get out of the attic. A better way — Cathal's way — was to celebrate and live the past as if it formed part of the present, as indeed it does.' Obviously, something in the past has never gone away, and whatever it is accounts for this affront right here." He jabbed at the paper as if he were poking its author in the chest.

There was something he had just read that set off a little tingle at the outer edges of my consciousness. I tried to bring it to the centre of my mind but I was interrupted by Burke, who had had enough. "I'm heading over to that bar," he announced.

The blues bar, he meant. "You go ahead. I'll call it a night, and catch tomorrow's performance. See you back at the hotel."

We went our separate ways. I hit the sack early but woke when I heard him come in at one-thirty or two, then dropped off again.

When I got up the next morning Burke was gone. I spent the day walking around the west side of Manhattan, stopping for a snack or a beer now and then, and thoroughly enjoying myself. But my mind was on the evening ahead; I had reached Rosemary and we had a date.

The blues bar, Colly's, was on Queens Boulevard, a five-minute walk from the Burkes' house. We got there ahead of Rosemary, whose arrival time would depend on getting her son, William, settled for the night. The bar staff all greeted Brennan as a regular and had a Jameson's poured for him before his bum hit the chair. I had a beer.

"So Burke. Was she happy to see you again?"

"Who wouldn't be? No —" he put up a warning hand, as the image of the disastrous evening with Sandra came back to us both "— don't answer that. Cassie gave the appearance of one who was not overly distressed to see me back in town."

"How did she sound?"

"She had me all ears."

"It was just your ears that pricked up, eh?"

Silence. Then, after a good long swig of whiskey: "We chatted a bit between sets."

"Oh?"

"Oh yourself."

"Has she recorded anything yet?"

"No, but she hopes to when she gets to Chicago. This move to Chicago she sees as a life-changing event. She had trouble with drugs

29

and booze, and hit bottom a few years ago. She has two boys; their father took them and left. She fought her way back through rehab and work, and she's been clean for three years. Can't wait to be with her kids in Chicago, and make up for lost time."

"She told you all this between sets?"

"No, she told me all this when I took her out for a bite to eat afterwards."

"Really! And did she tell you this in your role as kindly Father Burke, or —"

"She doesn't know what I do," he said shortly. "We were talking about her, not me."

"So you're just a mysterious stranger who pops up every once in a while to be serenaded —"

"You're getting a little annoying here, Collins. Go order me another Irish, will you? Once she comes out, I don't want to sit in front of her, swilling all night. Her having given it up."

"So you're going to get a few under your belt now."

"Correct. Now hop to it and buy us a round."

I got up to do the fetching, but I took vocal revenge by singing a few lines of "Long Cool Woman", a song about a man who had a life-altering moment when he heard a woman singing in a bar.

He affected not to hear.

"Ah," I heard him say then, and he rose to his feet. "Rosemary, is it?"

"Rosie!" She'd had her luxurious red hair cut into wavy layers since I saw her last, and a scarlet sweater set off her creamy skin with its light smattering of freckles across the nose. She smiled and plopped into her seat with a sigh of exhaustion. "What can I get for you?"

"A glass of white wine, Monty, whatever looks decent. I nearly didn't get here. William was feeling sick and, well, it goes on and on. How are you, Brennan?"

"The very best. Thank you."

I got us all drinks, and we talked until the band, South of Blue, came on and did very passable work on some old blues standards. A few of the songs I did with my own band back in Halifax. Brennan went to the bar and ordered a ginger ale. It was not until the next set that Cassie made her appearance. She had long ebony hair and lazy, half-closed dark eyes. She was not conventionally pretty but she had the look of a siren who could lure many a worthy ship onto the rocks. I estimated her age as late thirties or early forties. Her voice smoked and smouldered, and occasionally flashed to great soaring heights. It had its effect on Burke again; he looked like a man whose vital signs had measurably altered.

The set ended with a surprisingly toned-down version of the Janis Joplin number "Get It While You Can." Quiet, low, and wistful all the way through, very effective. Burke lit up a cigarette and sucked the smoke deep into his lungs as Cassie walked off with the band and reappeared with a glass of what looked like grape juice. She stopped at a couple of tables and chatted with the patrons. I noticed she was friendly to them, but kept her distance.

"Why didn't she come over to see us?" I needled Burke.

"She will," he informed me, as he stubbed out his cigarette and took a sip of ginger ale.

And she did. "Evening, Brennan," she said in a husky voice. "I hope I don't sound metallic on the high notes tonight."

He leaned back in his seat and looked up at her. "You sound like liquid gold on the high notes tonight, Cassie. Meet my good friend Montague, and this is Rosemary. They were with me last year when I heard you for the first time."

"Right. I remember now. And wasn't there someone else?"

Burke held her gaze and smiled. "There was nobody else."

I asked about her blues career, and she gave us a little history. Then she added: "It can be a crazy life and that started to wear thin after a while. Bad for the health. I'm hoping to settle down a bit. This will be my last set. I'd better go gargle something so I can get through it." She slapped the table in front of Burke, spilling his drink. "Wouldn't want to sound raspy on the fortissimos." She left us then to go backstage.

"What did you do, Brennan? Sit here last night and critique her work?"

"I just suggested she go easy on her voice today. She sounded tired last night."

"So, why didn't you let her go home to beddy-bye nice and early, instead of dining at the fashionably late hour of midnight? But perhaps she'll have an early night tonight."

"Perhaps she will," he answered impassively.

We chatted about this and that until Cassie came out for her final set and worked her magic on us all again. Her last number, she announced with a quick glance at Burke, would be her female — but not ladylike — version of "It's a Man's World." The song had left us stupefied last year when we heard it. Once again, her incendiary vocals issued a challenge to anyone in the room who might think he was living in a man's world.

It turned out that Cassie and Brennan had made plans to head to their now regular spot for something to eat after she said her good-byes around the bar. Rosemary and I stayed for one more drink. When we got to the restaurant we saw that things had progressed. Brennan was squeezed in beside Cassie in a booth and had his arm around her. Whatever he was whispering in her ear triggered an irresistible, throaty laugh. They didn't notice our arrival. Brennan turned Cassie's face towards him and kissed her on the mouth. By the time she opened her eyes and saw us standing there, they were practically horizontal on the bench. She gave him a gentle push in the chest; he righted himself, took a deep breath, and acknowledged our presence with a nod.

We made inconsequential conversation but, when the waitress arrived, Rosemary and I decided not to order anything to eat. It was clear that Brennan's mind was elsewhere. He had some part of himself in contact with Cassie at all times, and I realized he had not so much as touched her arm while she was working, while she was in public view in the bar. I realized as well that nothing had happened between them before tonight, and that he would be exactly where he wanted to be long, long before the crack of dawn.

My ambitions were more modest. I had billed the date with Rosemary as "getting together for drinks," which was as far as I was going to go with Maura and the kids due back the next day, and a possible détente on the horizon. Though when I thought again of Giacomo . . . But no, she wouldn't have arranged a rendezvous in Philadelphia, not with Tom and Normie there. The solution to my dilemma presented itself when Rosemary mentioned a midnight movie she wanted to see. We drove to New Jersey in her car, took in the movie, and picked up some food at a drive-through. I looked in my wallet and saw that I did not have enough cash to cover the $11.62 food bill. Smooth! But that's what credit cards are for. We parked and ate while gazing across the Hudson River at the skyline of lower Manhattan.

I got back to the hotel at three in the morning. Burke obviously thought I was gone for the night: when I walked into the suite, the door to his room was open. There he was in his bed, flaked out on his back, with Cassie asleep across him, her head on his belly, her long black hair forming a veil that might have been strategically placed by the Legion of Decency. I quietly closed their door and went to my room.

I dropped off instantly and didn't wake up until I heard the shower come on. I looked at the bedside clock and saw that it was seven a.m. It took me a while to remember who was there. Oh yes, Brennan. And? I heard Cassie's husky voice coming from the bathroom. "I'm in here trying to clean up my image, and you — again? How many times do you generally do this in the run of a night?" I didn't hear whatever answer he came up with to that. The last thing I heard before I clamped a pillow over my head was her saying: "Just don't drop me," and him, in a voice as husky as hers: "That would hurt me more than it would hurt you right now, darlin'."

When I awoke again it was nearly ten, and the room was bright. One of my suite mates was leaving. "I'll go down by myself, Brennan. I have to peel myself away from you some time. It might as well be here and now."

"I'm walking down with you." I recognized the tone all too well. It brooked no argument.

I was sitting up having a cup of coffee from the self-serve when he came back, dressed in jeans, a white shirt with the tail hanging out, and nothing on his feet. "When did you get here?" he wanted to know.

"I just walked in."

"Horseshit." I smiled at him. He kept going, nearly staggering, towards his room. "I'm going to bed."

"Again?"

"Feck off." He tore his pants and shirt off and threw himself face down on the bed. I suspect he was asleep by the time his nose hit the eiderdown.

I showered, dressed, and hung the Do Not Disturb sign on the door before I left the hotel.

Chapter 3

March 8, 1991

I may as well have been at work that Friday. I decided to check out the Criminal Courts Building in Lower Manhattan, and ended up spending the whole day observing a murder trial. Monty Collins, law nerd. Then it was time to meet the train from Philadelphia, get a cab to the hotel, and dress for the wedding. The Philly trip was by all accounts a success but, by the time we arrived in the hotel lobby, my irrepressible daughter had moved on.

"Can we go to the wedding now? I think I should put my hair up." She pushed her auburn curls into an up-do and squinted around the lobby for a mirror. "This makes me look older, don't you think?"

"Yeah, nine instead of eight," her brother replied.

"Ha ha, very funny. I think it makes me look mature."

"How are you going to see the wedding without your glasses, Normie?"

"Daddy, I can see."

As if to prove her point, she held my gaze with her big beautiful near-sighted hazel eyes. We had bought her enough pairs of eye-glasses over the years to outfit the entire membership of the Junior Mensa Chess Squad. She claimed she had no idea what had become of the pair we had bought her the week before.

Tommy Douglas had my dark blond hair and blue eyes; at the age of seventeen he was fast approaching my height of five feet ten. He was only with us for a week. His girlfriend, his rock band, his high school buddies — life for him would be unfolding in Halifax, and he did not want to be away for long. It was no accident, I'm sure, that he decided to be with us this week, when school was on, and would return to Halifax in time to have the house to himself for the school break. So, with time at a premium, he was anxious to begin his New York adventure, notably checking out the Greenwich Village and Harlem landmarks once frequented by his many musical idols. A wedding was nothing but an obstacle in the way of the real excitement ahead, but he was an easygoing lad and would make the best of it.

We got into the elevator, Normie pressed the seven, the doors closed, and Maura asked: "Is Brennan still here?"

"Christ," I muttered, "I hope not." I'm sure she was giving me an odd look but I was busy beseeching the Almighty that the room had been made up and Burke was not still passed out naked in a post-coital stupor. I had been so intent on the proceedings at the court house that I had forgotten my plan to call and roust him out. The elevator stopped, we emerged and walked down the hall to room 703, and I put the key in the lock. The absence of the Do Not Disturb sign gave me hope. We were in and, yes, he was gone.

Saint Kieran's Church was a neo-Gothic stone building with a triple arch leading to its three wooden doors, a large rose window with white tracery and a heavy square side tower crowned with finials. The taxi let us out across the street, in front of a block of low-rise apartment buildings. We crossed Botsford Street and climbed the steps along with hundreds of other guests. I noticed a young teenage girl giving my son the eye; he looked handsome indeed in his navy tweed sports jacket and pale blue shirt. Normie was wearing a pink frilly dress that did not suit her personality or her colouring, but I knew enough to keep my own counsel on the matter.

Night had fallen and the church was lit by a hundred candles. The light glimmered against the jewel-like stained glass windows in the nave. We managed to choose seats with a minimum of debate, and it was not long before the pipe organ announced the arrival of the bridal party. Katie Burke was a very young bride, eighteen or nineteen years old. Five foot two, with auburn hair and sparking hazel eyes; she wore a cream suit with a sprig of shamrock in her lapel. Young but obviously game for the big step she was taking; she was wearing a grin from ear to ear as her dad walked her down the aisle. Brennan's brother Terrence, father of the bride, was a very Celtic-looking man of around forty, with thick chestnut brown hair and bright blue eyes. The groom, Niccolo, was a short, broad young man with Mediterranean colouring; he rocked back and forth on his feet as his bride approached.

Father Burke, in vestments of white, looked upon his niece with unabashed tenderness and gently kissed her hand when she arrived before him. She held his hand and then went up on the tips of her toes to plant a big kiss on his cheek, which sent a ripple of affectionate laughter through the congregation. The priest made the sign of the cross over the gathering, and the ceremony began.

"Is Father Burke an angel?" my daughter whispered to me. "He's wearing white robes and there are spirits all around that altar."

Maura and I had long known that our daughter was able to see or experience things that most people could not. Like Maura's grandmother in Cape Breton, our daughter apparently had "the sight." Father Burke had picked up on it the first time he met Normie; it seemed they shared a moment of mutual recognition, a rich vein of ancient knowledge passed down from their Celtic forebears. For my part, I'd never had a clairvoyant moment in my life. If I had, I might have been able to predict what my clients were going to say on the witness stand, and saved myself a lot of grief.

"So, is he?"

"What?"

"An angel?"

"You'd know that better than I would, sweetheart. Now pay attention. You're going to get married some day and you'll want to know what to do."

- "Oh no. I'm going to do what he does. He gets to boss other people's weddings and he doesn't have to get married himself. Plus he gets to say secret prayers right to God, and he can sing by himself at the front of the church. Nobody tells him if he's singing the wrong notes."

"He doesn't sing the wrong notes, Normie. Listen."

Father Burke sang the simple, ancient and moving *Kyrie Eleison* from the Gregorian Mass of the Angels. I enjoyed the unaffected beauty of his voice, and not a note was out of place. As always, I was struck by the reverence and grace he exhibited in his sacramental role. The Mass proceeded, and he gave a short homily in English, Italian and — *Dia anseo isteach* — Irish: God bless all here. The marriage ceremony itself came next and we heard a few selections from soloists chosen by the newlyweds: a young woman who was a friend of Katie, and a man from the D'Agostino side. I noticed that Burke could not stop himself from giving the young female a little signal with a raised index finger, to sharpen her pitch. When it was time for Holy Communion we all lined up to receive the Host from Brennan. I looked into his eyes for the first time since the events of the morning. The priest's gaze was direct and unflinching. "Body of Christ, Monty."

"Amen."

The young couple made their exit in a barrage of flashbulbs, and we all gathered on the massive stone stairway of the church. Everyone appeared to be in a celebratory mood, with the exception of Declan Burke. He was standing off to the side, peering through the darkness at the roofs of the buildings across the street. Brennan's mother, Teresa, looked regal with her silver chignon and elegant dress in the same shade. She was tall, slim and oval-faced, with great dark brown eyes and an air of unflappable dignity. "Monty! What a pleasure to see you." She gave me a quick kiss on the cheek, and we spoke for a few minutes about the bride and the ceremony. When she was called away I went over to Declan.

"Mr. Collins."

"Mr. Burke. Good to see you again." We shook hands.

Declan was shorter than I was, and stocky, with thick white hair brushed from a side part. He had an aura of strength and power, and a disconcerting way of fixing you with his wintry blue eyes. A very vigorous man of seventy-three. His speech was Irish, terse, to the point: "Thank you for your efforts on my son's behalf last year. Without your detective and legal work, he'd be having his morning crap in a prison cell for the rest of his natural life. And we both know he's much too fastidious for that."

"Thank you for your kind words, Declan. That's all behind us now." His eyes turned from me and sought out the roofs across the street again. "Is there anything wrong?"

"Why would there be? Excuse me, would you?" And he moved farther away from the crowd.

Declan's worries, whatever they were, seemed to be groundless. The whole gathering moved to the reception in the gymnasium of the parish school, adjacent to the church. We entered a large foyer with glass cabinets displaying trophies going back to the 1950s. Ahead of us were the gym doors bedecked with white streamers, but Normie veered off to the left and then turned right, with two little boys hard on her heels. I made a detour and went after them down the corridor, which ran along the length of the gym. By the time I caught up, the kids were standing in the windows on the east side of the building, making faces into the dark outside. Tongues being stuck out at old aunts on their way to the reception? No, all I saw was trees out there. One of the windows looked as if it was ready to fall out of its casing. That was all I needed, my kid crashing out of the building and me stuck with the repair bill. Normie laughed when she saw me, but the smirk was wiped off her face when she caught sight of Declan Burke scowling at the end of the hallway.

"Uh-oh."

"Uh-oh, is right. Get off there, the three of you." One after the other, they jumped from their perches and ran to a side door to the gym, but it was locked. "Go back where we came in; that's the entrance."

Declan eyed the windows and the locked side door; then he turned back and entered the gymnasium.

I heard someone announce: "Family pictures!" The death knell for any hope of an early start to the party. Fortunately, the bar was open and doing a brisk business. After ordering a beer I took the opportunity to ask the bartender if he had ever heard of a brew called — I hoped I had it right — Lameki Jocuzasem. The beverage mentioned in the obit. He looked at me as if I were a pint short of a six-pack. Well, it was worth a try.

I made conversation with some of the other guests and was on my third beer by the time the wedding party entered, sat at the head of the room and invited the rest of us to choose our places at the elegantly dressed tables around the hall. Normie found four seats close to the action and hovered by them until we all got to the table and settled in.

A multi-course meal got underway, a well-designed mix of Italian and Irish, heavy on the Italian. The wine was plentiful and of excellent quality, a gift, we were told, from relatives in Tuscany. People stood to make toasts, including Brennan, who said what a lucky young man Niccolo was, and how much joy the young pair had in store for them over the years. "Love is a joyous event, or series of events — at least if my distant memories serve me well." This brought laughs from the crowd.

Maura leaned towards me and said out of the side of her mouth: "I wonder just how distant those memories are for Brennan."

I looked at my watch and said: "What time is it?"

Her reaction was instant and gratifying. "What are you saying!" I looked up and saw Brennan's black eyes on me, and I knew he had seen my little performance with the watch. He continued his spiel without skipping a beat and wound up with a toast to the bride's parents. There were more speeches, more fabulous food was produced, wineglasses were filled and refilled. Brennan, his brothers Patrick and Terry, and another fellow of similar vintage formed a quartet, got down on their knees in front of Katie and began to croon a number of old-fashioned love songs, including "True Love," with its assurance of a guardian angel for each and every one of us. It was hokey but it was good, and the crowd loved it. Katie was laughing and wiping tears from her eyes at the same time. Niccolo beamed with pleasure.

"Will you do that at my wedding, Daddy?" Normie begged.

"I thought you didn't want to get married."

"I changed my mind. Please? I want all those songs. Plus that one from my opera."

"'Casta Diva,' you mean."

"Right. Mummy can sing that one."

"I'd pay to hear that."

"You could hear it any time you wanted if you still lived in our house." I had to look away.

The quartet made way for the band, which would be offering a mix of Italian and Irish music. I took the opportunity to switch from wine, of which I'd had too much, back to beer. I heard Brennan ask for two double Irish whiskeys; he passed one to Patrick before moving behind me. Patrick and I got into a conversation about the music. Suddenly I lurched forward, spilling my beer on the floor. I had just been given a sharp clout in the back of the head. Brennan's retaliation for the watch incident.

Patrick raised his eyebrows. "What brought that on?"

"If I told you, I'd just get clouted again. Harder." I rubbed the back of my head. "I enjoyed the quartet. Good voices."

"If you enjoyed that, you'll have to hear our 'Lola' some day. You know, the Kinks song."

"Oh yeah."

"If you can ever get the Burke brothers tanked up enough to do it, you'll see a new side of Brennan's musicianship."

"I'll keep it in mind. Excuse me for a minute, would you Patrick?"

"Sure. Catch up with you later."

I had seen Maura crooking a finger at me to come over and join her. Just as I started in her direction, she caught sight of Declan and waved. As he recognized her from his visit to Halifax, his scowl gave way to a wide smile. He looked like a new man.

"Good evening, Badness!" he greeted her, and opened his arms. They embraced. He whispered something in her ear; she whispered back, and they shared a laugh. They chatted for a few moments, then she came my way.

I drew her over to a series of shallow storage cabinets along the east wall of the gym. They were about six feet high, made of plywood, and had padlocked doors; I supposed the basketballs and other pieces of equipment were kept in there. Standing beside the farthest closet in the row, we were partially sheltered from the eyes of the other guests. I leaned back against the cabinet, feeling the effects of the alcohol that was thinning my blood and impairing my judgment. My wife wanted something.

"Well? What was all that about? The business with the watch."

"Just a joke," I hedged, but the professor of law wasn't taken in by that, any more than a four-year-old would have been.

"We're all in this together, this little New York excursion you and Brennan cooked up. Part of the reason for the visit, aside from the nonsense you told me about Declan and that obituary, was Brennan's insistence on seeing Sandra again. I guess they've patched things up. He does seem a little different tonight. Why are you being so buttoned up about it?"

"How badly do you want to know?" I asked her. Fuelled partly by the alcohol and partly by the way her blue silk top set off her grey eyes and dusky hair, I put my arms around her and murmured: "You feel so good in this. Is it new?"

"All my clothes are new to the touch as far as you're concerned."

This wasn't going to be easy. But, stupidly, I persisted. I moved my hands down her back and pulled her against me. She must have recalled something she still fancied about old Monty because she relaxed against me and put her mouth close to mine. "Tell me what went on," she urged.

"Why don't we talk about it later?"

"Feels to me as if you're not going to last till later, Collins."

"I don't have much choice, do I? Considering we're in a room with three hundred people. Unless you want a quick and furtive encounter in one of these closets here."

"Right." She pulled back. "So tell me. Who made the first move? Did Sandra call Brennan?"

"I don't think he heard from Sandra."

"What? That was Tuesday; this is Friday. You're telling me he found someone else between then and now?" Her eyes were wide. The effects of our embrace were wearing off fast.

"Well, it was at this blues bar we went to —"

"A bar."

"Yeah, and this woman was a singer there. Amazing voice, very sultry, and —"

"She seduced Brennan with her voice, did she?"

"No, if anyone was the seducer, it was him."

"How do you know that? What did you do, watch?"

"No, no, by the time he was at the hotel —"

"The hotel? He was having it off with this woman at the hotel with you sitting there?"

"No! I wasn't there."

"Where were you?"

I looked around at the other wedding guests, hoping they couldn't hear us and wishing to hell I had stayed sober and intelligent for the evening. "Can we discuss this later?"

"There is no later." Fortunately, she was keeping her voice low. Low, but deadly. "You were with someone yourself. Less than twenty-four hours ago."

"No, it wasn't like that. I —"

"And you have the nerve to come on to me as if you sincerely wanted to reconcile! You flaming arsehole. You'll be singing the blues all right. You'll be holding a tin cup and singing 'Buddy, can you spare a dime' on Spring Garden Road before you get your hands, or any other part of your anatomy, on me again. You and *Father* Burke, trolling for women in a bar!"

"Mum!" Saved by our daughter.

"Yes, sweetie?"

"Can you come here? I need you. I don't know where to pee!"

"Right there, angel!" Maura assured her. "As for you, Collins, why don't you screw yourself all up tight, and burrow down through this floor till you get to hell!"

Why not indeed? I stood there for a few minutes trying to recover from my latest marital disaster, then straightened my clothes, yanked my tie into alignment and rejoined the party.

I stood with Brennan, Patrick and Teresa Burke; they pointed out various relatives and told me who they were. A mandolin started up and I looked to the stage, where I saw a tiny ancient man adjust the microphone and glare fiercely out over the assembled crowd before he began to sing:

O Father dear, the day might come in answer to your call
And each Irish man with feelings strong will answer to the call.

And I'll be the man to lead the band beneath the flag of green. And loud and high we'll raise the cry: *Revenge* for Skibbereen!

Teresa caught her husband's eye and spoke quietly. "Didn't I say there'd be none of that?"

"I didn't arrange the music and I don't even know the man!" Declan groused.

"Nor do I."

Mr. Burke started towards the stage, but was waylaid by a large man with a flushed face. I saw the singer walk out the door. Other musicians tuned their instruments and made ready to play.

"What was it?" I asked Teresa. "A rebel song?"

"It's about a family evicted from their home during the famine. It all runs together, though, doesn't it?"

A few minutes later, we saw Declan speaking to the security men on the door. Patrick went over to join them, but came right back.

"What did he say?" Brennan asked.

"He said: 'I don't like the face on you there, Padraig! Save your concern for your patients. They need it.' But the security men told me the troubadour left and they didn't notice his car. They did, however, check the building again. They found a window loose and they wedged something in it, so nobody can get in that way. The oul fella's obviously been more forthcoming with them than with us."

"Are you telling me this man came in and sang that one song, and nobody knows who he was?"

Patrick shrugged.

"So you're the lawyer!" A woman had materialized before me. She looked so much like the bride, she could have been her older sister. Same petite figure and colouring, though with darker hair, and the same mischievous look about the eyes.

"This is my sister Brigid," Brennan said. "Bridey, meet Monty."

"This is what I think of you, for getting him out of trouble." She reached up and put her arms around my neck, brought my face down to hers and gave me a long, leisurely, unsisterly kiss on the mouth. Someone who loved me more than my wife did. There was hope. When she finally drew back, I stared at her. The brothers laughed. "That's all you're getting. Don't let me lead you on."

"Not often he blushes," Brennan said. "Don't even think of pursuing her, Collins. She comes with a husband and seven children."

"I can see how you wound up with seven kids," I said to her when I got my breath back.

"And I wouldn't mind an eighth," she told me, looking me over critically. "Breed some blond good looks into my crowd."

"I'm at your service."

"I'll keep you in mind. But the person I really want to meet is that wife of yours. I'm told she has a tongue in her head that could slit the hull of a freighter."

"She's right there," I said. Maura had returned to the gym; with some trepidation, I beckoned her over.

Maura joined us, and I noticed that Brennan greeted her less exuberantly than he usually did. "Evening, MacNeil." He gave her a quick little hug and a peck on the cheek, then sat down on the corner of the table beside us, swinging his legs and sipping his whiskey. Maura gave him a searching look, which he determinedly avoided.

Brigid spoke up. "We were just talking about good-looking children. I can see you two must have bred a fine-looking houseful. I was rather hoping the wife would be plug ugly, someone I could compete with. Because I kind of have my eye on Monty."

"Well," Maura joined in with unexpected good humour, "I am kind of bulky and not necessarily in the places I'm told I should be. You could use that against me. I hear you have seven kids and you're just a little slip of a thing." I knew Maura was perfectly content with her figure as it was. I guessed this was a little ritual of sisterly bonding.

"You're not bulky. You're what we call *zaftig* down here. What would we do without Yiddish?"

"She's lush," Brennan put in.

"*You're* a lush," Brigid said to her brother. "Ease up on the whiskey there, Brennan. You're not allowed to notice what women look like below the neck."

"Hath not a priest eyes?" He wasn't lost for an answer but the body speaks a language of its own. He had been sitting with his legs splayed out over the corner of the table; now the legs were tightly crossed. I smiled. I saw that Patrick hadn't missed it either. He smiled back at me.

Meanwhile Brigid was speaking to my wife. "So, lush and pretty. Monty hit pay dirt when he met you. You both did."

"You obviously don't know about us then, Brigid. We don't live together any more. So I'd hang in there if I were you. Nobody ever goes away empty-handed after flirting with Montague. Just use him like you would a pull toy."

"Whoa!" Patrick exclaimed. "She's a handful!"

"I'm sorry!" Brigid said, genuinely contrite. "I didn't know. *He* never told me you were separated," she accused, turning to Brennan.

"What do I look like, a gossip columnist?" Brennan retorted.

"Never mind, Brigid," Maura consoled her. "It's all right. Let's go introduce your kids to mine." They went off together.

We drank and chatted for a while, then Brennan said: "Let's get some females out there on the floor, gentlemen." The three of us put our glasses on a table and went to find partners. Brennan cut in on Brigid, who was being pushed around the floor by an old fellow who had clearly made one too many trips to the bar. I asked Brennan's mum to dance and she obliged. Teresa must have been seventy but she was as lively as anyone on the dance floor. Brigid called out to her: "I think Da is on the lookout for your Young Man. I half expected him to turn up pretending to be a guest of the groom. Or to creep in behind a big bouquet of roses."

"Oh, Bridey. Give us all a rest, won't you?"

"Bet you didn't know that, Monty. Our mother has a secret admirer. Has had for years. Used to hang around the neighbourhood, watching her. Mack, we called him. The story is he worshipped Mam from afar but I think she's been having —"

"Monty isn't interested. Brennan, manoeuvre her out of my way, will you?" Teresa shook her head, then spoke to me. "What a case she is. She's always been like that. Brennan is crazy about her."

The Irish music wound down, and someone announced a break before the Italian entertainment started up. Everyone broke into little conversational groups. Brennan was three or four tables away with his father, and they were completely engrossed in whatever they were discussing. A few feet behind Brennan was Maura, digging for something in her handbag. That could take a while. All the children were at the other end of the room, sitting in a semicircle. They were intent on something; then I noticed Tommy Douglas was sitting with them, playing softly on his harmonica. I leaned on the edge of a table, contemplating another trip to the bar. I saw Declan nod at Brennan and move away to the unoccupied end of the room. Brennan watched him, shaking his head.

It happened without warning. A sound like "pop, pop, pop" against the wall facing me. I saw Declan drop to his knees at the same time I heard Brennan shout for him to get down. In the same instant, another couple of pops. Brennan whirled, put an arm around Maura's neck, and pulled her down, hard, onto the floor. He covered her body with his, lifted his head and ordered everyone in the room to get down. People were standing around confused; some seemed not to have heard the shots. "Get them down on the fucking floor," he yelled to his brother Terry. To my wife, he said: "Maura, stay down. It's at this end. The kids are fine." He got up and ran to his father, who was lying on his back. I was on my hands and knees by this time, crawling towards Maura, all the while desperately trying to spot my children. Yet I knew with a certainty that all the children were out of harm's way. The target was Declan, and he had stayed as far away from everyone as he could in the cavernous gymnasium. The shots had come from the side of the gym; I turned my head and saw that one of the plywood closet doors was splintered. The shots must have come from there. I turned again to Maura, who was just getting up. She appeared to be in pain. I helped her to her feet, and she said in a hollow voice: "I'll get the kids. You go help." She headed towards the children. I saw that the men in Niccolo's family had formed a phalanx around them.

I rushed to Declan. Brennan was kneeling beside him, trying to get his jacket off. "Da, where were you hit? Talk to me." He looked into the crowd. "Get an ambulance here. Now! Somebody make the call. Where's Patrick?" Declan's eyes were closing and he appeared to be trying to speak. "Where the hell is Pat?" Brennan demanded. I helped him remove his father's jacket, and we saw blood seeping from a wound in his chest.

Teresa arrived at his side. She fell to her knees and stroked his face. "Declan, stay awake for us. Stay with us darling. Talk to us."

Brennan and I removed his tie and shirt. Patrick appeared and took over. "It missed his heart," he said. "Looks as if one bullet entered his right side. Almost certainly went into his lung. And a second bullet grazed the skin on the left side, may have hit a rib and glanced off." He continued to examine his father and concluded that there were no more injuries. He bundled up the ruined shirt and pressed it against the bleeding wound. He looked up, and Brennan raised a questioning eyebrow. Patrick responded with a shrug that seemed to say: *Your call.*

"Someone get me some oil," Brennan pleaded. "Olive oil, whatever is here."

I heard a woman say: "Yes, Father." She returned seconds later with a cruet of oil.

Brennan began praying over his father in a low and urgent voice, and he made the sign of the cross in oil on Declan's forehead. He began whispering in his father's ear: "O my God I am heartily sorry for having offended Thee." He continued with the Act of Contrition and seemed to be waiting for Declan to speak. But Declan gave no sign that he was aware of his surroundings.

The police and medical team arrived within minutes, although it seemed like hours. Patrick and Brennan, doctor and priest, went with their father in the ambulance. Teresa and the rest of the family followed by car. I do not know what became of poor little Katie's reception after that, because Maura and I took our stricken son and daughter back to the hotel. On the way to Manhattan in the cab, Maura was virtually catatonic. She had her arm around our daughter as if she would never let her go. She had been brushed by the wing of that swift dark presence every parent fears: the darkness that will part us from our children forever. Normie looked around her at all the blazing lights of New York City, but was uncharacteristically silent. She didn't stir from her mother's side. Tom was simply dazed; he asked if he could phone his girlfriend, Lexie, from the hotel room.

"Sure, Tommy," I said. "Plan to sleep on the pull-out couch. That way you can stay up and talk as long as you like. Remember it's an hour later in Halifax; she'll be fast asleep. But I doubt she'll complain."

It was not until I was lying in bed alone, and had time to relive the whole scene, that I wondered how Brennan was able to pinpoint Maura's location so accurately. I had been watching everyone idly from my perch on the table, and I had not seen him even glance in her direction. When the shots were fired, Declan was beyond Brennan's reach. In a fraction of a second he had Maura down on the floor beneath him. Viewing the scene in slow motion, I could see him calling her name before he had even turned around. The incident left me too wired up to sleep. I experienced a rush of guilt for bringing my family into such a perilous situation. But I remembered why it had not crossed my mind to worry: I had dismissed out of hand the notion that there was anything ominous in that obituary.

It was just after two-thirty in the morning when I felt a soft little body snuggle up to me. "Are you all right, Normie?" I whispered.

"I woke up. I had shivers, and ladies were crying."

"It's all right. Go back to sleep, little one."

"Father Burke is sad."

"Of course he is. He's worried about his dad. Why don't you lie here for two minutes and think about the sights you want to see in New York. Then drift off to sleep. I'll tell Father Burke you were worried about him." She fretted for a few more minutes, tossing and turning, then slipped away into sleep. I carried her back to her own bed and tucked her in. And finally, I slept.

The phone rang beside my bed at eight-thirty. No need to wonder who it was. "Did he make it?" I asked by way of greeting.

"He made it. We nearly lost him. They had to resuscitate him in the middle of the night; his heart stopped. But they think he's going to be all right. *Deo gratias.* I'll be filling you in later. The police are here. Could you do something for me?"

"Of course."

"Could you go to my room? It's two doors down from yours. Well, I suppose they'll have to let you in. Bring me a change of clothes, shaving kit? Somehow I'm not in the mood for a shopping spree. I'll tell you how to get here by subway. You take the —"

"I'll cab it. The hospital or your house?"

"Elmhurst Hospital."

"No problem. Sit tight."

Maura shuffled into the room at that point; she looked as if she hadn't closed her eyes. She put her hand out for the phone. "Brennan. It's not often I have to search for the right words." Her voice was shaky. "But about last night, what you did — oh, I see." She looked at me and said: "He had to save my life because he hasn't been able to save my soul yet. Didn't want me to die in a state of mortal sin. Here, you talk to him." She passed me the receiver, just in time for Normie to make a grab for it. I hadn't even seen her slip into the room.

"Daddy."

"Not now, sweetheart."

"Please? Let me talk to him."

"I'm sorry, Brennan. Normie's been upset. She's asking —"

"Go ahead. Put her on."

"Father? Did your daddy's spirit get back into him last night? Father, can you hear me? I was worried because you were so sad. But he's back together, right? I'm really glad. Bye." She passed me the phone.

"All right, see you shortly. Brennan?"

"Mmmm?"

"What time did your father have to be resuscitated?"

"Ask the little Druid." Click.

I was let into Brennan's new room, and packed up a few of his belongings, then flagged down a cab. When I arrived at Elmhurst, I was told that Declan was still in the Intensive Care Unit so I headed there. Patrick Burke was coming down the corridor in my direction, unshaven and still in his wedding finery. He had both hands wrapped around a mug of coffee. We said hello and he began to fill me in but we were interrupted.

"Dr. Burke!" A nurse beckoned from a doorway, where a police officer sat observing me with a practised eye. "Your father is asking for you."

"We'll have to catch up later, Monty." Patrick hurried to the room. When he went in, Brennan and Brigid came out. She had not been home either. Tears that had been held in were now spilling from her eyes. Her brother put both arms around her and held her close. He looked over and saw me carrying his overnight bag.

"Ah. Monty. Good." He turned his sister around by the shoulders and gave her a little shove. "Bridey, go! There's nothing you can do here."

"I wish there was something I could do somewhere! I don't like being this useless."

"Call a taxi and go to Terry's. Get some rest."

She saw me and wiped her eyes. "Hi, Monty. I, well, I'd better get going." She walked slowly down the hallway, dabbing at her face with a tissue.

"How is he?" I asked.

"Getting crankier by the minute. Making progress, in other words. Would you like to pay him a visit?" I shook my head. Last thing I wanted. "Hold on while I go have a wash and change my clothes." I entered a small waiting room, sat, and flipped the pages of a magazine without taking in any of the images. Brennan joined me a few minutes later, still with a day's growth of beard but pink from a scrubbing. His hair was wet and he was in civilian clothes. He sat down next to me and stretched out his legs.

"Well, at least one of us feels better. Jesus, what a hellish night. Nearly losing him like that. And then when he was conscious again, to have to sit there while the old bugger kept his gob shut about who shot him. His first concern was for Katie and Nick, and Nick's family. We were instructed to issue apologies to them all. Well, I can understand it. We had to strong-arm Declan into attending the wedding in the first place. But whatever one might make of that death notice, who would have believed they — whoever they are — would try to hit him in such a public gathering? Poor Patrick is devastated that he'd begun laughing the whole thing off. But who can blame him really?" He looked at me. "Monty, I'm sorry."

"What do you have to be sorry about?"

"Bringing you and Maura and the children into this. I —"

"Brennan. You didn't know. As you said yourself, nobody could have foreseen what happened in that gym."

"The old fellow foresaw the possibility, though, didn't he? He wanted to forgo the wedding and when he couldn't do that, he tried to stay as far away from the rest of us as he could."

"But shooting someone at a public event with three hundred witnesses? Nobody's at fault but the gunman. And whatever he represents."

"What did you do for excitement before you met me, Collins?"

"It's been an eventful year."

"And we still have our mission to complete."

"But the police are on it now. Surely they are better placed than a couple of amateur gumshoes to —"

"They'll try to solve the crime that was committed last night. I don't expect them to get to the root of it all. Whatever it is."

"And that job falls to us."

"What did we come to New York for? To drink and get laid?"

I decided it might be wise not to answer that directly. "It's a reasonable alternative to playing detective alongside the mighty NYPD."

"They're not going to get all the answers. Declan will tell them only what he has to tell them, so he won't be seen as obstructing their investigation into the attempt on his life. Beyond that, he'll maintain the silence of the dead. Believe me. I know the man. And this won't end until we get to the bottom of it. So, back to that obit."

"I take it you've given the police a copy of the obituary." Silence. "Well?"

"No."

"And why is that?"

"Until we suss out what it means, and how it might implicate my father, I'm not giving them so much as a peep at it."

"I see. Did you come up with any new insights sitting in this place all night?"

He shook his head. "My brain isn't working. I said Mass for the family in the chapel here and I even screwed up the *Pater Noster*. I still can't decipher the part about Cathal — or Declan — sharing the song and drink. And I have no idea who the brother and the stepson are, Benedict and Stephen. If we just go by the names we get

Benedict, which means 'Blessed.' Saint Benedict was the founder of western monasticism. My father was predeceased by a monk? And Saint Stephen. The first Christian martyr. Somehow I suspect that line of thinking will get us nowhere."

"Martyred how?"

"Stoned to death."

"Sounds unlikely in this day and age. At least in the western world."

"I should hope so."

"Unless it was a drug-related death." He looked up sharply. "You know, died stoned. An overdose."

"We just don't know," he said helplessly.

"As for Benedict, maybe you're too much the Mick here, Brennan."

"How's that?"

"Think American, not Irish Catholic. What do Americans think of when they hear the name Benedict?"

"Benedict Arnold. The traitor."

"Right. Could Declan have been predeceased by a traitor of some sort? And the obit calls Benedict a brother."

Burke avoided my eyes. He got up and walked over to a nearby water fountain. Took a long drink. When he sat down again he didn't speak.

Who were Benedict and Stephen? The traitor and the martyr. "Do you have the clipping?" He pulled out his wallet, produced the paper and handed it to me. I skimmed it again. One word in particular struck me as being central to the entire indictment. "Brennan, what significance do you attach to the word 'predeceased'?"

He rested his head in his left hand and massaged his temples. "When we read it, Pat and I both had the impression that this person was accusing our father of murder. Or at least implying that he was responsible for the deaths of these two people. We didn't want to believe it. But now?" He lapsed into a brooding silence.

"Let's look at it that way then. Somebody tried to kill your father over this — whatever *this* is — so we have to face the fact that whatever happened was something very serious. We don't know who Benedict or Stephen were, so we'll go at it from another direction. Why do people kill?" Silence. "Very well. Why would someone *suppose* your father had killed —"

"Perhaps that should be: why would someone *claim* he had committed murder?"

"Whatever the case, let's get down to the basics of murder. What are the classic motivations?" I began to enumerate them. "Money."

"Nobody would ever think my father would kill for money. Money is not a motivating factor in his life."

"I agree he doesn't seem the type to be moved by greed. At least he doesn't seem that way to us. But we don't know how he might be perceived by someone else. Say this happened during the early years here in New York; wouldn't money have been a problem? Declan left Ireland under cover of darkness, on the lam from something, the way I heard it. So here he was, newly arrived in the United States with a wife and a young family to support."

"Well, I don't think it's likely that he knifed somebody for his wallet, or robbed a bank."

"No, but those aren't the only possibilities. Where did the money come from when your family got off the boat in 1950, to pay for a place to live, and all the other necessities of life? What did Sandra say the other night?"

"'Fuck off, Brennan'?"

"She didn't say that. She was telling us about her early encounters with your dad. Back in the fifties. She witnessed some kind of confrontation between your father and another guy. Didn't she say something about a big stack of dollars? What was it?"

"It was something like that."

"How did Declan come up with the money for a house in Sunnyside? After just getting off the boat from Ireland. What was going on back then?"

"I don't know," he answered in a quiet voice.

"We won't cross money off our list just yet. Other common motivations. Lust."

"Lust," he repeated.

"Right. Lust, love, jealousy. Right up there at the top of the list of reasons people do away with each other."

"It would help if we knew who is supposed to have been killed, I'm thinking."

"It would help enormously. Do you see your father as someone who would commit a crime of passion?"

"I don't see him that way. But I wouldn't; I'm his son. I was a child if we're talking ancient history here."

"The scene at the Met, the woman who accused your father of destroying her family. You say nobody ever told you what that was all about?"

"No."

"And that was when? In 1956?"

"Right."

"Well, I think we'd better proceed on the assumption that it's connected somehow."

"Bren." We looked up to see Patrick coming towards us.

"What did he want you for?"

Patrick waved a dismissive hand. "Don't even ask."

"I'm asking."

"He wanted to consult me for my arcane medical knowledge. That is, do I know if he can call long distance from the hospital phone without all the nosy old gossips on the switchboard listening to his every word. I broke the news to him that everyone in the whole communications system in this hospital has been waiting for the day Declan Burke would be admitted with gunshot wounds so they could hang on his every word. He told me to feck off so I was able to make a graceful exit. In front of a very attractive cardio resident who was just coming in the door."

"So, who does he want to call?"

"I said he told me to feck off, not to ring directory assistance. But never mind that. Are you two solving the case here? Let's move over to the other side, where there are three seats."

"Paddy, you've been here all night. Go home and sleep."

"You were here all night too. You need a break."

"I'm on holiday, Patrick. I planned to be up all night, every night. And I have been. I can sleep any time. Off with you. Oh, and give Brigid a call and tell her I thought of something she can do to help."

"What's that?"

"Get her to sit down with the telephone directories and go through all the Murphys — every one of them — to see if she can come up with a Cathal."

Patrick agreed and headed out. Brennan and I resumed our deliberations.

"I suppose it's pointless," I began, "to ask if you know of any other woman in his life."

"I can't imagine him with another woman. But then, I couldn't have imagined any of this."

"Moving on to other possible motives and circumstances. Self-defence."

"A possibility," Brennan conceded.

"Perhaps someone he had a long history with."

"Or a luckless stranger who jumped him outside a bar."

"Let's hope not. How would we ever trace something like that? But it's unlikely. An incident like that would not have stayed alive in someone's mind all these years, to the point where the person would craft this maddening little death notice and ignite the whole thing again." I took my turn at the water fountain. "How about revenge?"

"We certainly can't discount that. But who knows? We're not up on the history. This is so frustrating."

"Blackmail," I ventured.

"He'd never pay it. Never. Can you picture yourself sidling up to Declan Burke in a dark quiet spot and trying to wheedle money out of him with the threat to go public about some —"

"There you go then. Attempted blackmail. Exit one ill-starred blackmailer."

"We're talking through our hats here, Monty. We don't have anything to go on."

We had to get a picture of the kind of man Declan Burke was, the life he was living when he first arrived in New York, the people he knew. And why had he come here in the first place? What precipitated his sudden flight from the land of his birth? I put another motive on the table: "Patriotism. Love of country, killing the enemy. Does that strike a chord on the harp for you?"

"He's always refused to discuss that part of his life."

We were about to learn that, whether he discussed it or not, that part of his life was a matter of great interest to a number of people on both sides of the Atlantic.

Chapter 4

I was not yet eighteen when I went on the run
To win Ireland's freedom in the blaze of a gun.
Like the bold men before me, my choice I had made:
IRA, Third Battalion, Dublin Brigade.
— Hannigan Sweeney, "Dublin Brigade"

March 9, 1991

Tom and Normie wanted to get on with seeing New York. The lighter, less lethal side. When I returned to Manhattan we embarked on a day of sightseeing: the Empire State Building, Central Park, Strawberry Fields. By mid-afternoon Maura and Normie were keen to shop. Tom gave me the thumbs-up; it was time for the boys to hit the Village and see a number of places associated with Bob Dylan, starting with the White Horse Tavern and the Café Wha? All this helped keep the kids' minds off the harrowing event they had witnessed. We had dinner, then turned in early to catch up on our sleep.

The next morning, we were headed for the Fifty-Ninth Street Bridge in Terry Burke's car, with Brennan at the wheel. His face was pale and he was wearing sunglasses. An experienced New York driver, he ignored the traffic mayhem around him. Maura, though, had not yet adjusted. "I can't believe these people. The minute — the very microsecond — the light turns green, they're leaning on their horns. 'Beeeeeep. Get movin' — what are ya waitin' for, Christmas?' This starts at five in the morning and goes on, well, till five the next morning. Constant noise. It's a wonder they don't all die of a heart attack at forty."

"Ay, ya gotta chill out, babe," he responded in a New York accent that was not his own.

Maura and the kids were going to see the American Museum of the Moving Image, in Astoria. Brennan and I were on a mission to JFK International Airport, to pick up a mysterious stranger. We dropped the family off with a promise to collect them on our return from the airport. I now asked the obvious question: "Who's this guy we're picking up?"

"Dec won't even tell me his name. Or why he's here. Just said they 'served' together in the old days. Didn't say which Army had the benefit of their service, but I think we can safely assume it was the IRA. I got the impression this man was his commanding officer. Try to imagine the class of fellow who would be barking orders at my father."

"My imagination fails me. How's Declan doing now?"

"Still weak, but won't let on. Demanding to be released. My mother was laying down the law to him when I left."

We got to the airport, parked the car and headed for Terminal Four.

"How are we going to recognize this guy?"

"Declan said the man would know me. Must have given him a description."

We stood waiting for the passengers to make their way through the system. Brennan took his sunglasses off and put them in his pocket. I was shocked at how weary he looked. The area under his dark eyes appeared bruised, in contrast to the pallor of his cheeks. "When's the last time you had a night's sleep?"

"Not within recent memory. I'd like to sneak off to the hotel. Pass out for a day or two, I'm thinking."

"You should. Get this guy settled and disappear. You look like hell."

"Here they come." First off the Aer Lingus flight were a few impatient business people, who appeared to be Americans, looking at their watches and pressing their lips together. Then came a flock of priests and nuns, gawking around them with excitement. "Can't you see Mike O'Flaherty herding that crowd around?" I agreed. Father O'Flaherty, Brennan's pastor in Halifax, lived for the opportunity to squire gaggles of Canadian tourists around Ireland. A group of Irish clerics would be the *summum bonum* of his vocation as a tour guide. The priests were of all ages, the sisters mainly middle-aged and older. They were met by two co-religionists who shepherded them from the terminal. Then a few families and tourists straggled from the plane. Our attention was caught by a big pugnacious-looking man of indeterminate age, dressed in a tight suit in an unbecoming colour somewhere between forest green and black. He was either bald or had shaved his head, and his nose appeared to have been broken at some point in his life. Had Declan met his match in this hard-ass? He looked around with hostility, and Brennan stepped forward.

"Would your name be Burke, by any chance?" A quiet, clipped voice came at us from the side. We both turned to face a man who stood about five foot eight inches high, with a wiry build, thinning grey hair and snapping dark brown eyes. The man was in his robust seventies, mid to late, and was attired in black clerical garb with a Roman collar. He was looking at Brennan. "I'm Father Killeen. Now, which one are you?"

"Brennan. I'm happy to meet you, *Father*. This is Mr. Collins. Montague Collins, a good friend of mine."

"Collins, is it?" He searched my face. *"Miceál O Coileáin."*

Brennan just shook his head: *Don't waste your breath; Monty doesn't get it.*

"Hello. Father."

The old fellow did not say another word until we had walked to the car, put his bag in the trunk, settled him in the front seat, and driven free of the terminal. Then he began to reminisce in a strong old-country accent: "Brennan. Ah, yes. A dear little lad you were, too. You don't remember me."

"No. Did we meet?"

"Forty-two years ago."

"Oh?"

"In 1949 at the Bodenstown March."

"You met Brennan at some kind of parade when he was a child?"

The old man swivelled in his seat. "Mr. *Collins*. It was not 'some kind of parade.' This is the Bodenstown March we're speaking of here." He waited. In vain. "The annual march to the grave of Wolfe Tone."

"Leader of the 1798 rebellion," I said.

He looked gratified. "That's right. The founder of Irish Republicanism. In the old days, the national Army arrived first at the grave, paid its respects, followed by Fianna Fail. Then, when they'd cleared off, our crowd arrived and slagged everything the first two groups had done! If you paid attention to who was there and what was said, you'd have a leg up on the coming year's Republican policy. Like watching who's lined up in the Kremlin on May Day."

He lapsed into a contented silence for awhile, then: "That emphasis on your name, Mr. Collins, was not meant as a slur, and you have my apologies. Although I obviously took a different side in things when I became active, in my heart of hearts I believe we owed Michael Collins more than we could ever repay. He thought he was doing the right thing by signing the Treaty in '21. Thought it was the best he could get at the time, and it probably was. And of course the year that Mr. Burke here was playing guns at Bodenstown, that being 1949, the Republic was a *fait accompli*."

We drove on without conversation for a few minutes, then Brennan began to recite: *"Vere dignum et justum est, aequum et salutare —"*

Our passenger responded: *"Te quidem Domine omni tempore sed in hac potissimum die gloriosius praedicare, cum Pascha nostrum immolatus est Christus.* I always loved the Easter preface. Little wonder, given the historical significance of Easter for our people. Not your fault, Mr. Collins, that you were raised over here without a sense of history. Ah, how I miss those Latin prayers. I say the old Mass every chance I get."

Brennan directed a look of surprise at me in the rearview mirror. The man really *was* a priest.

Father Killeen said: "It stands to reason Declan's son would have been an altar boy. I hope you've stayed true to the Church, Brennan, a good Catholic, not like so many today."

"I have," Brennan assured him.

After a few more miles Brennan said: "We have one stop to make, then we'll drop you off at the hospital, Father. Where will you be staying?"

"Your pater has made some sort of arrangement for me."

"Good. He's under police guard, you know. They have a man posted outside his room."

"I should have no trouble getting past him." Father Killeen smiled.

When we got to the movie museum, Maura and the kids were not in sight, so I got out of the car, went inside, and spoke to the receptionist. I sweet-talked her into letting me in to find my wife and children. I pulled out my wallet and offered to leave my credit card with her but she smiled and told me to go ahead. Good thing: I didn't see the card in my wallet. I would worry about that later. It didn't take long to locate the family; they had one more exhibit to see, so I went back to the car. They trooped out a few minutes later. As soon as Father Killeen saw Maura, he gave up his front seat and squeezed in the back with me and the kids. Maura protested, to no avail.

"Don't be worrying about me; I've known rougher transport than this."

Brennan made the introductions: "Father Killeen, this is Maura, Tom and Normie."

"Pleased to make your acquaintance."

The priest smiled as he listened to the kids discussing the film clip they had edited, and arguing about which movie was the greatest of all time. When we reached the hospital, Brennan got out, took the old fellow's suitcase and made for the entrance. Father Killeen climbed out of the back seat, then turned and spoke through the open car window. "Your husband's a fine man," he said to Maura.

"You're too kind, Father," she replied in a voice loaded with meaning.

"I hope to see you and the children again before long, Mrs. Burke. And you, Mr. Collins. Good day to you now. God bless you." The priest walked jauntily towards his meeting with his old comrade in arms. Brennan was waiting for him at the hospital door, and they disappeared inside.

Maura twisted in her seat and made a face at me: "Maybe you'll connect with a compliment some other time, Collins."

I looked to my kids for support but realized they hadn't heard the exchange, so engrossed were they in some brochures they had obtained from the museum.

Brennan strode out to the car a few minutes later and took his place behind the wheel.

"How did the reunion go?" I asked.

"Effusive on the part of Killeen, wary on Declan's part. I couldn't follow it all, since Killeen started off in Irish. Of course, Dec wouldn't have caught it all either. Never heard more than a few words of the old tongue from him once we emigrated. Da gave me the eye. I took the hint and left."

When we were on the seventh floor of the hotel Brennan headed for his room, saying: "Da's getting out today so we'll all go over there this evening. Wake me at half six."

There was a Broadway musical Maura wanted to see, *The Secret Garden,* which boasted an all-female creative team: composer, lyricist, producer and director. We scored four tickets and enjoyed the show. Supper was deli food in the hotel suite. I went down the hall to knock on Brennan's door. It took him a few minutes to answer; when he did, he looked as if he needed another week of sleep. "I'll meet you in your room after I have a shower."

He joined us a few minutes later, looking considerably more chipper after a dousing and a shave. The five of us ate sandwiches, and we brewed some coffee. When I had eaten my fill I went into the bathroom to brush my teeth and, just then, the telephone rang. Maura picked it up.

"Monty?" I heard her say. I stopped the brush in mid-stroke. "No, Monty can't come to the phone right now. He's suffering from a very painful condition and he's too embarrassed to go and have it treated." *Oh, Christ.* "What's that? Brennan? Yes, he's here and he appears to be asymptomatic. So far. I'll put him on."

I then heard Brennan's curt voice. "Yes? No, not really. But I've a feeling he's going to lose the will to live when he emerges from the bathroom. Mmm. What's that? Ah, no. Gone. Chicago. No, I doubt it. I must be off. Oh. Just send it here. Bye." Click.

I thought of just staying in the bathroom of room 703 for the rest of my natural life. And why not? The alternatives were too grim to face. I took extra time to make my teeth squeaky clean, then opened the door. Four pairs of eyes locked on to me as I emerged. "So. Chez Burke, for some lessons in history," I tried.

Maura ushered the kids out with a deadly look in my direction as she passed.

"What was that all about?" I whispered to Burke when they had cleared the room.

"Didn't you ever hear the phrase 'I told you never to call me here,' Montague?"

"Rosemary, I take it. She's never called me in her life."

"You dropped your credit card in her car; she'll send it over. Don't be worrying about it now. Tonight should be entertaining enough to distract The MacNeil."

†

Declan was ensconced in a comfortable chair pulled up to the big card table in the Burkes' family room downstairs. The room was done in dark green with framed posters and photos on the walls; there was an impressive selection of Irish whiskeys on the bar in one corner, and there was beer in a small fridge. Flanking the invalid were Teresa and Father Killeen. Somebody had recently vacated one of the other chairs, if the empty shot glass was any indication.

"Is that a glass of whiskey I see in front of you there, Declan?" Brennan said in greeting.

"Will you people leave me in peace?"

"Surely you're not permitted to mix alcohol with your medication?"

"You sound like your brother Patrick. He's been hovering over me like a nanny ever since this happened. I finally put the run to him — the chair beside me is still warm from his arse — and now you're here tormenting me. Whiskey is not unknown to me; it has always perked me up. Sit down and stop giving out to me about my health."

"Maura!" Declan's eyes lit up. "Have you come to murmur kind, sweet words to us all? Start there with my worried little wife, and save the best for me. Have you met Father Killeen?"

"Yes, we've met. Evening, Father."

"Good evening. Please call me Leo. Ah, the children. Well, a young man, I should say. And a young lady."

The kids said hello. Then Teresa wisely suggested other activities that might interest them upstairs: a box of toys for Normie, a piano for Tommy Douglas. They were gone in a flash.

"We were just reliving old times," said Leo. "I'm sure your father has recounted many of these tales to you, Brennan, yourself being the firstborn son, but I'm hoping you'll indulge a pair of old timers if their memories tend to get repetitive."

Repetitive? Not much chance. Declan never recounted tales to anyone, birth order be damned. The firstborn son crossed his arms over his chest and raised an eyebrow at his father across the table. Declan looked down and took a sip of whiskey, then gratefully turned his attention to Maura, who was admiring a framed poster showing a number of Irish writers, among them Yeats, Joyce, Wilde, O'Casey, Behan, and dashing Flann O'Brien in a fedora. "When you've had your fill of greatness over there, come find a seat among some of the lesser lights of the Irish race."

"Lesser lights? Surely you're not speaking of anyone in this room," Leo Killeen protested.

"Just an attempt to put the girl at ease, Leo. She's a shy little thing, easily intimidated by powerful personalities such as ours."

"You're not fooling me for a minute," the old fellow laughed. "Here, *achree*," he said when Maura came to the table, "don't let me get between you. What God has joined together, let no man put asunder."

Everyone looked puzzled as he got up and moved so Maura could sit next to Brennan. I remembered then that Father Killeen had mistakenly assumed Maura was Brennan's wife. Brennan caught on and smiled. Teresa began: "Surely, Father, you didn't think Maura was —"

Leo interrupted. "You did say, quite discreetly, when I mentioned little Maura here, that they were having troubles and that Brennan was hoping the holiday would help them smooth things over." Declan sat quiet, obviously amused by the mix-up. "But never mind. I shouldn't have spoken. My apologies, Maura. You'll work things out. I heard in great detail about the events of Friday night, when — thanks be to God — the attempt on Declan's life was unsuccessful. I know young Brennan threw his body over yours to protect you from the gunfire. He wouldn't have done that if he didn't think there was something worth saving!"

The smile vanished from Brennan's face. But then he obviously decided a bit of bullshit was called for: "Nah. I yanked her body over mine. Figured she'd provide more cover than the skinny girl I really had my eye on."

Maura could not quite hide the emotion in her face, remembering the attack and her proximity to the line of fire. Suddenly, she turned in her seat and threw her arms around Brennan's neck. He embraced her and patted her hair. It was obvious she was in tears.

"Women!" Brennan said lightly.

Leo beamed a smile of satisfaction in his direction. "So, where was I when these young people came in? Oh yes, back in the Joy. Declan here did not make any friends among the screws on B wing —"

"Excuse me for just a second, Leo," Teresa said, "but would anyone like a fresh drink?"

"Oh, yeah," Brennan replied. "We all would, I'm sure." Teresa poured us each a whiskey and returned to the table.

"Isn't it a bit unusual," I asked Father Killeen, "for a man to leave off being a — a soldier in your organization to become a priest?"

Once again my ignorance set the old man reeling. "My dear Mr. Collins. May I call you Monty? I have to say it, as gently as I can, Monty: read your history. I am far from being the only man to make the journey from the Army to the priesthood. In some cases of course, it was the monastery. Who was the fellow, Declan, who started up a branch of the Legion of Mary while interned in the Curragh? No, no, that was after your time. The Curragh being the regular Army's headquarters, in the South," Leo explained to me, "where detention camps were set up. During the Emergency of 1939 to '45 our people had to rub shoulders with Germans and even some Brits! But let's not get into that. To return to your question, Monty, I'm not an unusual case at all. There was a very religious element in our movement, no two ways about it."

Maura decided that, since the knife was in, she should give it a little twist. Taking a swig of whiskey, she confided: "Monty has never been to Ireland. But I have."

Sadly, the old soldier shook his head. "He hasn't had your advantages —"

"Neither has Declan," Brennan interrupted, "not since he came here on the run in Anno Domini 1950."

"Well, I'm about to straighten that out for him, aren't I Declan?" Mr. Burke looked like a man who was longing to say: *Not in front of the children.* But he said nothing, and took a gulp of Tullamore Dew. "You understand that it was for his own protection, after —"

"Never mind that right now, Leo. We'll work all that out."

"We surely will. Now what was I saying before the prospect of a drink got us all distracted?"

"Something about B wing, wasn't it, Father?" Maura smiled at Declan, who refused to acknowledge her helpful inquiries.

"Oh, yes, Mountjoy Prison. In Dublin, as I'm sure you know. Well, yer man here could not be described as a model prisoner and took some blows as a result. But a model Republican he was to the end."

"What was it exactly that you were imprisoned for, Declan?" Maura asked sweetly, as if she had forgotten the minutiae of an oft-told tale.

Declan exercised his right to remain silent, and Father Killeen replied: "The Special Criminal Court, which of course your father-in-law, as a member of the Irish Republican Army, refused to recognize, found him guilty of being a member of an illegal organization. They swept a bunch of us up at the same time. Fortunately for everyone he only served — what was it, Declan? Six months? I wasn't so lucky, so I served a bit more time than that. Still, it was a slice of cake compared to what I endured in the Crumlin Road jail in Belfast years later. But that's all behind me now."

Teresa Burke was looking at her husband as if she had just heard the verdict all over again, and had no intention of waiting six months, or six days, for him to be released. But Leo had not come to the end of his reminiscences.

"Remember how rough around the edges some of our lads were, Declan? God forgive me for saying it, but for some of them the best thing that ever happened was a stint in prison. It was tough, but the education they got inside was just not available to them in their regular lives."

In response to the skeptical faces around the table, Leo explained: "It came to be known as the Republican University. Older Republican prisoners gave the younger ones classes in Irish, in history, in other subjects. I was something of a professor myself. Declan here brushed up on his Irish between shifts maintaining the distillery we set up inside, eh Dec? But these young fellows, some of them didn't know a thing when they went in. Like the lad on the pawnshop operation."

Declan shot him a murderous look but Leo missed it. "I don't know whether you've heard this one, Brennan."

"I suspect it's something I'll be hearing for the first time, Leo."

"Declan and this young boy were to rob a pawnshop to raise funds for our work. You'd be surprised how much money was sitting in pawnshops in those days. I think they got two thousand pounds, a lot of money back then. Of course that was not the sort of operation your father generally participated in. I know he felt it was beneath him, and he was none too happy about it."

"He looks none too happy now," Brennan remarked.

"He said he would put together a plan for a bank raid if need be. But orders are orders. The pawnbroker was notorious for his anti-Republican sympathies. The fellow who was supposed to go along with our young lad became unavailable very suddenly, so Declan was given the task. I hope you'll all excuse my language here, or Declan's language, I should say: 'If I wind up doing seven years for holding up a fecking junk shop,' he told his superior officer, 'I'll expect you to blast your way in to Mountjoy Prison, get me out, and then stand there like a man while I tear the heart and soul out of you with my bare hands.'"

"That would explain the little smile on Da's face," Brennan interrupted, "years later when he heard the news reports that a helicopter landed in an Irish prison yard and lifted some IRA men out."

"Ah, yes, 1973. A most spectacular escape from Mountjoy Prison. It was hard not to smile. Now stay quiet, *avic,* and let me tell about your father."

Brennan sent a barely perceptible wink in my direction. "Forgive me, Father. Go on."

Dublin, 1942
"What went wrong in the pawnshop, Declan? Young Shea was picked up last night."

"Young Shea couldn't keep his feckin' gob shut, that's what went wrong."

*"No need for that kind of language when I ask you for a report,
Declan. Now get on with it."*

*"In we go, the pair of us, with our face masks on. We draw our
weapons. I'm not saying a word. I point my gun at the pawnbroker's head and then I gesture towards the cash register just in
case he doesn't get it. The poor man is palsied with the shaking. He
doesn't even see I don't have my finger on the trigger; I'm not going
to shoot a poor man working at his job. But he hands me the cash,
all of it. I stuff it in my shirt. Mission accomplished. Time to go.
Or so it should be. But then I see young Shea goggling at something
in the show case.*

*"The lad pipes up: 'What's that doin' here? Where'd ya get that
necklace?'*

*"The man behind the counter can barely speak, he's trembling
so much. 'I, em . . . a young girl and her mother —'*

*"'She pawned the feckin' thing! I loved that girl with all my
heart. I want that back! Jazes!' Then Shea looks up at the man.
'How much for that necklace?'*

*"As if the lad doesn't have me crabbed enough by this time, he
then turns to me and asks for money!*

*"I'd maintained a proper operational silence up to then but I
couldn't help myself, Leo. I barked at the kid: 'We're robbing the
fecking shop, you little gobshite. Grab the fecking jewels and be
done with it!' Of course he got arrested, linking himself to the jewellery like that."*

"Luckily for Declan, nobody was able to identify him," Leo concluded.

"Lucky for him is right." Teresa spoke with ice in her voice.
"Because if they had, I assure you, there would have been nothing left
of Declan to identify. I would have seen to that myself."

"Understandable, Teresa, understandable. Some of this would not
have endeared him to you at all." Father Killeen then reached into his
pocket and produced a small leather-bound notebook. The brown
leather was worn, and yellowed papers stuck out on all sides. "Now
here's a rare sight, a photo of the man himself. That's me. I was OC of
the Third Battalion, Dublin Brigade, at the time. There's Declan, and

the other fellow shall remain nameless." It was a grainy photo of a young, hawkish-looking Declan, standing sentry with a machine gun at the ready. Leo Killeen stood in a doorway behind him. Thin and intense, dark eyes glaring at the camera, he had the look of a killer. It was difficult to reconcile the photo with the chatty cleric sitting across from me in Sunnyside.

Leo got up to "stretch his legs." Before he left the room, he took Brennan's hand and put it over Maura's, giving them both a little squeeze. As soon as the priest cleared the room, Maura turned to her "husband" and asked him whether he had taken the garbage out as she had asked him to do, over and over and over.

"If I take the garbage out and mow the lawn, do you think your headache will go away? Dear?" Brennan replied sweetly.

"Ever mowed a lawn, Brennan?" Maura answered, every bit as sweetly.

"I tried it once. But I didn't know how to work the machine."

"Where was this?" Declan wanted to know. "There's not enough grass around here to keep a rabbit alive. If rabbits eat grass."

"It was at, em, Sandra's summer place up in Nova Scotia. When I was visiting one time. Her father had this list of 'chores' for me. Old Worthington got a little frustrated and said to me: 'Burke. Don't you know anything but football, fucking and fa-mi-re-do?' That was the first glimpse I had of a sense of humour in the man."

"Brennan!" his mother exclaimed, but not without a hint of laughter in her voice. Declan smiled. "I wonder how Sandra is these days," Teresa mused. "Lovely girl."

Father Killeen walked in then. "What did I miss?"

"A story about this fellow's old girlfriend."

"Girlfriends, wives, you boys should try living my kind of life. You two wouldn't last a week," the old priest boasted as he picked up his glass and gestured first at me and then at Brennan. "No trouble for the likes of me, of course. A stint in the Curragh and hard time up north in the Crum, and you soon learn how to live without the comforts of female flesh. You boys are too attached to the worldly life, I can tell by the look of you."

Brennan smiled broadly and hid it in his whiskey glass. His parents looked highly amused. But Maura couldn't resist a little jab below the belt. "I know what you're saying, Father Killeen, but Brennan seems to have lived quite well without — what was it again? Starts with an F. Oh, right: football."

✝

The next afternoon Brennan contrived to capture Leo Killeen alone while Declan was occupied with a follow-up appointment at the hospital. Leo had spent his first night at the Burkes' but was moving on to new lodgings, a rectory at one of the local churches. Before Declan left for the outpatient department, his son assured him he would deliver their guest to his new abode. Eventually. For now, though, Killeen, Brennan and I had another destination in view. We walked down to Queens Boulevard and entered O'Malley's pub. It was a classic Irish watering hole, long and narrow, with the bar along the left side as you walked in and a narrow shelf along the right-hand wall. The place was done in very dark wood, the walls covered with framed black-and-white photos of boxers, pool players and other sportsmen. At either end of the bar was a glassed-in cabinet with more memorabilia. Ninety percent of the patrons were male, all smoking, and most of them were gathered at the front end of the pub; horse-racing was the subject of the day. Celtic music played in the background, but the regulars talked over it.

Leo brushed past the convivial group at the front and made for one of the high round tables at the back. The bartender called over: "And what can I get for you today, Father?"

Brennan started to answer, but the barman's eyes were on the only man in the room sporting a Roman collar. Father Killeen ordered a whiskey for himself and Brennan and looked questioningly at me. I asked for a pint of Guinness.

"Where's Mickey today?" Brennan asked the barman after he poured the drinks.

"At a wake over at Lynch's. I said I'd fill in for him. *Sláinte!*" We raised our glasses, and the man returned to his duties.

"So, young Brennan, your father has been modest about his service to his country." Leo took a delicate sip of the golden liquid.

"He keeps himself to himself, you might say," Brennan agreed, sitting back and fishing in his jacket for a pack of smokes. He offered one to Leo, who declined.

"It's about time somebody spoke for the record then."

It was as clear to me as it was to Brennan that Declan liked the record just as it was, a *tabula rasa* when it came to his history as a man bearing arms. But if Leo believed Declan had kept his son, and the rest of his offspring, in the dark out of a reluctance to boast of his military accomplishments, neither of us was about to disillusion him.

"Well, you've no doubt heard all about your grandfather's exploits at the GPO in 1916."

"I've heard a good sight more about my grandfather and granduncles than about my own father."

"Your grandfather, Christy Burke, burned with the Republican fire and he was there on Easter Monday with Pearse, Connolly and the other patriots when they took over the General Post Office. Unlike the patriots, poets and scholars who were executed by the British, your grandfather walked away a free man — after a stint in Kilmainham Jail.

"As you know, our people regrouped. And the public, who had been indifferent during the Rising, were outraged by the executions. The Tan War, the Anglo-Irish War, followed. You've heard of the notorious Black and Tans, Montague, the irregular force the Brits sent over to do the dirty work." I allowed as how I had.

"That's when Christy Burke took up with Michael Collins." The old fellow nodded at me, as if all Collinses the world over could share in the glory. "I don't see any resemblance in you, Montague, but you'll want to look into it nonetheless. Brennan here looks more like Mick Collins, in fact: tall, dark-haired, bit of the same kind of mouth. Collins was better looking." Brennan laughed. "But then, he was a lot younger than you. Never made it to his thirty-second birthday, God rest him.

"Now, your father surely told you that he met Collins. Well, I say met, but it would be more accurate to say he was presented to the Big Fellow by his proud papa. Declan was three or four years old. The way I heard it, little Declan kept pulling at Collins's trousers — one of those rare occasions when he was in uniform — and asking if he could see his gun! And Collins supposedly ruffled Declan's hair and told him he'd have no need of a gun by the time he was old enough to carry one."

"And was he right?"

Killeen shot Brennan a piercing look. "Obviously we didn't think so." He looked away and then took a slow drink of his whiskey.

We listened as the music switched from laments played on fiddle, whistle and bodhran to rabble-rousing ballads recalling old victories and defeats. "Ah, the old tunes," Leo remarked. "The Republican homes were where you'd hear the old Fenian songs. Even jail couldn't silence our lads. Many's the singalong we enjoyed under the noses of the warders back in the day. Your da loved a song. But what was most valuable about Declan was his ability to instill some discipline in the other Volunteers. He did a great deal of the training, with weapons and operations. There was no nonsense about him when he was working."

"I'll bet," Brennan muttered.

"And he was a crack shot with a rifle."

"I see. What happened?"

"Your father was ordered to, em, remove two traitors from our midst."

"Who gave the order?"

"One of his superior officers."

"You?" The old man glared into Brennan's eyes, then looked down at his hands.

Dublin, 1950

"What am I doing here, Leo? Where is everybody? When you summoned me to the usual spot in Parnell Street, I figured the entire command would be here."

"Never mind everybody else. I need answers from you, Declan, and I need them tonight."

"Why? What's happened?"

"I'm asking the questions here. Tell me about the raid."

"We headed north, crossed the border, entered the designated British Army barracks, lifted their entire supply of Lee Enfield .303 rifles, and returned to Dublin. 'Twas a grand time entirely."

"I don't like your attitude here, Declan. Give it to me in detail and tell me what I want to know. Don't waste my time, or your own."

"Am I runnin' short of time, Leo? All right, all right. The five of us went up there at night in two cars. McCann was driving one of them. I was beside him. I did my intelligence work beforehand, so I knew the layout of the barracks and where the rifles were stored. We left the cars way down the road, crept round the back of the barracks, cut through the perimeter fence and approached the Nissen hut where the armoury was located. We waited for the two sentries to go on their rounds, and we entered the hut. The rifles were secured by a chain running through the trigger guards. Our lads were prepared for that; we had cutters with us. We got away with two dozen rifles. Not the most spectacular raid, but a successful little mission. The raid didn't make the news, as far as I ever heard. I suppose the Brits didn't want to announce to the world that their defences had been breached yet again."

"There was another purpose to the mission, though, wasn't there? We had incontrovertible evidence that McCann was an informer —"

"I know that, Leo. I did my duty with McCann. That happened some distance from the barracks, but I took him — took his body — back and deposited him on the road leading to the hut."

"Good. He did us more harm than you'll ever know and he was primed to do more. Did you give him time to make things right?"

"How in the hell could he do that?"

"Not with us. With the Man Above."

"He said his Act of Contrition. Why are we alone here tonight, Leo?"

"You were given another order, weren't you. You had two informers to eliminate, not just one. Tell me about the arms dump."

"What about it?"

"You were supposed to go there with Quinn, stash the Lee Enfields, and dispatch Quinn while you were at it. What happened?"

"I drove out to Quinn's house in Terenure. And what was going on but a grand old hooley inside, a birthday party for his oul fella, *turning sixty. Quinn's mother invited me in, handed me a glass brimming with whiskey, and sat me down with the family. Quinn was in full flight on the fiddle. The wife was banging the piano so hard her arse was coming off the bench with every downbeat. Their little son was dancing and everyone was gathered round clapping and stomping their feet, and singing one of the old come-all-ye's. Then the little lad — seven or eight years old he was — sang one of the old, sad songs in the most beautiful voice you've ever heard. There wasn't another sound in the room, just everyone gazing at the wee child singing. Quinn picked him up afterwards, gave him a big kiss and danced him round the room.*

"Then the Republican songs started up, and everyone joined in. That's when I gave Quinn the eye. He stared back at me for a few long seconds as the music roared on around us. Then he bolted."

"And?"

"And nothing. I didn't make a move. I let him go."

"You disobeyed your orders, Declan. You let a known informer get away. And here's where it gets worse for you: Quinn found out, somehow, where the arms dump was and betrayed it to the authorities. So we lost all our hard-won weaponry from that dump. You look as if this is a surprise to you."

"You're fucking right, it's a surprise. You'd better not be telling me you think I whispered to Quinn where our stash was."

"You're in the soup at headquarters, Declan. What do you have to say for yourself?"

"I let Quinn go."

"Why?"

"Have you ever heard my little boy sing, Leo?"

Brennan took a long swig of O'Malley's best whiskey, then busied himself with a cigarette. He didn't look at me or Leo. He had to come to terms with something he had perhaps suspected all his life, and now knew to be true. I tried to picture the scene in the woods in Northern Ireland. Declan Burke with a gun, standing over "Benedict," the traitor. A man who saw the hit coming, a man who was given the opportunity to say his prayers before his death. Did he beg to be spared? Wouldn't we all? And the second informer. The worst he got was a threatening stare. I knew what a look you could get from Declan's icy blue eyes, even when he wasn't staring you down as a representative of the Irish Republican Army. But he didn't have a heart of ice; he couldn't bring himself to shoot a man he had seen in the company of his wife and children.

"Those two men," Leo said, "the informers, were guilty of the worst kind of betrayal. Terrible things happened to some of our lads as the result of their treachery. You have to understand that, Brennan."

"Did the IRA believe my father had given away the location of the arms cache?"

"They did. Your father hadn't given it away. He hadn't taken Quinn there. But there were many in the organization who thought Declan was an informer himself and he'd tipped Quinn off about the weapons. The truth is, we just don't know how Quinn found out. We're a talkative race. Maybe somebody else was informing, or just let it slip when he shouldn't have. Perhaps under the influence of drink. It's right there in the IRA handbook now, you know. The Green Book. Volunteers are warned against 'drink-induced loose talk and pub gossip.'"

"It's an Irish movement after all," I piped up.

"It is indeed," Father Killeen agreed. "And we have to recognize that. Though I think the Stalinists were a little harsh in their judgement."

I was even farther out of the loop than I thought. "What's that, Leo?"

Brennan answered my question: "Joseph Stalin said he couldn't take the Irish revolutionaries seriously because they hadn't shot any bishops."

Leo added: "That wasn't all. A couple of Communist agents looking into the Irish movement back in the thirties apparently reported to headquarters that the Irish were 'too Mexican' to be good revolutionaries! So we're not apparatchiks, we're not robotniks!" The old soldier was still smarting from the wound.

Brennan prompted him: "You were saying, Leo, before Joe Stalin offended you —"

"Yes, the night of the *ceilidh* at Quinn's house. Declan left the man's house, drove by himself to the arms dump and deposited the rifles. Well, except for one he kept for himself. Two days later the arms dump was in the hands of the authorities, and your father was on the run. You'd know this better than I would, Brennan, but I understand he spirited your mother and you children out of Dublin so fast you didn't have time to say a Hail Mary for the journey. He'd been holding a stash of money for the IRA, and he took it with him. That didn't help his case any at GHQ." Leo leaned forward and gripped Brennan's hand with his own. "But there have been so many changes — to put it mildly — in Republican forces since then, it's not the same organization at all. I honestly do not see a Republican hand in this. Didn't I come over here to assure him of that?"

Brennan did not look reassured. "What measures did Headquarters take in response to my father's actions?"

"Declan was court-martialled *in absentia.*"

"And the sentence?"

"It was a sentence of death."

Chapter 5

There's a broken heart for every light on Broadway.
— Fred Fisher/Howard Johnson,
"There's a Broken Heart for Every Light on Broadway"

March 11, 1991

We deposited Leo at his new headquarters, then went to the Burkes' house. Brennan asked me to wait in the family room and said he'd join me shortly, after he had a word with his mother. A few minutes later they came downstairs together. Teresa Burke held a tattered manila envelope in her hand; she looked exhausted. "It's all I have," she said. "And I don't know what it means. I have no idea how it could possibly be connected with your father."

Brennan's voice was gentle. "This is terrible for you, Mam, but we have to get to the bottom of it."

"This, these papers, may not have anything to do with what's going on now. The woman gave them to me, how many years ago? At the old Met."

"Maria Callas, 1956."

"Yes. A long time. Your father never read this — he couldn't find it." She smiled. "They say if you want to hide a book, hide it in a library."

She went upstairs, and we heard her go out the front door. "Visiting a neighbour," Brennan explained.

He opened the envelope and drew out a few sheets of yellowed paper, pages that appeared to have been sliced from a small journal. Thumbing through them, he said: "The dates are all jumbled, so we must be dealing with more than one year." He began to read out loud:

December 18. Christmas Concert. I was in the second row of the eighth grade choir. We were singing "Adeste Fideles." The lights were in my eyes but I picked out Mom and Dad. Dad was slumped over on Mom and he made this big snoring sound. Everybody looked at him. Then it was time for my solo in "Gentle Mary." I was really nervous! But I started to sing it and I was fine. Then — I couldn't believe it. Dad jerked awake, looked at the stage and this big stupid grin came on his face. He started giggling, like a little kid. I was so embarrassed I wished he was dead. I still do. He's nothing but an old drunk.

December 25. Christmas. Big deal. We had to go to Mass with the old drunk. He kept yelling out the responses ahead of everyone else. Once he said: *"et cum spiritu tuo,"* and the end of it came out like a burp. The people in front of us were snickering. And his breath stunk. I'm sure the whole church could smell it. I hate him. Jimmy says I'm lucky Mom doesn't send me down to the pub. She sends Jimmy to drag him home in front of all the neighbours. Jim says as soon as he gets enough money saved up he's moving away from us. Dad passed out before the turkey and Mom took a big screaming fit. How come? Because she's stuck with an old alkie for a husband. For the rest of her life. I bet she wishes we were Protestant so she could get a divorce.

September 20: Tenth grade, big deal. They asked me to join the band but I don't know. Maybe if Denise joins. Dad's away, and I have my fingers crossed that he never comes back. Mom sat me down all serious and tried to tell me where he was. I just said: "Who cares?" Jimmy found a job up in Boston and he never comes home. Lucky duck.

November 28: Guess who's back? Dad. He's different. I hope. He took me out for a walk. I tried to say no but he kept asking me. At least he didn't look embarrassing. He was clean, his hair was cut and he had on a nice sweater and tie. And a new coat. He said he had been away at some kind of drunk's hospital. (Thank God none of my friends were around when he said that!) He turned my face towards him with his hand and said he loved me, that he loved Mom and us kids more than anything in the world. That he was sorry for all the bad things he had done, that he had given up drinking (!) forever, that these monks or priests or doctors, whatever they were, had helped him stop. He promised he would be like a new father for all of us. Maybe he's serious because he didn't wink or give me a stupid grin, or any of the other dumb things he used to do.

December 12: Dad took Mom and me to a play. We got a babysitter for Beth and Kevin. It was this Irish play called *The Shadow of a Gunman*. I didn't get some of it, but Dad explained it at intermission. He told me all about this Sean O'Casey, how he lived in poverty in Dublin, and grew up to be a dock worker and write plays. Whoever would have guessed Dad knew about all these old writers?

March 17. Saint Patrick's Day, but Dad stayed home. Mom got a night out with some of the ladies. The Fitzes had a party for the little kids and ours went. Good riddance. It was just me and Dad home and he asked me if I wanted to learn to play poker. Said I could win money for college next year! You're supposed to have a "poker face," not letting on if you have great cards or lousy ones. Dad has a really good poker face; I just kept giggling. He was making me laugh. I never knew he was so funny. I would die if he ever started drinking booze and being an idiot again like he used to. But he won't.

June 28. Graduation was beautiful! I had a white dress and won an award in history. Shane kept smiling at me but I noticed Gianni Sodano was looking at me too. Sometimes I like Gianni better than Shane. The prom was great. The school wanted Mom and Dad to chaperone the dance but Mom couldn't go because Kevin was sick. Dad came anyway. It wasn't that bad. I actually danced with Dad and he was really sweet. He said: "Mary, I will love and protect you for the rest of my life." I started crying, I don't know why. But I was really happy. After the song was over, Gianni came up and was really polite. He said: "Mr. Desmond, may I dance with your daughter?" Dad said: "That depends. Are you light on your feet?" "Yes, sir." "Are you a good Catholic?" "Yes, sir." It went on and on. When I finally got to dance with G., he said: "Your father is a neat guy." "He's the best father in the world, so what?" I told him. I'm glad he likes Dad because I think things could become serious between me and Gianni.

July 3. I'll soon be Mrs. Gianni Sodano. I'm finally getting married! Mom says twenty-two is not old but it seemed to take forever for Gianni to finish college and me to finish biz school. Gianni fits right in with my family — what a relief! He even thinks the Irish are charming! A couple of weeks ago me and Gianni stayed up with Dad listening to him read from that book by the well-known author James Joyce. That was on "Bloomsday." I never laughed so hard in my life the way Dad imitated all those accents. He wanted us to stay up with him and have cocoa in the middle of the night like they do in the book but I couldn't stay awake. When I got up next morning, there was Gianni and Dad, asleep at the kitchen table with their cocoa mugs and a big puddle of cocoa spilt in the book! The wedding is going to be beautiful.

July 26. The wedding was beautiful, or so I see from the pictures. One good thing, my name isn't Desmond anymore. I hope Gianni and I can change apartments after a couple of years, to get farther away from — my ex-father! Where do I begin? How about when he got to the church just in time to walk me down the aisle? He didn't even come home the night before the wedding. Mom was frantic. Why even care? I couldn't believe it was the same person I'd come to respect and love over the past six years, fool that I was. Yes, it's him — the same person I hated all the years before that! I practically had to hold him up on the way to the altar. He had his chin kind of stuck down in his collar and he had on this fake solemn look as if he was trying to keep from giggling. When Mamma and Papa Sodano turned and looked at us I could hardly keep from crying. The expression on their faces was so kind, I wanted to throw myself in their arms. I hope they don't think our kids will be like that. I'll keep my fingers crossed for a girl first, to relieve everyone's mind. Who ever heard of a lady alcoholic? There is not enough space in this book to describe all the hideous things he did at my reception. But why bother? After your father jumps up from the head table, stumbles out into the hall, throws up and slips in it, and lies there giggling and sobbing, is there anything more to say? Is he still your father? NO! He's dead as far as I'm concerned. I'll have to ask Ruth about the thing the Jews have for someone who's disgraced the family way beyond the point of embarrassment. Chivas or Shiva or something. Now, for the good things. SEE the wedding album. Pictures carefully selected!

Neither of us spoke after Brennan finished reading. Who was Desmond? Why did someone — his wife? — storm up to Declan and Teresa and thrust this envelope into Teresa's hands? I finally said: "We have our first real names. Mary Desmond Sodano, sister of Jimmy, Beth and Kevin. Do you know them?"

"Doesn't strike a chord. And Mam says she didn't know the woman."

"Maybe this Desmond was a drinking buddy of your father's, and the wife blamed your dad instead of blaming her husband. Though it seems a bit extreme to go operatic about it. Wouldn't you think?"

"Maybe not. If this girl's diary is any indication, drink destroyed their family life, and the love that had blossomed between the father and his little girl. Must have been like a disease coming back after years of good reports."

"What are the chances your dad will sit down with us and reminisce about Mr. Desmond?"

"What are the chances Vatican City will win a year's supply of nappies for having the highest birth rate in the Western world? And is this diary even related to his current troubles?"

"Assume for now it is. So we're talking about a family named Desmond with a daughter named Mary, who married Gianni Sodano sometime before 1956."

"Morceau de gâteau."

"And the icing of course — we dare not overlook it — is another ruined wedding. So, Brennan, who do you have in mind to search the parish records?"

"I'll call in the services of my nieces and nephews. One of them will track it down for us."

"Oh? Your word is law with these kids?"

Burke raised one eyebrow as he picked up the phone, and assured me his word was "infallible."

That evening Brennan and I were still at the House of Burke, making small talk with his mother and debating where to go for a night out. The answer came to us soon enough. We watched from the living room as Declan made his way along the hall to the door, making every effort to walk like a man who had never required so much as a glance from a medical professional. He was pale but scrubbed, and his stocky frame was arrayed in a beautifully tailored dark blue sports jacket over a white shirt and silver tie. Teresa started to get up from her chair but Brennan put a restraining hand on her arm. "Where are you going, Da?" he demanded.

"Who will rid me of this meddlesome priest?" Declan snapped. "I am going out on the town with some old, old friends."

Brennan got up and loomed over his father. "Monty and I would be delighted to join the party. Let's go, gentlemen," he declared, holding the door open for us and neatly filching his father's car keys from his pocket. "Don't wait up, Ma."

There was no conversation in the car, other than Declan's terse directions.

We pulled up before a nondescript building on a commercial street in Long Island City. There was no sign on the door. To my surprise, a parking valet materialized to deal with the car. We were met inside by a maitre d', with whom Declan exchanged a rapid whispered conversation. He led us inside. A platoon of hulking doormen broke formation and allowed us to pass. The White Gardenia was a spacious club with a stage taking up one end of the room. Murals along the two side walls depicted elegant couples from the 1930s and 1940s dancing, sipping cocktails or strolling the boulevards of New York. Eye-catching young women glided between the white-clothed tables bearing trays of drinks. They were attired in men's black dinner jackets, and starched white shirts, their tiny waists cinched by brightly coloured cummerbunds. We were taken to a table at the far left of the stage.

Two men stood to greet us. One was of Declan's height and stocky build. He was expensively dressed in a charcoal suit, a black shirt and no tie. His hair was iron grey, brushed back from his forehead. He had large, deep-set brown eyes that were locked on Declan's blue ones. The other man was taller, younger, and bulky within the confines of a shiny black suit.

"Paddy," Declan said, extending his hand to the more senior of our two hosts.

"I could say the same to you," the man replied.

Declan gave a little laugh, and made the introductions. "Mr. Corialli, my son Brennan and our friend Montague."

"Call me Patrizio. Please," Corialli answered. We shook hands. "Sit. Will you have dinner? I have ordered a bottle of Irish for you, Declan. If your guests would prefer something else . . ." We shook our heads. Patrizio "Paddy" Corialli's voice was outer boroughs with a trace of southern Italy. I sat on his right facing the stage; the other man, who was not introduced, sat on the left. Declan and Brennan were across from us. In the background, we heard the voice of Luciano Pavarotti.

"It has been a long time, Declan."

Declan's glance took in his son and then me. "Patrizio was a friend of the Irish here in the older days, sort of a bridge between the two, em —"

"Immigrant communities?" Brennan offered.

A dark-haired Italian beauty appeared at our table in black tie, size six, with a bottle of Jameson's, and menus tucked under her arm. She looked like a dancer. "Good evening, Mr. Corialli. Will you be joining us for dinner?"

"Yes. Thank you, Angela. Bring two bottles of the Pio Cesare Barolo I have set aside. We'll look over the specials." She favoured us with a dazzling smile and went for the wine.

"What do you do, Brennan? Did you follow your father into business?"

"I'm a man of the cloth, Patrizio."

"*Benissimo.* I congratulate you, Declan. I alas have no sons in the church."

"Is this your club, Patrizio?" I asked him.

"No, my nephew owns it in partnership with two other men. It is almost like the old days when we were over in the East Fifties. Giorgio has captured the feel of the old club very beautifully."

Angela came with the wine and took our orders. Pavarotti ended his set. Declan and Patrizio chatted — uneasily, I thought — about old times and old timers. I started to say something to Brennan but the activity on the stage had caught his attention. Or so it seemed from a slight widening of his black eyes; otherwise there was no change in his expression. I looked over and saw the members of a brass band picking up their instruments. They were all women and they all had on spike heels, black silk panties, dinner jackets, brightly-coloured cummerbunds, black ties and no shirts. The band master was a very tall, Nordic blonde with a domineering manner. She tapped her baton and the band began with a rousing version of "In the Mood." They played passably well. I mentally thanked fate for plunking me into a seat where I could view the stage without having to wrench myself around. Though I noticed that Brennan and Declan managed to catch some of the show without completely turning their backs on the rest of the table.

Corialli said: "Not the most appropriate entertainment for a man of your profession, Padre."

"It's true," Brennan replied, "that I'm a choral director, but I enjoy something a little brassier once in a while."

Corialli smiled and raised his glass slightly in Brennan's direction.

Our dinner was sumptuous. I ordered seafood linguine expecting the usual mix of scallops and shrimp I would have been served at home; here, the ocean tossed up octopus and starfish along with other less recognizable denizens of the deep. I took the cannoli for dessert. Cigars were offered at the end of the meal, and Corialli, Declan and Brennan fired them up.

The band brought the tempo down with "Moonlight Serenade." Corialli nodded in their direction. "We have a history of high-quality talent here. Female talent. Those were glorious years for the female voice. The songs of the forties and fifties, even the thirties. Our little Evie met with great success, did she not, Declan?"

"Mmm," Declan agreed.

"She is here in New York, performing somewhere. Such a voice, such a presence. Evie always wore a white dress when she sang, and a white flower — I don't think it was a gardenia! — in her yellow hair," he informed us. "Did you know her well when she was with us, Declan? Was it not you who arranged for her debut out in —"

"I hardly knew her," Declan interrupted. "If I gave her career a boost it was off the cuff, but I'm happy to hear it."

When the girls in the band took a break, the room was quiet and Declan leaned over to Corialli. "There was an attempt on my life last week, as you may have heard." Corialli nodded, and Declan continued with considerable understatement: "I'm asking myself who might have been behind it."

"You have some possibilities in mind?" Corialli asked.

Declan glanced sideways at his son and turned back to Corialli. "I may have offended someone in your, em, family a few years back."

"Back when my brother was head of the family. Long time ago, Declan."

"Indeed it was."

Corialli turned to the silent man at his side. "Mr. Burke stepped on our toes once, long ago. But Mr. Burke made it up to us later. Go talk to Alfredo and find out whether there was a misunderstanding." Corialli turned again to Declan. "I do not see why this unfortunate matter would come back to haunt any of us after so many years."

Brennan certainly looked haunted, as we waited for the valet to bring our car around. Declan was taking no questions on the drive home.

Brennan moved across the river to his parents' house in Queens the next day. For my part, I decided it was time to rent a car. I was spending so much time across the river that it made sense to have my own transportation. So I arranged for a vehicle and was assured the hotel provided valet parking. My son gave me a bit of a rough time for acquiring a vehicle on his last day in the city; to compensate, I promised Tom he could take the wheel for a while once we got out of Manhattan. The four of us headed to the suburbs for a tour. We made our way north through the Bronx to Westchester County, through Yonkers up to Tarrytown, then across the county to Long Island Sound. Tom took over the driving. He chafed at the bit when his mother and I insisted on a leisurely pace so we could admire the stately old houses in Larchmont and the boats in Mamaroneck. We stuffed ourselves with seafood and made our way back to Manhattan. We stopped at the hotel, collected Tom's luggage, and drove him to the airport for his flight to Halifax. We assured him he would be loved and missed, then we laid on the instructions. Call us often, eat properly, don't drink, and remember: your home on Dresden Row is not a frat house. No parties. Right. I remembered when my brother and I had the house to ourselves; I kept that to myself.

The next morning I got a call from Brennan. "Progress. We've found Mary Sodano."

"Great. How did we do that?"

"Terry's son and my sister Brigid did some digging. Best of all we have a day, a month and a year. The marriage records show that Gianni Sodano and Mary Desmond were married July 12, 1952. And, by the way, Brigid's working through the Murphys in the phone book. The only Cathal she came up with was somebody's little boy. But there were a lot who didn't answer so she'll keep at it. Back to the Sodanos, Saint Brigid made a few calls and charmed some information out of them. I don't know what line she fed them but she learned that, although Mary and Gianni are away in Italy, Mary's younger sister Beth is in town. And we now have her address."

"And we're going to materialize on her doorstep behind a big bouquet of roses, right?"

"Something like that."

"So we know the big piss-up occurred in July 1952, Desmond hitting the booze, aided and abetted perhaps by your father."

"If a boozer can be said to need assistance."

"All right. So what do we say to Beth Desmond?"

"We'll think of something."

So that afternoon, Brennan and I were at the door of a boxy brick apartment building in Richmond Hill South, a working class area of Queens. It was a damp, windy day and I wished I had worn more than my Sunday go-to-meetin' suit. Beth Desmond Dowd answered our ring at one-thirty. She was an overweight and harried-looking woman in her middle fifties.

"Good afternoon, Mrs. Dowd. I'm Brennan Burke and this is Montague Collins. We're wondering if you can help us. We're trying to find a gentleman by the name of Barry McDermot. He was a member of Saint Finnian's parish back in the fifties and sixties. We've been asking around and we understand he was a friend of your father. We haven't had any luck so far and we're wondering if you might remember something that could put us on the right track."

"McDermot, you say? Doesn't sound familiar."

"Perhaps you'll recall the names of some of your father's acquaintances from those days, and we'll get a lead from that."

She looked us over and decided we were low risk. Must have been the Mormon suits. "Come in then. I'll see what I can do."

She led us to the living room of her ground-floor apartment. Every item had its place, and that place was at right angles to something else. A two-seater couch was flanked by two arm chairs at ninety-degree angles. The seating arrangement faced a mantelpiece with the fireplace bricked up. Magazines were lined up at each end of a veneered coffee table.

We sat, like twin suitors, on the tiny couch. I felt I should be twirling a hat in my hand.

"Tea?"

"Lovely. Thank you," Brennan replied with courtesy.

We were silent while Beth worked in the kitchen. She returned and poured us tea in dainty china cups. She set down a plate of Bourbon chocolate biscuits on the coffee table, six in all.

"Barry McDermot. I don't remember anyone by that name. Barry Casey I remember. He used to come around when I was little."

"I hope you'll forgive me, Mrs. Dowd," I began.

"Beth," she said.

"Beth. Is your father still —"

"Alive? I wouldn't know. Though they do say alcohol is a preservative. He may be pickled somewhere."

"You lost touch with your dad, then."

"He's the one who lost touch. With reality and with us. I haven't seen him since the late 1950s. Neither has anyone else in the family. But I did hear of a sighting maybe ten years ago. In a Salvation Army shelter for indigenous, no, what is it? Indigent? Indigent men. We were all indigent in this family, after our main breadwinner hit bottom. Oh, well. We did manage to get by. In a way."

"I'm sorry to hear it, Beth, what a shame," Brennan put in. "Had he been troubled by alcoholism all through your childhood?"

"My older sister tells me he was drunk nearly all the time when we were really young. During my formative years he was great. Sober, funny, responsible, hard-working. A man who loved to read. He was a great one for reciting poetry. Who was it, Keats? Was he Irish, or — who's the other guy?"

"Yeats?" Brennan supplied.

"Yeah. Apparently they called Dad 'the professor' at work. Wonder what they'd call him now."

"Where was it your father worked, Beth?" I asked.

"When he worked, he was a port watchman on the Brooklyn waterfront. But he lost that job. Not surprisingly."

"For drinking, you mean?"

"Chances are. But I think something happened. I don't know what. My sister got married and by the time the bills came in, the 'professor' was out of a job. I remember my mother begging him to go and ask for his job back so they could pay the family bills. I kept hoping she would shut up because Mary and Gianni were coming in the front door; I was mortified that Gianni might hear. Mom was saying: 'There are drunks on the payroll all over this city, but you can't expect to get a job anywhere after that.' Whatever 'that' meant. I'm not sure. It was a long time ago. I tuned them out after that. And then he was gone. Poor Mom. She should have been glad to get rid of him, but she just wasn't the same after he finally vamoosed. What a shrew she turned into. I'm sorry to be rambling on like this. You were asking about other friends of his. I'm sure we didn't know most of them, probably just other drunks. I remember Mr. Casey, nice man. I think he was from the church too. Ted O'Neill and his wife. They had eleven kids. Who else?"

"Did he ever mention a Cathal Murphy?" She shook her head. "Declan Burke?"

"I don't remember that name. Is he a relative of yours, Brennan?"

"My father. But he hasn't been able to help us."

"My mother might have known, but she died years ago. I haven't been of much use. But if I think of anyone who may be able to help, I'll call. Where can I reach you?"

"I'm at the Park Central Hotel. Collins. We appreciate your time, Beth. Thanks."

We went over what we had heard as we drove back to Sunnyside. Worked on the waterfront and lost his job as the result of an incident in the summer of 1952.

✝

Patrick was at the house when we got there, so we filled him in on our chat with Beth Dowd. For some unvoiced, communal reason we had all eschewed the harder stuff and were sitting in the family room drinking ginger ale. Brennan was puffing on a cigarette.

"Well," Patrick was saying, "maybe Beth has given us something to go on but it would be helpful to get some firsthand information about our father's activities back then. If only —"

"We did meet one of his old cronies," Brennan told him. "You haven't heard about our night at the White Gardenia. Ever hear of Patrizio 'Paddy' Corialli?"

"Sounds familiar. Known to the authorities, is that the man?"

"I'd say so. Our da had some sort of association with Corialli —"

"No!" Patrick interrupted.

"Yes. Spent time at his club. And Declan put a foot wrong with 'the family' somehow."

"I wonder if they sent someone around to straighten your father out. That could explain why a man showed up the time —" I was about to make reference to Sandra's story about a man who accused Declan of something. Theft? Whatever the case, it wasn't up to me to let Patrick in on the ill-fated night at the opera. He shot me a curious look, but waited for me to continue. "Didn't Corialli say Declan had made up for whatever he'd done?"

"At someone else's expense, perhaps," Patrick suggested.

"Who knows?" Brennan said. "We don't have enough information."

"Did any other names come up, anyone we can track down?" Patrick asked.

Brennan shook his head. I thought back over the conversation. "The only name that came up was some blonde siren who sang at the place. What was it, Brennan, Edie? Evie, I think."

"What was the story on her?"

"Nothing, really. Just that she had a great voice and was a looker."

"I wonder if she'd have anything to add. She might at least be able to give us some names of people Declan knew at that club," Patrick mused.

"I doubt it," his brother answered. "She would have been singing, not eavesdropping. And we don't know who she is anyway. It was decades ago."

"Corialli did say she's in New York for a concert, or a tour or something," I reminded him.

"Yeah, well —"

"Wouldn't it be grand," I said, in a bad brogue, "if yer oul da himself would display for us the renowned Celtic gift for storytelling and give it to us from start to finish. Save us from havin' to suss out all these witnesses to the life of the man when he's right here among us himself, God save him."

"Ah, damn his eyes," Patrick answered in the same tone. Then, more seriously: "Of course we have to look at this in light of his long-time membership — and indoctrination — in an organization that executes informers. Worst thing you can be, apart perhaps from being a member of a Brit-funded paramilitary group, is an informer. Loose talk was historically the bane of the Republican movement. Have you ever seen any excerpts from the IRA's Green Book?"

We shook our heads no.

"Fascinating document. So fascinating that I've always wanted to study it professionally, and study the membership as well. It's very well written, for the most part. And it warns away any recruits who might be joining up out of romantic notions and a desire for adventure. No romance to be found here, it says. It acknowledges mistakes made by the Army in the past — bombings gone wrong — and how they rebound against the movement. It gives volunteers detailed warnings of what they can expect by way of physical and psychological torture if captured. The book of course stresses the vital importance of security. Don't tell your family, your friends, your girlfriend that you're in the 'RA. Drink-induced loose talk is suicide.

"Even if the death sentence has lapsed, it would still gall a man like Declan to be considered an informer. I suspect that — regardless of his feelings about the IRA and his treatment at its hands — he prides himself to this day on maintaining his silence about anything connected with its activities. Or his activities on its behalf. If the shooting was a Republican operation, his natural inclination would be to tell the police nothing. And if it arose out of his dealings with some other organization, I think he'd take the same approach. All this combined with his own natural reticence —"

"Reticence!" Brennan exclaimed. "I prefer to call it —"

"I came as soon as I heard," a sardonic voice announced behind me.

"Francis!" Brennan looked up in surprise.

Patrick rose and embraced the newcomer. "Fran! Good to see you."

"Hi Pat. Hey Brennan, how's God?"

"Asking for you."

"Oh, yeah? What did you tell Him? To strike me down with a bolt of lightning?"

"I implored Him to take you by your little hand and lead you home."

"Fuck off. Where's the old man?"

"Out," answered Brennan.

"He's got an appointment with his doctor," Patrick explained. "So where have you been living, Fran?"

"Mexico. Place called Tlapa. Ever hear of it?"

"No," answered Patrick.

"Yes," answered Brennan. "I know one of the —"

"You would."

"How did you get the news?" Patrick asked him. "Nobody knew where you were."

"We get the papers, for Christ's sake. We're not completely beyond the pale down there."

Francis Burke was the only one in the family who sounded like a typical New Yorker; I wondered whether it was put on for effect. He was shorter than his brothers, and thin, with hazel eyes and unruly dark hair to his shoulders. Boyish good looks were marred by an expression of petulance.

Patrick made the introductions. "Fran, this is Monty Collins, a friend of Brennan's from Halifax."

"How are you doing? Another soldier of Christ?"

"Afraid not."

He shook my hand indifferently.

"Are you going to stay with us for awhile, Francis?" Brennan inquired.

"I doubt it. Do my paternal duty and then split."

"Filial," Brennan corrected.

"What?"

"Filial duty."

"You haven't changed any." He flopped down on the couch and closed his eyes. "It took me two fucking days to get here on standby.

I could use a drink."

Patrick got up. "What can I get you?"

"Got any tequila?"

"Not bloody likely," Brennan put in.

"How about a shot of Irish? Or a beer?" Pat offered.

"Gimme a brew. Thank you, Patrick. Well? How's the old coot? Out of danger?"

"The shot missed his heart."

"Guess the shooter didn't have the latest precision guidance system. It's not easy to hit such a small, hard, barely there —"

"Can it, Francis," Brennan interjected. We heard the front door opening, and Declan Burke's voice demanding to know who had piled all the shite in the doorway for him to trip over. "Ah. Here he is now."

"Hey, I've managed to piss him off already and he hasn't even seen me yet."

Declan came down and squinted into the dimly lit room. "There's a great lump of a knapsack up there. Have you boys taken up outdoor camping, or something? You'd be a fine pair out in the —"

"Hello, Da. How are you?"

"Francis!"

Francis got up and moved towards his father. He gave him a tentative embrace, avoiding contact with his wounded chest. Declan released him and looked him over. "How's the lad? This is a surprise. One of many over the past week. When did you get into town?"

"I just landed. How are you feeling?"

"Brilliant. Where have you been?"

"Mexico."

"Your mother was worried. Why didn't you let her know where you were?"

"The mail's unreliable. Takes weeks to get anything back and forth."

"Next time avail yourself of the telephone, why don't you. Reverse the charges."

"At it already. My boy Francis? He's the one who can't afford to make a phone call."

Declan sat heavily in an armchair. "Would you get me something to drink, Patrick? Just a soda. So. Francis. Are you home for good now?"

"I doubt it."

"Why the hell not?"

"I have a life, believe it or not. And it doesn't revolve around the great metropolis of Sunnyside, Queens."

"Tell us about it. Your life. Thanks, Pat."

"You wouldn't be interested."

"I just asked."

"Maybe Fran will fill us in later, Da. He's worn out from the trip. Took him two days to get here. Why don't you flop down on one of the beds, Fran, and have a rest."

"I don't need a nap, Paddy. Though maybe you could put me on the couch and get to the root of my attitude problem. I'm such a —"

Brennan spoke over him. "Ready to head out, Monty?" I had no idea we were headed anywhere, but Brennan obviously wanted to get clear of the house, so I nodded. He turned to the others. "See you fellows later. Dec, you look a little peaky. Get Patrick to give you something and take it easy for the day. And try to avoid any undue aggravation. If you can."

"Would O'Malley's be a good idea right now?" I said to him when we got outside.

"O'Malley's is imperative right now."

After a brief session at the bar, I returned to the hotel. That evening, Maura and I took Normie to Times Square, got treats, and revelled in all the activity. There was a telephone message from Brennan back at the hotel, so I called him.

"Ever hear of Vi Dibney?"

"Of course. My parents had her records. My father was a sucker for show tunes."

"Well, guess what?"

"What? Wait, I know. She's the same —"

"Right. She's in town on a concert tour and she used to go by the name Evie."

"No shit!"

"No shit. Pat got out the entertainment pages and found that Vi Dibney was the only performer of the right vintage and physical

94

appearance who's doing a tour. Apparently she tours the east coast every year. Baltimore last night. Here in New York tomorrow night. Pat charmed an appointment out of her entourage. You and I are going to the office of her publicist or her agent. One of her 'people.' Tomorrow morning. I'll pick you up at the hotel."

✝

And so we arrived at the midtown offices of Spencer and Talbot, publicists for Vi Dibney. After driving around the block three times to score a parking spot, we entered the towering glass building and rode up in the elevator. For the first time since we arrived in New York, Brennan looked well rested.

Miss Dibney was seated on a faux Victorian sofa when the agent, Pru Spencer, ushered us inside. If she had been singing at the nightclub anywhere near the time we were interested in, she was in her late fifties or early sixties by now. She was attractive in an overdone way, too much makeup, too elaborate a hairstyle, too skinny for the flashy clothes that hung from her frame. The hair was a frothy blonde, the eyes green, the skin showed the ravages of too much tanning. She looked up at us from under thick black eyelashes and put out a bejewelled hand.

"Gentlemen callers. How nice!"

"Miss Dibney, I'm Brennan Burke and this is Montague Collins. Thank you for seeing us. We've something of a mystery on our hands and we're hoping you'll be able to help."

"How exciting!" She leaned forward and spoke with an air of intimacy. "Tell me more!"

I cased the room while I stood there, checking out the framed photographs on the wall. Famous people grinning at other famous people. There were two pictures of Vi Dibney but none from the era we were investigating.

"May we sit?" Brennan asked.

"Of course, Brendan! You and Montgomery make yourselves at home." We sat on a pair of squeaky new gold leather chairs. "Now, Brendan, this mystery. Where do I fit in?"

"It's Brennan, and Montague. Now, Miss —"

95

"Oh, it's Vi, please!" She gazed across at him with wide open eyes.

"Fine, Vi. I believe you may have known my father some years ago. Declan Burke."

The name registered immediately. She was silent for two beats, then said brightly: "Declan! Of course I remember him. Such a sweet man!"

"Sweet, is it? Are you sure you've got the right man?"

Vi looked at her publicist, hovering in the doorway. "It's all right, Pru. I'll speak to these gentlemen in private." The woman was about to protest, then smiled gamely and closed the door.

"Declan, oh, yes. Did you say you're his son?" She made a show of examining him. "You're so tall, and so dark. You," she said, turning to me, "are more like him in colouring. But you, Brennan, seem to have his quality of, what shall I call it? Ruthlessness, I guess the word is. I hope you're not offended. His son! Well! Where does the time go? Tell me, how is dear Declan now?"

"He's been shot."

Her left hand flew to her heart. "I must go to him!"

"No. You mustn't."

She quickly masked a look of annoyance, and settled on a coquettish pout. Her lower lip went out and she asked: "Are you afraid my appearance on the scene might upset him?"

"He's already upset. The man's been shot."

She was silent for a few moments, and then came back to life: "Does the fact that you're here mean I could be implicated in some way, Brennan?" she asked, disingenuously.

"Did you shoot him?"

"Of course not! Brennan! How could you say such a thing? I haven't even seen him."

"There you go then. You're not implicated."

I spoke up. "So tell us, Vi, about your time at the White Gardenia when you knew Declan."

She splayed the fingers of her left hand out in front of her and brushed something off a lacquered pink nail. "Well of course Declan was in the club most nights. He was in charge of security. He never said much to me, though I often saw him talking with the other men who ran the place. The other owners were shameless flirts, shameless!

A girl had to be firm! But I always found Declan very polite. And he could be intimidating. Not to me, but to anyone who tried to cause trouble in that club. Nice looking, I have to say! I was dating one of the waiters, a young man around my own age, but — I hope this won't embarrass you, Brennan —" She laid one of her manicured hands on his knee.

"He doesn't embarrass easily," I said.

"Don't challenge a girl like that, Montgomery!" she warned with a tinkly laugh. "Anyway, what I was going to say was I developed a bit of a crush on Declan. An older man, handsome, with those penetrating bright blue eyes. I thought of him as very worldly. Older man! He must have been what? Thirty-five? How young that seems to me now! I'm fifty-nine, would you believe that?"

"Never," I assured her.

"I was always trying to think of excuses to speak to Declan."

> *New York City, 1952*
>
> *Is that Mr. Burke coming in? Yes! Declan. He said I could call him that. Swell name. All the men his age back home are named George or Wilf. Should I ask him for requests again, or should I sing "Just One Of Those Things" and look at him when I'm singing?*
>
> *"Good evening, Declan!"*
>
> *"Ah. Hello there, Evie."*
>
> *He looks like he's got something on his mind. Oh, no, here's that friend of his again. Every time this guy comes in he just drinks soda, and Declan barely touches his own whiskey, and that means he never loosens up. They huddle over a table together and talk all night. And Declan doesn't even glance my way. This guy looks Irish too, with that wavy reddish hair. He's cute. That's not really the word for older men, though. He's handsome but not as handsome as Declan. I'm beginning to think older men are my destiny! I'll sing "Younger Than Springtime." It's about a man with a younger girl.*
>
> *Oh, wouldn't you know? Here comes Ramon. I find him so immature now. I'll have to break things off with him. And here he is in his role as bodyguard for Declan and his guest. "Burke*

don't want no other company around his table tonight." Poor Ramon. Everybody knows he's from Puerto Rico, even though he tries to pass for an Italian. His English is terrible but he's going to language school to learn Italian instead! He loves being around the big shots in this place, giving them special attention, shooing the other waiters from their tables. He just wants to hang around them himself, hoping to overhear some Mob talk. Well, the heck with Ramon or this other Irish guy. I'm going over there.

"Any requests tonight, Declan?" He's thinking about it. What? That's a weird combination of songs. Well, if that's what he wants . . . My "Danny Boy" will make his eyes well up with tears, and I'll do such a sultry "Love For Sale" it just might make something else swell up! Oh, yeah, I've got their attention now. All eyes on stage!

It's been a long night. But maybe it's not finished yet. Declan is calling me over to his table. "That was brilliant, darlin'. Meet my friend, Danny. This is Evie. We're moving on to another bar, Evie. How'd you like to join us? Let someone else do all the singing, and you can sit and have a couple of glasses with us."

Do I want to go? Isn't this just what I've been waiting for? But I'll play it cool. "Sure, if you like."

. . . Where are we? Somewhere over on the West Side. Hell's Kitchen. I don't know how they've managed to fit a band into such a tiny bar, but they have. Irish music, the real kind. And I like this little room we have all to ourselves. It's called a snug. This stuff, Paddy Whiskey, is really strong. I'd better take it easy. It doesn't seem to bother Declan. I see Danny isn't drinking much. This is the first time I've heard Declan so talkative! He's telling us about the old country and how beautiful it is. And there are all these great Irish writers that are important to the literature of the whole world. Declan even used to drink with some of them in the pubs! Danny is just as spellbound as I am. Declan says Danny has a great love for Ireland, and he's going to help Danny find an affordable way to get there. "Don't forget about me, Declan, I want to go too!" It would be so romantic to go over there, just me and Declan, away from everyone in New York. I understand about Irish history now, how the English oppressed

the Irish for hundreds of years, and they're still there in the northern part of the country. Declan knew people who were murdered by the English. I can't help crying. Danny is upset too but, well, you know men! He can hardly sit there sobbing the way I've been doing.

Now Declan says he's all talked out, so we're getting a fresh round of drinks and listening to the band. He just gave Danny a big hint to ask me to dance. Why doesn't Declan ask me to dance himself? I might get somewhere with him if he does; I know I look good tonight in this dress. White, tight and lots of me in sight!

But no, I just danced with Danny. He told me his wife was always saying he had two left feet. I taught him a bit about dancing and it was fun. Declan just sat and smoked and watched us. Now Danny says he has to leave; his wife will be wondering where he is. There should be more husbands like that.

It's good Danny's leaving, because now Declan will have to drive me home. Just the two of us. Declan and Danny are in a deep, serious conversation together. There. Danny's gone.

Alone at last! He's not saying much but at least we're together. Here we are at my apartment. It's now or never. "When do I get my next instalment of Irish culture, Declan?"

"We could install a bit of it right now, I'm thinking." He's never said anything risqué like that before! And the way he's looking at me!

I just spent two hours in my apartment with Declan. The most blissful two hours of my life. I'm in love. In a way I've never been in love before. No more twenty-year-old boys for me.

"Declan, please don't go!"

But he's gone. And he was pretty damn quiet on the way out.

"For my remaining time at the club Declan was back to his old polite, distant self. I got a call from a hotel owner in Vegas, who said he had received a call from someone in New York, some Italian name I didn't even know, and this Vegas hotel guy wanted to hire me to sing in his place, and that was it. I was gone."

Brennan seemed not to hear her; he was gazing out the window.

"Do you have a last name for this Danny?" I asked her.

"Boy," Brennan muttered.

"No, I don't know who he was," she replied.

"When was this? When did this other man come into the picture?"

"That's an easy one. A few weeks before my big Vegas debut! I was off to the desert —"

"So that was when exactly?" I persisted.

"June of '52."

We were quiet for a few moments. Then it occurred to me to ask: "Was your move to Vegas something that had been in the works for a while? Sending out résumés, or demo tapes?"

She cast a quick glance at Brennan, who seemed to have lost interest. "No. The move came out of the blue. I always suspected Declan arranged it. I flew out to Vegas June the twenty-first. Morning flight, first day of summer, and it must have been a hundred degrees out there. I worked my last four shifts at the club. Normally, I would have had a night off. Not that week; I figured I'd need every cent I could get. I tried my best to avoid Ramon, and that was that. I was out of there."

"And things went well for you in Vegas? Your career took off after that?"

"Yes. Things went well." She put on a smile. "All that old stuff is just water under the bridge now." She turned again to Brennan. "I'm sorry to hear about your father. I hope he has a quick recovery. I suspect he will."

Burke and I stood outside the building, irresolute. "So, Brennan, what do you think? Is Vi a factor in this plot we're trying to uncover?"

"She had only a bit part in the drama but, like good bit players everywhere, she's made it possible for us to see the star, my father, in a whole new light. And she's given us another name to track down. Or is he somebody we already know?"

"The latter, I'd say. Unless we're way off, Danny is Desmond. The alcoholic who was fired, for drinking or for some other reason, from his job as a watchman on the waterfront. He was the real target of your father's efforts. Vi was just a honey trap, or a honey pot, whatever the expression is. And your father fell into the pot."

"Didn't fall, just took a quick dip."

Chapter 6

He had no veteran soldiers but volunteers raw
Playing sweet Mauser music for Erin Go Bragh.
— Peadar Kearney, "Erin Go Bragh"

March 15, 1991

Brennan's sister finally had a breakthrough with the name Murphy. She kept at it for a week, returning to those Murphys who had not answered their phones on the first, second, or third calls. And she came up with N.M. (Neasa) Murphy, an elderly woman who was cagey at first but who in the end broke down and acknowledged that Cathal Murphy had died some months before.

We stood crowding each other on the crumbling doorstep of a seedy house in Williamsburg, Brooklyn. It was a bright, sunny Friday afternoon. The Ides of March. The house was one of a row of attached frame houses, each one in worse shape than the next. There was a full ashtray on the stoop and a pile of dusty, curled magazines held down by a heavy, chipped mug. A sign tacked on the door advertised the upper flat for rent. Nothing happened in answer to our knock for two or three minutes; then we heard an irregular thump and shuffle getting louder as it approached. The door opened slowly, and a pair of small brown eyes glittered up at us. A chain barred our entrance. Unless, of course, one of us decided to give the door a forceful kick. The tiny woman leaned on a walker and waited in silence for us to state our business.

"Mrs. Murphy. I'm Brennan Burke and —" A truck barrelled down a nearby street and the noise blotted out his voice. He started again, then added: "And this is Montague Collins." The woman's expression did not change, and she spoke not a word. Burke went on: "I was wondering if we might have a word with you."

"A word about what?" It was the voice of a smoker, the accent unreconstructed Eire.

"About your husband."

"Burke, you say?"

"Declan's son."

She gave no acknowledgement that the name meant anything to her but she closed the door, fussed with the chain, opened up again, and stood aside to let us in. She could not have been more than five feet tall; she may have weighed ninety-five pounds with a cast iron frying pan in her hand. Her hair was short and grey; it looked as if she had just run the fingers of both hands through it. Her skin was wizened, like that of a woman who had passed many a long day out on her stoop, soaking up the sun.

The woman jerked her head towards a room beyond us, and shambled along ahead. Her pace seemed slower now than it had sounded while we waited on the doorstep. The floor of her living room was covered with a wall to wall green carpet that was too large and turned up at the baseboards. One theme dominated the room: horses. Every flat surface bore a statue or figurine of a horse; the walls were adorned with pictures of horses being groomed, ridden or raced. Above the archway leading to the dining room was a silhouette in unfaded tan paint, where a crucifix once had hung. The only personal photograph was a well-preserved black-and-white picture of two small children running through a field, the girl ahead of the boy, laughing and looking back at him.

Mrs. Murphy sat in an armchair beside an old-fashioned floor model ashtray, from the era when smoking accessories were part of the decor. This one had a large marble tray for the ashes and butts; it was topped by a bronze model of a DC3 aircraft with windows and moving propellers. I coveted the old Dakota but was not crass enough to try to buy it off her. The old lady lit up a smoke from a pack on the arm of her chair, and nodded to us to be seated on a small brown sofa. I took my place on it, still casting an envious eye at the DC3.

Brennan pulled a large chair over from the corner and made himself at home in it. He brought out a cigarette of his own, lit it and took a leisurely drag before speaking. He bypassed the usual formalities — and the usual priestly assurances — and got right to the point. "I was interested to read the obituary of one Cathal Murphy," he told her, never taking his eyes off her face. This was not the way I would have approached the interview.

"Interested in what way, Mr. Burke?"

"It appeared to contain a great many references that must have seemed obscure to all but a few readers."

"And would you be one of the few yourself?"

"Have you had many visitors show up on your doorstep asking about it, Mrs. Murphy?"

"You're the first to mention it, Mr. Burke. You'll have to explain the purpose of your questions." She inhaled a lungful of nicotine and emitted a harsh cough.

"Bless you," I said, since Father Burke didn't. "Who wrote the obituary, Mrs. Murphy? Did you write it?"

"Do you see anyone else here who might have written up the poor man's death? A niece with a pot of tea and a tray of cakes? A nephew up on a ladder repairing that leak in the ceiling?"

"What do you mean?"

"I mean the man had no family, nobody, besides me. Just me and my wooden leg." She rapped on the lower part of her left leg with her knuckles. "But I did my final duty. Hobbled in to the newspaper office and left the obituary and the money on the counter. What an exhausting day, me and my walker on the trains to Manhattan and back. Oh, well, all in a day's service to the dead."

"Should I conclude that things were not going well between you and your husband at the time he died, Mrs. Murphy?"

"I had no husband, Mr. Burke." She smiled, gratified by our reactions. Then she leaned forward and peered intently at Brennan. "I can see your mother in you. Tall and dark. Tell me, do poor lovesick women look after you in the streets? Trail around behind you, in the hope of even the slightest glance from those black eyes of yours?"

"Ah, no. I hardly think so, Mrs. Murphy. As a matter of fact, I —"

"I wouldn't want to get caught following you down a dark alley, for fear of what you'd do."

Burke and I exchanged a glance. What on earth was she talking about? Brennan said: "I don't understand you. What's all this about people being followed in the streets?"

"He escaped your notice, then? He must have perfected the knack of slipping through this life unseen."

"Who?" we both asked her.

"My poor pathetic article of a brother. Who else?"

"Cathal was your brother?"

"My twin. Charlie 'Cathal' Fagan and Neasa Fagan. They called me Nessie. My brother was Charlie Fagan over there, Cathal Murphy over here. I became a Murphy. I played along with the codology so long I tend to forget we ever had another name. That's the way he wanted it. Quite insistent, he was, about that."

"What codology? Why the change of name?"

"Undercover name, Mr. Burke. My brother had a mission."

"What mission would that have been?"

"Does it matter? I can't see how he ever got anything done. His devotions got in the way."

"His devotions?"

"To the blessed lady." She grinned, showing a mouth full of uneven yellow teeth.

"The blessed lady being —" I prompted, and Brennan looked at me as if my brain had just been washed of forty years of Catholic memory.

"The blessed, the beautiful, the divine Teresa Clare Montoya Brennan." At that, the woman took up and played an imaginary violin.

Brennan maintained a wary silence. Nessie Murphy was in no hurry to break the spell she thought she had woven for him. But I wanted to get on with it.

"How did your brother come to know Mrs. Burke?"

"From walking and skipping through the streets of Dublin, something he was able to do, but I was not. With my leg, you know."

"Dublin!" Brennan exclaimed.

"A lifelong love affair. On the part of poor Cathal anyhow."

"He knew my mother in Dublin?"

"Am I going to have to say everything twice for you, Mr. Burke? I thought it was just us oul ones who are hard of hearing. He moped around after her in Dublin and followed her over here. I don't know whether she ever caught sight of him in the new world. She knew a Charlie Fagan but I suspect she forgot his existence as soon as she boarded the boat for New York. I had to come too. What choice did I have? I could hardly support myself, could I? And what man would have married me, a one-legged bride?"

"My mother —"

"What happened to your leg?" I interrupted.

"It was when we were all killing each other. July of 1922."

"Yes?"

"They shot it off." She tried to sound matter-of-fact. Or perhaps she wanted to sound as if being matter-of-fact was an effort she could not quite sustain.

"Who shot it off?"

"The Irregulars."

Brennan rejoined the conversation. "Are you trying to tell me that the Irish Republican Army shot the leg off a little girl?"

"I was — what do they call it these days? — collateral damage. My father fought on the treaty side in the Civil War, and he was battling it out with the Republicans. He lost."

"How did you come to be hit?"

"We lived on a farm in County Meath, not far from Dublin. My mother had died giving birth to me and my twin. One day Cathal — Charlie — and my father were in the barn helping me with our pony, Finnegan. We had a new saddle and I was going out for a ride. I could ride at the age of five! We heard men coming. Da told us to hide, and he lay down on top of us. The men didn't know we were there until Charlie let out a little whimper of fear. The men started shouting, my father up and ran to lead them away from us, I panicked and followed him. When they shot him, I was in the way. My father died, and I lost my leg. All because of Charlie!"

"Your twin, a child of five," Brennan said.

"I managed to keep my wits about me! Charlie didn't. Here's the result." She raised her leg and let it thud to the floor. "After that, we were sent to live with Aunt Norah in Dublin. She was kind to us, kept us fed and got us through school. Where Charlie excelled and Nessie did not. Hard to concentrate on your sums when you're worried about who's laughing at you behind your back. Anyway, the poor woman did what she could, bless her. A staunch Republican she was. Like so many families, ours was divided by the Civil War. Norah had played a part in the Easter Rising. She and Charlie talked about it for hours on end; she had a convert in him. But she was getting on, and it was clear we couldn't stay there for all eternity. Charlie went out and got a high-paying job at Guinness, and we found a place of our own. I couldn't work of course."

Brennan opened his mouth to speak, but I cut him off. "And then?"

"And then Charlie saw Miss Teresa Clare Montoya Brennan making her elegant way down Grafton Street. The bollocks came home and told me all about it."

Dublin, 1936
"Wait till I tell you who I saw today, Nessie!"
"Who?"
"A girl in Grafton Street."
"Well, smack me in the gob! Imagine that."
"Not just any girl. She's brilliant. She has black shining hair and dark, dark eyes. She's tall and slight and carries herself like a queen!"
"Isn't that a fine thing for a Republican to be saying!"
"Oh, you know what I mean. And she looked right at me. Donal O'Leary was with me and she spoke to him! Donal says she comes into his father's bakery in Dawson Street, nearly every day. She has the grandest name: Teresa Clare Montoya Brennan. Her da is Spanish. He teaches at Trinity College, but he used to be a diplomat; they call him 'the Ambassador.' Her mother's one of the Brennans from Ranelagh. Donal told me all this, and he says his

da needs another young fella to help in the shop. So, since I don't work at Guinness on Saturdays, I'm going to work in the bakery."

Oh, here he comes from O'Leary's, with flour spilt all over his jumper and him not even knowing it's there. And the grin on his face — doesn't he look like he's been touched by the angels? Bad scran to him!

"I spoke to Teresa today, Ness! In the bakery. We talked a bit. Well, her and me and Donal. She's going to the opera tonight with her parents. Dublin's a grand spot for the opera, as you know."

"No, I don't know. If I had the money for the opera, I'd find a better use for it, so I would."

"We talked of other things as well. You'll love her, Nessie – she rides!"

"Oh we'd hit it off just fine then, Charlie. Half the fun of riding is hearing all about somebody else doing it when you can't do it yourself."

"Ah, well, now . . . Tell me this, Nessie. Should I ask to call on her at home? She lives in Merrion Square, you know."

"Ha! You with the arse out of your trousers going to Merrion Square. They'll have the Guards on you; you'll be thrown in the nick. Stay clear of there."

Isn't this a day to be treasured! Charlie is taking me out for a hobble round Stephen's Green. Knowing full well that one Teresa Montoya Brennan is known to promenade through this very spot. And sure enough, isn't she coming towards us now, with a younger girl. A plain little thing. Her sister? Bad cess to the pair of them. Now they're on the footbridge. In the shade of the trees, except of course where the sun breaks through in a blaze of glorious light around herself. And I see she hasn't spared any expense in her appearance. A royal blue dress, belted at her tiny waist, with a pleated skirt falling just below her knees. Soft leather shoes. She hasn't bobbed her hair like so many of the girls; she has it pinned up in an old-fashioned style. Janey Mac, will you look at Charlie beaming at her like an eejit. He's so dazed with joy he hasn't even remembered to speak to her. Well, I'll speak up for him. Oh, there goes one of my crutches . . . I'm slipping to the ground.

"Pardon me, Miss Brennan, could you help me up?"

"Certainly. Are you all right there?" Such a refined voice. "Good day to you, Charlie."

Listen to him stuttering. I'll do the talking here: "Did you happen to see my horse anywhere, Miss? He seems to have escaped me, the brute." Me, with the crutches!

Poor Teresa. As polished as she is, she can't quite hide the look of disbelief on her face. "I've seen no horse," she says to me, "but if I do I'll give him a crack on the arse and send him galloping back to you."

Oh, isn't that a sight, Charlie blushing from his collar to the top of his head to hear her say "arse."

That might have made him bold for their next encounter but alas! there's another suitor at her side now. Yes, somebody else has come along and ground little Charlie's dreams into dust. Charlie didn't witness their first meeting of course, though it's a wonder, the way he kept watch for her. But he saw the rogue today. In Grafton Street. Of course Charlie takes her part in the quarrel.

"He came right up to her in the street, Nessie. Full of himself, he is. Handsome in that swaggering way some of them have. They were having a row. I was nearby and heard it." Cowering in the shadows, no doubt.

"This fellow was trying to talk to her and she was putting him off. 'You have something of a reputation, Mr. Burke. And I don't mean for accosting young ladies in the street, though that doesn't commend you either.'

"'I didn't accost you in the street, surely, Miss Montoya Brennan. As I recall our meeting, I simply made a courteous greeting to you in response to a little smile I thought I saw on your lips.'

"'I don't smile at strange men, Mr. Burke. You are mistaken.'

"'I'll have you smiling at me before the day's out, Miss Montoya Brennan. I'll have you laughing so hard you'll be in fear for your linen.'

"'Good day, Mr. Burke.' And she turned on her heel and stalked away.

"But he persisted and walked after her! 'I apologize for that remark. It must be the company I keep. My mother's always telling me I should ingratiate myself with a better class of people. What do you think?'

"She didn't turn to look at him but said something like: 'I think running around with rifles and taking part in not-so-secret revolutionary organizations tends to coarsen a man.'

"And then he said to her, as serious as could be: 'I promise you that you'll never be touched by that part of my life. Hold me to it.'"

"Well, you know the rest. She married him. But still, Charlie had eyes only for Mrs. Burke, whether she was done up in fine style for the opera, or lumbering around with a big belly after Declan got her up the pole. All the same to Charlie.

"Until disaster struck. Declan committed a mortal sin and got himself excommunicated from the Holy Republican Church. And *that part of his life* bore down on the two of them like an armoured personnel carrier on the streets of Belfast, to the point where they fled Ireland in the middle of the night and left everything and everyone they knew behind them. Charlie didn't last a year without her."

The old woman began to croon: "Come back to Erin, Mavourneen, Mavourneen. Come back again to the land of thy birth! But she wasn't coming back. So my brother packed up and emigrated with a new name and an important commission from the 'RA to raise funds over here to send guns over there.

"My brother made a point of learning everything he could about your mother and that led him to all kinds of information about her husband. Including what oul Dec got up to in his first few years as a model US citizen. And give the devil his due, when Charlie set himself to learning something, he mastered it! Fool that he was in many ways, he was a very able fellow indeed when it came to his tireless work on behalf of Mother Ireland. I guess he had to do something with the passion that burned within him; must have compressed it all into the intense flame of Irish Republicanism." She looked at us as if newly reminded of our presence. "Did you say something?"

"How do you know what you claim to know about my father?" Brennan could not keep the anger out of his voice.

"Oh, a great man for the pen, was Charlie. *Cathal.* He saw, he heard, he memorized, he wrote. In his own peculiar shorthand."

"Who was Stephen? What was that queer drink, Lameki?"

"Oh, now, you'd have to ask Cathal all that. But, sadly, he's no longer with us. God rest his soul."

Brennan leaned towards her and demanded: "Who shot my father?"

A crafty look passed over her face. "I guess it was someone who can read better than you can, Burke."

Brennan launched himself out of his seat and loomed over her, grasping the arms of her chair with his hands. His face was only inches from hers. "Someone fired a gun into a room full of men, women and children at my niece's wedding! My father nearly lost his life. Because of you and your malicious little jest with the obituary. Your own father was shot. You were shot. How could you sit here plotting and scheming for the same thing to happen to someone else, someone you don't even know? I suggest you examine your conscience, and I also suggest you won't like what you find there. And after you've done that, you can let us know who is behind the attempted murder of my father. And make no mistake. You are every bit as guilty as the man who pulled the trigger!"

Gone was the insinuating smile, the smug amusement. Nessie Murphy shrank back in her seat, looking small and old and frightened.

"Brennan," I began, "let's all sit down and —"

"Get out of here!" Nessie cried. "Get out, the two of you, or I will scream the house down! The neighbours will call the police, and you'll be taken out of here in handcuffs. Frightening and tormenting an old woman in her home. Get out!"

I got him out of there but not before he turned and pinned her once more with his damning black eyes.

"Brennan, for Christ's sake!" I said when we got into the car. "The woman is seventy-three years old. You could have given her a heart attack."

"The poisonous creature! I'll get the answers out of her yet."

"How? By terrorizing her? We'll never get near her again. She'll call the police if she catches sight of us."

"She won't want the police around, the nasty old reprobate. Imagine being Cathal Murphy and being saddled with the likes of her."

"I wouldn't have envied him, I admit. No wonder he died!" Then my mind veered off in a direction it had not taken before. "Or did he?"

"Did he what?"

"Did he die? We know the obituary is in some kind of code. Maybe the whole thing is a fake. Maybe there wasn't even a death."

"Jesus Christ that died on the cross! What next?"

"We have to consider it. I think we can safely assume he really existed."

"Are you getting metaphysical on me now, Collins?"

"No, just lawyerly. I want confirmation that the man is six feet under. If not, did he finally act out his revenge on the man who took away the love of his life?"

"Why wait forty years?"

"Well, somebody did."

"I'll call Patrick, get him to look into the death records, however one does that. Then we'll know. There's no point speculating any further." We didn't say another word on the drive to Sunnyside. We went in the house and down to the family room, and sat at the card table. Declan Burke looked unconcerned as he dealt a hand of cards to the two men who were trying, without any help from him whatsoever, to unravel the mystery of his life and his near-death experience. Would I soon become so accustomed to this situation that I would find it normal?

"Who shot you, Dec?" Brennan asked. "Did you tell us and I wasn't after hearing you?"

"I believe I made it clear that I don't know who shot me, Brennan. Let's leave that to the experts, shall we? In the meantime, let's play cards."

"That obituary now, Dec, would you be so considerate as to offer us anything by way of an explanation —"

"Your oul da is alive; he intends to remain alive for a while yet. *Ergo,* no obituary."

"Would the name Charlie Fagan mean anything to you, Da?"

If it did, he gave no sign. "Would you ever fuck off with yourself and get serious about your cards? I'll be dead of natural causes before we get through this hand."

We heard someone on the stairs and turned to see Terry flying down two steps at a time, dressed in a suit and tie, his hair newly cut.

"Well, if it isn't Mr. O'Madden Burke!" his father exclaimed.

"Why O'Madden Burke?" I asked.

"Oh, I'm Mr. O'Madden Burke today," Terry explained. "Whoever shows up looking particularly well-tailored and respectable gets slagged. You know, from Joyce."

"A character in *Dubliners*, right?"

"And *Ulysses*, of course," Brennan put in. "That's where Molly got her nickname. Her real name's Maire but when she was a young girl she spent the good part of a summer lying about in bed, daydreaming about her boyfriend, who was out of town for the holiday. We started calling her Molly Bloom."

"I never read the whole thing," I confessed.

Terry stage-whispered. "Neither did I, but don't tell the rest of them. The *Baltimore Catechism* and the works of James Joyce were required reading in this house. No wonder we're all a little schizo. Do we celebrate Bloomsday or Corpus Christi? Do we rebel against the Church and all its works, or do we refuse even a sip of Kool-Aid before receiving Holy Communion?"

"Corpus Christi! I haven't thought of that in years. There used to be a parade."

"That's right." Declan joined the conversation. "And this fellow —" he jerked a thumb at Brennan "— before he became the Reverend Father Burke declared one year at the breakfast table that, since Corpus Christi also happened to be Bloomsday, we should spend the day walking around the city the way Bloom and Daedalus did in *Ulysses*, stopping at various pubs to eat and drink, and ending up at a whorehouse instead of venerating the Body of Christ."

"Ever get that conflict sorted out, Brennan?" I needled him.

"Not a problem unless Corpus Christi falls smack in the middle of June, on Bloomsday. Those years I'm torn."

Terry looked at his watch and sat down at the table. We settled in to a poker game and played for half an hour before the game broke up.

"I have to go," Terry said.

"Where?"

"Wine and cheese with the missus. Sheila told me if I miss this, it will be mac and cheese and no wine for me all week. Let's get together for a night out sometime, lads." We agreed, and he left us with a little salute.

"I'm off too," Declan announced.

"And where would you be off to?" Brennan asked.

"Someplace I'm not all that keen to go, to do something I'm not all that keen to do. But I'm lucky to be invited there at all. So I'm going."

"Where?"

"The bride and groom's apartment, to view the wedding photos. Your mother's there now."

"You will let us know if you see someone in the photos who shouldn't be there?"

"Anyone who shouldn't have been there will not be showing his face in the pictures. I think we're safe making that assumption. Find something to distract yourselves, why don't you?" We heard him shut the door.

Brennan looked at me. "Alone. At last."

"Your point being?"

"We can go through this place, with a crowbar if need be. There's got to be something here. Let's start in their bedroom."

"You start in their bedroom. Give me a more neutral assignment."

"Attic or basement?"

"Attic."

"All right. You'll see a door at the end of the hall up there; it leads to a narrow staircase to the attic. Watch your head."

I hoisted myself up into the attic. There was one bare bulb to light the place, and it did not do much against the fading light coming in through the one dusty window. The far end of the room was devoted to the storage of old furniture: an incomplete set of shield-back chairs, a banged-up mahogany china cabinet with mismatched tea cups, saucers and old tarnished silver, some wardrobes full of women's and children's clothing. A side wall was lined with book-cases. On the other side was a museum of children's toys from the last forty years: a wood-seated kiddie car, long tubes of Sta-Lox Building Bricks with white multi-paned windows and transparent green awnings, Tinker Toys, a tinkly baby piano, an old folk guitar. I had to remind myself I was there to work, not to play.

There was a large steamer trunk that I marked for future consideration. Everything else was stored in cardboard boxes. The first one I tackled contained framed photos of family groups, obviously in the old country, and crumbling black-paged family albums held together by laces. There were old Roman missals from various years back to the turn of the century, along with jet and wooden rosaries, crucifixes, holy cards and religious medals. I had to smile when I saw a church collection envelope with the words "Saint Bratty's" scrawled on it in red crayon, over the words "Saint Brigid's." A bit of sibling rivalry? Had little Brigid Burke been less than saintly, prompting one of her brothers to deface the envelope bearing her name?

The next box held photographs of the Burke family during the early years in New York. There was a smiling, blond Patrick as an altar boy. An older girl with black hair — Molly — held two smaller kids by the hand on the steps of a church. One little boy was trying to twist out of her grasp. Here was Brennan, looking angelic as a choirboy of twelve, with his black hair combed to the side and his mouth in a perfect O. A respectable-looking Declan and an aristocratic Teresa stood beaming as an older priest presided at the christening of one of their babies. Then there was an insolent-looking teenage Brennan dressed in skin-tight jeans and a black T-shirt. He was sprawled in an arm chair, cigarette dangling from his lips, looking lazily up at a slim, fair-haired girl who regarded him uncertainly.

My interest was piqued when I discovered a box full of documents relating to the house. The deed, dated 1950, and the abstract of title. The mortgage. Lawyers' correspondence showed Declan had scraped together a fairly good down payment. Old bank statements from the 1950s and early 1960s. Cancelled cheques for coal and then oil, electricity, telephone and all the other necessities of life. Regular deposits, and occasional cash withdrawals in varying small amounts. Nothing out of the ordinary. I pored over the papers for a long time but could not see anything of significance.

In the next carton I came across a long, flat box decorated with old Cadbury's Dairy Milk wrappers. It was filled with letters to Teresa Burke, with a Dublin return address. I opened the first letter; it was from her mother. They all were. I was about to close the box when something fell out from between two of the envelopes. I picked it up.

"Finding anything up there, Monty?" I started at the sound of Brennan's voice. "Not a thing in their room. I feel like a pervert." His head appeared and then he joined me in the attic. "I haven't been up here in years. Lots of laughs, I imagine. What's that?"

"These are old bank statements from late 1954 to early in '57. An account in Declan's name. Kept separate from the other bank records. Money going out of his account at nearly regular monthly intervals. These were cash withdrawals. Usually three hundred dollars. A lot of money in those days, when you have a family to support."

He sat down beside me, looking miserable and exhausted. "You're not suggesting blackmail! That's the last thing I would expect of him. Why in the hell would he keep the records?"

"He didn't. Your mother did."

"Jesus."

"And here's money coming in." I pointed to the entries. "For every payment he made, there's a deposit of money preceding it. He was obtaining, or diverting, money from somewhere to pay this. Then it stopped, in March of 1957. I wonder if Cathal Murphy was black-mailing him."

"Which Cathal? The competent, dedicated Republican organizer or the lovesick little man who was content to watch his beloved from a distance? Whoever did this would have to be one tough customer. Anyone Declan could intimidate would have failed in the attempt. We don't have enough of a handle on Cathal to know whether he'd have the bottle to blackmail the old man. Nessie herself would have, but physically she could not have pulled it off."

He was probably right. We were looking for a tough guy. And that led me back to the White Gardenia, home of mobsters, enforcers and hangers-on.

I had no trouble finding the club in daylight on Saturday. I didn't expect much in the way of dancing girls and, in fact, the place was fairly quiet. Canned music and a few scattered drinkers. An elderly maitre d' I hadn't seen before ushered me to the bar.

"I was here the other night with friends, and I was introduced to Mr. Corialli. I don't suppose he's on the premises this afternoon?" I may as well have asked whether the Pope was leaning on the bar, telling tales and buying rounds. "He had another man with him, kind of a bulky fellow."

"None of Mr. Corialli's associates are around today." The man looked Italian and spoke with a Brooklyn accent.

"This is quite an operation," I observed. "The club's been here for, how long? Forty years?"

"Forty-one. But not always here. Started out in Manhattan. East Fifties. Then moved over here to Long Island City, under new management. Took a while to get into gear again."

I looked at him. "Have you been working here long?"

"There and here. Since opening night."

"Really! What were you doing opening night?"

"Same thing I'm doing now. Maitre d'. Of course I was on nights back then. We weren't even open in the afternoon in those days. I worked Tuesday to Saturday till I was sixty, then I took kind of a semi-retirement. Or that's the way I look at the early shift. Not as much action, but easier on the old legs. Easier on the head too."

"I've been kind of fascinated with this place ever since I came in the other night. I'm a musician myself but I'd hate to have to follow the act I saw here."

"The girls are really something, I gotta hand it to them. They can play the instruments too. A popular act."

"I'm sure. Vi Dibney got her start here, I understand."

"Yeah, she did. We knew her as Evie. She really packed 'em in."

"She has a good voice. A looker too, I'll bet."

"She was a hot-looking broad. Come see for yourself." He led me to a corridor behind the bar, knocked on a door, got no response, and went inside with me at his heels. It was a large office with a cluttered desk, two telephones and a number of mismatched chairs. The walls were covered with photographs in cheap frames. "There's Evie."

It was an early colour photo of the singer in a low-cut white satin dress. Her lips, painted a bright red, were nearly wrapped around the microphone. Her frothy blonde hair was back combed and pinned up with a white rose tucked over her right ear.

"She must have had the guys eating out of her hand," I commented.

"Oh, yeah."

"So, did she meet up with a sugar daddy here in the club?"

"Nah, I don't think so. They made passes at her. How far she went along with it I don't know. If anything went on, it was after hours so I didn't see it. It wouldn't have gotten her a husband so maybe she didn't bother. You know Italians." He smiled in a proprietorial sort of way. "They might have been looking for a girlfriend but they weren't looking for a new wife. She was just a kid really, even if she didn't look it. She stuck with this guy around her own age who worked here. That's him there, Ray or something, his name was. Ramon." He pointed to a picture of the club's staff all grouped around a birthday cake ablaze with candles. "There it is. R. Jiminez. She was going out with him. Then one day he came in to work and she was gone. Without a word of goodbye. Got a job out in Vegas. This Ramon didn't say a word about it but you could tell he was steamed. He met a nice Italian girl later and quit the club. Couple of years after Evie left. Some story about wanting to join a band, or write plays or something. Maybe he was going to live off the new girlfriend. Wouldn't put it past him. He came back to us a couple of years after that though. He really hustled us about getting his old job back. You can always tell when a guy is in desperate need of money. Guess the new career didn't pan out. He stayed on for a while, but if he heard from Evie he didn't tell the rest of us."

"So she didn't find herself a rich Italian businessman. Maybe she should have tried for an Irish one."

"Irish?"

"Well, the guys I came here with last time were Irish, and one of them was around in the early days of the club."

"Oh yeah? Who's that?"

"Declan Burke."

The man raised his eyebrows. "Whoa!"

"You knew Declan?"

"Did anybody know him? Not exactly a back-slapping, lemme-show-you-a-snapshot-of-the-wife-and-kids kind of guy. But, hell, I don't know you either. What's your name?"

I put out my hand. "Monty Collins."

"I'm Al Dipersio. Did you say you were here with Burke the other night?"

"Yes. I'm a friend of his son. We sat with Mr. Corialli. They talked over old times."

"Yeah, well, Burke worked security here, at least for a while. Him and Mr. Corialli may have had other business. If they did, I never knew what it was."

"Al, did you know there was an attempt on Declan's life?"

"No!" His surprise was genuine. Not the kind of gossip that makes the day-shift circuit, I concluded. "Who did it?"

"That's what we're trying to find out."

"You and the NYPD."

"I imagine they'll get there first. But this may have been some kind of paid hit, and the gunman may not do much talking. It's all speculation, of course. We simply have no idea."

"Can't help you there."

"One thing we do suspect is that somebody was blackmailing him back in —"

Al snorted with laughter. "Not a chance. Burke would cut the guy's throat before he'd give in to blackmail."

I drove to Sunnyside after enjoying a solitary meal at the White Gardenia, and joined Brennan in the family room. I recounted my conversation with Al Dipersio. "So. Ramon was steamed about Evie's defection. When exactly was this, the doomed love affair between Evie and your father?"

"It wasn't a love affair," Burke snapped. "It was just a rub of the relic. A couple of hours in her flat."

"It was what? *A rub of the relic?* Is that what they call sex in sacramental Ireland?" He waved a dismissive hand in my direction and I continued: "All right, we'll call it the night with Danny, 'Danny' being a code name for the unwilling drinking companion, Desmond. The alcoholic. He apparently managed to stay off the booze till when, July of that year? Just before his daughter's wedding, according to her diary."

Desmond had resisted the luscious young Evie, showing her snapshots of his family while they danced. That sounded right. Mary Desmond's diary made it plain: Desmond loved his family. A fun dad, quoting the Irish greats. What had Mary written? He kept them up reading from Joyce on Bloomsday. And what had Brennan's brother said about Bloomsday? The family observed it unless it fell on the same day as a religious feast, or was it the other way around? Desmond and Declan Burke, not so different from one another perhaps, with one crucial difference: Desmond's fatal attraction for alcohol. What happened in July of 1952? Desmond lost his job as a port watchman. Just after the incident between Evie and Declan, a rare moment of weakness on Declan's part. Which may mean Declan was under stress at that time. Or, no, that wasn't July. What had Evie said?

"Brennan. When did Evie hop the wagon train out west?"

"Summer of '52."

"Yes, but when?"

"Didn't she say something about the first day of summer? It was steaming hot out in —" he shuddered "— Nevada."

"June then. Just how quickly did your father bundle her off?"

"Days, it sounded like."

"The middle of June." I tried to focus my thoughts. "When's Bloomsday? The same time as, what was it, the Corpus Christi procession?"

"Are you trying to catch me out here, Monty? The old fellow never let me live it down, the time I suggested we spend the day eating, drinking and whoring, when in fact it was Corpus Christi Thursday. But in truth we never actually did anything to observe Bloomsday. It's just —"

"What's the date though? Bloomsday."

"June 16, 1904. The day James Joyce and Nora Barnacle had their first —"

"June 16."

"Corpus Christi, on the other hand, falls on a different date every year because it is the first Thursday after Trinity Sunday, which in turn is —"

"It wasn't Desmond."

"What?"

"The guy in the club that night with your father and Evie, the guy they called Danny. It wasn't Desmond. We have to start looking for someone else."

"But —"

"I remember what Evie said. She worked her last four shifts, then flew to Las Vegas the morning of June 21. I think she said she didn't take any nights off. Worried about money, and no wonder. So her last four nights would have been the seventeenth, eighteenth, nineteenth and twentieth. Which means the night with Declan was June 16. But we know from the Desmond girl's diary that Desmond —"

"Spent that night — Bloomsday night — sober and slumped over a cup of cocoa at his kitchen table."

"Right."

"So. It was someone else being recruited at the club."

Brennan got up and went to the bar for a bottle of Jameson's, raised it, waited for my distracted nod, and poured us both a glassful. He handed me my drink and sat down, lit up a cigarette, inhaled the smoke and let it out with an exasperated sigh. "Are we going to get to the bottom of this, Monty?"

I shrugged and took a sip. And another. "We may have to face the possibility that we just won't find the answer, Brennan. What have you heard from the police on the shooting?"

"They keep saying they're confident, but they don't have a suspect yet."

"Well, I'm confident they'll pull somebody in for it. Maybe all we can hope for is that whoever did it will eventually talk. That may be the only way we'll hear the full story."

"Maybe we won't want this gunman to do any talking," he groused. "And the gunman isn't the only one who knows the story, don't forget. He got his cue from that obituary. Or so I assume, given the timing. There must be *something* in that obit, Monty. This fellow caught it; we didn't."

"So let's read it again."

He pulled out his wallet, unfolded the crumpled piece of paper and began to read. Something struck me, and I realized it had given me pause once before. "Brennan, read the last bit to me again. Start with the 'members of a generation' or whatever it said."

"'When the members of a generation pass away, the family is often left with little more than its memories; the telling details are locked away in a trunk and never get out of the attic. A better way — Cathal's way — was to celebrate and live the past as if — '"

I raised my hand and said: "I must be losing it. Like you. But I heard 'Attica.'" I reached over and gently slid it out of his grasp. "Locked away, never got out of Attica. Please tell me that doesn't make sense to you."

He removed the cigarette from his mouth and looked at me, unsmiling. "I hope we don't get to a point where it makes sense to either of us."

Once more, we lapsed into silence. We had limited time, we had an uncooperative client in Declan Burke, we had a gap of nearly forty years and now we were faced with a brand new avenue of inquiry.

"I can't imagine the authorities at Attica prison helping us with our ill-formulated inquiries," I grumbled, "especially since we don't have a name."

"A name would help."

"At least we know the time frame, 1952 or 1953, if the guy was caught soon after the event in mid-1952. So. Court records or some slogging through old newspapers."

"If we want to deploy my little army of Irish Volunteers, namely my young relatives, it had better be the newspapers. In the library. That, they can handle. What should they be looking for? Criminal cases in 1952 or 1953, involving Irish names and —"

"Guns, obviously. To think I ridiculed your suggestion that the names Brendan and Armand meant Bren gun and Armalite rifle. Sure, you're brilliant when you're daft. And the New York waterfront, if we haven't written off Desmond altogether. He did get fired as a port watchman. Of course the story has to end with someone being sent to Attica."

"I'll give the young ones their marching orders. Then we'll have to wait."

Above us, we heard people coming into the house; then the object of our speculations stumped down the stairs and greeted us.

"You fellows still here? When are your mother and I going to have some peace and quiet without you snooping around?" His face was flushed and his speech a bit slurred; he had been partaking of strong waters. "Go away and do good deeds."

"We'll be gone when we think you can take care of yourself, Da. When you come clean about who your enemies are, so we can help the police track them down, put them on trial and send them away where they can't harm a hair on your dear old head. The sooner you talk, the sooner we're out of your life."

"There's nothing to talk about. As I may have stated recently, I don't know who shot at me."

"He didn't shoot *at* you. He shot you. Nearly killed you. Now, who do you think it was?"

"Have you lost your hearing, Brennan? I said I don't know."

"Someone in the Corialli organization?"

"No."

"How do you know that?"

"I know. Forget it."

"How do you know, is what I asked you."

"And I told you I *know*. I got a message from Corialli after we went to the club. It wasn't any of his people. He made that clear."

"What about somebody else from your days at the club?"

"Like who, for Christ's sake?"

"How about that fellow Raoul?"

"I never heard of any Raoul."

"Not Raoul, Ramon. That was it. Could it have been this Ramon?"

"That gutless little gouger. He wouldn't have the bollocks to shoot me. Now piss off, the pair of you."

"Well, was there some —"

"Find yourselves another topic of conversation. Nobody's ever been at a loss for words in this house. Call on that gift now, why don't you."

"Let's try some other names."

"What did I just fucking say, Brennan?" The patriarch thumped his hand, hard, on the table. "Leave me alone. If I knew who was responsible, I'd have told the police. Eventually I expect the police will tell *me*."

"I wonder if the police have had any luck finding that mandolin player who gave us a song at the reception."

"They haven't. Oh, you had a phone call."

"Who from?"

"A Father Mac — what was it? Mackasey?"

"Dave Mackasey?"

"That's the man."

"What did he want?"

"He wants you to do what you're trained to do. Say Mass, perform the sacraments, not skulk around into things that are none of your affair. I wrote his number by the phone in the kitchen."

"At Holy Trinity?"

"No. He says he's at Saint Kieran's now. Pour me another thimbleful out of that bottle before you go, will you Monty?"

"Certainly, Declan."

We went upstairs and Brennan called his fellow priest. He agreed to say a Latin Mass at the crime scene, Saint Kieran's, later in the week.

"Shite," he said after he hung up.

"What?"

"That's the day Leo Killeen is flying home. He'll be coming over for lunch before his flight. I'll want to see him before he goes."

"You'll have time, don't worry about it. So. What do we make of that little exchange with your father?"

"That he knows this Ramon and doesn't hold him in high regard. For some reason."

"Right. He remembers some guy who was a young waiter at that club forty years ago."

"And we have the whiskey to thank for letting even that much slip. He considers Ramon gutless. Why? Did he swoon at the sight of steak tartare? Who the hell knows, Monty?"

"Gutless would not be the image he'd be aiming for, if he was really a wannabe, hanging around the fringes of the Mob."

"Or what he imagined to be the Mob. He may have wanted to

impress them. But surely not by rubbing somebody out forty years after the fact. I have an idea. Terry has friends on the police force. Maybe one of them will bend the rules and run a check on this fellow for us."

"Good plan. Al at the club said Ramon quit the White Gardenia, then came back again, desperate for money. Maybe his desperation for money brought him to the attention of the NYPD."

Chapter 7

They say there's bread and work for all,
And the sun shines always there;
But I'll not forget old Ireland,
Were it fifty times as fair.
— Helena Selina Sheridan (Lady Dufferin),
"The Lament of the Irish Emigrant"

March 17, 1991

Sunday morning I was up bright and early, strolling with my daughter on the Upper West Side. We went all the way to the Seventy-Ninth Street Boat Basin, where we walked along the river and speculated about life on one of the houseboats. A couple we saw sitting on bright yellow deck chairs, with a small black puppy frolicking around them, looked as if they had it made. A water view at a fraction of the cost. When we were back in the West Fifties Normie dragged me into a store filled with T-shirts and tacky souvenirs. Half the shop was devoted to all things green, ghastly and faux-Irish. Normie asked for a Central Park Zoo T-shirt and several other items. She and I were haggling when suddenly she screamed and grabbed my hand. An Uncle Sam figure had lunged out at her from the aisle and said: "Boo!"

"Hey!" I remonstrated. The mask was whipped off to reveal a gap-toothed boy about Normie's age. He grinned and took off behind a rack of leprechaun costumes.

"Who is that guy?" Normie asked.

"I don't know, sweetheart, just a boy playing tricks on you."

"No, I mean who's the mask about? The old guy with the beard and stars on his hat?"

"That's Uncle Sam. Symbol of the USA. I don't know whether you've ever seen those old posters: Uncle Sam wants you! Trying to get people to sign up for the Army in wartime."

"I wouldn't go in a war!"

"Watch it, kid. You'll never make it in this town if your loyalty to Uncle Sam is in doubt."

For some reason this exchange brought my mind back to the Cathal Murphy obituary. What was it? Some line about loyalty. "His loyalty to his Uncle was never in question." Brennan had interpreted it to mean Declan had stayed loyal to his Irish Republican relatives. But could Nessie Murphy have been making a remark about loyalty to Uncle Sam? Why would that be "in question"? There were a great many Irish Americans with an intense interest in the politics of the old country; such sympathies did not preclude loyalty to the United States.

Back at the hotel, Maura greeted us: "You just missed a call from Tommy."

"How are things?"

"Great, he says. He and Lexie are going out to dinner tonight. And his band has been asked to play at the Forum next weekend: young local bands playing for kids of all ages. No alcohol. He claims he's eating properly and getting some sleep. Who knows? Anyway, I'm glad you're back in time for the parade."

"Parade?"

"No reason you should know about it, *Collins*. It's not as if you've been in contact with any *Irish* since you've been here."

"Saint Patrick's Day! That explains — I hope — the ridiculous green items I saw on sale a few minutes ago."

"Sure and aren't you brilliant. So we'll have an early lunch and go to Fifth Avenue to watch it."

That sounded good to Normie, but she thought we shouldn't have the parade all to ourselves. "Call Father Burke!" she demanded. "He won't want to miss this!"

"He didn't mention it, sweetheart."

"Phone him, please! What if he misses it? He'll blame us."

Obediently I picked up the phone and punched in his number. He answered, and I noticed he didn't say "Top o' the morning."

"I have a little girl here who wants to make sure you don't miss the Saint Patrick's Day parade."

"Ah."

"Are you people regulars at this event?"

"I think it was only once I went to it. As a child. I'm just back from Sunday Mass, where they were giving out little shamrocks made of pipe cleaners, and a pipe made of what looked like chewed-up white candy. Sure didn't it make me want to burst out in song, and proclaim to the world that, yes, I am proud to be Bulgarian."

"You say you were passed over again this year?"

"What?"

"No, of course you're not too tall to be one of the little people. That's discrimination. There's nobody more suited to lead the parade. Yes, I agree. You do look good in a leprechaun outfit; has someone suggested otherwise? No, I understand. It's a shame. We'll go along to it anyway. I'll explain to Normie. What are you up to later?"

"Doing some prison visits, to tell you the truth. One of my fellow priests is under the weather, and I said I'd do his visits for him."

"No such luck you're going to Attica, I suppose."

"No, one of the local lockups. As for you, take the day, take two, go sightseeing with your family. Take in a show. I'll be wanting to see some holiday snapshots when we get back to Halifax, to assuage my guilt."

So off to the parade we went, and bought a tricolour for Normie to wave from the sidelines. It was a spectacle indeed and it showed that the colour green is not restricted to the places Mother Nature intended; I tried but failed to imagine any of the Burkes taking part. When even the youngest of us had seen enough, I suggested to Maura that we pay a visit to Sandra Worthington. We were only a few blocks from her townhouse in the East Seventies.

"This is more like it!" Maura exclaimed when we got to Seventy-Second Street. The outburst earned her a dead-eyed glance from a tall thin woman in tweeds, walking a long thin dog in a red sweater.

"Oh? The good socialist has a taste for the ritzier parts of town?"

"The quieter parts of town." She pointed to a sign that urged people not to sound their car horns except in a situation of danger. "I'd like to get hundreds of these signs and post them all over Manhattan, starting in front of our hotel."

"I'll help you, Mummy," our daughter offered.

Sandra wasn't alone when we arrived but she seemed genuinely pleased to see us, and she made a fuss over Normie, who beamed at Sandra and her splendid surroundings. We made ourselves comfortable in the elegant uptown apartment, with its high ceilings, panelled doors and carved marble fireplace. When I'd been there the year before, I had noticed a page from a musical score framed on the wall. This time, now that I knew her better, I would not be shy about taking a closer look. But right now we were being introduced to Reggie Baines. He was tall and expensively dressed, with a jutting chin and greying blonde hair brushed back from his forehead.

"Reggie is an old, old friend. Monty and Maura, and of course Normie, are new friends from Halifax, Reggie."

"Really. I've sailed up that way a few times. Fun town. I know some people at the Yacht Squadron. Do you sail?"

"Sold my boat."

"Trading up? What did you have?"

"A tub. Traded up for a Stratocaster."

"Stratocaster? Is that something just coming on the market? I'm not familiar —"

"It's a guitar."

Baines looked puzzled.

"We're friends of Brennan," Maura said. "That's how we met Sandra."

"Brennan? I don't believe I know the name."

"An old boyfriend, Reggie. Long in the past," Sandra said. Normie stared at Sandra with humongous eyes. Father Burke was somebody's *boyfriend*? "Can I get you anything? Scotch, gin, lemonade?"

"Lemonade sounds good," Maura replied, looking ready to settle in for the afternoon.

"Wait a minute," Reggie said. "Brendan. Was that the guy who took you away from Dody Spencer's birthday party? It was Dody's seventeenth and I remember it was almost like a debutante party. Though of course, with her birthday in April, it was out of season. Still . . ."

"Oh, Reggie, they don't want to hear about the days when I was young and foolish."

But Maura, one of seven children of a Commie coal miner from Cape Breton, looked as if there was nothing in the world she would enjoy more than hearing about Dody's deb party, in or out of season. "Do tell us, Reg. It's either that or the Saint Patrick's Day parade."

"Tell us!" Normie begged.

"Oh yes, it's that time of year yet again, when we're all confined to our houses by that crowd stumbling up the avenue." He sighed. "Where was I? Dody's party. We were all waiting for Sandra and this *boyfriend* —" he might as well have said *gigolo* "— and they simply didn't show up. Thanks to this Brian, or Brendan, or whatever his name was. What happened there, Sandra? That was just before I left for Yale, so I never did get the details. Or meet this *loverboy*. I heard you ended up with a bunch of tramps, in a bread line, or something."

He turned to us. "Did you say this Brian is a friend of yours? I would have thought he'd have imbibed himself to death or got knifed in a brothel by now."

Sandra spoke up. "I had invited Brennan to Dody's party. He didn't know most of the people there but —"

"I should say not."

"But we were going out together. So Brennan borrowed his father's car and came to pick me up. He was looking very elegant —" Reggie's expression told us he knew better "— in a beautiful dark suit he had saved to buy. Or maybe he stole it, I don't know. But when he arrived I was in a snit. About my shoes." She looked embarrassed, but went on: "I had ordered a new dress, and it was fine. Kind of a pale aqua —"

"And a pillbox hat to match," Maura quipped.

"It was after six, *dahling,*" Sandra corrected, with a laugh.

"So. No hat," Maura acknowledged. How did women know these things? Normie's eyes went back and forth between them, taking it all in for the future.

"Mother had sent my shoes out to be dyed to match my dress.

They weren't done until the day of the party, and when I saw them, I threw a fit."

"They'd replaced them with a pair of tooled leather cowboy boots!" my wife guessed.

"Almost as *bahd,*" Sandra agreed, in a self-mocking wail. "They were a bright turquoise, almost green."

"Frightful," I agreed.

"You're bad, Monty. You two know Brennan," Sandra stated. "You didn't know him then, but try to imagine him even as you know him now, listening to that story about my shoes."

New York City, 1957

"What's this you're telling me now Sandra? You had a pair of shoes dyed to match a green dress?"

"The dress is aqua, the shoes are green. I look hideous!"

"I don't understand this. What colour were the shoes before you dyed them?"

"They were white, what do you think?"

"So why didn't you just leave them white? Wouldn't they go with more of your outfits if they were white instead of green?"

"Brennan, it's April!"

"I'm not following you here."

"One does not wear white until after Memorial Day. Obviously. Oh, what's the point?" I can't bring myself to budge from the car. Anything else will be too horrid to imagine. But he's starting the engine. We're going to have to make an appearance.

"What's the difference?" he's asking me. "Who's going to notice?"

"Who's going to notice? Everyone! I'll be the laughingstock."

Brennan is looking at me as if he has no idea who I am or what I am doing in his car. He yanks the steering wheel, and the tires make the most embarrassing squealing noise. Right here in Upper Manhattan!

"What are you doing, Brennan? Where are we going?"

"You'll see what it's like to have some fecking hideous shoes, you little pussacon." I hate it when he calls me these Irish names. He calls me a pussacon when he thinks I'm being pouty. But I'm

just being normal. He's the one who's from another planet.

"You turn around this instant, Brennan! I cannot miss Dody's party. I will never live it down."

"Start livin' it down, Princess." Where is he taking me? We're on the bridge to Queens. Now where are we? What is this horrible place? It looks like an old warehouse and it's got a cross painted on the side. And who are all those people shuffling outside in a line?

"Where are we?" I hope he can't hear the panic in my voice.

"We're where I'm supposed to be tonight, but I bribed my little brothers to cover for me so I could take you out." He's parking. Is he serious? Now he's yanked off his jacket and tie. We're out of the car, and he's pulling me!

"Get your hands off me, Brennan." Inside there is a food counter and racks of obviously secondhand clothing. A man is ladling out soup, a woman is serving bread. There are cold sandwiches, and Jell-O for dessert. These people, you have to feel sorry for them. They appear to be absolutely desperate. I know I look out of place in my dyed satin shoes, skimpy little aqua dress with spaghetti straps, and my hair all done up.

Here comes his little brother Terrence. "Do we still get our money, now that you're here, Bren?" He's paying them to be here in his place.

"You'll get your money, you little gobshite. What are you supposed to be doing?"

"I've got the balls!"

"You what?"

"It's me that's puttin' the balls in the toy bags for the kids."

"So do it!" Brennan gives him a shove and sends him off.

Now it's Patrick coming over. He's so sweet. He's got a big spoon in his hand; his face and shirt are sticky with red Jell-O. "So you're here after all, Bren."

"Go get a clean spoon and keep it out of your gob."

"Oh, hello, Sandra."

"Hi, Pat."

"You'll be needin' some clothes, then? They've a whole bin full of sweaters there, Sandra. And don't worry; they won't cost you a cent."

131

Brennan is grabbing him by the arm. The poor little guy looks nervous. But Brennan just ruffles his hair and sends him off with a big wink. About me. Well, I guess I am the odd one out.

"Come here, Sandra. Spear some food onto people's plates and be gracious about it." I try to be, and it isn't really all that bad.

It's over now, and we're on our way to my place. He hasn't said a word. Now we're at my door. He isn't moving, he hasn't turned the engine off, he's just waiting for me to go. The only thing he says by way of good-night is: "Anybody comment on your shoes?"

"So that's where you were," Reggie said. "I never did get it straight."

"I told you before. It was a Catholic charity, Reg."

"Right," Reggie sniffed. "The Pope in Rome probably got half the money from it!"

"Half the soup, you must mean," Maura said.

"So," Sandra told us, "somebody learned the social graces that night." Reggie harrumphed at that, but Sandra went on: "It changed me, though I wouldn't give him the satisfaction of saying so." She spoke in a conspiratorial whisper: "Maybe I was the first soul he saved."

Everybody laughed, though perhaps for different reasons, if Reggie's expression was any indication. Then Maura brought the room down. "I don't know whether you heard, or maybe it was in the papers, Sandra, but somebody tried to kill Brennan's father."

"What? I didn't see anything in the papers. What happened?"

"I was there!" Normie burst out. "It was at Katie's wedding party. Somebody shot Katie's granddad, Mr. Burke. The guy got away!"

"Shot him in the chest," I confirmed. "Just missed his heart."

"My God!" Sandra was horrified. "Do they know who it was?"

I shook my head. "The police don't have a suspect yet. And if Declan knows who did it, he's not saying."

"Is he going to be all right?"

"Oh, yeah. He tries not to let on it happened."

I glanced at Reggie Baines. He looked as if somebody had just farted in the Knickerbocker Club.

Sandra chose that moment to offer us fresh drinks. Normie held out her glass for a refill, but Reggie declined, saying there was somewhere else he had to be. When he was gone, I went to the framed page of music on the wall.

"Tell us about this," I requested. The notes were done by hand. The sheet had been torn through the middle, then lined up again. The piece was written for traditional Celtic instruments and, when I sang the melody line to myself, it sounded like a lament. I gently removed it from the wall, took it over and propped it up so I could play the top line and some of the accompaniment on her piano.

"It's sorrowful, it's haunting, and it's so very, very Irish," Maura remarked, almost to herself.

Even in the small snippet we had, the piece managed to express an overwhelming sense of loss. "Where's the rest of it?" I asked.

Sandra shook her head.

"You lost it?" No comment. "You tore it up."

"I wasn't very receptive when I first got it. I should have been, I guess. It's the only piece of music anyone ever wrote for me, which explains why it's there on the wall. Really, I suppose, it was sweet of him to —"

"That's passion, babe, not sweetness," I snapped, jabbing the music with my finger. Even I was taken aback by the sharpness of my tone. "I hope you didn't underestimate him while you had him in your life."

Nobody spoke for a while. I played the piece again, this time picking out a different part of the accompaniment. Then I placed it carefully back on the wall.

"When did he write it for you?" I asked her, more gently this time.

"When we parted for good."

We were silent again. Then Maura suggested we all go out for dinner. Sandra joined us for a Saint Patrick's Day scoff of moussaka and kleftiko at a nearby Greek restaurant. She listened with wry good humour while Normie prattled on about her good friend Father Burke, who, despite his distant, unseemly past as a boyfriend, might some day be found worthy to join the heavenly host. Normie intended to conduct a discreet investigation with a view to having him declared an angel. His old flame kindly kept her own counsel till the conversation turned to more neutral topics. I did bring her back to the Burkes momentarily, when I asked her to recount the story of the man who confronted Mr. Burke at the house that day, back when she and Brennan were in their teens.

"You don't think something that long ago could be related to the shooting, do you?"

"I think the answer is more likely to be found in the past than in the present."

So she told us again about the man with a strong Brooklyn accent who had appeared on Declan's doorstep.

"He accused Declan of stealing, or called him a thief. He said something about Declan stuffing an envelope in his pocket. 'How can a man sink so low?' he said. Or: 'That's pretty low.' And I knew he meant something more than what my mother meant by 'low' — chewing gum or having fringe on your lampshades and sofa. Anyway, they had their argument. I can't remember what else they said. And they pushed each other around. Then the man went away, warning Mr. Burke to stick to his own turf, 'not ours.' The reason I remember that is I asked my father when I got home what turf was. And he gave me a whole bunch of meanings. I don't recall any of them except the kind of turf the Irish used for fuel in their fires. So I had an image of Declan hunched over his fireplace, face lit up by flames, and the other man doing the same in his own house."

"A turf war of some kind," I mused.

"Men!" Maura said, catching Sandra's eye. They shook their heads.

We walked Sandra home after dinner, and she told us she hoped to see us again before we left.

The next day was Monday, and Brennan called to tell me he had dropped his niece off at the local library, where she would spend a few hours looking at old newspapers.

"Shouldn't she be in school? Or are they on spring break?"

"She should be in school, but one day's mitching won't hurt her. You'll see what I mean. What are you up to tonight? Something entertaining, I hope."

"As a matter of fact, yes. It's father and daughter night at the opera. She's a little proprietorial about the druidic tale, given that

MacNeil and I saddled her with the name Norma after we saw it in Milan. Don't ever call her that, by the way. She answers to Normie, and that's it."

"Understood."

"Anyway, I promised that if the opera was good — and I'm sure we're agreed that it was, even if the night was a bit of a disappointment for you —" he snorted at that "— I'd take her to see it."

"She'll be enthralled. Have a grand time."

We took a trip on the Staten Island ferry that afternoon and ate lots of junk food, but Normie's mind was on higher things. She was indeed enthralled by the opera, as she reported to her mother when we got in. "They sang my song, 'Casta Diva.' It was beautiful. And the priestess — named after *me* — was in a sparkly robe and the lights were on her and she looked like a beam of light coming from the moon. We have to put the opera on at school, for our June concert! I'll play Norma, because I already know all the music, and Kim can be the other girl. Father Burke can be the guy, the Roman, and Daddy, you can sing in the background . . ." It took nearly two hours to get her wound down and ready to sleep.

On Tuesday morning I met another young girl, and this one probably *could* stage-manage an opera at school. It started with a call from Brennan: "Our little detective is here, with a sheaf of newspaper clippings. Would you like to come over?"

Traffic was light for some unexplained reason, and I arrived in Queens in record time.

Sitting at the Burkes' kitchen table with a cup of tea in front of her was an owlish-looking girl I remembered vaguely from the wedding. She looked like a young fourteen. "Deirdre, have you met Monty, my friend from Halifax? Deirdre is Pat's daughter."

"Hello, Monty. If you'd care to have a seat I'll show you what I've found. Would you like tea before we begin?"

"Tea would be great. Thank you."

Brennan winked at me and sat down. "I'll have a cup too, Deirdre."

"Certainly, Brennan."

Once we had our tea, the child got down to business. She pushed her round glasses up on her nose and straightened the stack of clippings in her hands.

"I think I can save you some time. I assume you are not interested in gang rumbles, domestic shootings, or Mob slayings unless the gangsters happen to be Irish. Am I right?"

"You are probably right, yes."

"You are not looking for a case in which the person was sentenced to death."

"I hope not," Brennan said quietly.

"You are interested in the waterfront but not in corrupt hiring practices and the investigations of that nature that were going on at the time."

"That's probably true," I agreed, and wondered if I could hire this child in some capacity at our law firm, "but you can show them to us."

"I will. But I think you'll be disappointed. So I'll start with the other things I found."

She slapped the first clipping on the table like a card in a poker game. "O'Farrell, John. Convicted in the beating and robbery of a storekeeper in Briarwood, Queens. Sent to Attica."

"What was the storekeeper's name, and what kind of store was it?"

"Mervish, Eli. Corner store. Cigarettes, groceries, candy, that sort of thing I gather."

"All right."

The next one was slapped down. "Doherty, Thomas. Convicted of shooting a security guard on the Lower West Side of Manhattan. Guard left disabled. Doherty sent to Attica."

"Does it say anything about Doherty? Any interesting connections, or was he just a lone bank robber?"

"He had done it before." Deirdre squinted at the paper. "In fact he had just been released from prison two weeks before this crime."

"Which happened when?"

"September 5, 1952."

"Never mind. That means he was inside in July. Next?"

Slap on the table. "Connors, Gerald. Convicted of robbery — armed robbery. Struck near-fatal blow to head of port watchman during a theft of weapons. Sent to Attica."

I looked over at Brennan. His eyes were on the clipping. "Let's hear more about this one, Deirdre."

Her lips curled up in a little smile. "Yes. This took place on the Brooklyn waterfront, Pier One. Some crates of guns — Smith and Wesson something or other — were supposed to be shipped to Japan, but they were stolen from the shed. The watchman got clobbered, and the thieves got away."

"How many thieves?"

"Connors and one other guy they never caught."

Brennan was sitting absolutely still, staring past the young girl and her papers.

I questioned her again. "The date, Deirdre?"

"The robbery took place July 12, 1952."

I slipped the paper out of her hand. Two men with their faces covered had pulled up in a truck outside the gate of the pier, got out of the truck, and were stopped by the port watchman on duty, Enzo Rinaldi, who grabbed one of them. The other had a gun. They tackled him, clubbed him over the head and left him unconscious. They were able to get into the shed, which had been left open. Police suspected an inside job but Rinaldi was not under suspicion. The two men removed three crates of .32 calibre Smith and Wesson "Chief's Specials" before fleeing the scene. Constable Seamus O'Brien stated this type of revolver was designed for close combat and extremely rapid fire. Police were able to place Connors at the scene because of torn clothing that matched items found on the pier, and he was arrested a few days later. Connors never admitted there was another man involved in the heist. Police believed the weapons were moved to another pier that same night and loaded on a ship bound for the Republic of Ireland. Connors was twenty-three years old, married, with two infant children.

"Do you want to see the rest of these?" Deirdre asked. I had almost forgotten she was there.

"I think we have what we're looking for, but let me glance at the others." It didn't take long. We had found the real "Danny," the man Declan was working on all those nights at the White Gardenia, with Evie as an extra attraction. What had she said? The man was younger than Declan, but older than she was? Of course. She was only nineteen or twenty; twenty-three qualified as "older." Connors turned out to be a stand-up guy, doing his time without informing on Declan. I looked again at the clipping. The court heard evidence of Connors's previous good character. He had no prior record. The sentence was seven to ten years. The words of the obituary chilled me when I ran them through my mind. Never got out of Attica. Why?

Brennan sat at the table staring at his hands. This was pretty much what we had expected, with the exception perhaps of the watchman bludgeoned and left unconscious, but it was obviously painful for Brennan to have his suspicions confirmed. I thanked Deirdre, and Brennan gave her a distracted smile. She left us with the assurance that she would be happy to assist if we needed her again.

"Well," I began.

"Why did he never get out of Attica, Monty?"

"That's the next item on our agenda." I picked up the clipping and took note of the defence attorney's name: Myron Rose. I also jotted down the name of the one police officer mentioned, Seamus O'Brien.

"Armed robbery," Brennan said. "They could have killed the man."

"I'm sure they didn't plan it that way, Brennan. They probably panicked. The story says it was an inside job. The warehouse was left unlocked, so they thought they'd get in and out —"

"It's never planned that way, is it? Yet everyone goes in carrying a gun. Jesus."

"This must have been the one big scheme your father had to compensate the IRA for the money he took with him, and maybe get the death sentence lifted. If he could pull it off, he'd be clear. That would be the end of it."

"But it wasn't the end of it."

"What do you mean?"

"He pissed the Mob off while he was at it. That night at the club, Patrizio Corialli said Declan had stepped on their toes. They may have had their eyes on this shipment of guns, and Declan moved in on their territory."

"Their turf. That may explain the visit from the man Sandra saw during your teen years. A Mob enforcer?"

"Chances are. Did my old fellow know what he was getting into?"

"Never know with Declan, do you?"

"You said a mouthful there."

"Whatever the situation, it seems Corialli isn't holding a grudge."

"Let's hope we can all achieve forgiveness of such biblical proportions. Let's call it a day here. I wish we weren't so short on time. We need a day to blow off steam. But we don't have it. Or I don't. You do. Take a day off, Monty. For Christ's sake, you come down here, shots fly past your family at a wedding, your wife reams you out —"

"Nothing new there." I stared into my teacup but found no answers in the dregs. "I'll go track down the lawyer."

Myron Rose had died in 1984, but his law firm was thriving. I stood in the twentieth-floor office of a concrete and glass high-rise on Sixth Avenue and gazed down at the landscaped plaza and blue fountain pool below. I had just identified myself to the firm's managing partner, Deborah Feldstein. She told me the Gerald Connors file was in storage, and it was confidential anyway. I understood that. She did, however, have a master list of all files and contacts. She would not give out any information, but she offered to try to find a member of the Connors family. If the person wanted to call me, fine. What exactly was my interest? I could have woven some kind of fantasy to cover my real purpose but I saw no reason to lie. I offered a short version of the truth, leaving out Declan's name. She nodded and said she would make her calls as soon as she had a free moment.

That evening Maura, Normie and I walked to D.J. Reynolds for an early supper. Normie brought a book she had purchased earlier in the day; she could not put it down. That was fine with me; we wouldn't have to hear "Can we go now?" halfway through the meal. Her mother and I each ordered a pint and settled in. The waitress had recently arrived from Ireland, and she had a few amusing tales for us about being a neophyte in New York.

"Not everybody had such a rollicking good time when they

washed up in the land of opportunity," Maura remarked when the woman had moved on to another table.

"Oh?"

"No. I had lunch with Teresa today. Took her out for a treat and we dropped Normie off to play with Terry and Sheila Burke's youngest daughter."

Normie's head came up momentarily from her book. "Christine. She's cool!"

"Teresa and I had a lovely time," Maura said. "But when the conversation turned to early days in New York, I was able to discern that it was not all the sweetness and light you'd expect from life on the run with Declan Burke."

"Imagine that! What did she say?"

"She didn't say anything specific about his activities or his 'troubles,' so we're none the wiser there, but she did reminisce a bit about life in Hell's Kitchen."

"Hell's Kitchen? I thought they'd been in Sunnyside all along."

"Oh, no. They got off to a rough start."

New York City, 1950
"Marry the likes of Declan Burke and you'll rue the day."
How many times did I hear that? Well, the day is here. We've just washed up on the shores of America with nothing but a rosary and the dirty, stinking clothes on our backs. Declan and me, five children, and we don't know a soul. I thought nothing could be worse than saying goodbye to our home in Dublin, roaring down the highway to Cobh in the middle of the night and leaping onto the ship just before it left port. Then came the interminable trip across the ocean with everyone weeping and whinging and sicking up. But this is worse. I'd as lief be back in the train station than in this place. Grand Central was grand indeed, the Shelbourne Hotel compared to this. Seven people in two rooms, the place is filthy, and the toilets and bathtubs are down the hall. We have to drag the children to get them down there. Then you see some class of enormous, terrifying insect scuttling about whenever you turn on the light. And the ructions that go on! All manner of gougers and gurriers run wild in the hallways day and

night. If Mam and Da could see us now, residents of a tenement in a place they call Hell's Kitchen.

Oh, didn't I give out to himself last night? I all but pinned him to the wall with my fury. "You got us into this, you get us out of it." He doesn't need me to tell him what I'll do if he doesn't get us a decent place to live; he'll not see us again until he creeps back onto Irish soil carrying that gun he smuggled out.

I thought Declan's heart was going to fail him, when I broke the news: Da and Mam are coming to New York! My father insists on seeing for himself that we're all right. And if we're not, I guess Dec will have to turn that gun on his own father-in-law to prevent him taking us all back to Dublin.

Jesus, Mary and all the saints be praised! Declan has us installed in a great brick house in a place called Sunnyside. And nearly everyone here is Irish. We moved just in time for my parents' visit. No coincidence there, I'm thinking. He sat there and told them about the business he's setting up, importing and selling Irish goods. I hope this means he can give up his job as security man at that nightclub. But I doubt it. He'll be working two jobs for a long, long time to pay off the loan for this house. I don't want to know where he got the money so fast, or how much he's paying in interest! I keep telling myself: this too shall pass.

"By that point," Maura told me, "Teresa and I had enjoyed a couple of glasses of wine. I asked her if she ever thought she should have married the boy next door. She just smiled and shook her head. Though one night, when things were a little strained between them, she suspected he had been with another woman. She acknowledged that this was not the most mortal of the sins he might have committed, but she said it was out of character. We didn't dwell on what might have been 'in character' for Declan. We talked some more. Then, with what might have been a pointed look in my direction, Teresa wrapped things up by quoting Saint Paul: 'Love bears all things, believes all things, hopes all things, endures all things. Love never ends.'"

†

The next day I heard from Deborah Feldstein, the lawyer. A few minutes later I received a hurried call from Judy Willman. She was the widow of Gerald Connors, and she was willing to speak to us. But her voice on the phone was no more than a whisper, and an overbearing presence was evident in the background. I could hear him interrupting her: "Who's that on the phone?" The woman said she had to go, but could we come around at two o'clock. So Brennan and I were suit-jacketed Mormons on the doorstep again, this time at a small, dingy apartment building in the Red Hook area along the Brooklyn waterfront, a few blocks from the Brooklyn Battery Tunnel. We pushed the button marked Willman and were buzzed in immediately. The building was run down; it smelled of piss and stale cooking. We trudged up a dark staircase to the third floor. The veneer on the Willmans' door was coming off in layers. We were greeted by a woman who appeared to be in her sixties. Time had not been kind. The skin around her small pale brown eyes was tired and wrinkled, and her lacklustre hair was dragged back from her forehead with metal hair clips. She was drying her hands on a tea towel.

"Come on in. Which one of you was I talking to on the phone?"

"You were speaking to me, Mrs. Willman. I'm Monty Collins and this is Brennan Burke."

The room was indifferently furnished; the prize item seemed to be a huge faux-leather reclining chair set about four feet in front of a large television set. The carpet around the reclining chair was worn, and littered with crumbs. An overflowing ashtray teetered on one arm of the chair.

"Come and sit down. I'm not sure I have the information you need. You may know more than I do," she said. She perched on the seat of the recliner; Brennan and I sat in armchairs.

"We know very little, Mrs. Willman. Brennan and I found out about this recently. But we're determined to piece together certain events that occurred back then. The reason —"

"Good. Because I was never able to piece it together myself. I finally gave up trying to find out why my husband died the way he did."

142

"Died," Brennan repeated.

"One minute we were here, a normal young family; the next minute he was gone. Arrested, put on trial, taken to that place. And murdered. It was a nightmare from beginning to end. I never knew what was going on. I still don't."

Never got out of Attica. Murdered. Burke's face had gone grey.

"Why don't you tell us what you remember," I said.

She took a deep breath and glanced towards the front door. "We were living over in Queens. Gerald, me and the babies. We didn't have a lot to live on but we were doing fine. Gerry had a steady job in a printing company and there was room to move up. He never missed a day's work. We were in a tiny flat, but we furnished it when we could, and it was cozy. Three years was the time limit we'd given ourselves there, then we would move on and up. Gerry —" her eyes darted to the door again "— was the sweetest guy you could imagine, a good husband to me, and he adored the kids. His dream was that the summer before Kathy started school, we would all go over to Ireland and see where his parents had come from. Somewhere in County Kerry. It sounded like a fine plan to me. I'm a mixed breed myself, never had any desire to go to any of the old countries my relatives escaped from. But for him it was different." She rose from her chair. "Can I get you anything? A soda? Coffee?" We both shook our heads. "I'm going to have a cigarette. Anybody mind?"

"It's your house, Mrs. Willman," Brennan said. "And I'm a smoker myself."

"Oh, would you like a cigarette? And call me Judy." She reached to a side table and picked up a pack. She opened it and appeared to be counting the cigarettes.

"Why don't you have one of mine?" Brennan suggested quickly. He offered her his pack; she took one out and he lit it for her. He lit one up himself, and leaned back.

"A few weeks before this all happened, maybe a month, I don't know, Gerry started staying out late. He'd never done that before. He wasn't drinking a lot, sometimes one or two drinks, sometimes nothing at all. I got worried and kept after him about it. He wouldn't tell me why he was going out, but he told me it was nothing to worry about. What he meant was he wasn't cheating on me with another woman."

She gave a snort of bitter laughter. "Like that's the worst thing in the world. Husband arrested for robbery with violence, sent to Attica and killed? At least he didn't have another girlfriend!" Her voice broke and she got up and walked out of the room. When she came back, she was wiping her eyes with a Kleenex.

"When he was in prison I would visit him. Sometimes I'd bring the girls. It was horrible. The other prisoners were terrifying. And all through that time Gerry wouldn't tell me what was going on. He didn't let me attend the trial, and I couldn't have anyway, with the kids and no money coming in. I know somebody got him into all that. He didn't go from being a law-abiding citizen one day to a violent criminal the next day without someone setting him up."

We heard a key scratching around the lock in the front door. Judy flinched, then dabbed hurriedly at her eyes. She tucked the Kleenex into her sleeve and set her face in what she meant to be a pleasant, welcoming expression. "Hi, Garth!" she called out brightly, in a voice too loud for the small room.

A large unkempt man in his sixties made a noisy entrance. A loud nasal snort sounded as if it would end in a gob of phlegm being expelled. "Who's this?" He directed the question at his wife, and jerked a thumb at her two visitors.

"Garth, we have company. This is Mr. Burke and Mr. Collins. They've come to —"

He turned on us. "Whaddaya want?"

Brennan looked as if what he wanted more than anything was to get up and tackle the man to the floor. He opened his mouth to reply, and I overrode whatever he was going to say. "Good afternoon, Mr. Willman. We're here to ask for your wife's assistance with —"

"She can't help you."

"Now, how would you know that, if —" That was Brennan.

Again, I talked right past him. "She may not be able to. We haven't had a chance to ask her yet. We just arrived." I shot a glance at Judy, and she stayed silent. The husband eyed the long ash on the end of her filtered cigarette. "We were hoping that some information about her former husband, so many years ago, might provide —"

"The jailbird! Forget about it. Gets her upset."

He parked himself on the arm of his wife's chair. She immediately slid out of the seat, and he took her place. She sat on the arm and busied herself with her fingernails. The husband lifted a huge hand and scratched his unwashed hair. A cloud of dandruff fell from his head and landed on his shoulders. I caught Brennan staring at it as if it were the bodily manifestation of a mortal sin.

"She has a lie-down at this time of day. Why don't you go in for your rest now? I'll answer their questions if they have any before they go."

I decided to shift the conversation onto another track. "Your children?" I looked to a pair of photos atop the television. One showed a wan-looking young woman with three squirming children seated on a rust and gold flowered couch. The other woman had done better for herself. She stood in the driveway of a double garage with an elaborately dressed little girl, an expensive car behind them, and palm trees in the yard.

"Those are my girls, yes. Our girls I mean, of course. They're Willmans now. That's Sheena with the three kids, and Kathy with the one. Kathy's down in Flor —"

"Kathy forgot you're alive," Willman butted in. "When's the last time you seen her? Seven years? She's got it made down there, him with his Pontiac dealership and her with her country-club membership. Rollin' in dough. But does she spread any of it around? Not up this way."

"And your other daughter? Does Sheena live in the area?" I asked.

Judy said: "Yes, less than a mile away. Life hasn't been easy for her, but she's starting —"

"She's livin' off taxpayers like me and you, that's what she's doin'. On welfare, the pack of them. Maybe the next boyfriend will get a job. Though why should he, with the welfare payin' the shot?"

I saw another photo display, on a table in a corner of the room. There were pictures of soldiers, along with medals, ribbons and other military paraphernalia. One of the photos was of Garth, in better days, standing with a young man in his late teens or early twenties. Both were in US Army uniforms. "Our son," Judy said.

"Private G.G. Willman," Garth confirmed. "I pulled some strings and got him into my old Army unit. I should take Sheena over to the sergeants' mess with me some night. See if she can meet a guy who's willing to get off his ass to serve his country and bring home a steady pay packet."

The final photo that caught my eye was Garth and Judy's wedding portrait. The date was emblazoned in gold script on the frame: May 7, 1955. Thirty-six years with Garth. Judy looked apprehensive even then.

"Now have you found out everything you want to know?" he asked with belligerence. Then to his wife: "Go rest. You're tired."

"I don't mind trying to help them, Garth. All they want to know is a bit of ancient history really."

"All this stuff from the past rattles her nerves, as you can see. So if you have all the information you came for, *adios.*"

"No, we haven't, as a matter of fact."

"I'm not sure Mrs. Willman can help us, Brennan. She didn't seem to know anything about the few points we raised. We should be going." I got up and he reluctantly followed my lead. "Thanks again, Mrs. Willman. Sorry to disturb you."

"Oh, that's all right. I'm sorry I couldn't help you."

The husband lumbered to his feet and corralled us to the door. Judy slipped quietly from the room. I started out the door, but Burke could not leave it at that. He turned to the glowering man and said in an undertone: "A word to the wise, Willman. Your wife has a tongue in her head and she can speak for herself. But just in case she's too polite to mention it: go and have a wash. You'll be doing her a kindness, and one that's long overdue." He turned on his heel and walked away. The slam of the door reverberated behind us.

"Imagine putting up with the likes of that," he fumed as we left the building. "And of course he'd arrive on the scene in the middle of the conversation."

"Whether we like it or not, she thinks she does have to put up with him. So we don't want to make it any worse for her. And anyway, I suspect she doesn't know anything more. Whatever started her former husband on his criminal course, she wasn't privy to it."

"We can't just leave it! She thinks Connors was murdered. We have to know what happened."

"We're not going to find out today."

We didn't find out the next day, either. When I called her number, Garth Willman answered and hung up when he heard my voice. I tried again a few hours later and got Judy, but she whispered: "I don't know. I never did." The call ended with a soft click. I phoned Brennan to let him know that we wouldn't learn anything more from Judy.

"I'd like to know more about this Willman."

"Just because he has dirty hair doesn't mean he's a criminal."

"There's something about him I don't like."

"Yes, I was able to infer that with my sharp lawyerly mind."

"Well, one inference I'm trying desperately not to draw is that my father had something to do with the death of this young fellow in prison. To silence him. I can't allow myself to think that."

"Brennan, we don't know that." Though it was hard to avoid the suspicion. I knew exactly how he felt.

It was Thursday. Maura and Normie announced their intention to spend the afternoon and evening shopping for gifts for Tommy Douglas and everyone else back home. Normie seemed to think that everybody, young or old, would be more than happy with something from F.A.O. Schwarz, the toy emporium. And she was probably right. I had a late lunch and settled down in front of the television to watch a movie. This was something I rarely did but I could never resist *Dr. Strangelove.*

In the evening I drove to Queens to see what Brennan was up to. Turns out he had a plan, and he was dressed for the occasion, in faded jeans, a worn-out T-shirt with Italian writing on it, and a battered black leather jacket. He hadn't shaved. "You're just in time, Monty." He grabbed the keys to his father's car from a hook by the front door.

"We're going down-market?"

"Possibly. I'll fill you in on the way." We got into the car, drove to Queens Boulevard and turned left. "Patrick counsels a group of ex-convicts. As you can imagine, the composition of the group varies from session to session. He remembered that one of the ex-cons was in Attica in the early fifties. This fellow is supposed to be attending therapy but he never shows up. Pat said he'd try to get the man into the office. But we're not going to wait for that. I got a phone number from Pat, the number of a place where this man is a regular. I called, and he's going to meet us there."

"As simple as that."

"Sure."

We pulled up at a one-and-a-half storey house with a tin awning. Yellow light glowed in the front window. It didn't look like a rough place to me.

"Come on." He turned off the engine, and we got out and went up the walk. Brennan rang the bell, and an elderly man came to the door, wearing a beige cardigan over a shirt and tie. Ex-cons come in all guises.

"Brennan, good to see you, lad! Step right in."

"Ed Gillespie, Monty Collins. My brother's here, I understand." We followed Ed into the living room where two tables of bridge were underway. All the players except Terry Burke were in their seventies. They did a double take at the sight of Brennan's dressed-down ensemble.

"Got stuck with an extra ticket to the fights, did you Brennan?" one man said.

"Let's hope it doesn't come to that. I need to borrow this fellow," he announced.

Terry put on a little show of regret but he did not look overly disappointed to be called away from the bridge party. Ed said he would take Terry's place. We said goodbye and trooped out to the car.

"What's going on, Bren?"

"We need some extra muscle."

"I'm your man."

As we drove across the bridge to Manhattan and headed south, Brennan told his brother why we were going to a Lower East Side bar to meet an ex-convict named Earl. Someone leaned on his horn and gave Brennan the finger when he pulled into the only parking space near the dingy bar that was our destination. The place was just as dingy inside. We asked for Earl, only to be informed by the bartender, who looked as if he might have been inside an institution or two himself, that Earl was not there. He would probably be back. Or he'd phone in. Earl was a little "paranoid, man" and sometimes phoned to see if anybody was looking for him. We sat down, ordered beer and waited.

When we had our drinks, Terry took off his sweater to reveal an eye-catching T-shirt. It showed an airline pilot in uniform and cap standing behind a jumbo jet; the jet was going up at a forty-five-degree angle from his body. Below it were the words: "Pilots get it up." The shirt caught the attention of two women who were obviously from out of state. It wasn't long before Terry was leaning over to their table, telling them he had been a pilot for years until the airline destroyed his career; they fired him because he intended to go public about something he had seen "up there." There was a conspiracy among all the top airlines to silence him. When the women asked what he had seen, he raised his eyebrows and said: "Think about it."

I spoke quietly to Brennan: "Is he really a pilot?"

"Yes, and he's still employed. It's all pub talk. Wait till he gets wound up; he'll be at it half the night if Earl doesn't show."

Earl didn't show. But he called the bar, and Brennan asked the bartender to hand over the phone. Earl said he'd meet us at his place if there was something in it for him. So we drank up, paid up and went out to the car.

"Where's he meeting us?" Terry asked.

"Some hole on Avenue D."

"Alphabet City! Lock your doors, boys."

We didn't have far to drive before we found ourselves surrounded by abandoned buildings and stripped-down cars. The streets were populated by derelicts, some hovering by fires burning in oil drums on the corners. On every block there seemed to be a guy with a pit bull on a leash. We stopped at a crumbling tenement building, which had suffered a fire and was partly boarded up. I jumped when I saw a man with his face so close to the car window it steamed up with his breath. He said: "Smoke, dope, coke, smoke, dope, coke" over and over again until he finally lurched away.

Brennan looked a little less cocky than usual, but he put a brave face on the situation. "You two stay in here with the doors locked and the engine running. Terry, get into the driver's seat. I'll take a quick look for our man."

"I thought you brought me along as an enforcer. So now what? You're going alone?"

"You're my little brother, Terry. Ma would never forgive me if —"

"Fuck off."

"We'll all go, Brennan," I said.

"Three of us together will spook the man. Stay here for now." Terry gave an exasperated sigh, but got out of the back seat. Brennan vacated the driver's seat, and his brother took his place. "If anything happens, take off and call the police."

"Yeah? What will be happening to you while we're out looking for a working pay phone?"

"I walk with God. Remember?" He laughed and strode towards the flophouse, opened the door, and stepped inside. We heard a cry of pain from an upper window, and Terry and I exchanged an uneasy glance.

It wasn't long before Brennan appeared in the doorway. He had a firm grip on the elbow of a man who must have been Earl; Brennan practically dragged the man to the car. He opened the back door, shoved Earl into the seat, and got in beside him. Terry and I turned to gawk at the captive.

"Assholes," was all he said to us.

Earl looked about seventy, with deep lines in his face, but Brennan told us later he was closer to sixty. His hair was grey and combed straight back from a square face with a wide, prominent forehead and small, deep-set eyes. A tattoo was visible where his shirt opened at the neck, and he had familiar tats on his knuckles: "love" on one hand and "hate" on the other. He stank of sweat, smoke, dirty clothes and Christ only knew what else.

"Get moving, Ter!" Brennan ordered, and Terry put the car in gear and peeled away from the curb. Brennan tried to persuade Earl to accompany us to a bar or restaurant for a decent meal but Earl did not respond.

Terry offered a comment on our surroundings: "I hear this place is supposed to be the next trendy neighbourhood. Place to be for yuppies in the nineties."

"Cocksuckers."

We drove to a park beside the East River and stopped. We opened our windows a crack to admit some much-needed fresh air. Earl sat in silence, his leg jiggling non-stop. Brennan gave him a cigarette but he obviously needed something stronger.

"Tell us what happened that day in Attica, when the young fellow was killed."

"Motherfuckers."

"All right, who were the men who did the killing?"

"Low-lifes."

"How was the young fellow killed?"

"Shivs."

"Stabbed to death?"

Earl doubled over with a hacking cough, and Brennan looked ready to heave right there in the car. But he went on with his questions.

"What was the name of the young man who was killed?"

Earl stared into space for about two minutes, as if he had tuned us out. Then he said: "Connors."

"Why was he killed?"

Earl shrugged. "Tensions."

"Tensions related to what?"

Earl sucked so hard on his cigarette I thought it was going to shoot right down into his lung. Then he coughed again. Big time. Terry laughed at the sight of his brother turning a sickly grey.

"Earl," Brennan persisted, "were these fellows involved somehow with the crime that landed Connors in prison?"

"Strangers."

"They were strangers to Connors? So the killing had nothing to do with whatever Connors had been convicted of?"

"Brains," Earl said, pointing to Brennan's head. As if he was saying: "Go to the head of the class." He let out an immoderately loud laugh. It went on and on, then stopped as if someone had slapped him in the face. But nobody had.

"So, Earl, this was a random killing? Connors just happened to be in the wrong place at the wrong time?"

Earl took another deep drag of his cigarette. This time, instead of hawking, he brought up a whole sentence: "Shit happens."

Chapter 8

*Though we're not free yet,
we won't forget until our dying day
How the Black and Tans like lightning
ran from the rifles of the IRA.*
— Unknown, "Rifles of the IRA"

March 22, 1991

Brennan Burke was hammered when I met him at O'Malley's Friday night. I didn't have to be a psychoanalyst to infer that Earl's revelations of the previous night accounted for Brennan's presence in the bar, at a table by himself, with an ashtray full of butts and a skinful of whiskey.

"A Guinness," I said to the bartender, "and a glass of chocolate milk for my friend here." The bartender laughed and started to pour him a shot of whiskey. Burke, his eyes at half-mast, waved a weak hand to fend off another drink.

"Mickey, no, no. This is Monty." Never mind that Mickey and I had already met. "Mickey is the Brian Boru, the high king, of bartenders. He served me my first legal pint."

"Good to see you, Monty," the man replied diplomatically, in an old-country brogue. I noticed he made it a point to have a bottle of Tullamore Dew at hand, and took a nip whenever he served a customer. It kept him in good cheer.

"It's not often I see you in this condition, Burke," I began, as I took my seat beside him.

"It's not often," he answered in a slurry voice, "I get the news that some poor fellow, a young husband and father, loses his life in a completely random, vicious attack that could have happened to anyone, but happened to him just because he was in the wrong place at the wrong time, put there by my father, who seduced him into taking part in an armed robbery for what the poor lamb of a misguided idealist believed was a good cause, and —" He ran down at that point, and fumbled to light a cigarette. He smoked moodily for a few minutes, then started up again. "I can't explain to myself why this troubles me more than if the man had been killed by someone in the organization, to keep him quiet. I don't know what's wrong with my thinking, that that would have been preferable somehow. Maybe I'd console myself with some kind of rationalization: he knew what he was getting into; this turned out to be part of it. But what happened didn't have to happen at all. He would have done his few years — terrible enough, to be sure — and then rejoined his wife and children. Ah, I don't know what the fuck I'm talking about. And for Declan just to sit back and let this fellow suffer all the consequences by himself —"

"Your father couldn't have predicted what happened in the prison. I don't make light of it, obviously, but he would have thought along the lines you just expressed: imprisonment was the risk, part of the deal. Same way he did his own time — and undoubtedly kept his own mouth shut — when he got caught in Ireland. And by the time this waterfront heist took place, Declan was supporting a house full of children, in a new country. I'm not trying to put on a defence for him; it's just, well, I'm sure your father must have been devastated to hear what happened."

"I hope you're right. I believe you're right. He was a good father, essentially a good man. Not without blemish, but — but, Jesus Christ, this isn't the only death he has on his conscience. He killed that fellow in Ireland. I wonder how he justifies that in his mind."

"Who says he does?"

"He'd say he was at war. But was he? He'd say the traitor had caused the deaths — the torture, who knows? — of his brother Republicans, and taking this man out of action probably prevented the same happening to others. But still, it's murder. No two ways about it." He rested his head in his hands and massaged his temples, his cigarette burning dangerously close to his hair. "I'm not doing myself any good here, Monty. Not doing good for anyone. I should be down on my knees in prayer, not legless with drink."

"Well, in that case I'd better get you home, Father."

"Oh, Christ. Has it come to this? I'm like those fathers who have to be dragged out of the bar by their poor mortified sons. 'Come along now, Da. Mam's waitin' supper for us.'"

"Yes, I'm sure we all knew somebody like that. Who was the guy we read about? Desmond. One of his sons . . ."

"The young girl's diary, right. Said her brother was forever being sent to the pub to roust the old man out. What was his name? Kevin?"

"Maybe. Or, no, Kevin was the baby. I don't know. Look it up in the diary. But that's not your problem right now."

"Got to get to sleep."

He pushed himself up and crushed out his cigarette. After pulling out his wallet and dropping it, bending over and banging his head on the table, he produced a wad of bills and smoothed them out on the bar. He gave Mickey a salute and followed me out the door; we turned and headed for his father's house. It was a beautiful cool night and the stars glimmered through the haze of light rising from the city.

"I don't suppose you'll be queuing up to spend a holiday with me again any time soon," he mumbled.

"Father O'Flaherty's Begob and Begorrah Tours of the Emerald Isle are looking damn good about now. But then, you'd probably end up on the tour bus beside me. You and me and a couple of church ladies who haven't had their bones jumped since Saint Patrick was in charge of the sheep dip."

"Tha's all right. We'll hijack the bus and hand it over to Leo Killeen. Famous arms dumps of Ireland. You know how keen O'Flaherty is on reading about the police and crime and history. Here, Michael, here at last is where the bodies are buried. Ah, fuck it." He stopped to light up a smoke. "I'm sure we'll both be glad to get clear of all this and get ourselves back to Halifax. Work will be a relief. Of course, it helps that my work happens to be music."

"Speaking of music, I saw a page of the piece you wrote for Sandra. Do you still have —"

"I don't want to hear about Sandra," he growled.

"Do you think you'll try to see her again before —"

"Are you daft?"

"I'm sure that, if you gave her a call —" I wasn't sure at all, but I soldiered on "— the two of you could at least have a meal together, and talk things over."

"Am I not making myself clear to you, Collins? Why would I put myself in the way of all that aggravation?"

"Aggravation? Did I hear you say aggravation? Ever since I met you, you've been trying to get me together with the world's most aggravating woman, someone I cannot get along with for more than two hours, regardless of how hard I try."

"She's your wife, the mother of your children."

"Aha. So that's it. You just don't think families should split up. Period."

"No, that is not it. I don't think your family should split up. There's no need of it. Where are you going to find anyone who suits you better than MacNeil?"

"You're the daft one now. We could walk back to Queens Boulevard and cull a weak one from the edge of the herd; chances are I'd get along better with her than I do with MacNeil."

"You're just being stubborn, the pair of you."

"You're being stubborn about Sandra. Of course, so is she, but —"

"My calling in life does not allow me the luxury of a Sandra Worthington. We've had this conversation before."

"And the conversation ended with you opening the door to seeing her."

"And the cool wind of reality has blown the door shut once again. I'm glad we had that excruciating evening together; it made me realize what an *amadán* I'd been, to have kept her in my thoughts all these years —"

"An *amadán?*"

"A fookin' eejit. She had the right idea: move on. And that's what I'm doing."

We arrived at the house. I jingled my car keys in my hand. "Well,

156

I think I'll just go out for a cruise and find myself a better wife. Nighty-night."

"K.M.R.I.A. And I don't think I need to translate. Oh, Christ, I hope the oul fella isn't in sight; I couldn't face him in the humour I'm in. The sooner I can pass out — Oh, before you go. Terry called, said he got the word on this Ramon. What was his last name? Martinez? No, Jiminez. Do we even care, now that we know about Connors?" With something constructive to focus on, he sounded more sober.

"We care. We need everything we can find."

"All right. Ramon Jiminez has a few theft charges on his record back in the mid-fifties. Nothing else. Well, a speeding ticket last year."

"He's still around?" I was surprised but could not have said why.

"Why wouldn't he be? They looked up Willman as well for me."

"You asked for info on Garth Willman?" I couldn't keep the amusement out of my voice.

"Sure I did. The cop gave Terry a list of Willmans who've been convicted of crimes. There was an Albert Willman, a Gehrhart, a Patrick, a Sean, and if I could think straight I could remember some others. But no criminal record for Garth." Brennan shrugged.

I wondered about the Willmans with Irish first names. "Did the Willmans have a son?"

"Girls," Brennan said. "Two daughters. Was there a boy as well?"

I remembered the photos on the television, the one daughter down on her luck, the other standing in front of an oversize garage in suburban Valhalla. Judy said how horrible it had been taking the girls to visit their father in Attica. There was a son, photographed with Garth, side by side in US Army uniforms. Hard to imagine Willman Junior mixed up in Irish Republican highjinks. "What did Terry say about the Patrick and the Sean?"

"Not much, but whatever it was didn't fit in. They were too young. Or, one was too young and the other's in jail and has been for a long time. Something like that. Besides, old Willman didn't strike me as a son of Erin, Monty. You couldn't imagine him reading Joyce to his children over a cup of cocoa on Bloomsday."

"No." Another dead end.

"Now," Brennan said, "yer man Ramon will be easy to find. Turns out he's in Manhattan, has been for years. And he's still in the bar business."

"I think I'll pay him a visit before I call it a night."

"I'll come with you."

"The night's over for you. Go in and sleep it off."

✝

After patiently eliciting directions from a sobering but exhausted Burke, directions that made allowances for the fact that I was not blessed with an intimate knowledge of New York, I managed to locate Ramon Jiminez in the bar he ran not far from Madison Square Garden. The place was rundown and cheerless with half a dozen morose drinkers scattered throughout the room. The only attempt at decoration was a garish, badly painted mural on the wall across from the bar; it showed Rocky Marciano delivering the knockout punch to Joe Louis in 1951. I was assailed by a blast of cheap musky aftershave, and my nose twitched as I turned from the picture.

"I was there. And I saw Marciano beat Walcott a year later. Undefeated, how 'bout that?"

The man was five foot six and thin, but he had been working on his biceps and on his hair, which was coal black without a touch of grey. He was wearing a Little Italy sweatshirt over a pair of black jeans; a large gold ring glittered on the baby finger of his left hand.

"Mr. Jiminez?"

"Yeah."

"My name is Monty Collins. I'm the music reporter for the Montreal *Morning Globe,* and I'm working on a biography of Vi Dibney."

"Oh, yeah?"

"Yes, and I know from the interviews I've conducted so far that you and Miss Dibney knew each other when she was here in New York some years ago."

"You might say that."

"I was wondering whether you'd be willing to give me a bit of your time, so I can round out my portrait of Miss Dibney by talking to someone who knew her when she was starting out."

158

"Yeah, I knew her back when she was just little old Evie."

"You worked in the same club, I understand."

"Yeah. The White Gardenia. It's still there. Well, different location. Classy joint. A lot of guys were wishing they were in my shoes. You've seen her, so you know what I'm saying."

"Right. What kind of guys were around the club back then? What was the clientele?"

"It was frequented by Italian businessmen. Italians with a lot of money to throw around. Some big movers in, let's just say, certain circles."

"I see. Now your role there was what?"

"Most people thought of me as a waiter; others considered me more of a confidante. A lot of big deals went down in that club. And I had the inside dope on more than a few."

"Patrizio Corialli was one of the owners, wasn't he?"

"Oh, yeah. Major owner."

"Who else had a piece of the club?"

"Couple of his associates. Italians. Some other people invested from time to time."

"Like who?" He shrugged. "So tell me about you and Evie."

"She was a great kid. Real looker. And she could belt out a tune. I was fond of her. But I had to let her go."

"Is that right?"

"Getting too serious, too attached. You know the type. I was young, I had plans, I wasn't getting corralled at that time in my life. I tried to let her down easy."

"But it was hard for her, I imagine. The breakup." *The breakup she didn't even tell you about, you bullshitter.* I kept my thoughts well out of view.

"It was rough on her. Emotional. You know how they get. But you might say I gave her career the boost it needed. She took off for Vegas to make a new start, away from her memories of me, and the rest is history."

"Yes, she certainly made a name for herself. How did she link up with the hotel out there? I forget the owner's name, but wasn't he an acquaintance of somebody back here?"

"Yeah, an Italian connection."

"And she mentioned somebody by the name of Burke who had a hand in it as well."

The name hit home; Jiminez was instantly on his guard.

"Is that name familiar to you?"

"That scumbag."

"This man offended you in some way?"

"You might say that."

"Well, Vi implied that he was helpful in getting her started in Vegas, but —"

"Evie says a lot of stuff about a lot of people. Doesn't mean she knew what those people were all about."

"You're making me a little nervous here, Ramon. I don't want to leave out any important links in Vi's career but I don't want to, you know, write glowingly about this man if he wasn't what he appeared to be."

"What he appeared to be was a smooth-talking, blue-eyed Mick. What he really is, is a piece of shit."

"You say 'is.' So, he's still kicking around? I got the impression from Vi that he was older. I thought —"

"He's still kicking all right, despite somebody's best efforts to take him off the board."

"What do you mean?"

"Somebody tried a Paddy-whack on him, but it didn't take."

"You sound as if you wish it was you! Maybe you'd have done a better job."

"I would have. When I start something, I finish it. And I sure as hell wouldn't have tried to shoot him in a room full of people at a wedding. What a loser, whoever pulled that one."

"Well, obviously I've been given some bad information. I'd better check him out further. So, what did he do to earn your undying hatred?"

"Fucking blackmailer!"

"What? This Burke was blackmailing you?"

"You heard me."

"When was this?"

"Decades ago, 1950s. Bastard knew I didn't have the money. Well, I sure as hell had to come up with it."

"What was he blackmailing you about?"

"None of your fucking business."

"You're right, Ramon. I apologize. Let's forget Vi's trip to Vegas and whoever did, or did not, help get her there. Let's move on to something more pleasant: her music. Which songs do you remember her for?" I carried on with the charade for a polite interval, then finally thanked him profusely for his time and made my escape.

†

We were back in O'Malley's the following afternoon, a Saturday: Brennan and I and Maura. Normie was at Declan and Teresa's, playing with their granddaughter Christine again. Mickey was in place behind the bar, shot glass filled with Tullamore's, racing sheet in front of him on the polished wood. He and a sober Brennan talked over old times until three pints of Guinness were decently poured, then we settled in at a back table.

I wasted no time, given that Declan was to meet us there in half an hour. "I had a talk with the wise guy wannabe waiter, Ramon."

"What's he wanna be, a wise guy or a waiter?" Maura asked, after sampling her pint and finding it satisfactory.

"It's the oddest thing. This guy is head of one of the primo crime families in New York. He lives in a massive compound flanked by security cameras and guard dogs and, after I'd been with him for five minutes, he broke down sobbing, and said all he ever wanted was to be the wine steward at Garçon-Garçon!"

"Point taken," my wife conceded. "So what did he say?"

"Unfortunately, we're back to blackmail again."

Burke looked up sharply. "I saw the bank records and I still can't believe the old fellow would pay —"

"It's worse than that, Brennan." He was absolutely still, right hand poised over his pint as if an invisible glass barrier held it up. "This Ramon says your father was blackmailing *him.*"

"Oh, Jesus Christ who suffered and died for our iniquity!" His head dropped heavily into his hands and he worked at his greying temples as if he could expunge the memory of what he had just heard.

Maura laid her hand briefly on his arm, then asked: "What was

Declan supposedly blackmailing him about?"

"Wouldn't say. Told me it was none of my business. But then, that's the thing with blackmail, isn't it? It doesn't work if you don't mind somebody knowing whatever it's about." I took a sip and went on: "Brennan, you're going to have to sit your father down and insist that he come clean about this. Otherwise, we'll never —"

"I can insist all I want. I can threaten to excommunicate him and hound him to the portals of hell. He won't talk. Haven't you learned that by now, Monty?"

"The bank records were with your mother's things. I wonder if she —"

"I'm not putting my mother through any more of this. It was hard enough getting her to give over that diary. The Desmond girl's journal. I looked at it this morning, by the way. We were trying to remember the lad's name, the son who was sent to fetch his father from the bars. Jimmy, his name was. He left New York as soon as he was old enough to get away."

"That's right. I wonder how things turned out for him."

"Well, I hope, God save him. Now let's change the subject. MacNeil, entertain us here. Swill that pint down and give us some improbable tales from Cape Breton."

Maura thought for a few seconds, then said: "This fellow shall remain nameless, because he was reputed to be the keeper of a still. Making his own moonshine and bootlegging it around the county. Our man got word that the Mounties were on their way, and dismantled his still as best he could. By the time the Mounties arrived, all that was left were some pipes and other paraphernalia.

"'We're going to charge you for operating a still,' they told him.

"'Do you see a still anywhere around here, b'ys?' he challenged them." She spoke in a broad Cape Breton accent.

"'No, but we see the parts for one,' the Mountie replied.

"'Well, you may as well charge me with a sex crime then. I've got the parts for that too!'"

We were still laughing when the door opened and Declan stood glowering at us from the doorway.

"Declan! *Dia duit!*" Mickey called out.

"*Dia is Muire duit.* The usual, Mickey, and set up those two *amadáns* at the back table."

"Three of us, Declan! Don't leave me out if there's a free round coming."

"Maura! I didn't see you, *a chara*, with that great son of mine hulking in the foreground."

I got up to help with the glasses, and Declan sat down with us. Brennan looked at his father as if trying to find what he had been missing in him all the years of his life. The old man ignored him, and directed his attention to my wife. "When are you going to shake these two hooligans so you can salvage what's left of your time in the big city?"

"I've been trying to lose them all week, Declan."

"Well, you're in luck, MacNeil," I improvised, "because, as I started to tell you earlier, Brennan promised to take me to a second-hand shop that has a huge collection of vintage harmonicas. Cheap."

She was a quick study. She said to Declan: "He's a bluesman. Even if he won the lottery he'd buy his music, his instruments, and the drinks for his groupies on the cheap." I let it go. MacNeil would have a better chance than anyone of opening the old boy up.

"Use the back door; it will get you out of here faster," was Declan's only comment.

"So, Brennan," I asked when we were outside, "where's the mouth organ district?"

"I have a better idea. Let's pick up the girls and go uptown."

"The girls?"

"Normie and Christine. I was going to suggest this before. We'll take them on a monster tour."

We found them in the family room, drawing the planets in coloured chalk on a portable blackboard. Christine was a petite girl of ten or eleven, with long chestnut braids and a ready smile. Half an hour later we were standing on Amsterdam Avenue on the Upper West Side, gazing at the gargoyles that ruled the roost at Saint John the Divine. Or, as the cathedral is known locally, Saint John the Unfinished; they've been working on the Gothic-style masterpiece for a hundred years. But it wasn't only churches that had been colonized by gargoyles and grotesques, greenmen and griffins; the creatures could be spotted all over the neighbourhood if you knew where to look. The girls squealed with delight at each new sighting. By the time our tour was done, they had seen demons and winged beasts; angels and babies; gargoyles reading, cooking and gobbling. And Father Burke had risen a little closer to heaven in my daughter's eyes.

When we returned to the Burkes' house, Normie and Christine went in search of laundry powder, which they swore could be mixed with water and formed into gargoyles. Brennan and I found Maura flaked out, eyes closed, on the living room couch.

"Well?" Brennan asked Maura. "Did you get anything out of him?"

"A couple of pints of Guinness," she replied without opening her eyes. "Which I didn't need." It was more than a couple; her face was flushed and she was clearly feeling the effects.

"Anything else?" I persisted.

"Nah." She slowly raised herself to a sitting position. "When I brought up the subject of blackmail, in my own little way, he knew exactly who I was talking about. But get this. He said: 'That little gouger tried to blackmail me. I took him by the throat, scared the bejazes out of him, then persuaded him to donate to a worthy charity I happened to know about.'"

"What charity?" I asked.

"I tried, but he wouldn't tell me. 'Charity' was in vocal quotation marks, and I don't know any more than that. I got the feeling, though, that he wanted to tell me. The temptation was there, to let it all out. But he just couldn't. He's not made that way."

"Tell me about it," Brennan muttered.

"We got up, said our goodbyes to Mickey, and set off for the walk home. I asked him whether he thought the blackmail had anything to do with his being shot. He just looked at me as if to say: 'What do you think?' I stopped walking then and said to him: 'Why don't you tell us, Declan? Nobody in the family is out to hurt you. Come clean about it.' And for a moment there was such pain in his eyes I could hardly stand to see it. I wrapped my arms around him and he held me very tight, but he didn't say a word. Just pulled gently away, took my hand in his and started walking. After a few moments he began talking about the neighbourhood and the house. He virtually admitted he had to go to a loan shark to borrow the down payment! And that's why he took on the nightclub job in addition to the business he set up. He told me what it was like when they first moved into the house, how he had all these children and no beds for them. They put all the kids to sleep in a pile of blankets. He laughed and said the first bed he got was for him and Teresa. 'The little lads kept crawlng into the bed with us, and Teresa refused to put the run to them — her way of ensuring we didn't make another one that year!'

"When we got back to the house he said: 'I hope Teresa doesn't look out and see me hand in hand with another woman. Hasn't she had enough to put up with? I nearly lost her once. I nearly lost my family.' He wasn't joking any more. Anyway, we went inside. Teresa was waiting for him and they went out somewhere.

"So, I did my best. But he's not talking. Part of him wants to come clean but he just can't bring himself to do it. He's kept his secrets all these years. He doesn't want Teresa to know. As he said, he nearly lost his family over those secrets — or over his behaviour — in the early days. What will she think of him now, if it's revealed that he stayed involved and maybe compounded his errors in the years following their emigration? What are his sons and daughters going to think of him? There is also the simple fact that he genuinely does not know who pulled the trigger at the wedding party."

"And," Brennan added, "we have to concede that a man who goes through life with a death sentence hanging over his head, as the result of a wrongful accusation of being an informer, might, over time, fall into the custom of maintaining the silence of the grave."

Maura slumped over on the couch. "Oh, Christ, I need a nap to sleep this off."

I went downstairs to collect my daughter. She and Christine had a box of soap flakes and a bowl of water on the card table; their hands were covered with white, sweet-smelling goop.

"No! I can't go yet, Daddy! We haven't made our gargoyles yet!"

"Why don't we promise that you'll come play with Christine again, and you can do your sculptures then?"

"Aww!"

But with the promise of a follow-up visit, she did not protest too fiercely. I got my wife and daughter into the car and drove to the hotel; MacNeil slept the whole way. Normie and I accompanied her to the suite, then went out for fish and chips while Maura continued her nap. She was up when we got back, and she relayed a conversation she had just had with Brennan on the phone. "He said: 'Terry's coming by to pick me up. Says he has something to tell me, but won't say what. I'm of a mind to give him a clout in the side of the head when he shows up.' So there you have it. They're on their way over here."

They were at the door twenty minutes later. Terry greeted me: "Hey Monty, we just had dinner with Earl and his mother over on Avenue D. She was asking for you. I don't know what we were eating but it tasted like chicken. How are you, Normie? Christine said you guys had a lot of fun today."

"We did!"

He glanced from Normie to Maura. She got the hint. "Normie, why don't you get the F.A.O. Schwarz bag, take it into your room, and decide who's going to get what for a present when we go home."

"You said I couldn't get into that stuff."

"You can now."

What would be better, rooting through a bag of new toys or listening to whatever the grown-ups wanted to keep from her? She went for the toys and retreated to the bedroom. Maura gently closed the door behind her.

Terry wasted no time: "Here's the news. I was with Da and we had a visit from the police. They found the gun."

"Where?" I wanted to know.

"A maintenance crew spotted it near JFK Airport. Buried under some rubble. They were clearing a patch of land and found it. It was wiped clean of prints."

"How do they know it's the same gun?"

"The ballistics are a match. It's a Lee Enfield rifle, a bit of an antique. And, get this: they believe it came over from Ireland."

Maura shook her head. "I thought Leo Killeen swore up and down it couldn't have been the Irish after all this time."

"Leo was sincere. I know that," Brennan said.

"So somebody managed to get the rifle into the country, but wasn't going to chance it on his way out. Little wonder," I remarked.

"And that's not all," Terry continued. "In the gym at Saint Kieran's, where the shots came from, there was a bit of torn clothing or material, something that was dropped or snagged. Whatever it was, the police ran it by a fabric expert. The tests haven't been done yet but the expert is almost certain it's from the Irish Republic. I'm not sure if it's the fabric itself that's Irish or something else they have. The cop said something about 'traces'; could be soil, or I don't know what."

"Jesus," Brennan muttered. "What was the old fellow's reaction?"

"I thought he was going to pass out. It was just the two of us at the house. He didn't so much as look at me. Just stared at the cop."

"So, Terry, what did Declan tell the cop about his own Irish history?"

"Very little. He was desperate to keep it to himself. He admitted he had been involved with the IRA before he came over here. But the cop already knew that. And Da allowed as how he might have offended them. How badly had he offended them? 'Mortally,' Dec answered. But he stressed that it was forty years ago. The officer wanted to know about any Republican activities he might have been engaged in over here. None. Gave it all up when he got on the boat. What else could he tell the officer? Nothing. Declan wished he could be more helpful. He knew the police were doing their best but he had no idea why this would come back to haunt him after all these years, and he certainly could not name any individual who would want to cause him harm.

"Did he know anything about the guy who appeared at the wedding and sang 'Skibbereen'? No. The police found no match for the prints on the mandolin, which suggests the old lad has no criminal record. Nothing for us there."

"Wait till poor Leo hears this," said Brennan. "I wish I hadn't told Dave Mackasey I'd do his Mass for him tomorrow. Leo's coming to the house for Sunday lunch before he flies to Dublin. You're all invited. I'll do a quick and dirty Mass and boot it for home."

"Quick and dirty sacraments. That sounds like the seedy barfly of a cleric I've come to know."

"Bite me, MacNeil."

"The man saved your life," I reminded her. "You'd better cut him some slack."

"I'm sure he knows there are some things that leave even me

without words." She leaned over and kissed him on the cheek. "Seedy and unshaven."

The phone rang and I answered it. Tommy Douglas, calling from Halifax. "I may as well tell you now because you'll hear about it anyway . . ."

"You got that right. What happened? Are you all right, Tom?"

"I'm okay. What happened was, I had a few people over and then some more people showed up . . ."

"You had a party. Which we told you not to do. Go on."

Maura's eyes were locked on to mine. Normie had appeared, and transformed herself into a four foot, one inch, red-haired listening device.

"We didn't plan it this way," Tom said. "But word must have got out . . . And a couple of guys had booze and then some other people had, uh, coke and, well, one guy got into an argument with another guy and his friends. And it spilled out into the street and then . . ."

"And then it became a police matter. Anyone arrested?"

"A couple of guys I don't even know."

"And you?"

"No!"

"Good. Any drug charges?"

"No, just for the fighting. And they told us to shut it down. So we did."

"What kind of damage to the house?"

"Just some stuff spilled on the furniture and on the carpet." He paused. "One lamp got broken." Another pause. "Well, there was kind of a cigarette burn on the kitchen table."

Maura appeared to be on the verge of a stroke, and I put a hand up to reassure her that it wasn't as bad as it sounded.

"Get everything fixed and cleaned up before your mother and sister get home. If it costs money, pay for it."

"I will."

"No more parties, no more people over, no more anything."

"Got it."

"Take care of yourself."

"Okay, Dad."

"Bye."

Maura snatched the receiver but it was too late. "Is he all right? I wanted to talk to him!"

"Let him get on with his housework."

"Tom's in big trouble, isn't he?" Normie asked, trying but failing to sound more sympathetic than fascinated.

"He's learned his lesson. Any of this sound familiar to you, Brennan?"

"It puts me in mind of a few incidents in my youth, yes."

Normie regarded him warily. Could angels be fashioned from such stuff as this?

†

On Sunday morning I offered to drive to the rectory where Father Killeen was staying, and pick him up for lunch at the Burkes'. When I pulled up just before noon, he was waiting outside in clerical suit and collar, a Gladstone travel bag in hand. He moved a subway map and a chocolate bar wrapper off the seat and got in beside me.

"Good morning, Montague. You know, I'm almost reluctant to leave. In spite of all the trouble here, I've enjoyed getting reacquainted with the Burkes. And isn't it grand to see New York! Where's our friend Brennan today? Off with the children somewhere, I expect."

"No, Leo, actually Brennan is at Sunday Mass. The noon Mass is in Latin."

"Ah, a fine lad. Will he be joining us for lunch afterwards?"

"He will."

"Latin, did you say?"

"That's right. He said it was the old Mass."

"What time's Teresa having lunch?"

"Twelve-thirty, one o'clock, she said."

"I'll go in and give her a quick call. You and I are going to Mass. It'll do us both the world of good. Even though I said my own Mass early this morning!" He got out of the car and skipped up the stairs to make his call. In less than a minute he was back, all smiles, and got himself settled in the car again. He dug around in his bag and produced a scuffed old Roman missal. "Teresa was delighted to hear

169

we're going to celebrate the Eucharist before we arrive for lunch."

"I'm sure she was," I said, as I put the car in gear.

We could hear the bell pealing in the Norman tower before we were in sight of Saint Kieran's. I found a parking spot and we speed-walked to the church. The priest was at the back of the nave setting out booklets with the Latin responses for the congregation. The place was half filled; it struck me as a good crowd for a noontime Mass. Brennan finished with his booklets and turned around. His Roman collar peeked out above his vestments, and he was wearing a biretta on his head. He saw Leo, and I followed his glance. The old priest was making the sign of the cross at the font of holy water. I caught his expression when his eyes focused and he saw Brennan. He stared at him, astonished. Brennan smiled and moved towards the older man with his arms held out. They embraced.

Father Killeen finally found his voice: "Why didn't you tell me, Brennan?"

"You never asked." Leo was shaking his head, and Brennan went on: "That routine with me and the children and, em, Maura, wasn't planned, Leo. You misunderstood, and nobody corrected you. But the joke wasn't on you."

"No," Killeen answered, regarding Brennan with a shrewd look, "it was on you, wasn't it?"

A shadow seemed to pass over Burke's face before he laughed and said: "Maybe so."

"All right, *avic,* let's hear how good your Latin is."

"Better still — you celebrate; I'll be your altar boy." The old fellow's face lit up and they walked together *ad altare Dei.* Five minutes later the two priests emerged — one big, dark and deceptively hard-looking, the other slight, grey-haired and deceptively mild — and sang the ancient Tridentine Mass in Latin.

When it was over my two companions joined me on the steps of the church; their sense of peace and well-being was palpable. Since meeting Brennan, I had spent a lot of time wondering how he could give up so much in order to be a priest of the Roman Catholic Church. But I knew the answer lay somewhere beyond my powers of comprehension. Whatever it was, it was with him now. I was reluctant to break the spell. But mundane matters intruded anyway.

"Where did you park, Monty? I came by cab so I'll go back with you and Leo."

"Just around the block."

"So this is where it happened," Father Killeen remarked, directing his gaze to the school. We all stopped and looked over.

"We have some news, Leo," Brennan began. "The police found the gun, and some other evidence they won't reveal."

"Did they now. Are they any closer to an arrest?"

"They think the gun can be traced to Ireland."

Leo stared at Brennan. "I don't believe it."

"It's not just the weapon, it's where they found it. The gunman turfed it at JFK. Well, took a bit of time to conceal it in some rubble, according to the police. So it looks as if —"

"What kind of a gun was it?" Leo interrupted.

"Something old. Do you remember, Monty?"

"A Lee Enfield."

"In that case, with any luck they'll trace it to England!"

"They seemed quite sure there was an Irish connection. Perhaps whatever other evidence they found —"

"No," the old fellow interrupted again, "this was not an Irish hit. Not IRA anyway."

"You're sounding quite sure of yourself there, Leo."

"I am. Look elsewhere."

We were all still gazing at the school, so it seemed natural that one of us would say: "Let's go see where it happened." It was Leo.

The school gym was open and unoccupied, and we went inside. We stood where Declan had been standing when the shots were fired. "They came from over there." Brennan pointed to the row of plywood cabinets along the wall.

"Is that right? I would have expected the gunman up there." Killeen indicated the long glassed-in area on the second floor, where people could observe what was happening in the gym. "But of course, much harder to escape from the upper floor."

We walked over to the cabinets. The door of the last one in the row, which had been splintered during the attack, had been repaired.

"He was in here," I explained to Leo. The cabinet had a shiny new padlock. "The guy must have got the original lock off in order to get in there. But then he couldn't have replaced it or put one of his own on from the inside, and the security people surely would have noticed if there was one lock missing or open. So —"

I walked around; the cabinets were about eighteen inches out from the gymnasium wall. I wondered why they were not flush with the wall but then I saw an electrical panel behind the cabinets. The panel would have to remain accessible. Obviously a makeshift solution to a storage problem. It then occurred to me to wonder why the cabinet hadn't moved when I leaned against it during the wedding reception, during my doomed effort to seduce my wife. That's when it hit me.

"The gunman was in there while Maura and I were — I was leaning against it and I had her —" I realized I had my hands out as if I were grasping her hips against mine. Leo and Brennan were looking at me with great interest.

"Go on," Leo encouraged, with a twinkle of amusement in his eyes.

"She went off in a huff," I finished.

"Story of your life," Brennan remarked.

"The point I'm trying to make is that this flimsy cabinet didn't move with my weight against it, which means the shooter was in there at the time."

"Yes, he would have taken up his position before the reception got underway, and waited anxiously for his target to appear," Leo said. "He may have removed the back panel of this cabinet to get in. Well, he must have, if he didn't come bursting out the front door of it after the shooting."

"He didn't. We didn't catch even a glimpse of him," Brennan replied. "How he got in and out would all be in the police reports but we haven't been privy to them."

"Have you asked to see them?"

"Well, no."

"Why haven't you?"

"I suppose because we've been concentrating on motive, not method."

"And have you been sharing your thoughts with the investigators?"

"No."

"So. A Lee Enfield," Leo stated, in a businesslike tone. "If it's the No. 4 MkI, I've fired that weapon myself. In training." Sure. "The barrel is this long —" he held his hands about two feet apart "— and this cabinet is considerably less than three feet in depth. So I would have — the gunman would likely have positioned himself like this." The priest got into a firing posture, holding an imaginary rifle and peering intently through an imaginary gun sight. A shiver ran through me as I watched him. "Everything at an angle. He must have poked a spy hole in the door here. Not an ideal position at all. No room to manoeuvre. But he didn't want to chance the second floor so this is what he was stuck with. He must have been very patient. And very determined. Now he may have used the No. 5 with the shorter barrel. I heard that model has quite a kick so his shot may have been off . . . Where did the bullets go? Declan is what? Five foot ten or so? And he was hit in the chest. What was the angle of fire, do you know? I mean, did the round enter his body on an upward trajectory, downward, or what?"

"I don't know, Leo. But the police have all that information."

"I do think the fellow would have to be standing. Very uncomfortable if he was a tall man. Not a lot of room to crouch here without his arse sticking out or pushing the loose panel out of the back of the cabinet. Where was the scrap of clothing found?" Brennan and I looked at each other and shrugged. Leo continued: "It's a small space behind here but I don't see anything that would have impeded his movement, or caught his clothing. Do you? Nothing metal sticking out. And I would assume the inside of the cabinet is just plywood. What was the man's escape route?"

"Through the window in the corridor right behind him," I answered. "There's nothing but bushes on this side of the building. Perfect screen. The police say he had prepared things well in advance. Came one night and took out the window. Put it in with just a bit of putty. He came in that way the day of the shooting, replaced the window somehow from inside — I don't know how, I'm no carpenter — and went out the same way. Left the window lying on the ground, jumped in his car and was gone before the security guards made it to this side of the school."

"So no jagged glass to snag him on his way out. Is it an actual piece of cloth we're talking about, or a few threads? Or microscopic fibres the technicians were able to pick up?"

"Terry didn't say. And we didn't ask. We will now. Aren't we due at lunch, Brennan?"

"Ah. We'd better be off."

✝

Maura and Sheila greeted us at the front door. I could smell lamb. Irish stew?

"This fellow has left you for the Lord above, *a cushla machree*," Killeen said to Maura, jerking his thumb towards Brennan. She snickered and responded that the Lord had his hands full.

"You seem to be taking it well."

"Easy come, easy go."

"So it's young Montague you have to patch things up with." Another snicker from my wife, this one much more cynical than the last. "Of course, when I picture your children, especially Tommy, I can see he's a ringer for his da. Declan, *Dia duit.*" Leo lowered his voice. "In spite of what the police have found, I don't think for one minute —"

"Ah, leave it alone, Leo. Enjoy your last meal here, without getting into that. Come inside."

People were packed in around the mahogany dining room table; an extension must have been added, and chairs brought in from other rooms. Normie was sitting with Christine; somewhere they had come up with identical pink hair bands. Patrick and his daughter, Deirdre, were helping Teresa set out the plates. Terry and Brigid were sharing a laugh; she raised a glass and grinned when she saw me come in. A bottle of wine had already been consumed, and a couple more were set to go. All in all, a relaxing, convivial setting. There were three places waiting for those of us arriving fresh from the sacraments and the scene of the crime. I looked forward to hearing more tales from Leo, his lighter side, I hoped. He opened with the traditional blessing, and everyone raised a wine glass to his presence and his safe journey home.

"I'll be anticipating a visit from each and every one of you, now that we've become reacquainted. Don't all come at once; I don't have a table this big. Which puts me in mind of a story. You're not going to like it, Declan, but I'll be telling it anyway. It was meal hour in the Joy and the screws —"

"A party? For me? How thoughtful!" The voice was sarcastic and vaguely familiar.

"Francis! Darling! We'll find you a chair. Terry, bring one up from the family room. Here, Francis, let me fill a plate for you, dear." Teresa got up, kissed her son and headed for the kitchen.

"Leo," Declan said, "this is my son Francis. Fran, meet Father Leo Killeen."

Leo stood to shake hands with the new arrival, who took his hand distractedly and said: "Two of them in the same room? Well, they say the Irish are a priest-ridden race."

"They also say we're a charming race," retorted Leo. "Shows you how misleading popular notions can be."

"Sorry."

"You'd better be," Declan admonished his son with barely controlled fury. "Here's your seat. Sit on it and try to be civil, why don't you."

"Yes, Your Graciousness. If only I had your pleasant, easygoing manner, hell, I'd be head salesman at the —"

"Oh, feck off, Frankie," Brigid told him. She and Francis had the same colouring, dark hair and hazel eyes with a prominent black ring around the iris. "Now, where were we? You were saying, Leo?"

Maura chimed in: "Bridey, I haven't been introduced to your brother."

"Don't bother, Maura. He'll leave in a snit halfway through the meal. Now, Leo —"

Patrick tried to pour soothing oil on the roiling waters. "What have you been up to, Fran?"

"I've been working my arse off, Patrick. All for nothing, as it turned out."

"You were working?" Terry asked without bothering to mask his surprise.

"What do you think I've been living on, scraps from the bin outside?"

"Here's a wee scrap for you," Teresa announced, putting a heaping plate of stew and boxty in front of him. "Eat up, darling."

"Thanks, Ma." To Terry, he said: "I was working at a printing company, and doing a better job than a lot of the old stiffs who have been on the payroll since Jesus was a Jew. But the boss was a Class A jerkoff and I told him to stuff it."

"Why doesn't that surprise me?" Terry said. "Every time this guy lands a job, the boss is a jerk. The résumé of Francis Burke: I quit, boss was an arsehole; I quit, boss was an arsehole. Does he coincidentally find every shithead of a supervisor in North America? Or could the common factor be — could it possibly be Fran himself?"

"Terry, you're not helping matters here. Why don't we listen to what Francis has to tell us?"

"Oh, Pat, you're such a sweetheart, but don't waste it on that little gobshite," Brigid snapped.

"Paddy and a whole team of psychiatrists couldn't help this clown," Terry added.

"I need a shrink? I thought all I needed was the warmth and love of my dear, dear family."

"I'm of a mind to get up and belt you around the head, you little *glamaire*," his father threatened. "It's bad enough the family has to listen to your whinging and complaining, but to act like this in front of our guests — you're insufferable."

"Why don't you get up and clock me, Dec? That was your solution in the past. His Holiness over there felt the rap of your knuckles a good many times and look how he turned out." Brennan fastened his black eyes on his brother as if he were a serpent climbing up from the depths of hell.

"Brennan needed correction a few times, certainly. He was a boozing, drug-taking little skirt-chaser, but he's all right now. As you can see."

"I doubt it. He's probably still at it. I can't see him, of all people, living up to a vow of celibacy. In fact —"

"I'm sure he does the best he can," Declan answered shortly. "More than I can say for you."

"Declan, don't mind the young *boicín*," Leo said. "Isn't it likely he's been given *bata agus bóthar*, and is a little *cantalach* as a natural result?"

"No, he's always like this."

"Do you think I'm too thick to understand what you're saying? No, I wasn't fired. I've never been fired from a job in my life. As hard as it is for some in this room to believe."

"You're an Irish speaker then?" asked Father Killeen.

"I know a bit of the old tongue, yes."

"And where did you pick it up?"

"I spent some time over there."

"Oh? When was this?" Brennan asked. "First I heard of it."

"It's news to me as well," Declan said.

"Sure and isn't there a great lot of information we've never been given about your own time over there, Da? It might surprise you, Father Killeen, to hear that Declan wasn't always the mild, gentle *paterfamilias* you see before you today, smiling fondly at his adoring children. He had a darker side. But then again maybe you're his confessor, and know a bit about the old sinner after all."

Father Killeen regarded Francis with his sharp brown eyes and then said: *"Bhíomar sna hÓglaigh le chéile, a mhic."* Which was translated for me later as: "We were Volunteers together, my boy."

Francis's face lost its sullenness, and he looked at the priest in astonishment. "You and the old man in the IRA together, and you a priest?" The old man gave a curt nod, and returned to his dinner.

"When were you in Ireland, Francis?" Brennan asked.

"A while back."

"Doing what?"

Terry answered the question in a stage accent: "Liftin' a dacent pint and shaggin' the local colleens, if it's any of your business, you fookin' eejits."

But Francis merely said: "Touring around, doing a bit of studying, odd jobs." He shrugged.

Everyone was suddenly hungry, and it looked as if peace would reign. Several conversations started up, and I sent up a silent prayer of thanks that Maura had uncharacteristically stayed out of the fray. My daughter had looked on in fascinated silence. Our own family strife must have looked dull and benign in comparison.

But Francis couldn't leave well enough alone. "So. Bridey. How's Larry Lunch Bucket?"

"Steadily employed, is how he is," Brigid snapped.

"Well, that's all that counts, isn't it? Brings home a paycheque to keep all those childer in shoes. Why'd you leave him home — again? More fun without him, right?"

"What?" Brigid stared at him.

"I notice you can't keep your eyes off this guy." Francis pointed his fork in my direction.

"What on earth brought that on, Francis?" Patrick asked with unfeigned concern.

But Bridey was well able to speak for herself. "Monty knows I've been warm for his form since I first laid eyes on him. He also knows, tragically, that I'm spoken for."

"Larry. That plodder. 'What's new on the construction site today dear? Nothin', Bridey, still waitin' for the drywall. Same ole, same ole. Is my bologna sandwich ready yet?' If you'd held off, finished college and played your cards right, you could have had someone like this." Now it was his knife that pointed me out.

Brennan had had enough. "Why the hell don't you grow up, you little *garlach*? We've all gone out of our way to make allowances for you, Christ only knows why, and every time you show up, we have to endure your whinging and your tiresome little rants. So far today you've insulted our father, our guest Leo, your sister, her husband, me as usual — and for no fucking reason at all. Well, that's over. This is the last time we're going to put up with this shite from you."

"Oh, a decree has gone out from Father Burke, has it? Are you the moral authority of this family now? I hope not, you fucking hypocrite."

Leo broke in. "Francis, how can you talk to your brother in such a way? Fine man that he is, you should be seeking his guidance. Between him and Padraig here, they —"

"Fine man! Him! God's anointed. Ask him about the time I went to see him in Rome. I worked at the airport, in the blistering sun, every day for one whole summer, to save up and go visit him at the Vatican or wherever the fuck he was supposed to be staying over there."

"What were you doing in Rome, Brennan?" Leo asked, as if in the middle of a perfectly civilized conversation.

Brennan turned reluctantly from his brother to Father Killeen. "I did my STL at the Greg, STD at the Angelicum. When I had time I did some work at the Pontifical Institute for Sacred Music. In the seventies."

"Well done! Did you meet the Holy Father?"

"I did. I struck up a friendship with Cardinal Muratore, and when the Pope —"

"Yeah, right," Francis drawled. "You and ten thousand other clerics. You can't swing a cat over there without hitting a pair of priests. Well, in between hitting the books, singing like an angel in the choir, and licking the Pope's ring, he was shacked up with some lady in waiting, or social secretary, or something —" all eyes turned to Brennan "— and he barely had time to see his own brother. Well? It's true, isn't it? Why don't you come over here and give me a fat lip so I'll shut up, like you did when we were kids. I know you're dying to."

Brennan was looking at him with fury. "If I go over there, they'll have to dig me out of you."

"I don't hear you denying it."

"Denying what?"

"That you were too busy living *la dolce vita* in Rome to spend a token amount of time with your own brother. If that was the only occasion you blew me off I might have forgotten it, but that's what always happened with this guy. One time he even —"

"This is the first I'm hearing about the slight you claim to have suffered in Rome. I thought we spent quite a bit of time together; I was happy to see you. As for the high living you think I was doing, what can I say? You have the air of an informer about you today, Francis. Not a popular breed with certain people at this table. Of course, if you are morally superior to everyone else in the room, maybe you should take Holy Orders yourself. But until you do, I've got a word of advice: get over yourself and grow up, you peevish little prick!"

"Brennan, Brennan," Leo interceded, *"quam tristis et afflicta fuit illa benedicta."* Brennan looked at his mother, who had maintained a stunned silence throughout the meal. The pain in her face was visible for all to see. Brennan reached across the table and took her hand in his.

"Finally, someone he listens to," Francis got in. "Maybe you can teach him —"

"Shut up! Just shut the fuck up, Francis!" Declan roared.

Nobody looked at anybody else. The silence was unearthly. Unfortunately, it was my little girl who started the next round. She slid from her chair, went over to Francis, reached up and tried to put her arms around his shoulders. His angry face did not turn in her direction. "Don't cry, *leanbh mo chroí*. Don't be sad. They all —"

"Leave me alone, you little four-eyed *caillichín!*"

Normie looked at him, stricken, then started to wail and ran from the room. Any allusion to her glasses went straight to her heart. I started to get up but Christine went after her. "Normie!"

"How did she know that?" Teresa said with wonder. "That was the pet name I called him when he was a little boy. 'Child of my heart.'"

"She has the sight," I said, surprised I still had the power of speech. "I don't know if I'd call it a gift."

"You!" Declan bellowed at his son. "Apologize to that child. Now!"

"Fuck you!" Francis leapt up, knocking over his chair, and ran from the room. The front door slammed hard behind him.

Finally, we heard from Maura. "Isn't this where you're supposed to rise in dignity, Teresa, and say: 'We'll have our coffee in the drawing room'?"

"I was thinking of something a little stronger, actually, Maura."

"Right, then. Brandy and cigars in the living room. For the women. While the men clean up. After all it was one of their number who brought the whiff of unpleasantness into the room."

I went downstairs to find Normie sitting on the couch, glasses clenched in her fist, tears streaming down her cheeks. Christine was at her side, and had a comforting arm around my weeping daughter.

"Normie, sweetheart," I said, "you know he didn't mean to hurt your feelings about your glasses. They look very pretty on you. You just touched a nerve and he thought of something to say he knew would make you leave him alone. He was upset that you knew he was sad, when he wanted everyone to think —"

"— that he's tough and cool."

"That's right. Are you going to come upstairs?"

"I don't think so."

Christine said: "Forget about it, Normie. Uncle Fran's a real dork. Let's make some gargoyles now!"

"Okay!"

I left them to it and dutifully went into the kitchen, where the men were doing the dishes. "No, Leo, we'll finish them up," Terry was saying as I walked in. "You sit. Have your tea. We're very efficient at this. An extra hand will throw us off." Pat was looking as if he were about to be sick. Brennan and Declan had murder in their eyes.

Declan finally spoke. "Leo. I'm so sorry you had to witness that. I don't know what's wrong with him."

"Declan, there's no need to apologize. It's the family that's been hurt, not me. I just pray he'll find the help he needs before he goes beyond words. Brennan, I know you'll be praying along with me, for your poor brother. And for your own ability to minister to him with love and forbearance."

Brennan looked about as prayerful as a Mob hit man, for whom all the joy had gone of out the job. His father went over and gave his shoulder a little squeeze. "Bren, put him out of your mind. For some reason the little prick can't help himself."

"Da," Patrick said, "I tried for years to get him into therapy, but he —"

"Paddy, we know that. Now put the silver away so we can join the ladies before they swill down the last drop of brandy out there."

When we entered the living room we heard my wife singing a tune familiar to me, coming as I do from a big Navy town: "No, Bridey, it's 'The cabin boy, the cabin boy, the dirty little nipper, he filled his ass with fibreglass and circumcised the skipper.' Now, repeat after me —" She caught sight of the male contingent, and went smoothly on: "Knit one, purl one, don't drop a stitch and you'll have the loveliest little tea cozy. Oh, hello, boys." I was relieved to see a smile on Teresa's face, in anticipation of knitting a tea cozy or regaling the ladies in her bridge club with a few rousing lines of "The North Atlantic Squadron."

Leo looked around and remarked: "All the family together, a perfect time to say the rosary." Silence. "I'm coddin' ye. I just want what everybody else wants: a good stiff belt of brandy."

The party, such as it was, began to break up. Patrick had to go to his office in Manhattan and took Maura with him. I stayed on, in the hopes that I might pick up another tidbit of information from Leo about the shooting, but I didn't get the chance before it was time for him to go.

"I'll run you out to JFK, Leo," Terry offered.

"I want to talk to Leo," Brennan declared in a tone that cut off all avenues of discussion. "Terry, I'll drive you home and take Leo out. Let's motor."

"All right. Normie, you come and play with Christine. How about a sleepover?"

"Yay!" the girls exclaimed in unison.

"We'll bring our gargoyles and make some more at my house," Christine said.

Leo said goodbye. I was sorry to see him go.

I got up to leave, too, but Brigid asked me to wait. "Monty, could I ask you to take me over to Terry's house? I can't go now because I want to talk to Mam without the whole crowd of them around. I won't be long, though."

"Sure. Take your time. I'll be outside."

I sat in the car and listened to music. Brigid emerged twenty minutes later. "I'm sorry, Monty. I didn't know we'd gab that long. But I rarely get a chance to talk to her, and I'm going back to Philadelphia today."

"That's all right," I assured her, as I pulled out from the curb.

"You'll be glad to see the tail end of us."

"Nah. My life was boringly predictable before I embarked on this adventure. Where are your girls today?"

"They're at Patrick's, playing with their cousins. I hope there's something to eat at Terry's. I couldn't eat at Mam's. Lost my appetite when dingledoink showed up and ruined the lunch."

"You're hungry?"

"I am now."

"Well, let's get you something to eat. Where do you suggest?"

"We could go to Horgan's, right there on Queens Boulevard."

P.J. Horgan's was a more elaborate bar than O'Malley's, with stained glass lamps, booths along the left side and tables at the rear. We sat in a booth. Brigid exchanged pleasantries with the bartender, who had come over from County Meath years before, and lived nearby. The waitress arrived and took our orders: beer for both of us, a club sandwich for Brigid. When we were alone, Brigid issued a command: "Ignore everything Francis said at the table."

"Easy for me to ignore him. A little harder for the rest of you."

"You can particularly ignore his suggestion that I was looking at you."

"Oh. I was hoping that was the only kernel of truth in his little tirade. The long, lingering kiss you gave me at the wedding reception is the only sex I've had since I arrived in New York."

"I'll bet that puts you ahead of Francis! And speaking of that, I don't believe a word of what he said about Bren being shacked up with a woman in Rome! Do you?"

I gave a noncommittal shrug and was saved from answering by the arrival of the waitress with two pints of lager.

"So. What were your brothers like when you were growing up?"

"Brats!"

"Well, why not? 'Brat' is just 'brother' in Russian."

"How do you know that?"

"I studied a bit of Russian when I travelled over there."

"When was that?"

"Years ago."

"You were allowed to go to Russia?"

"What do you mean, allowed?"

"I don't think we're allowed to go there. To a Communist country."

"You mean there are travel restrictions in the Land of the Free? Just like in Soviet Russia!" I mimed a conspiratorial look around the bar, then spoke out of the corner of my mouth: "Don't let this get out, but I did see a few Yanks over there. Cuba's verboten too, isn't it? That's how the Germans and the Canadians get all the best spots on the beach."

"You're taking the piss, right? Making fun of me."

"A little." Which was hardly fair. A girl who got married out of high school and started having children right away could hardly be expected to be a world traveller. But I couldn't resist; I leaned towards her and whispered: "Don't tell anyone around here. But my father-in-law's a Commie."

"You're shittin' me."

"I'm not shittin' ya. You come up to Nova Scotia some time, and I'll introduce you. That's the only way you'll meet him. He's not permitted to enter the USA." Her eyes were wide. "But how did we get off on such a subversive tangent? Oh, right. Your brothers were brats. But the fact of the matter is: I heard you were the bratty one."

"Who told you that?"

Who *had* told me that? I thought about it, then remembered: I had seen it written in a childish scrawl. "Somebody crayoned over the name on a Mass card or something. One of the collection envelopes for your church. It said Saint Brigid's, and they wrote over it, Saint Bratty's."

"Liar. There's no Saint Brigid's around here. We always went to Saint Kieran's. The church, the school, and the high school. So there. And picture this: I had Brennan as a teacher in high school! Just after he got out of the seminary."

"Brennan used to teach at —" I almost said the crime scene "— Saint Kieran's?"

"Yeah, when Terry and I were there. That fearsome creature stalking the halls in his soutane — the other kids couldn't believe he was our brother. Terry used to tell his pals about Brennan: 'Burke's my brother — don't even think of fucking with him.' God, that man knew how to instill fear! But we sure as hell learned our religion."

"What did he do to keep the students in a suitable state of terror?"

"Well, those were the days of corporal punishment in schools, as I'm sure I don't have to tell you. But he didn't do much of that. Mainly, you'd have to face his withering remarks if you didn't know your stuff. Or stay after and do your work with him scowling at you. I was hanging around one afternoon and I heard him blasting some big dolt: 'I'm working overtime here to teach you the peace and love of Christ, so get it done, for God's sake!'"

"Did he ever keep *you* in after school?"

"Once."

"What did you do to bring that on yourself?"

"Oh, God, it was embarrassing. I sat beside this girl named Claudia Fiore. She passed me a note one day; I answered it and passed it back, and so on. He caught us.

"'Brigid Burke and Claudia Fiore, stand up! What are you doing back there?'

"'Nothing, Father.'

"'What's that you have in your hand, Claudia?'

"'It's a note, Father.'

"'Read it.'

"'Oh, no, I couldn't. I —' She was on the verge of tears.

"'Read it!'

"So she had to. The note said: 'Brigid, we should get HIM to teach the HEALTH class. We'd pay more attention to him than to Sister Herman-Joseph.'

"I wrote back: 'Yeah, he could teach Sister a few things. He used to HAVE a GIRLFRIEND, if you know what I mean.'

"'Really??? NO!!!'

"'YES!!!'

"Poor Claudia. I myself was paralysed.

"'Both of you! After school!'

"So we had to stay after. Claudia was shaking. The two of us stood there till all the other kids had left; they all stared at us on their way out. When they were gone, he said: 'Claudia, you may go.' She bolted for the door. He glared at me and said: 'Smarten up.'

"'I will.'

"'Answer this question!'

"Oh, God, what was he going to ask me?

"'What's our mam cooking for dinner tonight?'"

I laughed, then said: "Hard to imagine the same man inspiring such love in you and such, well, whatever it is Francis feels for him."

"Too many males under one roof! Horns inevitably get locked."

"Which airport did Francis work at in the summer?"

"I don't know."

"What would he have been doing?"

"Leaning on a shovel with his butt crack showing, and whining about how hard the job was."

"Does he have a girlfriend, a circle of pals?"

"Fran?" She rolled her eyes. "I can't even remember the guys he used to go around with. Jerks, I imagine. He went with a girl named Marta for years. She was okay; I don't know what she saw in him."

"Who do you think tried to kill your father?"

She shook her head. "I have no earthly idea. It came right out of the blue as far as I was concerned."

Bridey's sandwich arrived and she glommed onto it, taking an enormous bite. Then, with her mouth full, she made a sound that must have meant "Want some?" and pointed to her plate. I shook my head. I smiled at her, remembering what a character she had been at the wedding reception before gunfire shattered the family's joy. I recalled dancing with Mrs. Burke, and Bridey had come waltzing by. Her mother told her to get lost because — "What did you mean at the reception, when you said your mother had a secret admirer?"

"Oh," she said, swallowing her food, "that was an old joke. We saw this man a couple of times in the neighbourhood, watching. We nicknamed him Mack. Terry and I used to tease my mother, saying Mack worshipped her from afar. But it was decades ago. I mean, there was a guy following me around all through high school. I'm sure they were both harmless."

I resisted the urge to question her further. She had come to New York to enjoy her family, and had seen her father shot and her brother compound the family's pain with his obnoxious behaviour. Why upset her any more? And what would she know about her father's history that her older siblings didn't know?

We finished up at Horgan's and drove to Terry's house, which was a mile or so from that of his parents. It was one of the few wood-cladded detached houses on the block, and either he or Sheila had turned the small front yard into an eye-catching rock garden. Brigid tried the door but it was locked. She dug a set of keys out of her bag, opened the door and called out: "Terry! Sheila? Nobody home. Must have taken Christine and Normie out somewhere." We went inside.

"Well, I'll be on my way."

"How much longer are you in New York, Monty?"

"Not much longer. I have a lot of criminal clients who count on me to keep them free to roam the streets."

"What kind of criminals do you defend?"

"All kinds. Most of them are just no-hopers. Occasionally there's one who gives me the willies. You may want to rethink that invitation to Nova Scotia, Bridey. Between my clients and my Bolshevik relatives, I'm a dangerous guy to be around. I'm no good for you, baby."

"You're fecking right you're no good for her!" Shit! Brennan, with Terry on his heels. I hadn't heard them come in the door. I didn't even want to think what spin they would put on my remark.

Bridey rolled her eyes, mouthed the word "brats," then sprinted up the stairs. She came down again a minute later, banging a small suitcase behind her.

"Brigid!" She started at the sound of Brennan's voice. "You're jumpy today. Terry's taking you over to get the girls, and then to the station. Are you ready?"

"Yes, Father!" she said, and winked at me.

"Respect, at last!" Brennan replied. "Have a good trip, darlin'." He gave her a hug and said goodbye.

She gave me a sisterly peck on the cheek and departed with Terry.

Brennan did not allude to my goofy remark, and I did not allude to the fact that I was having dinner that evening with Sandra. Maura and I were, that is. Sandra had called with the invitation the day before. So, following a pint at O'Malley's, over which Burke and I relived the events of the day, I headed back to Manhattan and he went to his parents' place. He was planning to attend Compline at Saint Kieran's. Perhaps the chanting of the ancient prayers in Latin would restore some of the peace and contentment he had achieved after Mass earlier that day.

"No children?" Maura and I had arrived at Sandra's townhouse.

"No, Tommy's back in Halifax and Normie is over in Queens with one of the Burke kids. Terry's daughter."

"Terry. He was a real character. What's he doing now?"

"Airline pilot."

"Yes, I can see that. Good for him. And Patrick grew up to be a psychiatrist. A highly regarded one too, from what I've heard. What about the little girl, Brigid?"

"Mother of seven children in Philadelphia."

"And Molly's still overseas? I don't think she ever took to life in

North America. And there was another boy. What was his name?"

"Francis."

"I never really knew him, for some reason. Well, let's have a drink and make ourselves comfortable. What would you like?"

I asked for a beer, and the women decided on gin and tonic. When we had our drinks, Sandra asked: "How's Declan?"

"Full of piss and vinegar," Maura replied.

Sandra smiled and raised her glass: "Here's to Declan."

"To Declan," we chimed in.

We sat and yakked about New York and listened to amusing tales about Sandra's neighbours on the Upper East Side. It was not until we had nearly finished our baked stuffed lobster, and were on our second bottle of Chardonnay, that Maura gave voice to the question on both our minds: "Well? Are you going to see him or not?"

"I rather doubt it."

"Why?"

"The simple answer, Maura, is that I'm not a stupid woman."

"We're all agreed on that! But —"

"I can see the writing on the wall — I saw it clearly that night at the restaurant. He made his decision twenty-five years ago. When I saw him last year in Halifax I toyed with the idea that maybe he'd done his time, given half his life to the church, and now it was time to return to the secular world. I was tempted to call him but, of course, I didn't. I was afraid I was deluding myself. I'm not cut out for the role of jilted lover, or delusional hanger-on! When he called me, he said he was coming to New York 'for a brief visit.' I thought that was rather a pointed remark, but I may have over-analysed it. He had tickets for *Norma*. Was I interested? Sure. He phoned when his flight got in; would I like to have dinner? I made an excuse, he saw through it, and coolly said he'd see me at the Met. When I got there I couldn't think of any common ground where we could begin a conversation. I know he was disappointed, but all my training in the social graces failed me! It was excruciating."

Maura nodded sympathetically and said: "I know it was difficult for you."

"Then, the dinner. Just when things started looking up, that man arrived, and Brennan got into a long song and dance about

Gregorian chant. The fact that he immediately introduced himself as a priest spoke volumes to me. If he had been out to lull me into thinking he was the same old Brennan, he could easily have glossed over that. But what put the kibosh on the whole thing was him sitting down and hearing that woman's confession. If his primary objective was a night with me, the Brennan I knew would have quietly told the woman he'd meet her the next morning, then rededicated himself to the goal of getting laid. But no. He is first and foremost a priest. A man who believes — hundreds of millions of people believe it, I know — that he has the power through God to absolve people of their sins, and to lift the veil between heaven and earth at communion time. That kind of sacramental mysticism, or whatever it is, is way beyond me. It's as if he lives part of his life in another dimension. I grew up as an Episcopalian, and I don't mean a high church type. We made polite obeisance to God just in case he really was pulling the strings, and the whole economy might come crashing down if we got too self-satisfied. But the Roman Catholic Church: that was way out there, according to what I had been taught. And of course it makes inhuman demands of its ministers. Bren's a very, um, physical sort of man. If he's given that up — which I find difficult to imagine —"

Sandra must have caught something in my expression because she stopped and waited, with her eyes on me, as if she expected me to make a remark. But I wasn't about to comment on this, of all subjects.

She resumed speaking: "If in fact he has given it up, then whatever he has found in its place is not something he's going to abandon. Almost an argument for the existence of God, you might say! So. He can't have me, or any other woman, and stay in the priesthood. And I would not even consider accepting anything less than marriage or a close equivalent. If he thinks he's going to whip his cassock off and unite his flesh with mine once a month or something, he's been inhaling too much incense!"

"I don't imagine he's thinking that," I offered in his defence. But in truth I had no idea what he was thinking. When it came to Sandra, I suspected he was unable to project beyond the moment. Seeing her in Halifax had no doubt thrown him into turmoil, and he hadn't managed to sort any of it out by the time he called her about the opera.

"You two know him, or you're getting to know him," she said. "He's not a man you take lightly. You don't love him lightly; you don't hate him lightly. It would be devastating to me to fall in love with him and lose him again. I have no intention of doing either. More wine?"

Chapter 9

The youth has knelt to tell his sins.
"Nomine Dei," the youth begins.
At "mea culpa" he beats his breast,
And in broken murmurs he speaks the rest.
— Carroll Malone (William B. McBurney), "The Croppy Boy"

March 25, 1991

The telephone rang the next morning in the hotel suite. Normie made a grab for it. "Hello? Yes, it is!" Maura reached for phone. "It's for me, Mum, not you!" Normie spoke into the receiver. "Oh. Okay, I won't." She looked at me and then her eyes immediately slid away. She turned her back on us and lowered her voice. "Uh-huh. Oh, that's all right. I'm not supposed to be so sensitive about my glasses. Really? Do you think so?" Her hand went up to pat her hair, preening in response to whatever compliment was being offered. "Thank you! Yes. I understand. I'm sorry too. I have to learn not to say those things out loud. What's a call-a-heen? You don't mean a wicked little witch! Oh, good." She was thoughtful for a moment. "How did you figure out my phone number? Your mum, right. Well, thank you for calling. Bye." Click. She tried to look nonchalant as she sashayed back to her bed.

"Who was that, sweetheart?"

"I can't say." But she couldn't maintain a complete silence. "I can tell you this, though. I'm trying to find evidence that Father Burke is an angel, and the person on the phone is not someone I would even think of asking."

Normie was jolted two feet in the air at the sound of the phone jangling again. She made a move in its direction, but I got to it first. It was Brennan. "I just got a terse call from Leo in Dublin."

"What did he say?"

"'Drop it.' That's what he said. When I asked what he meant he said: 'Leave it alone.' Then he rang off."

"Didn't take him long to make contact with someone. He just got back there last night."

"Right."

"That pretty well confirms the Irish connection, I'd say. Must have come as a shock to the poor man. Leo was so sure it could not have been the Irish."

"I know. Gotta run."

I wondered if this meant we would learn no more about the mystery of Declan and the attempt on his life.

I banished the whole thing from my mind as I headed out with the family for a walk on the Upper West Side. Everything was in blue that morning: a ninety-four-foot blue whale and the Star of India sapphire at the American Museum of Natural History, and the deep indigo sky luminous with stars at the Hayden Planetarium. We walked around all day, sightseeing. Then we hoofed it back to the hotel, got ourselves all dressed up and secured a table at the renowned Russian Tea Room. It was the last week of March; Maura and Normie would be returning to Halifax in a few days' time, and I wanted to give them a big night out. Maura and I were able to converse like the rational, intelligent adults we were; come to think of it, she had not berated me lately about any of my recent marital blunders. Perhaps there was hope for us after all. Normie spent the time mentally renovating her mother's Halifax kitchen with red leather banquettes and chandeliers. She conceded, however, that she would not be demanding caviar again any time soon. For my part, I would be in no hurry to drink vodka again.

I passed out when we returned to our suite at ten o'clock, and didn't have another conscious thought until I heard a quiet knock at the door. I ignored it and sank back into sleep, but it happened again. I looked over at the clock. It was only eleven-thirty; it felt like three in the morning. Finally I got up, pulled on a pair of jeans and stumbled to the door. It was Terry Burke, not looking much better than I did.

"Monty, I'm sorry but this is urgent. Can we go downstairs and talk?"

"Sure. Hold on."

I grabbed a shirt and shoes, and we took the elevator down to the bar. I could feel the tension emanating from my companion. He didn't speak until we had two beer in front of us. I couldn't look at mine.

"I have a friend in the police department. Gabe. He arrived at the house tonight, told me to come out to his car." Terry took a long swig of his beer, and I noticed a slight tremor in his hand. "Gabe told me he was doing me a favour. He was telling me something he shouldn't, and I had to promise not to breathe a word to anyone in my family. I agreed. I don't suppose it occurred to him I'd spill this to anyone outside the family."

In spite of my queasy stomach, I took a sip of beer.

"The police got a tip or learned of this somehow — anyway, they found a box that was brought over from Ireland. There are traces of soil and plant matter in the box."

"Yes?"

"Remember I said they found traces of Irish dirt or something on the gun or on the scrap of clothing that was left behind?"

"Yes. So they think this may be how the gun was transported."

"Right."

"Where was the box found?"

"He wouldn't say. But that's not the point. They found fingerprints on the box."

All my senses were alert now. I looked at him and waited for the next shoe to drop. He wouldn't be here if the prints belonged to some anonymous Irish smuggler.

Terry took another sip and wiped what could have been tears from his eyes. "They ran the prints and found a match. With my brother."

"Your brother."

"Francis."

"Jesus Christ."

"Exactly. They had his prints from an old narcotics conviction, years ago. You know fucking well the soil tests are going to show the gun was in that box. The gun was wiped clean of prints but now they have the container. With Fran's fucking prints on it. I imagine they'll have to do a bit more investigating before they — if they're going to arrest him, right?"

"Maybe," I agreed. "But we don't know what else they know."

"Christ Almighty. We have to get to Francis before the police do. But we can't, you know, try to spirit him out of the country —"

"Forget it."

"We have to question Francis without him catching on. Because you never know what he'll do if he's cornered. I mean, you saw how he was at a family luncheon! Still. As much of an arsehole and a fuckup as he is, and as much as the old man rubs him the wrong way, I can't believe he'd try to kill our father. At a wedding with the whole family there? And another thing I really can't believe is that he'd manage to pull it off. Get away, I mean."

"There may be some other explanation," I offered. Sure: the kind of other explanation I was forever trying to flog to the courts in my efforts to acquit my guilty clients.

"How are we going to handle this, Monty? I can't very well go and take the little Christer by the throat and question him. I'll lose it. And when it's over, one of us will be dead on the floor. But if you talked to him, you being a lawyer . . . If we still have some time, before the police get their soil samples tested, you could approach him on some pretext. After all, he doesn't know what the cops have found. He's been hanging around as if everything's business as usual."

"What reason could I possibly have for talking to him, that he would believe?"

"You'll think of something!"

I sighed. "Where does he live?"

"I'll try to find out."

Terry was a worried man when he left the hotel bar. I tried to get back to sleep but was assailed by images of Francis Burke's angry face at lunch; his sardonic manner when he showed up a few days after the shooting; Leo at the crime scene, wondering how the scrap of material had been snagged; the gun wiped clean of prints. The gunman had likely worn gloves, and he would have wiped everything down. That would take a cool head. What did he wipe everything with? Something from which the scrap of fabric had come? How long had he been waiting behind that plywood door before his victim — his father? — had come within his sights in the gym? Then various pretexts for talking to Francis came into my mind, some so nonsensical that I laughed at them even in my dreams.

Late the next morning Terry called to report he'd had no luck in finding his brother's current address. But he did have the phone number of Fran's old girlfriend. I told him I would call her and carry on from there. Maura and Normie headed out to the Children's Museum of the Arts; I stayed behind and made a date with Marta Lesnik to meet in a Brooklyn pub. I fabricated a story about a court case in which the defendant had given me Francis Burke's name as a possible character witness. I wanted to find him and I wanted to know what kind of person he was.

†

The Between the Bridges Pub was situated, as the name suggested, between the Manhattan and the Brooklyn bridges. A red awning shaded the length of the bar from the glaring sun. A lighted Guinness sign beckoned from the window, and I could hear rock music coming from the sound system. I went inside. Three men were arguing and gesturing with their glasses at the bar on the right. There was only one single female in the place, and I made a beeline for her table. She got up when I approached, and we introduced ourselves. Marta Lesnik was tall and athletic with dark blond hair pulled back in a high ponytail; the style accentuated her Slavic features. We ordered beer and engaged in a bit of small talk; then I asked her about Francis Burke.

"Oh, God, I went with Frankie on and off for years. I don't know why. I can't see what either of us got out of it. Where he'd be now is anybody's guess. He travels a lot on the cheap, bumming around Mexico or Ireland. When he's in town he usually crashes with friends or lives in a rooming house. And there's no need of that; he could have done a lot better for himself. The rest of his family did well. Frankie is a nice guy deep down, but he's a mess."

"How do you mean?"

"Well, he was always quitting his work, then taking courses at some college or other, then quitting those. At one point he was taking psychology. A lot of good that did him. Ever notice some of the people who get real keen on psychology, and can't see their own problems, which are practically stamped on their foreheads for the rest of the whole world to see? That was Francis." She shook her head. "And sometimes — sometimes things didn't go all that well between us. As guy and girl. You know."

This I didn't want to hear. "Yeah, well —"

"But other times he was perfectly normal. When we had problems it was usually after some ruckus with his family. Or he'd drink too much and start yammering on about his brothers or his father. On those nights, I just put on my flannel nightie and let him talk himself to sleep. Anything else? Fuggedaboudit."

"He didn't get along with his father?"

"Who did? From what I hear anyway. Tough old buzzard. I only met him a couple of times. Frankie went around in circles to avoid taking me to his house. The only place I ever saw his brothers was in this bar. It's near my work so Frankie would meet me before my shift and we'd have a couple of beers. His brothers came in once in a while. That would ruin Frankie's day of course but I got a real kick out of them. One time they all trooped in and sat up at the bar beside me and Frank. They were half in the bag already, and so was I. Probably didn't make my shift that night. Anyway, I said: 'Good afternoon, Father.' One of the Burkes is a priest. 'I see you're worshipping outside the parish again today.' The parish being O'Malley's, the pub they practically live in, over in Queens.

"So Brennan, the priest, says: 'I heard there were a lot of sinners in this area, so I came over to hear confessions. Anything you'd like to tell me, young lady?'

"And I said — like I told you, I had a buzz on — 'I had lustful thoughts about a young man, Father, someone sitting at this bar right now.'

"Brennan says: 'Did you act on these sinful thoughts, my child?'

"And I said: 'God knows, I tried to!' Francis turned scarlet! I just meant it as a joke, the kind of thing anyone would say; I wasn't talking about our problems. Jesus, he was sensitive. They wouldn't have known anyway, unless they saw him turn red and get all upset. But he was always like that about those guys. I used to refer to Brennan as 'Father What-A-Waste,' the standard joke about a handsome priest, right? Frankie thought I had a crush on Brennan. Hell, I'm a little Polish girl from Greenpoint; I respect priests! And he has a brother Patrick who's a psychiatrist; I used to call him the sexologist. No reason, just a joke. Again, Frankie thought I had my eye on Patrick. And the airline pilot, Terrence, well, naturally I must have been scheming to get into the cockpit with him.

"That day I'm telling you about, when they came in and Frank got upset, Patrick's wife showed up. Dressed to kill. She was one of these icy blonde types. 'Patrick! Why do I feel as if I'm in a particularly baaahhd Irish film, having to park our vehicle in this sort of neighbourhood so I can drag my husband out of a bar? You look drunk, just to complete the scenario.' She commanded him to leave.

"And she stalked out, without even speaking to the rest of them. It was funny, they all lifted their pints at the same time, all eyeing her sideways as she went out the door. It looked choreographed but it wasn't, just brothers with the same habits. Even Francis. Patrick got up and pretended he was being dragged out by his tie. 'Henpecked Husband Disorder. Hirschfeld and Rosenblum in their monograph on the subject stated blah, blah.' What a bitch. Frankie told me Pat had a really nice girlfriend all through high school and college, then he met up with this ice queen when he was in med school. As my mother used to say, she was looking to get her MRS.

"That night Francis was all weird, accusing me of telling his brothers about his 'infrequent' difficulties. But I hadn't told them! You didn't have to be Doctor Freud to know he was intimidated by these high-powered brothers, and the tough old boot of a father. Come on!"

"So you haven't kept in touch."

"Not for a year or so."

"Any idea where he's living now?"

"There's a house he stays in from time to time, in Astoria. One of those illegal basement apartments. He and the landlady don't get along, so he comes and goes. Here's the address if you need it." She grabbed a coaster from the table, took out a pen and wrote it out for me. "You know, I hope he's met another girl. Ideally, someone from out of state, so he can keep her apart from his family! If that's still a problem for him."

Still a problem indeed.

✝

So there I was at the door of Francis Burke's basement apartment in a red-brick two-family house in Astoria. The house was in need of maintenance but it was swept and scrubbed. I had worked out a pretext and tried to ignore the pang of conscience I felt for using my little daughter's name in such a sordid affair. The door opened in answer to my knock, and Francis did a double-take when he saw me. He was unshaven but clean, and was wearing a pair of cut-off jeans and a faded T-shirt. There was a faint smell of dope in the air. Neither of us spoke for about thirty seconds, then he came up with something to say.

"Let me guess. You're here to defend my sister's honour." What? Oh yes, the ill-starred luncheon. "But you needn't have bothered. I called and apologized to her. I have nothing against Bridey. Though she *was* stealing glances at you across the table. In case you're interested. I never got along with her husband, so I don't give a shit. He's not good enough for her, never was. So. If that's all, I'll let you get on your way."

"That wasn't it, actually, Francis. May I come in?"

He looked wary, but shrugged and moved aside. The room was like the building: rundown but not dirty, except for a few beer bottles that had not been rinsed. There was a small collection of books in the studentesque brick-and-boards bookcase: Irish history, radical politics and a bit of psychology. His music ran to Celtic, heavy metal and — I was surprised to note — Gregorian chant. There was only one photograph that I saw: of his mother looking very young and exceptionally attractive.

"I made three calls of apology in a single day," he said, "one to my

198

sister, one to my poor long-suffering mother, and one — as you probably know — to your daughter. She seemed to take my apology in good grace. I didn't apologize to that prick Brennan or to Declan. The old *sagart* — the priest — had left by the time I was in a mellow enough mood to pick up the phone. So. Why are you here? Want a toke?"

What to say to that? "All right."

"Shit, I don't have any left." He looked as if he really was sorry; obviously, he had not expected an affirmative answer. "But I can get some really fast if you're keen."

"No, that's okay."

"So. What do you want?"

"Well, you mentioned my daughter and that's why I came."

"She's a sweet little kid, and a spooky one. I'm sorry I hurt her feelings."

"She understands that. She wanted you to have this, but was too shy to come with me." I reached into my pocket and produced the portrait I had hastily forged over her signature that morning, using crayons and my memories of her artwork at home. It showed a red-haired girl with enormous dark eyes framed in spectacles, and a dark-haired young man, standing side by side, grinning. A bright orange sun, also grinning, shone on them from the top left corner of the picture.

Francis took it gently and stared at it. "That's cute. Thank her for me." He went to his dresser and placed it carefully on the top, then came back and offered me a beer. He popped two open and motioned for me to sit in one of his two chairs. His was near the window, and he leaned back in it.

"How long have you been a lawyer?"

"Over twenty years."

"Like it?"

I just shrugged: *comme çi, comme ça.*

"I have to get myself into something decent. Brain work of some kind. I've wasted enough of my time on bum jobs and low wages. Or maybe it's too late, I don't know."

"It isn't." *Unless you're going down for the attempted murder of your father.*

"I also have to find a decent girlfriend. Someone marriageable. Not like the one I have now. She's gotta go."

"Why?"

"The simple answer is: she's too dumb. She's cute, but that's neither a necessary nor a sufficient reason to maintain the relationship. Let's just say she wouldn't be able to hold up her end of the conversation chez Burke if the subject of Thomistic philosophy came up. As it sometimes does with certain people over there."

"So what? How many people would be able to hold their own on that subject?"

"It's not just that subject, obviously. She thought Ireland was where Wales is, for Christ's sake. All she does is watch sob stories on television and read those women's magazines with the health scares in them. I don't have a college degree but at least I pick up a book once in a while, look at a map, get off my arse and travel. Jesus. If I didn't have the hots for her I'd have said sayonara months ago."

"Where have you travelled? This is as far as I've got in years, but I used to travel a lot. I intend to take Father Killeen up on his invitation to Ireland."

"Good plan. We've all made trips over there. Except for oul Dec. He hasn't been back."

"Why not?"

"No idea," he answered quickly.

"Speaking of Declan, how did you learn about the shooting?"

"As I said before, Mexico is not beyond the reach of the American press. We get the papers, I read them."

Francis turned to the subject of his oldest brother. "I don't see what you get out of hanging around with Brennan. Jesus! I can't believe someone would associate with him by choice."

"And I don't see why he gets under your skin. I know he can sometimes be a bit — how should I say it?"

"Brusque? Arrogant? Superior?"

"You take too dark a view of him. And he certainly did not deserve the shelling you gave him the other day."

"Yeah? What about the shit bombs he dropped on me? Well, at least he finally declared his true feelings. As if I didn't already know."

"Come on, Francis! No wonder he let fly at you, after the things you said to him."

"Look — he's my brother, and he barely acknowledges my existence. Like that time in Rome. Now he says he doesn't even remember sloughing me off."

"I'm sure he was busy —"

"He was busy getting his ashes hauled."

"— getting his doctorate. So, you have two Doctor Burkes in the family."

"Three. There's Molly as well. But only one of them can cure what ails ya."

You should be putting yourself under Patrick's care, I thought. I said: "Plus Brennan was studying music, working in a parish, performing some sort of function at the Vatican, and —"

"And attending the opera, scurrying back and forth between the Teatro dell'Opera — don't ever get him started on that — and La Scala in Milan. He took me to meet Graziella Rossi at her posh domain in the Parioli district of Rome. You know who I mean? The soprano."

"Yes."

"Great voice. Brennan says when she gets out of control she has a vibrato you could build a roller coaster on, and I have to agree with him for once. Usually, though, she's top notch. But what a shrew!"

"Oh yeah?"

"Yeah. She made a big show of greeting Brennan: *'Caaarrrrro Padre Burke!'* He spoke to her in Italian for a bit, then switched to English and introduced me. She looked at me as if I had just come off trotting the bogs, and was tramping the stuff all through the house. Then she turned to the subject of her social secretary, this woman Annunziata; she's the one Brennan was shagging when he was there. Typical."

"Not typical at all," I countered. "The occasions when he breaks those vows are few and far between."

"If you say so. Later I heard that La Rossi fancies herself quite the femme fatale, and she had set her sights on my brother. He blew her off. Not because he is righteous and holy the way he's supposed to be —"

"Who can be righteous and holy every minute of his life? If he has to let loose once in a while, who's the poorer for it?"

"Yeah, yeah, right. So he blew off the songbird because he liked the look of her assistant. This Annunziata had five kids and her husband had left her, but when Brennan started eyeing her the diva fired her in a jealous snit. The night we were there, she tore a strip off Brennan, going on and on and on in Italian. It just rolled off his back. 'Don't be histrionic, Grazi, save it for your performance.'

"Bren and I made our escape and polished off the night at an Irish bar. I have to say, we had a few laughs together. That's the kindest thing I can say about my brother, at least while he's still alive."

"For Christ's sake, Francis! I hope you're not wishing him dead. To say that, after the shooting!"

He leaned towards me. "Maybe somebody just meant to scare them."

I stared at him. "Scare *them?*"

"You're right, 'Our Fathers' don't scare easy, do they? But a bullet beside the old man's heart — came a little closer than planned perhaps. Brennan emerged unscathed as usual."

"Francis, are you saying —"

"Frankie! Hi, honey!" The voice came from the street outside his window.

Francis rocketed out of his chair, whipped around and stared out at the sidewalk. He gave a half-hearted wave and muttered: "Jesus."

"You have women calling to you from the streets?"

"It's my girlfriend."

I got up and joined him at the window. She was a bit on the chunky side but if I were in love I would call her curvy. Not classically pretty, but a sweet, open face. Her shoulder-length blonde hair was held back with a headband.

"Frankie, I brought you lunch! I thought we could go to the park with it. Chicken and ribs. Grandma's recipe."

"And that's another thing —"

"What?"

He called out to her: "Bring it in."

"Okay!"

He turned to me and said: "I think she's shittin' me about her background."

"Why do you say that?"

"The story she tells is, well, improbable. You'll see. I'll get her going on it."

The knock came a minute later and he let her in. "Hi, Frankie! I missed you last night." She placed a basket on the floor.

"Ay, Shirl."

"Mmmm," she murmured, as she hugged him around the waist. The way she smiled at him I knew there were no "difficulties" between them. And his hazel eyes absolutely sparkled as he looked at her.

"Uh, we have company."

"Oh!" She started and turned in my direction.

"Monty, this is Shirley."

"Pleased to meet you, Monty."

"Hi, Shirley."

"Whatever you have in there smells tempting," Francis said, ogling the basket.

"I told you, hon, ribs and chicken. With potato salad. And buns. A picnic."

"Squirrels," Francis muttered.

"Pardon?"

"That's what my brother calls people who eat outdoors. Squirrels."

"Oh, is that the brother who's a preacher?"

"He is not a preacher, he is not a parson. He is a Doctor of Sacred Theology. An ordained priest of the One Holy Catholic and Apostolic Church. Just put the meat and salad in the fridge for now, so it won't go off."

"You make it sound like it's going to blow up!"

"Here, sit down, Shirl." He gave her his armchair and sat down on an empty red plastic milk crate. "Monty's a lawyer, from Halifax."

"Where?"

"East coast of Canada."

"Oh. A lawyer, isn't that interesting. So, did you patch things up with your boss, hon?"

"No."

"Well, in that case, have you thought any more about coming out to meet my folks?"

Francis looked at me and mouthed the word "folks." His expression said: *Here it comes. You be the judge.*

He asked her: "What would I do out there, if I went to visit?" He settled back against the wall with his arms folded. Like a cop about to hear the same lies he's been hearing for twenty years from an old lag in the interrogation room.

"There's lots to do out home. My heavens! We could go for long walks in the fields —"

"Fields? I get hives if I go to a baseball stadium with anything but Astroturf."

"Really, Frankie? Do you suffer from hives? I was just reading an article —"

"Of course I don't have hives! I don't even know what they are. What else would we do?"

"We could go to the dance."

"The dance. Okay. Tell Monty about your family, Shirl."

She smiled. "They'd just love Frankie! My dad's retired now, just putters around the house getting underfoot, my mom says. She keeps trying to talk him into taking up golf, except for there's no golf course. My sister Jolene is married and has three children already, all boys! They're trying for a girl. I help her with them whenever I'm out there. My brother Fred runs the feed store."

Francis raised an eyebrow as if to say: *How likely is that?*

To Shirley he said: "Let me get this straight. *The* feed store, your brother runs that. *The* general store, somebody else runs that. Somebody else has the diner. Then there's the bank, the barbershop, the insurance, the pharmacy and I imagine Old Doc Perkins is still making house calls. I'm sure there's a bar on the outskirts of town where I'd get my head kicked in. Someone runs that. They all have a couple of employees. What the hell does everybody else do?"

"Who do you mean by everybody else, Frankie?"

"The rest of the population."

"Well, aside from the merchants on Main Street and the farmers, and their families, there isn't really anybody else there."

He looked at her and then at me, as if to say: *I rest my case.*

"Theme park," he said. She appeared puzzled. "You're really from Jersey, aren't you Shirl, and you've come up with this —"

I interrupted: "What brought you to New York, Shirley?"

"I came to study geriatrics, Monty, because I just love old people."

"I've got an old person who could cure you of that in a jiffy," Francis announced.

"How's the geriatrics course?" I asked.

"Hard! You wouldn't believe the subjects we have to study. I wasn't very good at science in high school." Francis rolled his eyes. "But I'm plugging away at it. I've passed all my courses so far."

"Well, there you go." I gave Francis a pointed look.

"Of course, what I really want," she said in a wistful tone, "is a family of my own. Raise my babies, then go back to work when they're in school. But, try as I might, I can't really see Frankie coming out home, marrying me and settling down there. Can you, Monty?"

I tried to form a mental image of Francis in overalls and a straw hat or, perhaps closer to Main Street, in slacks and a golf shirt. The Burkes visiting, Declan scowling from a rocker on the front porch, Brennan perched in a little white wooden church listening to a fire-and-brimstone sermon from a corn-pone preacher, Terry chatting up the locals in the bar on the outskirts of town. Shirley was smart enough to know that wasn't in the cards.

"So maybe I'll stay here instead. Lots of old people in New York, too."

"Millions," Francis agreed.

She turned to me. "Frankie teases me about my family. Sometimes I get the impression he thinks we're a bunch of hicks!"

"Dang! What's the point of all my Jesuitical subtlety if she sees right through it?"

"But he won't even talk about his own family. Let alone invite me over to meet them. And most of them are right here in New York."

"Forget about it. You wouldn't like them."

"I like everybody!"

This brought a stunned look to her boyfriend's face. He managed to recover, then said: "You haven't encountered my old man. I don't want to disillusion you."

"Come on, Frankie. How bad can he be? He's not in the — the Mafia or something, is he?"

Francis and I exchanged a look. I had no idea how much he knew. Or, now, what his own involvement might have been.

"He loves his mother," Shirley said, "that much I know. But it wasn't very nice what you said about your dad that time, Francis. These things have a way of coming back to haunt us. I know you didn't mean it, but think how you'd feel if something really did happen to him. Wouldn't you —"

"Forget about it!" he snapped, cutting her off.

I stayed for a few more minutes, then left the apartment with some unsettling impressions but no useful information.

✝

I called Terry when I got back to the hotel. He sounded uncharacteristically tense. "What did you find out?"

"It was a bust, Terry. I couldn't find out anything. We got interrupted. His girlfriend arrived."

"How did he manage a girlfriend? He's not the smoothest lizard in the lounge, if you know what I mean. What's she like?"

"She's . . . wholesome. A country girl."

"Well! What was he like with her?"

"Not bad, aside from needling her about her family. He was quite affectionate towards her. I'd say he really loves her. There was one thing, though, Terry, something very off-kilter that he said."

"What?"

"He was going on about Brennan and some evening they'd spent together. He told me they had 'a few laughs,' and then he said: 'That's the kindest thing I can say about my brother while he's still alive.'"

"Jesus Christ! That fucking arsehole!"

"That wasn't all. I made a remark about the shooting. And Fran said maybe somebody just wanted to give them a scare. *Them.*"

"Who? The family?"

"No. In the context of the conversation, he meant Declan and Brennan."

"*What?* You mean the shooter was after *both* of them?"

"I didn't know what to make of it."

"That goddamn — then what happened?"

"That, unfortunately, is when Shirley arrived."

"Shirley."

206

"The girlfriend. And that was it."

"We're going over there. Tomorrow."

✝

It was late the next afternoon by the time Terry was free to pay a visit to Fran's basement apartment. We met outside, knocked and heard Fran's voice in reply: "Come in darlin', it's open. And I've got something for you!"

Terry blasted the door open and charged in, with me right behind him. Francis was standing before us, a dumbfounded look on his now clean-shaven face. He was holding out a huge, raggedy bouquet of flowers and grasses.

"That's not what I expected to see sticking up in my face when I walked in," Terry stated.

"Flowers. The latest and most creative way to disappoint your family."

"They look like a bunch of weeds."

"They're wildflowers. I thought she'd like them."

"They stink, for Christ's sake. Prob'ly full of bugs. Turf 'em out the window. Where in the hell did you dig them up?"

"You wouldn't fucking believe what I went through to get this stuff. I rolled out of bed at the crack of dawn. Climbed up into a big honking motorbus headed for Jersey thinking I'd get off when we left civilization and pick the wildflowers lining the highways. But there was hardly anything there. Maybe the time of year, I don't know. So then I had to wait out there like the last man alive till another great bus came by, then I —"

Terry interrupted him: "That's not what we came to talk about, Romeo."

"No? I thought you stopped by to check out my girlfriend. She'll be —"

"Shut up and listen. The police found your prints."

"Where?"

"On a big, long, heavily laden box from Ireland."

Francis blinked once and looked away, then went into action with his flowers, searching intently for a vessel in which to display them.

"Put those goddamn stinkweeds down and talk to me."

"I don't know what you're on about."

But he did, and all three of us knew it. Terry spoke again: "So far nobody else in the family knows about this. So start talking. When were you in Ireland?"

"Late last fall, leading up to Christmas. Before I went south."

Terry was about to ask another quesstion when we heard a knock on the door. "That'll be herself. Come in, Shirl."

Shirley walked in and came to a sudden halt when she saw the three of us. "Oh, hello! Hi, Monty. And this is?"

"This is my brother."

"Oh! Which one are you?"

"I'm the cute one," Terry replied, "with the left-handed guitar."

The look she gave him was blank. Francis shook his head as if to say: *Don't bother, she doesn't get it.*

He introduced them, and Terry gave her a distracted smile. Her eyes went to the kitchen table and lighted on the flowers. She opened her mouth to speak but Terry said: "Listen, sweetheart, we need a few minutes here. Why don't you — here, take my keys and sit in the car while you're waiting. Listen to the radio." He gave her the keys, described the car and its location, and she left, looking once over her shoulder as she went out.

"Sit down, Francis."

"We'll all sit down," I suggested, and positioned myself on the red milk crate. They each took a chair and Terry started again.

"Tell us about the box."

Terry had insisted on doing the talking. I urged him to resist the temptation to ask leading questions, about the gun for instance; if you want someone's story, don't plant your own. I could see Francis weighing the advantages of brazening it out, or admitting what we seemed to know anyway.

"And just why am I being interrogated by my little brother, Terrence?"

Terry rose and towered over Francis. "Why me? Would you rather Brennan? Or do you think it's nobody's concern at all, that you're the one —"

"Terry, let's keep our heads, all right?" I reached out and gave him a gentle shove into his seat.

"Are you here as a witness, Monty, or a bodyguard?" Francis tried for a light tone but did not quite manage to carry it off.

"The box, Fran. Get on with it."

His eyes darted to me again, then he said: "I met a guy in a bar. I'd seen him there a couple of times. One night we got talking. The subject of the old country came up."

"Who brought it up?" I forgot I was there as a witness/bodyguard. Old habits die hard.

"Don't remember, Monty. Anyway, this fellow said he knew of some artifacts that had been stolen by the British, or maybe they were found in an area controlled by the British Army in the north. The soldiers were looting the site and selling the stuff back in England." He fell silent.

"So?" his brother prompted.

"He knew a guy who had access to the site. He and this guy came up with a plan to rescue the artifacts."

"What kind of artifacts?"

"Old stone crosses, other carvings in stone. They wanted to bring the stuff over here."

"Why here? If this fellow in Ireland was such a good Samaritan and could get his hands on the stuff, why not take it to a museum in the Republic?"

"Why do you think? I didn't say it was an angel I met in the bar. These guys saw the opportunity to make a profit."

"What was in it for you?"

Francis looked defensive. "A trip to Ireland, with them picking up part of the tab. He said there was no way anybody would be able to trace the stuff to me."

"And you believed him."

"Just because you've never uttered a word of truth in a bar, Terrence, doesn't mean —"

"That's what bars are for. A place where you can go and lift a pint and tell lies all night long."

"I would not have believed him if he said he was doing it out of the goodness of his heart."

"Why didn't he make the trip himself?"

"He couldn't. Some kind of history, criminal record, some fucking thing."

"And this is your story."

"Yeah."

"You weren't smuggling guns, you were smuggling artifacts."

"What? People are smuggling guns *into* the United States these days? Last I heard there was no shortage of weapons in this country."

"Well, now there's one more, isn't there? The police found your fingerprints all over the box that contained the gun that was used to shoot our father. And you expect us to listen to this horseshit!"

Francis was perfectly still. His face was the colour of oatmeal.

Terry leaned into him. "Right. We know, you fucking psycho. If our mother weren't alive — and thank God she still is, though it's a wonder — I'd have the police here with me. But she is alive and she couldn't survive having this made public. As if she hasn't been through enough."

Francis finally found his voice. "How did they find the box?"

"How did they find the *box?*" Terry shouted. "That's all you can say?"

"Terry, I swear to you! I had nothing to do with that gun. I just brought these artifacts over."

"Must have been one hell of a long, modern-looking cross in that crate."

"I didn't see what was inside."

"Oh, Jesus Christ. Now he didn't even look in the box."

"I didn't. When I picked the box up, I could barely lift it. And it was all strapped with packing tape. I didn't open it."

"You just picked it up somewhere and lugged it to the airport. Didn't you think to wear gloves to keep your prints off it?"

"Gloves? It was sixty degrees out! I looked suspicious enough as it was."

"How long would this tale stand up in court, Monty?"

I shook my head.

"Monty!" Francis turned to me and pleaded: "It's true, believe me. Help me get this sorted before they find out."

"The police are already —"

"Bren and Declan. The family."

We were quiet for a few minutes, then Francis spoke again. "Maybe we can find this guy."

"Sure we can," Terry replied. "Go into a bar, pick out a drunk. Look, it's him! But, Jazes, with the drink taken, sure he can't remember the conversation."

"I spent several nights drinking with him."

"Where?"

"The bar was Vin Hennessy's."

"Never heard of it."

"It's here in Astoria. And this guy eats, drinks and sleeps there as far as I could tell. I'd know him if I saw him. I never knew his last name, but his first name is Colm."

"Don't waste our time, you little louser."

"I'll describe him for you. I'll draw you a picture. We'll split up and look for him."

"We're not splitting up so you can leave the country."

"No, really. I'll —"

"Go ahead," I interrupted, "draw him."

Francis got up and dug around until he came up with a sheet of paper and a pencil. He swirled the pencil around on the corner of the page to dull the tip, then began to draw. Terry could barely contain himself. "You're lucky it's me here today. You know that, don't you?" Francis nodded in acknowledgement and kept working.

I gaped at the results. Francis looked at me with hope. "You recognize him? You've seen this guy?"

"No, but this sketch is amazing. How long have you been doing this?"

"Doing what?"

"Doing portraits?"

"I don't do portraits! I just want to show you the guy's face so we can —"

"It's too bad," I mused. "You could have had a career as a forensic artist."

"Do you think? Maybe I still can." The hope and pleading were in his eyes again.

You'll have plenty of opportunity to draw criminals' faces where you're going, I said to myself.

We left Francis pale and sick-looking in his room. Terry warned him not to leave the country. Or was it a veiled plea to do just that?

Not for the first time, I wondered how long it would take the New York papers to reach the remote area of Mexico where Francis claimed to have been. He had surfaced in New York within days of the shooting. How did he phrase it when the subject came up? Carefully, I thought. Was he keeping track of his stories?

We got to Terry's car and were both taken aback to see Fran's girl-friend sitting in the passenger seat, bobbing her head to the music on the radio. We had forgotten her completely. She turned the radio off when she saw us, then got out of the car.

"He's all yours, sweetheart," Terry told her.

When we started up the car, a wailing country tune washed over us.

I drove to Astoria again that evening. Vin Hennessy's bar wasn't easy to find, eclipsed as it was by the bright lights and joyful music blaring out of the Greek restaurants and tavernas nearby. There was only a dim light coming from a side door, and I missed it on my first pass. Finally I found it, parked, and went in. But there was nobody who looked like Fran's sketch, nobody even in his age group. There was a line of scowling old men along the bar, grousing with Vin, the ancient publican, and two tables of newly legal young drinkers. Nothing in between. I didn't ask the bartender about Colm because I did not want to set anyone's antennae quivering.

My luck wasn't any better the next day at lunchtime. I decided to risk talking to Vin, who was behind the bar again; had he even gone home? He must have been at least eighty.

"Hi. Could you pour me a Guinness?"

"Do you see a Guinness sign in here, *avic?*"

"Right. A Murphy's then."

"That's better." He performed the pouring ritual in silence.

When I had my pint of stout, I took a sip and asked: "Is Colm around these days?"

"Who?"

"Colm. He used to come in here."

"Can't say I know the name." I shrugged. There was no point sitting around waiting for someone who might not even exist, so I drank my pint as quickly as was decent, and left the bar.

†

This was Maura and Normie's last full day in New York. When I rejoined them in our suite, Normie had found the drinks coaster I had taken from the Between The Bridges Pub, with Francis Burke's address scribbled on it. The address was of no interest to her but the coaster was, with its depiction of the two great bridges as a backdrop to the bar.

"Which one is that?" she asked, pointing to the Gothic-arched towers.

"That's the Brooklyn Bridge, which some people called the Eighth Wonder of the World when they built it."

"When?"

"Over a hundred years ago."

"Can we go see it?"

"We can walk right across it if you like."

"Really? Let's go!"

"Why don't we go at sunset? In the meantime, how would you like to spend the afternoon running around and seeing kids and dogs and street performers and all that?"

"I want to do that! Where?"

"Washington Square Park. It's in Lower Manhattan. We'll go from there to the bridge."

The three of us enjoyed the park. Then we walked across the water and were treated to a spectacular view of the East River and the skyscrapers of Manhattan, as the sun went down in a blaze of red and gold, and the lights came on all over New York.

After that it was time for another look at Vin Hennessy's bar. If nothing panned out, I would wait a day or two and try again. Unless I convinced myself in the meantime that "Colm" did not exist. It was nearly ten o'clock when I arrived at the pub. There was a larger and more varied crowd than there had been the night before. My attention was drawn to a big man being greeted by the bartender.

"Haven't seen you in a while, Sully."

"A Morphy's if you please, Vincent," the man answered, in a broad Irish brogue. "I've been out of town. Merchandising trip."

"Ah."

"They're fine and *súgach* over there," Sully remarked, indicating a table of young women laughing and singing. "Think I can pick one of the young ones off before the night's out?"

"I'm going to cut them off, the lot of them," the barman growled.

"Give me the heads-up when you do." Sully turned and scanned the room for a seat. He was wearing a sloppy sweatshirt that read "feck you" in Celtic script. His hair was a mass of red curls and he had a heavy beard, but he was easily recognizable from the sketch Francis had done. The same eyes and nose; Fran had captured his expression and even his attitude with uncanny skill. The only thing wrong was the name.

"Sully," I said to him. "I thought I might know you as Colm."

"If my mam had her way, you'd know me as Aloysius."

"That would be Mrs. Sullivan, I take it."

"It would. Do I know you?"

"No, but you seem like a sociable kind of guy. Maybe you'd be willing to extend a helping hand to a stranger. My name's Collins. Let's talk privately, shall we?" I pointed to a table, sat down and waited for him to join me.

He sat but his eyes, green and piercing, regarded me with suspicion. "What is it you think I can I do for you, Collins?" The Irish voice had taken on a rough edge.

I said quietly: "I've taken a recent and sudden interest in Irish artifacts."

"Is that right?"

"Right. Know where I can find any?"

"There's a lot of Irish craft stores around, so why come to me?" His eyes did a quick sweep of the bar.

"I want things that haven't been dusted off yet."

"That kind of thing is a minor sideline for me."

"Oh? What's your main line of business?"

"Cut the crap, Collins," he said, without altering his tone of voice. "I know why you're here."

"Is that so? Why am I here?"

He took a quick look around the bar again, and lowered his voice almost to a whisper: "That little chickenshit is in trouble now, and he's looking for someone to frame. But guess what? Not going to happen."

"Who are you talking about?"

"We both know the answer to that: Frankie Burke."

I decided to switch to a more direct approach. "How do you know Frankie?"

"Met him here. I moved to a place close by and started coming to the bar. This guy was always sitting with his girlfriend, blabbing away. When he got well-oiled, he tended to talk a little too loud. I'm not surprised he blew his cover. I knew it was a mistake getting involved with him, but what the hell. I made sure they couldn't trace anything to me."

"I found you."

He laughed. "You found me but you won't find a trace of me anywhere near those items Frankie brought over."

He was probably right. I asked him: "If he was that much of a wild card, why pick him to go on this escapade?"

Sullivan looked at me in surprise. "Pick him? What are you talking about? He picked me!"

What? I knew I was about to sit there and watch Francis Burke's story disintegrate before my eyes. Then what would I do? "He picked you," I repeated, lamely.

"Yeah."

"How did that happen?"

"Well, I listened to this guy Frankie go on and on about his troubles —"

"What sort of troubles?"

"Family shit. His old man was a prick, his brother didn't understand him, blah, blah. His girlfriend would try to tone him down. Sometimes he was okay; he'd be sober and wouldn't go off on a tangent. One of those times we started shooting the shit. Couple of nights after that, he said he'd heard something about me. I don't know where. He heard I was able to get my hands on something he very much wanted to have."

"Some kind of artifact."

"Depends on what you mean by artifact. Doesn't 'artifact' mean something somebody made?" He laughed and leaned towards me in a mock conspiratorial pose. "This one was artifacted in the 1940s by the Royal Small Arms Factory in Enfield, UK."

I had spent years constructing a facade to cover this kind of moment in a courtroom. Well, I wasn't in court now and I didn't even bother to hide my reaction.

"Bad news?" Colm Sullivan asked with insouciance. He lifted his empty glass in a friendly gesture. I shook my head, and he went for a refresher for himself.

He returned to the table and resumed his casual dismantling of everything I had wanted to believe about Francis. "The kid — he's probably my own age but I always thought of him as a kind of kid — asked me to follow him outside the bar one night. I was on my guard. If he had brawling on his mind, I knew I could pulverize him. But no, he'd heard I had a working knowledge of weaponry, here and abroad. He wanted a gun that couldn't be traced, unless it was back to Ireland. He didn't mind if it had been used over there. In fact, you didn't have to be Einstein to know he wanted it traced to the old country for some reason of his own."

Now I was trying to hide my feelings on the subject, outrage on behalf of Declan and his family, fury at Francis for stringing me along when I was trying to give him the benefit of the doubt.

Sullivan continued: "He asked how much it would cost him and I thought I'd charge him as much as he could afford, which wouldn't be much, judging by the look of him. I'd get him to bring my archaeological treasures over on the same flight. If anything went wrong, only one of us would lose, and it wouldn't be me."

I felt sick. Sullivan went on.

"Burke gave me some line about trying to reconstruct an episode in his family history. Was going to get uniforms, whatever. I didn't give a shit. It's not in my job description to ask what the guns are for. But I'll tell you this much: when I heard there was a Declan Burke who got shot at a wedding in Queens — go ahead, call me an idiot — I couldn't believe this guy Frankie had done it. He's just too much of a hothead to plan the thing, shoot the guy, then get himself out of the building and disappear. My idea of a Frankie Burke hit would be, his old man is railing at him from his armchair some night and Frankie goes out to the car, grabs the gun, comes flying back inside and blasts the guy's head off then and there. Giving out to him the whole time: 'I've hated you for years, you old fecker, so take this.' I spent about two minutes wondering if Frankie had hired a professional. But no professional would have taken the job. Not in that location. And poor old Frankie wouldn't have the greenbacks to pay for a hired man. Maybe Frankie did yoga and got himself 'centred' before his mission! Who the fuck knows?"

Drop it, Father Killeen had warned. An Irish connection indeed. Declan's own son. I walked along the crowded thoroughfares of Astoria, listening to bouzouki music coming from the lively Greek restaurants that lined the streets. The smell of lamb and garlic made my mouth water. But I was too preoccupied to enjoy the atmosphere. I found my rental car and drove to the hotel. What in the hell had Francis been trying to pull, with that story of himself as merely the carrier of Irish carvings? I thought I had caught a glimpse of something genuine in him beneath the abrasive facade. The pleading look on his face: *Give me one chance here and I'll straighten things out, become a courtroom artist.* You'd better become a courtroom artist, Frankie! Better still, hire one. And fast. It had been nothing more or less than the pleading look I see over and over on the faces of my clients. *Get the judge to gimme one more chance; I won't fuck up again.* I never fall for it; what was wrong with me this time?

What puzzled me, of course, was why he had set me straight on the trail of Colm Sullivan. He must have known Sullivan would give him up. I wanted the answer to that question before I told Terry Burke about my encounter with Sullivan, but I had to tell him something. I would make a point of seeing Terry tomorrow.

Friday was departure day for my wife and child. Terry and Sheila had invited Normie to spend the hours before her flight with Christine. We packed all the bags, threw them in the car and headed to Queens. When we arrived Sheila told us Terry was at his parents' house, so MacNeil and I continued on to the familiar house in Sunnyside. I had not told Maura anything about Francis. She would hear about him soon enough if there were any more developments.

Terry was the only one at the house. He was in his pilot's uniform, which earned him a look of undisguised admiration from MacNeil: "Fly me to Havana and nobody gets hurt. Except me, I'm hurting already! I can't believe Sheila lets you out of her sight in that outfit."

"She checks my altimeter whenever I get home, to see if anything went up."

"Where is everybody?" I asked him.

"They're on their way to Horgan's for something to eat. I said I'd join them in a minute. Have you two had lunch?"

"No."

"Good. We'll all go."

"Perfect, and it's going to be my treat!" Maura piped up.

"You don't have to do that," Terry protested.

"Did you see how much food I stuffed into myself when I was here the other day?" she countered. "I'll just run out to the car and get my bag."

"So, what's happening?" Terry asked as soon as she was gone.

"There's nothing to tell. Not yet anyway. The guy didn't show."

"Oh, for Christ's sake."

"Yeah, I know. We'll find him, don't worry. And if the cops move on Francis, we'll put them on to Sullivan."

"God knows what he'll tell them."

You said it. "Well, we sure as hell can't keep him to ourselves if Francis gets arrested."

"True enough."

Terry pulled some papers from his pocket — photocopies of his brother's sketch of Sullivan. "I'm taking a good, long look at this clown. And I'm going to do a lot of barhopping over the next few days. How big did Fran say he was?"

"Five ten or so, heavy set," I answered, fresh from my face-to-face meeting.

"Looks like some kind of paramilitary freak with the buzz cut and the —"

We heard someone coming in, and Terry went to the door. I grabbed the photocopies and stuffed them into my pocket.

"Your mother forgot her glasses," I heard Declan say. "As if she doesn't know the menu off by heart. There they are. You coming or not?"

"I'm coming. Monty and Maura are here."

"Good. Let's get a move on."

We walked to the restaurant and the five of us crowded into a booth.

Maura decided to make the best of her last day with Mr. Burke. "Tell us more about the screws on B wing, Declan. You did say, I believe, that you had spent some time in the lockup."

"Hanam 'on Diabhal, you little clip!"

"Which means?"

"It means 'your soul to the devil!' And your memory is faulty. I didn't say I was in the lockup. Father Killeen said it. But yes, I did a stint in Mountjoy Prison. And when I got out, I'd no home to go to. Wasn't that a sight now — a man on his doorstep after six months away, finding himself locked out and his family gone."

"Declan," Teresa chided him. "You say that as if I didn't leave you a forwarding address."

"Word never reached me."

"Isn't that queer — all the makings of poteen reached you in there, and the components of a still. Cakes with files baked in them reached you —"

"I got out and you were gone!" His voice had risen a notch in volume.

"Gone to a far better place, Declan."

"You moved into exactly the same damned house in a different street. You moved because you didn't like the name."

"The name. The Mountjoy Burkes, you mean? The name the children were being called when they were outside playing?"

"We lived in Mountjoy Street, for the love of God. They called them that to differentiate them from the Burkes of Blessington Street."

"Did they now. And here I was thinking it referred to their father being in Mountjoy Prison up the street. I took advantage of a place that became available in Rathmines. The difference was we were no longer living next door to Christy Burke's Pub, and all the associations that place had for us." She turned to Maura. "An IRA pub with a secret door in the back, a stash of rifles, the chance of a raid at any minute, the sounds of spies being thumped after being caught in there. Declan's brother and his cronies with the bar stools surgically implanted up their rear ends, guzzling porter from noon till night and plotting the destruction of the state. The state now being run by their former brothers in arms." Teresa shook her head. "Life with Declan in the 1940s, Maura . . ."

Dublin, 1943

I'm standing in Mountjoy Street, looking north. Partway up the street on the right there's a tall spire. That's the black church — it turns black in the rain. Just north of that, across the side street, is a pub. It's a cream-coloured building on the corner, with black trim and gold letters saying "Christy Burke's." To say it's the family local is to understate things considerably: Christy is Declan's father. Beyond Christy's the street curves away to the west, and it's lined mostly with Georgian-style townhouses, three storeys high. Rows of chimney pots, multi-paned windows and brightly painted doors under demi-lune fanlights. The brick looks lovely in the warm golden sunlight from the west. Farther up, Mountjoy Street becomes the Berkeley Road; up there is the Mater Misericordia, the hospital. Now that's a fine majestic building with rows of Palladian windows and Ionic columns at the entrance. But there's a serpent in the garden. Because if I were to walk around to the back of the Mater and look across the North Circular Road, I'd be looking at Mountjoy Prison. Where ten of our patriots were executed by the Brits in 1920 and '21. And where Declan is serving six months in a cell.

Now I'm in the new house in Rathmines Road. Declan has just come home. He's thin, and he's agitated. "I've just spent six months in prison, Teresa, one hundred eighty nights trying to avoid the sin of impurity thinking about you! And when I get home, hopin' for a bit of the how's-your-father, you're not there. Now I'm standin' in a new house, with all our furniture piled in the corner, and the last thing I feel like doing is moving chairs and hanging pictures. You came this far without me, you can finish it without me. Now I'm going to make a call to Finn."

His brother. They'll be heading up to Christy's, I suppose. What's he whispering about? The move, of course. He sounds even more perturbed than usual! Ah, well, he'll get over it. There. He's off the telephone. "It's not all here, Declan," I tell him. "There are still some things we have to pick up from the old place."

"What's that?"

"I left some things in the basement of the old house."

"Is that so! Sure, we'll go up there right now and get them, Teresa. I'll call for one of the furniture vans."

Blessed mother of mercy! It's as if I just told him we've struck gold and it's all going to be plowed under if we don't move instantly to mine it. "There's no hurry, Dec. The new owner is the very soul of kindness. She told me I can take my time clearing out the basement. She knows my husband was away. Somewhere. She herself is a young widow with three children."

"Who would she be now?"

"A Protestant lady by the name of Bowles."

"Well, let's go and get all our old things out of her way." And there he is on the phone again, this time to Burke Transport. They'll be snapping to attention; it's the first time they've heard from the boss in six months.

So here we go, roaring down Rathmines Road into the centre of the city, across the river and up to Mountjoy Street. I'm hanging on for my life. What's the rush? Here's the old house. And Mrs. Bowles is at the door. Such a lovely person, in a brown shirt-dress and a permanent wave. She invites us inside. What's this? Who is sitting in the parlour with a cup of tea and a plate of scones before him but Finn Burke himself! If ever there was a smiling chancer in this world, it's Finn Burke. A handsome-looking divil too. Didn't he make good time getting here after that telephone call! And why on earth is he here at all?

Now don't the two of them have the widow charmed! There they go, down to the cellar to get what they came for. Mrs. Bowles and I can hardly hear ourselves speak with the banging and the ructions going on down there. It seems our old house has two cellars, one dug below the other.

Back in the van we go, over to Rathmines. Our furniture is carried into the new house. A few big boxes remain in the back of the van, and the Burke brothers are off again. To another destination, a secret one, where they will squirrel away their artillery or rocket launcher or whatever has been lying beneath the old house all those months.

"Ah, bejazes," Terry remarked in a thick brogue, "nothin' ever goes away, does it?"

"Home sweet home," Teresa continued, "and Declan's memory serves him faithfully indeed. The new place was identical to the old." She opened the clasp of her handbag and pulled out a plastic folder of snapshots. "Here it is."

Maura took the folder, and I looked over her shoulder at a creased colour photo of a brick townhouse with a yellow door and spanking white trim, one in a row of similar dwellings. Looming over the streetscape, a few doors away, was a large stone church with a columned portico and a green-roofed dome. Running across the lintel were the words: *"Sub. Invoc. Mariae Immaculatae Refugii Peccatorum."*

Teresa smiled. "I moved the family away from Christy Burke's pub and planted them right next to —" she paused for effect "— the Church of Mary Immaculate, Refuge of Sinners!"

After lunch, we walked back to the Burkes' house and I asked Terry what he was up to for the evening. He said he and Patrick had been planning to go out, but the airline had called and asked Terry to substitute for another pilot who had taken ill. It was a short flight but he wouldn't be back in time for an outing. Perhaps, he suggested, I'd like to go along with Pat; it was rare that his brother was keen on a night out. That sounded good. Maura and I went to collect Normie for the trip to Halifax. She and Christine had a long goodbye hug with promises that they would write, and visit each other again soon. There were a few tense moments — and the inevitable cacophony of car horns — when I nearly missed my turn at LaGuardia and cut across a lane of traffic to reach my destination. But we got there, found a parking spot and made it to the departure terminal with time to spare. Maura didn't fire any parting shots at me, and I took some encouragement from that. But Normie's behaviour was strange. I suppose it was understandable, considering the events she had been witness to in New York. She took me aside and made me squat down so we were at eye level.

"You're going to be careful, right, Daddy?"

"I'm always careful, sweetheart."

"No, you're not!"

"You had a terrible fright, Normie. We all did. But Mr. Burke is fine now, and the police will catch the guy who committed the crime."

"What if it happens again?"

"It won't."

"It might. Don't go anywhere alone!"

"If I'm by myself, sweetheart, it won't happen. Because nobody's after me. Right?"

"I don't believe you! I think you're going to get in trouble!"

"Nope. So, give me a hug. I'll be home in a week, and I'll miss you every day till then. Have fun on the plane, and give Tommy a big kiss for me."

"Ha! I love you, Daddy." She flung her arms around my neck and held on.

"I love you too, Normie. See you soon."

When I got to the hotel I called Patrick, then Brennan. Pat and I agreed to meet at Colly's. Brennan had been asked to sing with a Gregorian choir that evening, so he would not be joining us at the blues bar.

I sat down on the bed, looking forward to a few hours with nothing to do. When I bent over to remove my shoes I felt something bunched up in the front pocket of my jeans. Terry's copies of the Colm Sullivan drawing. Not copies, I saw, just one. The other papers were the obituary, tattered and marked up, and some handwritten notes. I noticed the name Ramon Jiminez. This was the information Terry had received from his friend in the police department; he must have scribbled the notes during a phone conversation with the cop.

And here was the name Willman. Right. Brennan said Terry had checked and there was no record for Garth Willman. But the cop must have given Terry the goods on all the Willmans who came up during the search. Yes, I remembered; I had asked Brennan if there were any with Irish first names.

Here they were. Patrick, born November 1965: string of car thefts, parole violations. Too young. Sean, born May 1959: sex offender. I saw that Sean was in prison at the time Declan was shot. I skimmed through the other names. Albert Willman, born 1922: murder, still inside. Gehrhart, born 1930: porn. Gerard, born 1953: house breaks, assault in the second degree. Norman, born 1961: rape, ten years. Trevor, born 1970: drugs. William, born 1942: racketeering and related offences. Nobody with a conviction relating to firearms.

But we knew somebody who did have a gun. Brought in specially from Ireland. I made up my mind. It was time to confront Francis Burke. I got the car and drove across the river once again, to Astoria, so I could ask him in person why he had given me Sullivan's name. But I didn't find the answer. I found something else: a For Rent sign on his apartment door. Francis was gone.

Chapter 10

Some on the shores of distant lands their weary hearts have laid,
And by the stranger's heedless hands their lonely graves were made.
— John Kells Ingram, "The Memory of the Dead"

March 29, 1991

That Friday evening, Patrick and I were seated in Colly's, pints in front of us, talkin' blues. I didn't mention Francis. I was telling Pat about my band, Functus, and what a great time we had once a month on Mondays. "If not for blues night, I'd be balled up on a couch talking to a guy like you."

"Blues night sounds like a better time, with better results."

"So how do you work out your frustrations, Patrick?"

"Who says I have any?" he asked with a wry smile.

"You must meet even more aggravating people in the run of a day than I do. I can't imagine how you put up with them all."

"I'm a very, very patient man."

"I've noticed. Don't you wish, deep down, that you could lash out at the next family luncheon? You're the one who tries to keep the peace, to keep the others from doing too much damage to each other. Wouldn't you like to get up and let 'er rip?"

"Only when Francis is there. No need otherwise. But what could

I say to him that hasn't been said by everyone else? That scene you witnessed — you may not believe it but that's the first time in years that Brennan has lost it with Francis. Poor Fran. In big families there always seems to be one who gets lost in the shuffle. I'm actually working on a paper on that very subject. For an American Psychiatric Association conference. Hope Francis doesn't get wind of it. He'll have an even bigger chip on his shoulder."

"Is that a psychiatric term, 'chip on the shoulder'?"

"Sometimes a homely cliché serves the purpose better than a mouthful of psychiatric jargon! Fran just never carved out a unique role for himself in the family. Molly, Brennan and I were top students. Of course Bren only studied when he felt like it. But still. Molly became a professor, Brennan entered the priesthood and went to study in Rome. And of course he has all that musical talent. I became an MD and then a psychiatrist. Brigid was the baby of the family and the youngest girl. Everyone doted on her. Terry was the youngest boy, and he was cheerfully indifferent to school. He never wanted to do anything but fly airplanes, and who can blame him? Francis is just a year older than Terry. He wasn't blessed with Terry's nonchalant attitude to life."

"Terry's the kind of guy I'd like to have along on a road trip."

"Oh, yeah. And he can provide the transportation. Poor Fran. Nobody would want to be with him on the road. Even as a little kid, he felt out of things. He ran away a few times when he was really small. Somebody must have made fun of him or something. Problem was, the first couple of times he took off nobody noticed! So what's the point?"

"How come nobody realized he was gone?"

"He and Terry shared a room with bunk beds. Francis slept in the bottom bunk and he liked to turn his bed into a tent, with sheets hanging down. Sometimes he would hide in there all day, and he kept nearly everything he owned in there with him. So once it was lights-out, nobody would notice if he sneaked off.

"A couple of times he got caught sleeping in the car. That was okay till he peed on the car seat; that was the end of that. He told me he spent the whole night in the car. He didn't wake up till morning, when he heard the front door bang shut and the engine start up. Declan was at the wheel. Francis slid down behind Da's seat and didn't make a peep. Apparently, Da drove all over hell and creation before pulling in at a church for early Sunday Mass. He parked and went inside. Fran stayed in hiding for a few minutes, then ventured into the church. He had to pee. But he couldn't figure out where the toilets were and got all upset. So he went back to the car, where he couldn't hold it in."

"There must have been hell to pay that time."

"So you'd think. But I remember Fran telling me Dec was in a forgiving mood that day. The grace of God working in him! He just told Fran not to mention it to anyone and neither would he. Which, as you can imagine, suited Fran just fine. It was years before he told me the tale. Just the thought of anyone — especially Brennan — hearing that, instead of embarking on a big adventure of his own and having the family worried sick, Fran slunk back to the car and peed on the seat —"

"But Francis was just a little boy at the time. Brennan would not have ragged him about it surely."

"Of course he wouldn't! But Francis couldn't see that. He used to worship the ground Brennan walked on. Anything Bren did, Fran wanted to do. They were far apart in age so that wasn't very realistic. When Brennan went into the sem, Francis didn't know what to do. He started acting out, getting into trouble, the usual."

"If he couldn't be as good as Brennan, he'd damn well be bad, eh?"

"Well, that was part of the problem. The family already had a black sheep and that was Brennan himself. Until God booted him into the seminary. Up till then, if anyone was a likely candidate for the priesthood, it was me, not Bren. You name it, he'd done it. And he'd done more of it than all the rest of us combined. So Fran could not even be as bad as Brennan, let alone as good. Any time they're in the same room together, it sets Fran off. He can't help himself."

"And then there's Declan," I added.

"What do you mean, 'and'?" Patrick said with a laugh. "Let's get things in perspective here. In the beginning, there was Declan. And all who came after him would bear his mark."

"With a father like that, it wouldn't be easy for some guys to stand up and be counted."

"Absolutely."

"What was it like growing up with him glowering at you from the head of the table?"

"Actually, he's not as much of a hard-ass as he might seem. He's tough, no question. But very loving in a gruff sort of way. He wasn't one of those distant fathers who never showed affection or anything like that. I see a great many patients who grew up with that sort of parent. And he was never the kind of man who always had to win, or prevail on every point. I'm sure you know that type. We all argued with him, once we got old enough to take our chances. And he would give in on occasion too. Now he might not say: 'I've considered your arguments, my son, and I can see that you are right. I'm wrong and I apologize.' It would more likely be: 'Go ahead then, you stubborn little gobshite, but don't come wailing to me afterwards.' Of course we did go wailing to him afterwards but —"

"He wouldn't say 'I told you so'?"

"Of course he'd say 'I told you so'! But then he'd help us out of whatever scrape we were in. Our mother is a very strong woman and so we grew up knowing there was a counterweight to the old fellow. We could handle him. Or the rest of us could. Francis had the roughest time with him, not that Declan singled him out. Hell, it was Brennan who got knocked around the most. In those days it was just accepted, in many families anyway, that your father would give you a clout if you didn't behave. I don't condone it, of course, but in those times it was the norm. He threw Bren up against the wall a few times and smacked him, when he caught him misbehaving."

"Did Brennan hit him back?"

"Are you *well?* Of course not! I was spared most of the time because I was a goody-two-shoes. Terry got whacked the odd time. The girls never. No matter what they said or did! But poor Fran. He used to see this going on, with Bren and the old boy. One time Fran did something bad. Told Declan to fuck off; maybe even took a swipe at him. Declan hauled off and clocked him, gave him a black eye. And he felt terrible afterwards. Took Francis for an outing. All day, just the two of them. But the thing was, all Fran boasted about was the shiner, not the trip to Coney Island or wherever it was. 'Look at this, the old man gave it to me.' Fathers and sons, Monty, fathers and sons." He shook his head.

"How many children do you have, Pat?"

"Two girls. I'm the biggest pushover that ever lived. I've got to watch it or they'll be spoiled princesses. Unfortunately they live half the time with my wife. Former wife. I didn't live up to her social ambitions. We share custody."

"I hear you. I'm in the same boat, though not for the same reason. Any chance of you getting back in the matrimonial bed?"

"I'd rather be home with a glass of Jameson's in one hand and myself in the other."

"Well, that pretty much sums it up."

"Mmm. Before I forget: I did some detective work on yer man Cathal's death. He really died, last fall."

"Of what?"

"Congestive heart failure."

"That's a relief, I suppose. Do we know anything else?"

"Not about his medical condition. He had a funeral but nobody went. Or almost nobody. I spoke to the funeral director. The old lady insisted on a church funeral, but the place was empty apart from her, an elderly woman who accompanied her, the priest doing the Mass, and an ancient priest in a walker, who hobbled to the front and gave a little eulogy. What a faithful and generous parishioner Murphy had been. Attended Mass several days a week. That was it. Oh, and one other man who came and sat in the back of the church. The undertaker wasn't sure whether he was part of it."

I thanked Patrick for his investigative work, and wondered about the man who sat at the back and observed the funeral of Cathal Murphy, formerly known as Charlie Fagan.

I got to bed late and slept till mid-morning. In that confused state between sleep and wakefulness, I heard one phrase echoing around and around in my head: "Fathers and sons," Patrick's voice was saying, "fathers and sons." A memory surfaced, of my own father sitting beside me in a movie theatre, as we watched some kind of historical saga. He was saying: "Kill the father, kill the son." Otherwise, he explained, you never knew when the son would return to avenge the father's death. What sons did we have in our own saga of death and retribution in New York? Cathal Murphy didn't have a son. Judy Willman, widow of Gerald Connors, had a son and two daughters. I remembered the photo of one girl who had done well in life, another who hadn't, and Private Willman with Garth in their Army togs. Willman's son would not be out to avenge his mother's first husband. My mind returned to the daughters, and I imagined the tongue-lashing I would get from Professor MacNeil for concentrating on sons and dismissing daughters as possible actors in the drama. She'd have a good point: why wouldn't a woman take revenge for the loss of her father? And then there was the Desmond family. Mrs. Desmond certainly blamed Declan Burke for her husband's downfall. The drunkenness, the loss of his job on the waterfront. And we knew from Mary Desmond's diary how profoundly the girl had been affected by her father's return to the bottle. Desmond had sons, too. Brennan and I had spoken about them recently. What was that conversation about? Right. Young Desmond being dispatched by his mother to drag his father home from the bars. Kevin. No, Jimmy was the older boy. And then we had Francis, prime illustration of a whole other chapter of father–son relations. I slipped beneath the rim of consciousness.

I was jolted awake in the morning by a knock on the door. I tried to ignore it, but there it was again. I stumbled from the bed and realized I was still in last night's clothes. It was Brennan at the door. Great. Another encounter with a member of the Burke family and I still had not come clean about Francis. I stood there trying to think of something intelligent to say. Brennan helped me out: "Are you going to invite me in?"

"Come in."

"Looks as if you had a good time for yourself."

"Drinking with Patrick. Have a seat while I take a shower. Help yourself to a cup of coffee or whatever you can find in the little fridge."

When I was clean, bright and dressed, I sat down and looked at my guest. "What's up?"

"I want to lean on that old boot Nessie. She knows more than anyone, with the exception of the man with the gun." The gun.

When was I going to lay it all out for them? "Let's go over there and rattle her chain."

"Brennan, do you really have the balls to show up there again, after telling her off and being kicked out of her house?"

"I've been turfed from better places, by better people. Let's go."

It was worth a try. If she would talk to us, I might get some sense of how the obituary fit in with Francis and the gun. Or was it conceivable that the two events — the publication of the obituary in December and the shooting in March — were unrelated?

We left the hotel and got into a small silver car, which Brennan had left double-parked in the street. "Whose car have we got today? This isn't Terry's."

"Paddy's."

"Good thing they didn't come along and tow it away."

"Doctor's plates. Everyone should have them."

He pulled into the line of traffic, and someone leaned on his horn; Brennan ignored it.

"Did we ever establish whether Nessie knew any of the players, besides her own brother?" I asked, trying to recall our conversation with the old woman. "Did she know Desmond, or Gerard Connors, or —"

"Gerald Connors."

"Hmm?"

"*Gerald* Connors. You said *Gerard*. And who knows whether she was acquainted with any of them? We'll make it our business to find out."

It was a brilliantly sunny day. I rolled my window down but the din of traffic, horns and air brakes was deafening, so I rolled it up again.

"I got a call from Brigid," Brennan remarked as we headed onto the bridge. "I think you can imagine how unimpressed she was with what happened the other day. She delivered herself of a few choice words about male aggression and competitiveness. Well, what could I say? To have her embarrassed like that in front of you, and Leo, and the rest of us — but, *mirabile dictu,* the arsehole called and apologized to her."

"Did you get an apology yourself?"

"Did the sun become black as sackcloth and the moon become as blood, and the stars of heaven fall unto the earth?"

"I'll put that down as a no. You certainly let him have it in return. Can't say I blame you."

"Leo took me to task for that. Gently."

"Sent you off to say three Hail Marys, did he?"

"Something like that."

"Well, I don't know what sins you might have confessed to him. But I'd move heaven and earth to hear Leo's confession."

"I didn't hear it, I can tell you that much."

"Just as well."

"Given the identity of his accomplices," Burke acknowledged. "Right. Speaking of which, should we come right out and ask oul Nessie if she knows the other names we've come up with?"

"Mr. Desmond and Gerard Connors. *Gerald,* I mean. We'll play it by — Brennan, pull over!"

"What?"

"Pull over to that pay phone."

"Now?"

"Now."

He gave me a raised left eyebrow but turned into a parking lot and stopped the car. I walked to the pay phone, saw with relief that it was in working order, dialled directory assistance, got the number I needed and then stood outside the booth, waiting. She came along about two minutes later: a tough-looking young woman with a case of beer under one arm and a set of car keys in her other hand. I could see Burke peering at me from the car.

"Excuse me," I said to the girl. "Would you do something for me?"

"In a phone booth?" she asked incredulously, in a strong Brooklyn accent. "What are you, some kind of weirdo?"

"No, no, I'm not. Really. I just need somebody to help me make a call."

"Why can't you make it y'self? Is there something wrong with you?"

"I don't want her to hear my voice. It's personal."

"Yeah, right, isn't it always? Gimme the number. And don't even think about rubbing up against me in that booth."

I showed her the number I had written on my hand. "Just ask for Gerry Willman, then hand me the receiver."

"What if he's there? You gonna go over and beat the shit out of him? In front of her?"

"No."

"'Is Gerry Willman there?' That's all you want me to say?"

"Yes, but if you could say it . . . in perhaps a more friendly tone."

"Now he gets picky. You're not from here, are you?"

"No. So I have to rely on the kindness of strangers."

She gave a bit of a laugh, shook her head and dialled the number. In a perkier tone than I would have hoped for, she asked if she could speak to Gerry Willman. She looked at me and shrugged. Nothing happening.

I took the receiver. After a few more seconds of silence I heard Judy Willman's quiet voice: "I'm sorry. Gerry doesn't live here anymore. He hasn't lived here for a long, long time." Then she clicked off.

I went back to the car. "What was that all about?" Brennan demanded.

"Got any quarters?"

He dug around in a small pullout container beneath the car radio. "Who are you calling?"

"Right now I'm going to call Terry. Where can I reach him?"

Brennan gave me the phone number and started to speak, but I ran off with an assurance that I would explain later. I called Terry. The person who answered gave me another number, and I reached Terry there. I filled him in and asked if he would be willing to get hold of a skip tracer to track down Gerard Willman. Then I returned to the car.

"I got the name Gerard from notes Terry took of all the Willmans the police checked out. When we were at the Willmans' place, Judy told us about her daughters. And I saw the photo of a young guy in uniform with Garth. Private G.G. Willman; I thought he was Garth's own son. But no. Terry's notes show that Gerard Willman was born in February 1953. That makes him Gerald Connors's son, born after Connors went to Attica."

"Jesus. What now?"

"Now we deal with Nessie. And we'll ask her if she knows a Gerry Willman."

†

Nessie was sunning herself on the stoop like an old lizard when we arrived. She shaded her eyes as she looked up.

"You again. Didn't I put the run to you before?"

"You did," I admitted.

"Well? To what do I owe this imposition today?"

"We're helping the police with their inquiries. This may not be your last interruption."

"A fine lot of help you two must be. Well, the police are welcome to stop by. I've done nothing more than write up an obituary for my dearly departed brother — God rest his soul."

"Do you know someone by the name of Gerry Willman?"

She looked from me to Brennan and back. "Help me up here." Brennan took her arm and steadied her while she stood and reached for her cane. "It's a gentle touch you have, Mr. Burke; I wouldn't have expected it. Come inside."

When we were seated, she said: "So you're on to young Gerry. Very well, no need for me to protect him anymore!" And, leaning forward in her chair, she began the tale she had been longing to tell us from the start. After all, it showcased her craftiness, and she seemed to think we wouldn't try to implicate her when we had better suspects in our sights.

"This fellow came to see us, well, to see Cathal. But Cathal had gone out to do the shopping. I can't get around, as you know. So we got talking, and it turned out this Gerry was trying to find out what happened to his da many years ago. The lad had put together part of the story, that his da — also named Gerry, though I think he was a Gerald and his last name was different — had got caught up in a gun-running operation that went wrong. My brother was involved in it somehow. It seems the young fellow got Cathal's name from someone in the old country. I suspected young Gerry had made a few gun runs himself, if he had contacts like that in Ireland. Anyway, somebody over there knew Charlie Fagan was Cathal Murphy. Gerry seemed to know that whatever part Cathal had played, he was not the one who had got the father in the soup. Or maybe he just told me that. Anyway the father, Gerry the elder, had gone to prison and didn't last a year in there. This boy was born when his father was in the stir.

"So we waited for Cathal, and young Gerry told me a bit about himself. His mother had taken up with a man by the name of Willman after her husband died. Willman was an old Army man, served in the Pacific during the Second War. He tried to make young Gerry over in his own image. The two of them clashed from day one; the old man made life hell for his stepson. Gerry got into trouble with the law; after that, Willman finally frogmarched him into the Army. Gerry went into 'Intelligence work,' as he called it. He didn't last long in the Army, but he loved codes and word games, puzzles, that sort of thing. I told him all I could do in that line was the cryptoquotes in the paper.

"Anyway, Cathal came in with the shopping and I introduced him to the young fellow — well, he would have been in his thirties. Cathal looked so miserable. He wanted to talk to this fellow but not in front of me. So, a lady first and last, I announced that I was tired and headed off to my bedroom to rest. Really, to eavesdrop. In the apartment where we lived then, my closet bordered directly on the living room wall. And poor Cathal, bless his soul, was going deaf at the time. Like many deaf people, he thought he had to talk loud to make himself heard. So I settled in and listened.

"Somebody had run afoul of the IRA, and was anxious to put himself right with them. My brother didn't say who. No informer, our Cathal. This unnamed individual — I later figured out it was Declan Burke — had assassinated someone in Ireland, an IRA informer. Then he botched some other assignment, or refused to carry it out, and was under suspicion himself. He absconded and took a bit of start-up money with him, out of the organization's coffers. With one thing and another he managed to wind up with a price on his head. From the moment he arrived in New York, he was looking for a way to make amends. Eventually he learned of a shipment of guns that was supposed to be going overseas somewhere. Declan came up with a plan to steal the guns and reroute them to Ireland. There was some man he knew who worked as a port watchman on the waterfront here in Brooklyn. This fellow, again unnamed —"

"Desmond," I put in.

"Desmond, was it? This Desmond was a real *pótaire*, a drunk, so it wasn't hard to sweet-talk him into helping the cause. He unlocked the shed and left it open for Declan and his accomplice, who was of course the ill-fated Gerry Senior. But Desmond left his post, and another guard filled in for him. The other guard tried to stop the robbery, and was knocked unconscious in the fray. To hear Cathal tell it, this Gerry had never been in trouble in his life. Burke seduced him into it somehow and had the poor young man so indoctrinated that, when the police caught up with him, Gerry refused to name his partner in crime and took the whole rap himself. He got a stiff prison sentence because of the violence. Declan Burke sat back, kept his mouth shut and let it all happen. The poor young man was butchered in Attica prison by hooligans he didn't even know. It could have been anyone; he was in the wrong place at the wrong time. That was the end of Gerry the father, and the beginning of a long, slippery slope for Gerry the son. I heard the young fellow begging Cathal to give him the name of the man who had let this happen to his da, but Cathal was firm: he was sorry, but he couldn't give the name.

"I came out of my room before the lad left, and I whispered to him: 'I'll find out. And when he goes —' I meant when my brother dies '— when he goes, I'll let you know.' I was sure Cathal would have the information somewhere. He wrote everything down, and he kept the most embarrassing diaries. He needn't have done, because he was one of those people with a photographic memory. But there he would be at the kitchen table, scribbling away for hours. This would be weeks' or months' worth of his activities; he kept all the facts in his mind and then wrote them down. Why, I couldn't tell you. And he locked all his papers in a strongbox. A detail man, I suppose he was. Too bad he hadn't used some of that talent to give him a leg up on the American dream. Two legs up! He'd have made a grand businessman and earned great pots of money. He could have provided his only relation — his twin! — with a life of comfort instead of this."

She glared around at her mean surroundings, then continued. "I planned to get into Cathal's papers and give Gerry the heads-up. Sure enough, when Cathal died I got into his box and read his journals. There was a lot of blather about Teresa Burke. And Cathal's mysterious activities on behalf of Irish Republicanism. And there was no doubt that Declan was the man behind the robbery on Pier One. You almost have to feel pity for Dec: he had to make reparations to the IRA, and he had to get on with supporting his family. It must have taken Burke a good many years to climb out of the hole he'd dug for himself. Mind my words, he was in holes he didn't even know he was in! Tsk tsk." Her eyes glinted with malice.

The hateful obituary was beginning to make a kind of sense: the stepson Stephen was Gerry Connors Senior. Brother Benedict was the IRA traitor Declan had dispatched in Ireland. Both had "predeceased" Declan. We had been right about Attica.

"Are you still carrying that obit around with you, Brennan?"

I turned and saw him looking at the old woman with mask-like impassivity. I could sense his wrath, even if she couldn't. Without changing his expression or taking his eyes off Neasa Murphy, he reached into his wallet, pulled out the tattered paper and handed it to me.

I read it quickly, then asked Nessie: "What on earth is a pint of Lameki Jocuzasem? I've spoken to many a pint-lifter over the past few weeks and nobody has ever heard of it."

"You two should do a stint in Army Intelligence. Learn about codes. I did, in order to assist young Gerry. Didn't sign up for the Army but I did hobble onto a bus and go to a library. I couldn't move the next day, I was so exhausted." Her eyes darted to a dusty bookcase in a corner of the room. "Anyway, when Cathal passed on and I learned the name of the man behind all the death and destruction, I couldn't find young Gerry. Tried to get his phone number or address. No luck. And I had moved house since his visit, and the listing is in my name. I knew he wouldn't be able to find me. So I hit upon the idea of putting a coded message in the paper. I had to grab his attention. The only thing I could think of was that I had promised I'd get the name for him when my brother died. If the message had my brother's name in it — the announcement of his death — that might catch Gerry's eye. Obviously, it did. Unless somebody else has it in for Declan, too! From what I know, the man could have a whole nest of enemies!"

"So Lameki Jocuzasem gave Gerry Declan's name? What was the code?"

"Did you see the 'nine' in the text? 'Dressed to the nines.' Code buffs always look for numbers. That was a clue that the sequence of letters started with I, the ninth letter of the alphabet. The alphabet goes in order after that to the end, then starts again with A, and finishes with H. I to H instead of A to Z. Using the alphabet that way, 'decburke' is spelled 'lmkjczsm.' I couldn't just put it in like that — it isn't a word. So I stuck the vowels 'aeiou' in. It came out like something real, didn't it? Lameki Jocuzasem. Young Gerry took a while to get it. Or maybe he didn't see the death notice right away."

Or maybe he never saw it at all. Francis didn't need the obit to act against his father. What was Gerry Willman's role?

"I'm quite proud of it," Nessie said. "The rest of the obituary I just decided to have some fun with, and I put a little capsule history of yer man Burke in there for all the world — the clever, sharp-eyed readers of the world — to enjoy."

"And just how many clever readers have there been, do you suppose, Mrs. Murphy?" I asked her.

"It disappoints me to say there have been none."

"Present company and young Gerry excepted."

"What did I say, Mr. Collins? You don't hear so well for a young man. Now if you'll excuse me, I have nothing better to do than chat with you gentlemen, and I'd like to get on with it. Help me out to the stoop, Mr. Burke. I'm relieved to see you've controlled your temper this time. Maybe I'll survive your inquiries after all."

I stood to follow them out but took a detour to the bookcase Nessie had glanced at. There were two books on codes, one fairly elementary, the other much more advanced. The old lady turned and caught me looking. I said: "Codes before the world of computers."

"Some of us are too poor to own a computer, Mr. Collins. Turns out there was no need for anything that complicated; the easy code book did the trick. Amn't I right? Gerry deciphered the code and you didn't."

We left her, and got into the car. Brennan's anger was palpable. His hands gripped the wheel as if it was somebody's throat. He didn't say one word during the drive to my hotel.

†

It was Saturday night, March 30, Easter weekend. Brennan would be attending the Easter Vigil, the high point of the Catholic liturgical year. The church would be in darkness, then the candles would be lit one at a time. The light returning, bells ringing out, and more alleluias sung over the course of three hours than are heard all the rest of the year. I hoped it would bring him some peace. The weekend for me was not so joyful. Normie was still at the age where the hunt for Easter eggs was a high point of her year. She might not believe they were brought by a rabbit but somebody obtained them and scattered them around, and she relished the search. Every year she relied on Daddy to arrive with extra chocolate. Not this time. When I called her in Halifax, she fretted about how Easter morning would go. Would Mummy know the appropriate quantity of treats to buy? Was it conceivable there could be a shortfall? And it wasn't just *that;* she missed her dad.

"I miss you, too. Put Mummy on the phone, would you, sweetheart?"

"Okay."

"Everything's under control here," MacNeil assured me when she came on the line. "I have extra provisions."

"Thought you would."

"What's happening there?" I started to fill her in on our visit with Nessie Murphy. "Back up!" she pleaded. "I thought you guys were hallucinating about the obituary, and Attica, and the other improbable aspects of the affair, which turned out to be based in fact. So I missed a lot of it before I really tuned in. Give me the rundown. Briefly."

"All right. Here's what we know so far. Declan was supposed to eliminate two informers in Ireland."

"I find it so hard to believe that Declan's a killer," she said.

"Was, forty years ago. He would have considered himself a soldier at the time, or so I assume. And it's not a role he enjoyed. He disobeyed his orders to kill the second traitor. The second guy betrayed the IRA to the authorities, and the IRA thought Declan was in on it. He wasn't. But he was sentenced to death. He took some IRA cash and fled to New York. Life was hell for Teresa and the children, as you heard, and the tension escalated when Teresa's parents announced they were coming to New York. Declan panicked and came up with the down payment for a house in Sunnyside. He told you he borrowed it from a loan shark. So then he started working nights at the White Gardenia. This was in addition to his day job, a legitimate business he set up importing Irish goods.

"It was probably at the Gardenia that he learned of the stash of weapons lying in a warehouse on Pier One in Brooklyn. Thinking this might be the way to make things right with the IRA, he conscripted Mr. Desmond and young Gerald Connors into helping him steal the guns and ship them to Ireland." In my report to Maura, I skipped over Vi Dibney, the attempted seduction of Connors, and Vi's one-night stand with Declan. "The people running the Gardenia almost certainly had their eyes on the guns, if that's where he heard about them, so he was unpopular in that arena for a while too. I got the impression he had to work for free for a while to make up for it. A young waiter at the club, Ramon, got wind of Declan's activities, and tried to blackmail him about them. Declan turned the tables, and extorted money from Ramon. The bank records in the Burkes' attic showed that Declan was spending this money somewhere as soon as he received the payments. He told you he was supporting a worthy charity with the money. Who knows what he meant by that? Meanwhile Gerald Connors, who was convicted in the waterfront heist, went to prison and was stabbed to death by strangers.

"Cathal Murphy, who had immigrated to the US to do some serious gun-running of his own, knew all or most of this history. When Gerry Connors's son learned how his father died, he found out about Cathal through his own contacts in Ireland, and went to see him. What Cathal wouldn't tell him, Nessie did when she published the obituary after Cathal's death in December. She put a coded message in the obit, giving Connors's son Declan's name. Declan was shot in March. Simple, really."

I left Francis out of my account. If the whole story ever came to light, she would hear about it then.

I couldn't unwind after my conversation with Maura. We had pieced together a chronology of events but there were gaps in our knowledge. We didn't know how Francis fit in with the obituary, if in fact he did. Nessie knew nothing about Francis, I was almost certain, because she would not have held back if she had such explosive information about Declan and Teresa's son. And I didn't think she was aware of the Mob connection. There was nothing about that in the obit. I had suspected Declan may have got involved in criminal activities with Patrizio Corialli, but now I didn't think so. That, at least, was not in Declan's character. True, he had been desperate for money and had gone to a loan shark. That's when he learned of the White Gardenia security job, which he needed to supplement his income. He committed one crime, the waterfront heist. The Mob considered the gun cache their own property, so Declan fell out of favour over that. Maybe he worked at the club for free after the gun fiasco. But Corialli obviously considered that a minor matter, long forgotten. Declan was acquainted with Mob figures, but he was not one of them.

Yet Nessie Murphy knew more — about something — than she was telling us. She had left us with the taunt that nobody had deciphered the entire obituary.

And there she sat, smug and hostile in her flat, in possession of the diaries and other secret records that could explain — and expose — the whole sinister affair. I entertained myself that night visiting a number of bars in lower Manhattan, but I kept a clear head. My mind had homed in on a single point: the collection of papers in Nessie's flat. I didn't know how I was going to do it, but I was going to walk out of there with the papers in my hands.

I was in a foul mood by the time I arrived at Nessie Murphy's place the next morning. What were the chances she would give up, or peddle for an extortionate price, the incriminating papers? The day was hot and bright, but she was not in her regular spot on the stoop, basking lizard-like in the sun. I rapped on her door. No reply. I rapped again, louder. I did not want to make two trips — I never wanted to see her again — so it had to be now. I tried the doorknob and pushed. The door swung open. I called her name as I stepped into the hallway. Silence.

When I looked into her living room, I reeled backwards in shock. The room was a shambles of blood and chaos; the smell of death overpowered the stale odour of smoke that hung in the room. I fought down the urge to be sick. My first thought — and it shamed me — was: *What have I touched?* My second thought was to look down at my feet to make sure I had not stepped in anything that would show up in a shoe print. Nessie Murphy was face down on the floor, blood pooled around her head. There was spatter on the walls and the couch. Lying on its side near her body was the DC3 ashtray stand; ashes and cigarette butts littered the floor around her. The bronze propellers of the old aircraft were bent and broken. The heavy marble ashtray rested against her head. I didn't have to be a forensic investigator to know it had been used to club her to death. Her horse figurines were nowhere in sight. Books had been yanked from the bookcase in the corner. The scene suggested she had been dead for a while. But not that long: I had been there myself less than twenty-four hours ago. Was that why she had been killed, because I had been here?

Every instinct told me to bolt. But I steeled myself to go through with my plan, to retrieve the papers. I was treading on dangerous ground, interfering with a crime scene and plotting a theft of what would be key evidence for the police investigating her death. But I took a deep breath and told myself to get moving. Then I noticed a pair of worn bedroom slippers sticking out of the hall closet. I removed my shoes and socks, and shoved my bare feet into the slippers. Let those be the footprints they find, if any. As I made my way to the back of the flat, I was relieved to see that the blood and gore were confined to the area immediately around the victim. I peered into the first bedroom. Like the living room, it had been tossed. An old-fashioned jewellery box had been upended on the bed; the mattress was askew as if someone had groped beneath it. On the floor beside the bed was a plastic shopping bag with photographs spilling out of it; I dumped the pictures and wrapped the bag around my right hand before touching any items in the room. No papers. I proceeded to the other bedroom. Here again all the items had been rifled. Two battered leather briefcases had been wrenched open and left empty. I searched every drawer and shelf but found no documents, no diary.

I had just entered the kitchen when I heard a sudden creaking sound, and my heart banged in my chest. I stood perfectly still, covered in a sheen of sweat. Nothing happened. After a few tense moments I resumed my quest but again found nothing. How long till someone came to the flat? I grabbed a paper towel from the holder and left the kitchen. I looked ahead through the hallway to the front door and saw a car slowing down in front of the house. I held my breath. It moved on. Probably just on the hunt for a parking space. I searched the front closet, only to confirm what I already knew: the papers were gone.

I was so desperate to get away I felt my heart might give out before I got clear of the building. I toed off the slippers, grabbed my shoes with shaking hands, shoved them on my feet, kicked the slippers back into position, looked around again to reassure myself I had not left behind any markers visible to the naked eye, then wiped the doorknob with the paper towel, closed the door, removed the plastic bag, stuffed it along with the paper towel in my pocket, and walked as calmly from the house as if I had been there to sell the obstinate old woman a life-insurance policy. I did not see anyone about, but that did not mean there were not curious eyes behind the curtains of the dilapidated houses on the street. I got into my car, fumbled and dropped my keys, finally got the car going, and drove away from the neighbourhood. My eyes were drawn obsessively to the rearview mirror; where did that white van come from? Good, it veered off. After motoring aimlessly for half an hour, I stopped several towns away and threw the paper towel and plastic bag in a Dumpster. Convinced at last that it was safe to return to the hotel, I headed in that direction, narrowly averting a collision that would have been entirely my fault. When I got to my room I showered and changed, then collapsed on the bed. When I finally felt calm enough I got up and drove back across the river, went to a pay phone close to the Brooklyn Bridge, called 911, reported Nessie's death in what I hoped was a generic New York accent, hung up and hightailed it to the Burkes'.

What did it mean that the papers were gone? Had Nessie destroyed them herself before falling victim to a murderer's hand? Was this a simple break-in, someone preying on a crippled old lady, taking a few keepsakes to be sold at a flea market? Unlikely. The burglar had one purpose and one purpose alone: the retrieval of the records that had been a threat to somebody's security for forty years. The theft of her trinkets was a cover-up. Was the murder a by-product of the need to get the papers? Or was it a planned execution?

†

Brennan was the only one home; his parents were still at church. He came to the door carrying a book, which I saw was a breviary. I was about to shatter his mood of peaceful contemplation.

"Nessie Murphy is dead."

He stared at me. "Dead!"

"Murdered."

"God save us! How do you know this?"

I described what I had found. "And I did not cover myself with glory at the scene."

"What do you mean?"

"I sneaked around the house while she was lying there, covered my hand with a plastic bag and proceeded to search the place. Looking for the obituary, the diaries and whatever other papers Cathal had and Nessie found. Which is what I went for in the first place."

"And?"

"The papers weren't there."

"I see." He looked beyond me to the window. "Christ only knows what was in those papers. I wonder how easy it would be for someone to make sense of them. Nessie knew her brother's writing, and obviously had a sense of whatever shorthand he might have used. Perhaps his scribblings won't make sense to anyone else."

"Somebody wanted them badly enough to kill for them. That individual will be able to decipher them." I thought for a moment. "Those code books on Nessie's shelf. The ones she used for the little bit of encryption she did in the obituary. There were no library stickers on those books, nothing on the spines. She didn't hoof it all the way to the library in her walker. That little scene never happened."

"So she bought them."

"You didn't see them, Brennan. Those books were well past their 'best before' date."

"Secondhand book shop? No," he replied in answer to his own question, "she couldn't have assumed there would be code books on offer, and she wouldn't have done all the standing that is part of a trip to a used book shop. So, old code books in the apartment. Cathal's?"

"Could be. If they were hers, and she had a long familiarity with them, I don't think we would have heard so much about how she devised an easy code for someone she knew to have worked in Army Intelligence. She wouldn't have explained it. So yes, I'd say they were Cathal's. And now they're gone. Other books were left behind, but not the code books. Were the IRA into that kind of tradecraft?"

He shrugged. "I wouldn't know."

How would the IRA and its supporters have operated in those days? It was probably a minor point and I did not want to turn it into a research project. Maybe there had been some information in the news clipping about the waterfront heist. Had the story mentioned IRA codes, or subterfuges of that nature? I didn't think so. The news story gave the name of an investigating officer, I remembered, but the robbery had occurred nearly forty years ago. What were the chances the cop was still alive? Well, Declan was still kicking, and Nessie Murphy had been, until yesterday. What was the officer's name? Rose? No, that was the lawyer.

"Brennan, where's the clipping your niece found, the news story about Gerald Connors?"

He left the room and came back with the photocopy. I scanned it: a straightforward report of crime and punishment. No details about the clandestine operations of the IRA. The police officer was a Constable Seamus O'Brien. A constable could be any age, given the large numbers of cops and the limited opportunities for promotion.

"So, where did you go after you found the body?"

I looked at Brennan and turned my mind to the present. "I went back to the hotel, showered, changed my clothes, drove to a pay phone in Brooklyn and made an anonymous call to 911 about Nessie, then came over here. Jesus Christ! I just left the woman lying there, I tried to steal evidence —" My voice had risen and I willed myself to calm down. "All right, Brennan. Who knows about our visits with Nessie?"

"I'm not sure."

I waited, but he had nothing to say. Finally, I asked: "Do your brothers know?"

"I don't think so. The only one I would have told would have been

Patrick. And I don't think I did."

"Terry?"

"No. I wasn't speaking to Terry about it."

"How about your sister?"

"No."

"Was Francis in on any of the discussions about this?"

"Not with me."

I let a few moments pass. "And Declan. Does he know?"

He looked at me sharply. "We don't know what he knows, but he didn't get any of it from me."

"Right." Now, last but not least: "Did you tell Leo Killeen?"

He gave me an appraising look, then answered: "No."

"I mean, in confessional mode or in any other —"

"No."

"So, what do we do now?"

"Now we drop it."

"What?"

"It's Easter. You're missing your family. You'll be going home soon. Enjoy the rest of your time here."

"But —"

"You've been exposed to a shooting, now a murder. If you'd turned up there sooner, you might have ended up with Nessie on the floor. In fact, you may be in danger anyway because whoever killed Nessie and took the papers may know that you —"

"And you, Brennan. But I don't think so. I'm not able to think straight today, but if I were betting on this I'd say the killer got what he wanted: the papers. If he knows we're involved, he knows why we're involved. We're in it for Declan. And if he knows Declan, he knows the man wouldn't talk about this business even if his life depended on it. The killer knows we're not going to appear on the six o'clock news. Nessie was the tattletale, the informer. Now she's been silenced and her brother's papers safely removed from prying eyes."

"What are you saying? That this isn't the same man who tried to kill my father? We've got two maniacs running around attacking people? I don't take much comfort from that thought." He was quiet for a few seconds, then picked up the thread again. "But I suppose the fact that the two attacks were so different — my father shot by a meticulous executioner with a gun, the old woman hit over the head with a piece of furniture —"

"Oh, I don't put any stock in that, Brennan. I think Nessie's killing was an execution. I think it was made to look like a burglary to muddy the waters. Our killer — if there is only one — is doing damage control. He knows she had the goods on the Irish operation back in the 1950s."

"But who, aside from my father, would care about all that now? As far as we know it's only Declan who would lose if his role were exposed. The other man, Connors, paid the price years ago."

It was a good point and it made me think. What were we missing?

Brennan continued: "We've always taken the position that my father was shot in revenge for his part in that heist, shot by someone whose life was altered as a result of it. And I still think that's true. We have to find Gerard Willman."

I made no comment. I was not yet ready to announce that the attempt on Declan might be personal. That it came from the very heart of his family. And that the obituary might represent another avenue of inquiry altogether, whether parallel to, or intersecting with, the path taken by Francis. Was it possible Cathal and Francis knew each other? Where did Gerard Willman fit in? I would have to check with Terry to see whether the skip tracer had found him.

I heard Teresa and Declan coming in the door, and my thoughts returned to Cathal. I thought of Nessie's mean-spirited account of her brother's obsession with Teresa Burke, an obsession that impelled him to uproot himself and his sister from their home, so he could follow Teresa to New York. How much did Teresa know about Cathal Murphy, or Charlie Fagan as he was called in Ireland?

I eventually got Mrs. Burke on her own, and wasted no time in getting to the point: "Teresa, when you showed Declan the obituary of Cathal Murphy, did you know who Cathal was?"

"No, I didn't."

"Do you know who he is now?"

"My husband recently — belatedly — gave me a terse explanation that this was a fellow by the name of Charlie Fagan, from Dublin. Declan wasn't very forthcoming, but I gathered it had been a man we had seen around the city. I remembered him after that."

"But before that — before Declan's outpourings on the subject — did the name set off any bells in your mind? When you first read the obituary?"

"No. Cathal is a common name in Ireland. It's a common name in the Irish Republican Army, for that matter. Or was."

"Tell me about Charlie Fagan when you knew him in Dublin."

"I hardly knew him at all, Monty. He worked in a shop. I used to say hello to him. He was a nice young man, but I didn't know anything about him."

"Did you know he was in love with you?"

"I wouldn't go so far as to say that. I noticed he was shy whenever I was around, but if I'd thought about it I'd have assumed he was like that with all young women." She gave a helpless shrug.

"Were you aware that he had followed you over here?"

"No!"

"Were you ever aware of a man following you or watching you here in New York?"

"The children used to cod me about a secret admirer. 'He was out there again, Mam!' I paid them no mind. I'm sorry, Monty, I'm of no use to you here. To more pleasant subjects now: Terry and Sheila have invited us all over for Easter dinner. Patrick and his little girls will be there. I hope you'll be joining us."

Either that or I'd be moping around by myself somewhere. "If you can bear the sight of me any longer, I'd love to come."

"You're a part of the family now, Monty. I only wish Bridey could come up for it. I don't quite know whether I should wish for Francis or not!"

Bridey yes, Francis no. Francis never, if you knew what I know.

Teresa left the room and Brennan came in. I recounted my talk with his mother. "Bridey was teasing your mother at the wedding reception, about a secret admirer. Bridey called him Mack. Do you remember any of this?"

"I vaguely remember a joke about it. Didn't pay much attention. Here." He picked up a pen and paper and wrote down a number. "Give her a call."

"Bridey?"

"No, Saint Dymphna."

So I dialled the number and a young boy answered. "Hi. Is your mother there?"

"One second please." A series of bangs and then Bridey came on the line.

"Hello?"

"Hello, Bridey. It's Monty."

"Oh! How are you, Monty?"

"Fine. Listen. Brennan and I are wondering if you can help with something."

"Sure. Ask away."

"Do you remember, when we had lunch together —" Brennan looked at me "— I brought up the secret admirer you were teasing your mother about, but I can't remember exactly what you said."

"You don't think this guy had something to do with the shooting! Please don't tell me that!" Her voice had risen half an octave.

"No, if it's who we think it was, he's dead. But I'd certainly like to hear what you remember."

"It's just that when we were kids we saw a man kind of sauntering along a few blocks behind us when Mam would take us out somewhere."

"How many times did this happen?"

"Only two or three. That I saw, or remember. One time Terry and I were playing a few houses down and saw him watching our mother hanging out clothes."

"How old was he?"

"Oh, Monty, you know kids. A grown-up is a grown-up. He could have been thirty-five; he could have been fifty, for all we knew."

"What did he look like? How did he act?"

"I can't remember what he looked like, honestly. Just a man. Nothing unusual about his clothes. I picture him in a shirt and tie, with a sweater and a tweed jacket. He wore one of those hats the men all wore in those days. What do you call it, a fedora? He didn't do anything. Just stood there with his hands linked behind his back."

"You mentioned a nickname you had for him. Mack, was it?"

"That's right. I can't remember why, maybe just because that was a common word back then. Got a light, Mack? Get lost, Mack. I don't know."

"Anything else?"

"No. Does Bren recall any of this?"

"Apparently not."

"Terry might. He and I got into a big fight in connection with this man, but I can't think what the fight was about. Shit. What was it? We got in trouble and, typical brother and sister, each of us tried to blame the other. We followed him! My God, I haven't thought of that in years. Terry and I set out to follow the guy. And we were late getting home. Somehow we ended up in a big snit, and I punched Terry in the face. I have no idea what any of that was about. Ask Terry; I'd love to hear it!"

"I'll give him a call. Where did you follow him to? Mack."

"I can't remember anything else about it, where we went or anything. I'm really sorry. But try Terry."

"Thanks, Bridey. Well, bye for now."

"Good luck!"

"They followed him!" I announced to Brennan. "She and Terry, but she can't remember where or what happened."

He picked up the phone to call his brother. But Terry's memories were even more foggy than Bridey's. Brennan filled me in as the conversation went on. Terry barely remembered the jokes about the secret admirer or the one attempt to follow him. The fight didn't register: "He's supposed to remember every time he took a punch from one of his siblings? It's all a punch-drunk blur!"

Then Brennan said: "Grand. I'll tell him." To me: "You're invited for dinner."

"Thank him." He did and hung up.

"I wish we could hear more about those two young operatives," I remarked, "when they put the tail on Cathal. Let's hope Bridey gives it some thought and brings forth some more details."

"We'll get Patrick to put her on the couch and hypnotize her; bring back all her repressed memories."

"Are you serious?"

"No."

"Does he really do hypnosis?"

"It's not an everyday occurrence, from what he's told me. Are you serious?"

"I'm not going to sit here and tell you to have your brother put your sister under a hypnotic spell. But if you suggest it, I'll be happy to go along. We need all the help we can get."

"We'll have him put Terry under too. Though I'm not sure I'd want to listen to whatever he'd say in a trance."

†

Easter dinner was sumptuous. Nobody mentioned the crisis, nobody mentioned Francis.

I awoke the next day with a longing to be back in Halifax. It looked as though I would not have the satisfaction of solving the riddles surrounding Declan Burke before I left New York, and I found that vexing. I had one more lead: the name of a cop, Seamus O'Brien. Would he still be around, nearly forty years after the investigation? I wouldn't get anywhere calling the police department and asking for the home number of one of their retired officers, so I went down to the hotel lobby and asked for copies of all the New York borough telephone directories to be delivered to my room. I had breakfast and went up to start working through the O'Briens. The responses to my calls varied wildly, but I finally got through to a Seamus in Brooklyn, who parried my questions for about two minutes, then admitted he was Lieutenant Seamus O'Brien's son. The "Loo" was still living in New York. The son would call him and, if the Loo was interested, I'd hear from him. If not, fuggedaboudit. So I gave my cover story, and hoped for the best.

A bit of touring was in order so I headed up to the Bronx, where I had a look around the campus of Fordham University, then checked out Yankee Stadium. I had an early supper at a place called Dominick's, where I shared a table with friends of the family that had been running the place for a quarter of a century. I could hardly move by the time I got up to leave.

I placed a call to my own family in Halifax that evening. Tommy Douglas and I discussed music, specifically, whether I thought he'd look like a "hot dog" in front of his friends if he played a sax solo he had written. I said he wouldn't, especially if he just eased into the number without announcing it. He put Maura on the phone and we chatted about the day's activities until I asked for Normie.

"She's not here. She's staying at Kim's for the night."

"So, what's the occasion that Normie gets a sleepover on a school night?"

"Does there have to be an occasion?"

"Well, she usually doesn't stay out on a school night, considering how tired she gets."

"I'm going out."

"I see."

"What do you mean, 'I see'? You make it sound as if I opened a hoor house as soon as I bundled the child out the door."

"I didn't make it sound any way. I just wonder what came first, Kim's invitation, or —"

"Or the big shipment of oysters and opium at the container pier."

"All right, all right. Just make sure she catches up on her sleep and settles down to her schoolwork."

"Oh, I won't have to. I imagine Children's Aid will have stepped in before sunrise tomorrow."

"For Christ's sake!"

"I hate to break this up but I have to go rouge my lips before my Moroccan gigolo gets here."

"So much for the pretence that he's a Roman consul."

"Piss off." Click.

I slammed the phone down and it immediately shrilled back at me. Could she do that? I picked it up and shouted into it: "What!"

"Exhibiting a little hostility this evening, are we? If you'd like to come and see me, I could help you work through it." Patrick Burke sounded highly amused.

"Oh hi, Pat. I wouldn't have been so rude if I'd known it wasn't my wife!"

"I won't offer any further professional comment. I spoke to Bridey and she loves the idea of being put under a spell. Says she wants me to ask her about everyone who attended that notorious family luncheon, so she can say what she really thinks and not be blamed for it." I hoped it wouldn't come to that. "She's arriving late tomorrow, so if you'd like to come up to the office around five or so we'll see what she remembers about our mother's mysterious suitor."

"Thanks, Patrick. I'll see you there."

I hung up gently that time, but my thoughts returned to my wife. I had been hoping the New York holiday would bring us back together, and there were times when the mood had been relaxed and non-combative. I had even started to plan the opening lines of a conciliatory speech. But the vacation had a perilous start — the call to Giacomo, the misunderstanding about the evening with Rosemary. Now this. Perhaps it was time to draw the papers up and admit defeat. Some marriages should be taken out and shot; maybe this was one of them. I threw myself on the bed and tried to decide what to do that evening. One thing I knew: I was determined to have as good a time as Maura MacNeil was having, or better. After all, *I* was in *Manhattan*.

But I didn't call a lady of the night. I called my priest instead.

I travelled to Queens by subway this time because I knew my blood alcohol level would soon exceed the legal limit. I met Brennan at O'Malley's and we sat side by side at the bar. Neither of us had shaved and both of us were in jeans and T-shirts. Mine was plain grey; Brennan's was black with white lettering: *"da mihi castitatem et continentiam, sed noli modo."* A plea to God from Saint Augustine: *make me chaste and celibate, but not yet!* Burke seemed to have taken the same approach to drinking. That made two of us. But, typically, he had more to say on the subject. When he remarked on the condition we were in after two hours in the pub, I made the mistake of offering a theological opinion: "Well, it's hardly a mortal sin."

He twisted around on the bar stool to face me. "Are you not aware, Montague, that drink is immoderate and intoxicating?"

"Uh . . ."

"Would you rather be drunk than abstain from drinking?"

"Tonight, you mean?"

"Are you aware that morals take their species not from things that occur accidentally and beside the intention, but from that which is directly intended?" He paused for a mouthful of whiskey, and continued: "A man willingly and knowingly deprives himself of the use of reason, whereby he performs virtuous deeds and avoids sin, and thus he sins mortally by running the risk of falling into sin."

"Says who?"

"Says Saint Thomas Aquinas in the Secunda-Secundae of the *Summa Theologica.*"

"Oh." We turned back to our drinks.

Sandra's name came up during the course of our musings; to be more accurate, I brought it up. "You can't just leave things the way you did with Sandra."

"Why not?"

"Get together with her. Clear things up."

"They're clear now. The woman walked out on me. Wouldn't you be able to take a hint if someone . . . em, well . . ."

"Aha," I pounced, "you don't want to pursue that line of reasoning, do you? You just about gave it away: the truth that old Monty, who's been walked out on more times than he can count, by the mother of his children, should finally admit defeat and bring the curtain down on his own charade of a marriage. While you —"

"I think no such thing about Collins and MacNeil. There is, on the contrary, no Father Burke and Miss Worthington. The left side of my brain has known that all along, even if other parts of me were temporarily confused."

"If you never intend to see her again, tell her."

"She doesn't care. How thick are you, Monty?"

"Go see her. Maybe you'll be surprised." Probably not, given Sandra's admission to me and Maura that she would never take the risk of falling in love with him again. But maybe there was hope if they were face to face. I never give up.

"There's no future in it," Brennan declared.

"Then tell her."

"She can tell me, if she thinks I'm stupid enough to have missed it the first time."

That is how we ended up in a cab, heading to the East Seventies in Manhattan. Burke had grabbed one for the road, a pint of Guinness. We heard a siren screaming and saw an ambulance bearing down on us from the cross street on our left. The cab driver cursed and swerved, and Brennan's pint spilled all over his shirt and pants.

The normally fastidious priest did not seem to notice. In fact, he nodded off just as we approached the Upper East Side. I nudged him and he jerked awake when we pulled up in front of Sandra's townhouse. He fumbled in his wallet for the fare and we stumbled out.

I rang the intercom and was buzzed in without having to identify myself. Was she expecting company? She was indeed. The door was ajar when we arrived. There were half a dozen people in the room, dressed for an evening out. I smelled coffee brewing, so I concluded they had been out to dinner and had come back for a cup and a chat. But it was more than that; it was soon evident that we had blundered into a meeting of sorts. Seated in an armchair, Sandra looked effortlessly elegant in a pair of cream linen pants and a silk sweater in pale aqua. She didn't notice our entrance because she was writing in a notebook. Without looking up, she said: "Pamela, that's when you'll introduce Reggie to the rest of the board."

A tall woman with expensively styled silver hair picked up a clipboard and consulted it. "I have here: 'The gallery is pleased to welcome Reginald Bagley Baines. Reg and his family have been serving their country since his mother's ancestors came over on the *Mayflower* and disembarked at Plymouth Rock.' That won't embarrass you, I hope, Reggie!" Reggie Baines was standing by the marble fireplace, looking anything but embarrassed.

"My family came over on the *Piss-a-bed* and disembarked at Hell's Kitchen!"

Shocked faces and elaborately coiffed heads swivelled in the direction of the boozy Irish voice. Only then did the board of directors realize their meeting had been crashed by two dishevelled drunks. Sandra stared. "Brennan! Good evening, Monty. What a surprise."

"Brendan?" Reggie demanded. "Sandra, is this the individual who caused you so much grief and mortification in the past? If so, it appears he hasn't improved with time. Should I call security?"

"That won't be necessary, Reg. Coffee, Brennan?"

"Would ya have a wee drop of anything to put in it, darlin'?"

"I'd rather not."

"Forgive me for saying so, Brennan or whoever you are," Baines said then, "but it's guys like you who give a bad name to an entire race of people."

"Ah, now, Reg, don't be makin' all the Puritans look intolerant. It's not as if it's a mortal sin to have drink taken."

"This man is hopeless."

"How's your dad, Brennan?"

"The gunshot wound is healing nicely, thank you, Sandra. But it's the scars inside that never heal, isn't it? Mild, sensitive soul that he is, my oul da can't understand why anyone would have a grudge against him."

Sandra smiled in spite of herself. "Why indeed?"

"Your father. This is the man who was shot at a family wedding, am I right?" Reg asked.

"He's 'a man' who was shot at a family wedding. I'm sure it happens all the time."

Not among our sort, Reg refrained from saying. But his expression said it clearly.

Brennan plopped down heavily on the pale yellow chesterfield, causing the clipboard woman to jolt upwards, then fall over against his shoulder. She jerked away and clung to the arm of the couch. He gave her a loopy smile.

"Let us carry on, shall we?" Sandra said. "Excuse me for a moment while I pour the coffee."

The clipboard woman consulted her notes. "I have our letter to the gallery in Florence. And I had a friend translate it into Italian; I thought that might be a nice touch, posing the request in the curator's mother tongue. Now apparently the curator, Signor Falda, is reluctant to lend us the artist's entire oeuvre from that period, but I think we should insist. That was our starting position, and I felt we had the agreement of the government person I spoke to."

"Is this the Uffizi you're talking about?" Brennan inquired.

She favoured him with a condescending smile. "The Uffizi is the most famous gallery in Florence but it's not the only one. We are dealing with the National Museum."

"Right. The Museo Nazionale in the old Bargello. You're looking for sculpture, is it? Ceramics, that sort of thing? I don't know the curator but you may want to call Luca Carracci."

"Really."

"Really."

"His name again . . ."

"Give me your pen and I'll write it out for you." He leaned over, she drew back, but she shoved the pen and the clipboard into his hands.

He scribbled at the top of the page. "This is his name, this is where he works." He peered at the letter. "What's this now? No, no, you can't say that. It means 'what we want is.' That would sound rude and pushy to an Italian. You need the conditional tense there. We'll change it to *'vorremmo avere,'* which is 'we would like to have.' And here, where you say you're going to give the ministry an assurance of this or that. It would be less awkward if you changed the indirect pronoun *gli* to *glie* and combine it with the direct-object pronoun *lo* to get *glielo*. Then you should stick it on the end of the verb, so you have *darglielo*. That's better. And, oh no, here's something that's not spelled right . . ."

He went through the entire letter, rewriting it from top to bottom. Was the man drunk at all? Reg stared at him, baffled. Unseen by Brennan, Sandra peered in from the dining room. Reg caught her eye and, with a terse nod, she gave him the news: whatever the sozzled Paddy writes will be correct. She then called out that the coffee was ready. "I hope you'll be having some, Brennan."

"No, don't trouble yourself, Mavourneen. Young Collins here hasn't yet enjoyed a pint over at P.J. Clarke's; we'll be headin' in that direction now."

Sandra saw us to the door. She took Brennan's left hand in her right; he didn't move. "Be sure to look me up next time you're in the city, Brennan."

"I will."

Each gave the other a long, long look before he turned and walked away.

He lit up a smoke when we got out to the street. "Well, there's an end to a pathetic twenty-five year delusion on my part."

"What do you mean?"

"I'll be putting her out of my mind for good. And she'll be happy to be rid of a drunken Irish priest. No loss for her there."

She knew damn well he wasn't as drunk as he appeared to be; she'd seen him with the letter. So I persisted: "She said she wants to see you next time you're in New York."

"She was lying."

"Well, you told her you'd look her up."

"I was lying."

"But . . ."

He gave me a pitying look. "You have a lot to learn about the world, my lad."

Chapter 11

Confiteor Deo omnipotenti . . . et tibi Pater,
quia peccavi nimis cogitatione, verbo, et opere,
mea culpa, mea culpa, mea maxima culpa.

I confess to Almighty God . . . and to you, Father,
that I have sinned exceedingly in thought, word and deed,
through my fault, through my fault, through my most grievous fault.
— Confiteor, the Mass

April 2, 1991

I got a call the next afternoon from a rough-voiced man who said he was Lieutenant O'Brien and he was in McQuaid's bar on Eleventh Avenue if I wanted to meet him for a drink. I left the hotel and walked west and down. A wind had come up and it blew sheets of rain into my face. I was soaked by the time I got there. McQuaid's Public House was a small corner brick building with an awning over the door and shamrocks painted on the outside wall.

Seamus "Shammy" O'Brien was in his late sixties, long retired. He was several inches over six feet and must have weighed in at two-fifty. He sported an iron-grey crewcut, and had the face of a fighter who had taken a good many hits in the ring. Delivered a good many too, I suspected. There wasn't a drop of rain on him; he'd been here awhile.

"Lieutenant O'Brien, thanks for seeing me. I thought you lived in Brooklyn."

"Spent all my working life over there, but I grew up here in Hell's

Kitchen. Place like this, it calls you back." He gave a snort of laughter, then signalled for the bartender. "What are you drinking?"

"A Guinness would be good."

"Two pints, Denny. So, what can I do for you?"

"I'm interested in some of the gun-running that was going on in the 1950s. Over on the other side of the river."

"Oh yeah? What got you interested in that?"

The hapless Desmonds were my cover story. I had no intention of linking Declan's name with the waterfront heist. "I'm a friend of the Desmond family. Does that name mean anything to you?"

"A lot of Desmonds around."

"These people are trying to find out what happened to their father. Big boozer. Drifted off and the family lost touch. The daughter told me something happened on the waterfront when he was a port watchman."

"A lot of stuff happened on the waterfront."

"I hear you. This was in 1952, an incident on Pier One, when some guns were stolen. Desmond was supposed to have been on duty at the time."

"He wasn't. The watchman on duty was an Italian guy. I don't remember his name."

"Rinaldi. I saw it in the news clippings. Which is where I got your name. So Rinaldi was on duty, and he's the one who got clobbered. Was there any mention of a Desmond?"

"Not that I can recall."

"That's good news, I guess, but I was hoping to get more information about this Desmond. The watchman position was the last work the family knew he had."

So the Desmonds were in luck, even if they didn't know it: the police did not associate his name with the crime. But since all this was just my cover for contacting O'Brien, I had better move on.

"Your beat was the waterfront, was it, Lieutenant?"

"That was a good part of my career, yeah."

"You must have come across some real characters."

"Yeah, you could say that. Organized crime makes for some interesting characters. The Cosa Nostra kept me busy in those days. Never a dull moment."

"How about the Irish Mob? How well-organized would they have been? I'm thinking about code books, or —"

"*Organized?* They're Irish!" He raised his pint and wiggled it; a gold Claddagh ring glimmered on his right hand. "Organized would not be the word. Code books? I doubt it!" He shook his head.

"The Desmond woman mentioned a name, but I couldn't find out anything about him. Cathal Murphy. Ever hear of him?" O'Brien shook his head. "He also went by the name Fagan, she thought."

"Fagan, you say?" I had his attention now.

"Yes. I don't know why he had two names."

"I do, if it's Charlie Fagan you're talking about. He was running stolen guns out of here for years. Or so we suspected. I never knew him as Murphy. He stayed in a little rathole in Williamsburg. Lived like a monk. The Irish Republican movement was part of his religion. He was good, I'll say that for him. Quite the operative. We could never catch him meeting with anybody in the gun racket. We figured he was using a go-between, a courier, to take the money to the suppliers. But we never saw it happening. We never saw him socializing. He worked in a manufacturing plant, came off shift and went home. We kept an eye on the plant for a while but, as far as we could make out, he didn't have any Mick contacts there. He spent the occasional evening in a pub but all he ever drank was soda, and he didn't have any regular pals."

"How did you know he was moving stolen guns if you never caught him at it?"

"Well, I shouldn'ta said 'never.' We nailed him once. We were following an Irishman who we knew had flown over from the old country specifically to set up an arms network. This guy met with Fagan. But even then we could only get him for illegal possession of firearms. We couldn't pin anything on the guy from Ireland. Fagan copped a plea, did his time like a man, didn't give anybody up. He wasn't inside very long."

"When was that?"

"Early fifties. Fagan must have become a lot more sophisticated after his experience in the clink. We believed he was still at it for a long time after that, but we never had enough evidence to charge him."

"When you say he lived like a monk, how do you mean?"

"Lived alone in this one-room dive near the waterfront."

"Alone?"

"Yeah, he wasn't married. I had a warrant to search his place one time. A little cot of a bed and a hot plate to cook on. Didn't bother to hide his inclinations: the only reading material was Irish history, Irish saints and church stuff. Missals, holy cards, that kind of thing. The guy went to Mass every day of his life, far as I know. We had guys tail him into Saint Bridey's a few times but he was just praying and attending Mass; he wasn't hiding or slipping out the back door."

So Cathal had kept two apartments, one of his own and one for Nessie. Maybe he couldn't afford to drink!

"What kind of job did Fagan have? Manufacturing, you said?"

"Yeah. He spent his workday in the warehouse, shipping and receiving. The outfit made aviation parts or something. Desailes Inc."

Picturing the arms smuggler in Mass every day reminded me of a detail Patrick had dug up about Cathal Murphy's funeral. "Did you attend his funeral?"

"What?"

"Fagan's funeral. You weren't among the mourners, were you?"

"Not fucking likely. I didn't know he croaked."

So O'Brien wasn't the lone man at the back of the church.

"One other thing, Lieutenant. What about women?"

"We never saw him squiring any dames around town. He paid a lot of visits to this crippled girl. Relative of some kind. But, like I say, a real monkish type."

"So. Not the type to follow women around."

"Where did that come from?"

"Just something that came up," I said, unconvincingly.

"I don't know what you're driving at. But if you're talking about Fagan following somebody and he was spotted, it's because he wanted to be seen. Otherwise, nobody would ever have known he was there."

✝

It was time to scoot up to Patrick Burke's office. It was in a red-brick Victorian row house on the Upper West Side, with a bow window and a flower box. Patrick arrived at the same time I did, and we entered his waiting room.

"Is my sister here yet?" he asked his secretary.

"Not yet. There are a few telephone messages for you." She handed him a stack of pink slips. "And here's another one: 'Tell Doctor Burke he's a fraud and a quack and I have no intention of putting myself in his hands. T.' Can't win 'em all I guess, Doctor."

"That would be my brother Terry. Long years of training and experience lead me to the conclusion that he will not be participating in our session today."

Shit. "That's too bad," I said.

"Think about it, Monty. Would you really like to see an airline pilot go into a hypnotic trance in response to monotonous sights and sounds? Would you ever fly again?"

"You've got a point there."

"We'll get what we can out of —"

"Hi, Paddy! Put me under, put me out, put me down, I don't care. I've had the most aggravating day. Oh, hi, Monty! I'd give you a big hello kiss but not under the watchful eyes of Doctor Freud here. He probably took note of whether your pupils dilated at the sight of me. Did they?" she demanded of her brother.

"No, I didn't see anything get bigger."

She dropped a heavy handbag on the floor and collapsed in a chair.

"How are you, Bridey?" I asked her.

"Don't ask. How many kids have you got?"

"Two."

"Don't have any more."

"Not much chance of that."

"All right, sweetheart," her brother said, "I explained to you on the phone what we're going to do here. Would you like anything before we start? Tea? A glass of water?" She shook her head. "Just make yourself comfortable and I'm going to help you relax."

She closed her eyes. Patrick began to talk to her in a soothing voice. A couple of times her eyes opened, and she looked over at me. Her brother caught on and turned towards me. I was a distraction.

"I'll wait outside, Pat," I said and left the office. Sooner than I would have expected, his secretary came out and beckoned me inside. Patrick motioned for me to sit behind Bridey's chair, and he got her started on her recollections of the man who had followed her mother decades before.

"Me and Terry have money to go to Zuckerman's for a treat. We're s'posed to bring something back for everybody."

"How old are you now, Bridey?" Pat asked her.

"I'm seven! There's that man again! He's on our street. Now he's moving away. We're following him to the bus stop. He can't see us hiding behind the tree. Me and Terry are getting on the bus. Everybody thinks this lady with the shopping bags is our mother. When we get home we're going to tell all about this man and where he lives. Mam will give us chocolate milk. Fran will be jealous. The man's not even looking at us. Boo! No, we don't want him to know. He's staring out the window. We're going a long ways from home. Terry's pointing out everything he sees. I tell him to shut up. We're secret agents! Oh, the man is getting off here. Us, too. He's crossing the street. Red light! We can't go. But we keep watching. Now we go. Long walk. The gardens! Bren and Molly took us here before. Brooklyn Botanic Garden, Terry says, reading the sign. Shut up, Terry. We sneak in behind some people with a bunch of cameras around their necks. We should have brought Paddy's camera. It's beautiful in the garden, with all the trees and flowers. Good places to hide! There he goes. Now he's sitting on a bench, reading the paper.

"The man is just sitting there. I'm hungry and Terry is making me mad. He's climbing the trees and you're not allowed to. I hope he gets in trouble. This is no fun. The man didn't go to his house, so we can't find out where he lives. Da is going to kill us for being away so long. He'll give Terry a crack on the arse and send me to my room. I have to pee. I already did, Terry says. Where, in the bushes? Look! The man is getting up. He's following that other guy that just walked past the bench. Terry is whispering that our guy is Number One and the new guy is Number Two. Bet they wouldn't like those names! There they go, out of the park. That's Number Two's car. There's a bunch of boys peeking in the windows of the car. They're gonna get in trouble. Number Two is yelling something at them; I can't make it out. The boys are taking off. Both the men are getting in the car. Driving away. Now we can't follow them. Now we have to find the bus home. What number was it?"

We could see Bridey becoming agitated, a little girl in Brooklyn, with no idea how to get back to Queens.

I signalled a question to Patrick. *The car?*

"What does the car look like, Bridey?"

"Black and shiny. Brand new."

"What's happening now?"

"I'm scared. We're at the bus stop. Terry's telling this lady we're orphans and the Sunnyside Orphanage bus forgot us and we don't have any money. But we do! The lady is patting his hair and giving him two bus tickets. We're waiting. She's giving us two candy bars! She says get on this bus that's coming now." Bridey stopped abruptly.

"So you get home . . ." Patrick prompted.

"And we're in trouble. Mam was worried. Lucky Da's not here."

What had Bridey said the other day? Something about Terry, and a fight. It sounded like the kind of day that would wind up in a crying spell. I found a pen and paper and scribbled a note: *She and T had a fight.*

"Are you and Terry talking about what happened?"

"We're in a fight. We were going to make a big announcement at dinner time, that we followed the man who loves our mother. Now we don't want to tell. And Terry's saying it wrong."

"Saying what wrong?"

"Some word. I just punched Terry in the face. He's mad and he says he's saying it right. But we both gave the guy his nickname, Mack. That's where it came from."

"Where did it come from, Bridey? I don't understand."

"From Potomac! That's what it is. I say it's 'Po-TO-mac' and Terry says it's 'POT-o-mac,' but it's okay because both ways you get Mack, and that's what we're going to call the man from now on."

Patrick looked at me and shrugged. I mouthed a question: *Why Potomac?*

"You're telling us about Potomac, Bridey. Why did that word come up?"

"His car. Man Number Two's car. It had a sticker on the back that said 'Potomac Auto Rental.' We got all excited, because you can rent any car you want. We're going to get Da to borrow one a lot fancier than our car and take us for a drive."

Patrick brought her out of her hypnotic state, and the three of us sat in his office trying to fit the new information with what we already had. I would have to be careful not to let anything slip about Francis.

"It sounds to me as if Cathal — the man following your mother — was playing a double game," I said. "The police knew he was running guns to the old country. But they couldn't catch him at anything except a minor offence. Now we have him meeting, and following some kind of tradecraft, with a guy from Washington. Imagine how that would go over back home, their man in New York meeting an FBI agent. When did he turn informant, I wonder. And now, all these years later, Cathal's sister is murdered." Drop it, Leo had warned. Whatever the Irish connection to the shooting of Declan, and whatever Francis's role in it, there was no longer any doubt in my mind that the Irish were involved in the death of Nessie Murphy.

I was about to speak again when a low-pitched, pleasant ring issued forth from Patrick's phone.

"Yes? Put him through. Terry! Change your mind? Care to put yourself under my power and — I'll take that as a no. Yeah, I think we did. A Washington connection, it seems. Just to muddy the waters even more. Yes, he is. Here, I'll put him on."

"Hi Terry."

"I heard from our skip tracer. We've found Gerard Willman. Why don't we meet at O'Malley's and figure out where to go from here."

Terry, Patrick, Brennan, Bridey and I shoved two tables together at the back of O'Malley's, where we sat with pints of Guinness and shots of whiskey according to taste. Mickey was presiding as usual, and regulars lined the bar, poring over their racing sheets in the dim light. At one point they all roared a greeting to a man who was the head of something called the Hay Ho Haitch, which, I was told, was an approximation of the initials of the Ancient Order of Hibernians.

Patrick was the first to get down to business. "All right. What are we going to do about this fellow Gerard?"

"Break his kneecaps," Terry suggested.

I looked at him as if to say: *The kneecaps you break may be those of your brother.* He closed his eyes and raised a hand as if to ward me off. I knew he had built his hopes up about Gerard, and who could blame him? But the fact remained: brother Fran had imported the gun. And skipped town.

"What do we do about the police?" Patrick continued, as if his brother had not spoken.

"We can't keep this information to ourselves," I answered, "if it turns out Willman is connected."

"What do you mean, *if?*" Brennan asked.

"But we do have a problem," I went on. "What is he going to say? More to the point, what is he going to say that will implicate your father?"

"Obviously, we have to get to him first," Brennan declared.

"Let's go round him up now. A posse of four." Terry again.

"Four? There are five of us by my count. Does this mean you're chickening out, Terr?" Bridey asked with deceptive sweetness.

"I won't chicken out if you go in first. You seduce the guy and when he's preoccupied, I'll jump out and —"

"Let's be serious here," Patrick urged. "One of us will meet him and it won't be you, Terrence."

"Fine with me. It shouldn't be hard to pick one of you three to do the job. People confess to Brennan, they tell Pat all their problems, and Monty cross-examines them for a living. Brennan knows sinners, Pat knows loonies and Monty knows criminals."

"We don't know what we're dealing with," I said. "So we can't discount the possibility that something will set him off. If emotions are going to run high, that's more likely to happen with a member of Declan's family than with an outsider. Even though I'll have to make it clear I'm representing the family."

"We've put you in harm's way once too often on this trip. Let's not do it again," Brennan stated. "I'll go."

I shook my head. "You don't have the patience. I don't even want to think about you in the same room with the guy who tried to kill

267

your dad." What I didn't say was: *I already saw you in the same room with Francis, the guy who probably did try to kill your dad; you didn't even know it and you laid waste to him.* "Forget it. I'll do it. But I'll try to engineer the meeting in a safe place."

"He may not go along with that."

"We'll have to see, won't we? Where's the phone? Let's hope he's there." They all pointed to a pay phone at the back of the bar.

"He's there," Terry promised.

"How do you know that?"

"Because I called his number just before I got here."

"Now for the small matter of what to say, to lure him to a meeting."

"How well do you do voices?" Terry asked. "Maybe you can imitate the old doll over the phone. He probably doesn't know she's dead, so —"

"We can't assume that. We can't assume anything. We don't know Gerard Willman, or what he's done, or what else he knows by now."

"Tell him you saw him at the wedding reception, or you have proof that he was there," Bridey suggested.

I shot a glance at Terry, who seemed to be avoiding my eyes. Like me, he had good reason to doubt that Willman had been anywhere near the Saint Kieran's gym when Declan was shot. It was Francis who had imported the rifle. And it was Francis who let slip the implication that there were two targets that night: "Maybe somebody just meant to scare them," he had said to me. What role Willman played — but I was being prompted by my companions. They had come to an agreement.

"Give him the old line, that you have the photographs," Brennan suggested.

"Nobody saw the guy. How could anyone have photographed him?"

"He can't be sure of that," Brennan countered. "It should cause him concern that you've linked him to the wedding reception. Give it a try."

I got up and dialled the number. It rang and rang. No reply. Deflated, I returned to the table.

"Nobody there."

"Sit awhile longer, then try him again," Terry advised. "So, Bridey, what did you tell Doctor Strange-Spell today? Nothing about how your brothers are the root cause of that little twitch in your eye, I hope?"

"I don't have a twitch in my eye."

"You will now. Just thinking about it will bring it on."

"Feck off."

I tried to steer the conversation back on course. "Let's return to the scene in the Botanic Garden, Bridey, when the stranger showed up in the Potomac rental car."

"Okay."

"What did the man look like, the one who had the car? How was he dressed?"

She was silent for a moment. "I just picture him in a suit and tie. I think he had short light brown hair. I'm not sure how much of this is memory and how much is imagination. I wish I could be more specific."

"And you didn't hear him say anything."

"He yelled something to the boys hanging around his car. It was loud but I didn't understand it."

We sat and nursed our drinks for a while longer, making small talk. Eventually I got up to try the phone. It rang for a long time again. I was about to hang up when the receiver was finally picked up and a pissed-off voice came on the line.

"Yeah?"

"Mr. Willman?"

"Who's this?"

"This is a guy who's standing here looking at a grainy photo of you, Mr. Willman. It shows you someplace you weren't supposed to be, doing something you weren't supposed to do." That should cover it, if he had been up to anything untoward at all.

Silence.

"Mr. Willman?"

"What?"

"I thought you might like to see my photos. Before I take them downtown."

"Fuck you."

"The police don't know about you yet. But I do."

"I don't know what you're talking about," the Brooklyn voice insisted. "So, like I said, fuck you!"

Slam. End of conversation. I reported to the others; we stayed on and drank a few more rounds, but alcohol did nothing to ease the frustration.

The next day I had another conversation on the phone, and it took all my lawyerly acting skills to hide my surprise. "Declan!"

"I just got a call from someone named Sullivan. An Irishman. Says there's something I should know about Francis." Declan seemed to bite off his words almost before he got them out. "And that, if I want to find out what it is, I have to meet him in the gymnasium where I was shot."

"Declan —"

"Don't interrupt me, Montague. Sullivan said Francis left something for me in the gym. 'Unintentionally,' because, as Sullivan put it, 'you can't expect perfection from Frankie.' I told him Francis was in Mexico at the time of the shooting and Sullivan laughed at me. Said my 'private dick' must not have filled me in. I asked him who the fuck he was talking about, and he said: 'The blond guy with the accent.' That must be you, Montague, with the Canadian accent. What the fuck is going on? Do you know something about Francis you're not telling me? You've got some explaining to do and you can start when you meet me there at seven, with this man Sullivan."

"Declan, there's a lot about this I don't understand and —"

"Understand this, Monty. I expect to see you there at seven." Click.

I would do better than that; I would be there early. Sullivan would likely arrive ahead of Declan in order to have the advantage. To position himself in the spot where he said Francis had left something behind. With any luck, I would be able to deal with Sullivan and defuse what could be an explosive situation.

There was nobody in sight when I got to Saint Kieran's gymnasium. I stood by the main door and waited as dusk began to fall. Then there was a loud bang as someone slammed down on the bar and sprung the door open from inside. A man stepped out.

"What the fuck?" he exclaimed in a thick New York accent.

He stood in the doorway facing me. Despite the late hour, his eyes were obscured by sunglasses, but I had a feeling he had me in his sights like a sniper. Obviously, my presence was an unwelcome surprise. The man had a shaved head and overdeveloped muscles, which could be seen straining against his black polo shirt and the cheap sports jacket he wore over it.

He didn't ask me who I was. I looked at his face in the fading light. There was something familiar about him. But I wasn't prepared for what he said next.

"We meet again, Collins. Only this time my name's Willman. By the way, I didn't like your attitude on the phone."

Gerard Willman! But we hadn't met. And I hadn't given him my name over the phone. Yet I was sure I knew the guy.

"Take off the shades, Willman."

It took him a few seconds to make the decision. Then he whipped them off. Without the wild red hair and beard, he was the spirit and image of the man in Francis Burke's sketch. This was how he looked when he met Francis all those months ago. The bright green eyes regarded me with amusement. Colm Sullivan was Gerard Willman. Always had been.

The Sullivan brogue was nowhere to be heard. "You're not the guy I wanted to see here tonight, Collins. I'm waiting for Burke."

My telephone call had obviously flushed Willman out, and he intended to confront Declan. This wasn't about Francis at all.

"Bet you thought you were pretty fucking clever tracking down Colm Sullivan, am I right, Collins?"

"Maybe."

"You couldn'ta done it without me ratting Frankie out to the cops. Giving them a tipoff where that box could be found. I figured Frankie's prints would be all over it. I also figured he'd rat me out."

Willman's eyes swept the area around the gym as we stood there, him half in the building, me outside. He said: "So once I set things in motion by directing the cops to the gun box — also filled with worthless chunks of stone and soil, the better to trace that gun to Ireland — I practised my act as Colm Sullivan. The accent, the feigned surprise at the notion that the smuggling scheme was my idea."

Now I had the answer to a question that had been plaguing me all along: why had Francis given me Sullivan's name? Because he thought Sullivan would confirm his story, a story Francis thought was the truth. That all he was smuggling into the country was a box of Irish artifacts. Poor Francis was just a dupe, after all.

Gerard Willman had been convincing as Sullivan, just a guy with a little scam going, a guy who had no interest in trying to point the finger at Frankie Burke. He led me to believe he did not think Frankie was up to the job, but he made sure he left me with no other conclusion to draw.

"How did I do?"

"You did a good job. A good job all round."

"Like I told you, that wasn't a Frankie Burke kinda hit."

It was an enormous relief that this had not been a Frankie Burke kinda hit; at least Declan and his family were spared that. It reminded me of something else, though.

"Were you after Brennan too?" I asked.

"Who? One of the sons? Why would I be after him?"

"Never mind." A couple of shots must have gone wild. If Francis thought there had been an attempt on both his father and his brother, that said more about Francis's frame of mind than it did about the events as they unfolded so quickly in the gym. I remembered Leo Killeen saying the shooter's location was less than ideal.

"How much did you know about your father when you were growing up, Gerard?"

"Not much. Judy was fucking clueless."

"Your mother."

"Yeah. She had no idea what happened. But I remember her saying there was money coming in. She thought it was from the IRA — right, Jude! — a payoff for the guns that were sent to Ireland. Like I said, clueless. Then the tap was turned off and the family standard of living took a dive. Down to where you'd expect it to be with my stepfather, Garth Willman, at the helm. Useless shitball. You know, you hear about these girls who want to have a kid and raise it by themselves — they don't need a husband — and it pisses you off. Then you look at a loser like Willman coming into the house and you think, hey, we would've been a lot better off just three kids and a mother. He treated me like shit. Nothing I did was good enough. I wanted to be an actor! Well, old Garth wasn't going to let that happen. All he wanted was for me to join the Army and rise through the ranks. I finally did join and I hated myself for giving in. Lasted a few years, then got discharged."

"When did your mother take up with Garth?"

"It was around the time I was one and a half, two. I think he sniffed out the money — followed it right into her bedroom."

"You said the payments stopped at some point."

"Oh yeah. I know exactly when they stopped. A few years ago I paid Judy a visit when the old motherfucker was out of the house. She said my father was murdered in Attica. She didn't know who did it, why, how. Guess it never occurred to her to look into her husband's death. Ay, these things happen, right? Anyway, she said: 'And then they stopped paying.' I asked her when this happened and she kinda laughed and told me to dig out the old photo album. She thumbed through the black-and-whites of us as kids till she got to this colour picture of old Willman with a big grin on his puss. Only time I ever saw him in a good mood. Standing at the tail end of a brand new '57 Chevy, hefting a set of golf clubs into the trunk. It was right around then that the money stopped coming. I think you can draw your own conclusions."

I could. Declan Burke's worthy charity — Judy Connors — had been downgraded to unworthy status thanks to the conspicuous consumption of Garth Willman. The family had a wage earner, and Burke was not about to finance his car payments or his golf dues. Must have come as a relief to Ramon Jiminez, whose efforts at blackmail had been turned against him, and who had unwittingly bankrolled Judy and her family up till then.

Willman was getting edgy. I wanted to keep the talk flowing. "You must have spent a fair bit of time around here casing the place before the wedding."

"You think I walked around the gym in overalls and a tool belt posing as a handyman, Collins? Nobody at the school caught a glimpse of me. You could build a row of condos between the gym and the bushes out there, nobody would see them. I did my advance work at night. Loosened a window so I could get in and out. Didn't take the time to do that tonight — I just broke one. Anyway, I went in and removed the back wall of that plywood closet. What a shitty place to hunker down for five hours. Not the best vantage point for a sniper. Fortunately for Burke. Oh, by the way, the old guy I hired to sing at the wedding reception has no idea who I am or why he was there. I imagine these days he's lying low."

I looked at the man standing in front of me, tense and agitated. "I think we'd better end this here, Gerard. You have nothing to gain by any more —"

"Where the fuck is Burke?"

"I have no idea."

"He tipped you off about this meet, and you told him not to show!"

Gerard's hand went to his pants pocket then came out again, swift as lightning. It took me a moment to realize that I was looking into the barrel of a gun.

I fought to stay calm. "I don't know where he is, Gerard. He said he was coming. He's expecting to hear something about Francis. Don't make this any worse than it already is. Declan doesn't know anything about Gerard Willman."

"I'm about to set him straight on that."

"Walk away, Gerard. There's no physical evidence tying you to the shooting."

"You got that right. All they have is a gun box with Frankie Burke's prints on it, and an obituary written by a little old lady who's not going to do any favours for Declan Burke. So until you walked onto the stage in this drama, Collins, there were no witnesses. Nobody to badmouth me in front of a jury. Now there's you. What —"

Willman stopped speaking and cocked his head to the right, then took a step forward. He pointed the gun at my stomach and spoke in an undertone: "Here's Burke. Keep your mouth shut if you want to stay alive. Mr. Burke!" he called out. "Over here."

I turned my head and felt the gun pressing into my flesh. Before

I could decide how to handle the situation, or even decide whether I had any options, Declan was beside me and Willman moved back. Only then did Declan see the gun.

"Inside! Both of you."

"Do I look like a fucking *amadán?*" Declan retorted. "I'm not going in there with you, Sullivan, or whoever the hell you are. And whatever your problem is, this fellow had nothing to do with it." He inclined his head towards me.

"You don't know who I am, Burke?"

"No."

"My name's Gerry Willman. If my father was still alive, I'd be Gerry Connors."

Declan looked as if the bullet had been fired and, this time, had found his heart.

"I can see you recognize the name. So maybe I don't have to bore you with a big, long explanation of my activities. Now, get a move on. I want you both inside that building."

"Whatever you're going to do, do it out here." Declan didn't move.

"You're not in a position to give orders, Burke. The man who carries the gun into the meeting has the floor. Go!"

"No."

Willman reached out, grabbed Declan's arm and gave him a shove. But Declan flattened himself against the glass door and resisted being forced inside.

"You know, Burke, until this Collins guy threw a fuck into things, I was finished with you. I didn't manage to inflict a fatal wound but all in all I was pleased. I made a statement and I got away. Even tonight, if it was just the two of us, I wouldn't be all that concerned. Because, as I mentioned to Collins before you joined us, I'm not really worried about being hauled before the courts for this. You know why?" No response. "I said, do you know why?"

"No."

"Think what it will take to get this case before a jury. It will take Declan Burke sitting down and grassing to the cops about why somebody named Gerard Willman would want to see him dead. Because the only evidence against me is motive. And it's you, Burke, who would have to provide that evidence. The whole fucking story of what you did when you were with the IRA, why you had to shove your family on a boat in the middle of the night and flee the old country, what you did on Pier One in Brooklyn, leaving one watchman in hospital, another without a job, and leaving my father to go to Attica alone, where he died in a vicious attack that left his family fatherless, and left me with a brutal, moronic stepfather. That's how I got where I am today. Do you think you'll want to get up and tell that story?

"But now there's this guy." Me, he meant. "He tracked me down, he phoned me up, and now he's here. It's no longer just between you and me. And that makes me nervous. Nobody wants to leave a witness walking around. Not when there's a charge of attempted murder hanging in the air."

Declan didn't answer. Neither did I.

"Problem is, Burke," Willman continued, "if I eliminate Collins, you become a witness to that. You see where this is going."

"There's something I want to tell you, Connors," Declan said.

"My name's Willman!"

"To me, you're Connors. Your father's son."

Gerard blinked, but his hand didn't waver.

"What I want you to know is . . ." Declan's voice faltered. He put his hand to his head, and began sliding down against the door until he was on his knees. I had never been more alert in my life; he was fading before my eyes.

"Declan!" I shouted, and Willman whirled on me with the gun.

"Get down there beside him, Collins, now! And don't try anything. I have Army training; you don't. Now get down."

I looked at Declan. His eyes were on me. A warning not to get down. He started to speak in a faint voice. "When your father went to prison, Gerard . . ."

"I can't hear you! Speak up!"

"As soon as your father was sent to Attica . . ." Declan's head flopped back against the door. His eyes closed, and his voice was barely a whisper.

Willman leaned close to the old man. "Tell me! Don't have a fucking stroke on me, Burke!"

There was a sudden movement, the deafening crack of a gunshot, and a yelp of pain. Willman was down on the ground, and Declan was struggling to stand. I launched myself onto Willman's back and grasped his right hand. It was empty. Declan got to his feet and stood over us. He had the gun in his hand; it was pointed at Willman's head.

"Don't move, Gerard," Declan commanded, as he backed away to a safer distance.

Gerry Connors's son twisted his head to look into the chilly, unblinking blue eyes of the old Irish outlaw. Gerard wasn't the only one with Army training.

"It's all right, Monty. Get off him."

"Declan," I said, as I cautiously released the man, "is he —"

"Nobody got shot," Declan interrupted. "The gun went off but the bullet went wide. I lured him in close, kicked his leg out from under him, and he went down.

"We don't have much time, Gerard. That gunshot will be reported. I want you to know this: from the time your father arrived in Attica, I had a lawyer working on an appeal. And I arranged for protection for your da inside, through people I knew in the world of organized crime. There were fellows in the prison keeping an eye out for him. But they couldn't foresee a completely random attack, and they couldn't stop it. I'm sorry, Gerard. I've been sorry for forty years and I'll be sorry till the day I die. I don't expect forgiveness. Ever. And you're right. I won't be giving your name to the police. Neither will my lawyer here."

Gerard was the picture of misery, anger, grief. Declan backed away, then removed the clip from the gun, extracted the bullets and dropped them one at a time onto the ground. I counted five rounds. Gerard started to move, and Declan pointed the weapon at him again. Gerard sank back to the ground. There must have been one round in the chamber ready to fire. Then Declan took out a snowy white handkerchief and wiped the gun free of prints, pushed the barrel into the grass, fired the last round where it could do no harm, and laid the weapon on the ground.

"That's it," was all he said. We walked away.

†

Francis appeared, as if on cue, the following day. I had packed and checked out of the hotel and was spending my last afternoon haunting the premises of Declan Burke. I had just finished describing last night's drama to Brennan, who absorbed the news in stunned silence, when Terry called to say he was picking Francis up at Penn Station. Would anybody like to come along? So we headed in to Manhattan. There was only one topic of conversation on the way. Terry and Brennan reluctantly conceded that, if Declan did not want to press charges against Gerard Willman, they would go along with his wishes.

When we pulled up outside the station, Brennan said: "I didn't even know Francis was out of town. Where did he go?"

"Iowa."

"Iowa!"

"His girlfriend is from there."

"Ah."

We caught sight of Francis then, limping towards us with a knapsack on his back. His shoulder-length dark hair had been cut short. It looked good on him, or would have if the effect had not been marred by a cut lip and bruising around his left eye.

"Oh, good!" he exclaimed when he saw Brennan in the car. "The high priest of brotherly love."

"What happened to you?" Brennan barked at him.

"They don't like strangers," Francis replied in a twangy accent.

"Who? Her family?" Terry asked.

"No, no. The dudes in the Circle Jerk."

"The what?"

"The Circle J. A bar on the outskirts o' town."

Brennan stared at him. "What happened, they thumped you for no reason?"

"They may have misunderstood something I said."

"That sounds more like it."

"Christ, can we stop for a dacent pint? Nobody has ever heard the holy name of Guinness out there."

After we found a bar and a parking spot, we all ordered drinks and settled in. "So, what was Shirley's family like?" I asked.

"Real nice and quiet round the dinner table. 'Pass the ribs there,

Mother. Tell me, Frank, what's your line?' I told them I was curator of the Museum of Modern Art. I later met her brother Fred, who really does run the feed store, and told him I'm an undercover narc who works the subways all night. He gaped at my bloodcurdling adventures underground.

"Anyway, we were sitting at her parents' table, just the four of us, not a sound to be heard — I thought for a while I'd been struck deaf, maybe thanks to your intervention with a higher power, Brennan — and the old man said: 'Well, Frank, what would you like to watch?' I'd pretty well resigned myself to a tractor pull or a steer-roping contest. Or maybe they rope the tractors and pull the steers. What are steers anyway? I thought it was cows and bulls."

"I think a steer is a bull that's been castrated," I put in.

"Why in the fuck would anybody do that?" Francis wailed. Nobody knew. "Doesn't matter anyway, because the old man meant the tube. 'What's on tonight, Mother?' She produced a scrap of paper from her pocket and read what I took to be a list of television programs. That's when brother Fred stopped in. He asked if I wanted to go out 'four-wheeling.' I didn't know what he was talking about so he invited me to step outside. I thought I was going to get pounded right then and there, but he just wanted to show me his 'rig.' A massive vehicle with a big rack of lights along the top. The kind of thing that turns up in the movies just after aliens have left a big radioactive circle out in the woods. I climbed up into it and I felt the onset of vertigo. Shirley beamed at me from the doorway and waved goodbye. There were a couple of yokels in the back. I kept up a stream of bullshit till we got in sight of the bar, then I got them to let me off.

"Not long after that, I was set upon by two big bruisers. Guess there was something about me they didn't like."

"Which was what, exactly?" Brennan asked.

"I walked in and asked the barman to pour me a Guinness. Since he was so far from the source, I gave him detailed instructions on how I wanted it poured. Then he told me he didn't have Guinness. I told him what I thought of that. These two rednecks started laughing and one of them said: 'Go back to the Bronx, asshole.' So I turned around and pointed to the other one and said: 'Is this guy your brother, or your cousin, or your brother-in-law, or all three?' It took them so long to get it, I forgot all about it. Then they were on me. Guess I should have kept my mouth shut."

"At long last, the scales fall from his eyes," Brennan remarked.

"So after they finished pounding me and they roared off in their truck, I dragged myself up to the bar and asked the barkeep to call a cab for me. He just laughed. 'Gonna take that cabbie a long time to get here from Fifth Avenue, son.' I walked all the way back to Shirley's place, bleeding and in pain. Took me two hours. There was nothing out there. Nothing. Have you any idea how spooky that is? But it was better than hanging around the bar, waiting to get beaten to a pulp again. Half the guys in the bar had cowboy hats or ball caps on, over hair that was halfway down their backs. Hence the new look." He patted his shorn locks, then took a long, long swig of stout. "And that was about it. So, what's new with you guys?"

"Nothing much," Terry said.

"So, what about Shirley?" I asked him.

"Hard to say."

"I got the impression you were quite keen on her."

"Oh, I am. As a matter of fact, all my stuff's at her apartment now, because my landlady kicked me out for being behind in the rent. So I'll stay at Shirl's for awhile, see how it goes.

"Perhaps you guys will be interested in some scribblings I did on the way back east in the stage coach." He directed his remarks to me. "Since you liked my work before. Any arrests made yet? Did you manage to track down my suspect? I think I captured him pretty well on paper."

I tried to send him a "don't ask" signal, but it was intercepted.

"What suspect?" Brennan's tone was sharp.

"You mean Sullivan," Terry said.

"Who the hell is Sullivan?" Brennan demanded.

"Didn't pan out," I answered. I mouthed the word "later" to him and then to Francis I said: "Let's see what you have here."

He hauled his knapsack onto his lap. I leaned towards him and whispered:

"Tell me something. How did you really hear of the shooting? You didn't read it in a newspaper in the wilds of Mexico two days after it happened."

"Nah. I keep in touch with my sister Molly in London. She called me. I figure if the rest of them know where I am, I'll be bothered by all kinds of blather from them. Now, have a look at these."

He carefully removed what looked like a couple of posters rolled and secured with an elastic. On the first sheet of paper was a charcoal sketch of Shirley. Technically, it was well done, though he had taken some liberties and shaved a few pounds off her. She was accompanied by three young fair-haired boys.

"Her nephews. Cute little peckerheads," he remarked.

"You did this?" Terry asked.

"Why not?"

He put the picture aside, then flattened the second page with his hand. This one showed his own family seated in the dining room. Francis was at one end of the table, looking comically perplexed, one hand to his chest as if saying: "Who, me?" The table was littered with broken crockery, and a burning cherry bomb was flying towards the other end of the table, where there were two figures. Declan was portrayed in a military uniform and beret. His eyes were hidden behind the kind of dark glasses I had seen in photographs of IRA funerals. At his side was Brennan in his Roman collar, looking down his nose in a caricature of arrogance. These two figures cast a shadow that travelled the length of the table and enveloped Francis completely. All the other figures were half in and half out of the shade. A closer look revealed something that appeared to be the laurel crown of a Roman emperor over Brennan's head. There was the shadow of a rifle over his father's shoulder. With his back to the artist and his head turned to his father and older brother, Terry sat with a pint of stout in his hand, his mouth twisted as if he was telling an amusing tale. Beside Terry was Teresa, her face turned towards Francis; she favoured him with a loving smile. On the other side of the table, an adorably beautiful Bridey laughed with mischievous glee at her clever brother Fran. Standing beside her was Patrick, his face radiating kindness, his right hand raised in a gesture of benediction over his assembled family.

Nobody spoke; we were riveted by the tableau before us. There was no subtlety in it, but that was not his intention. I stole a glance at the artist. His attempt at a casual expression did not mask his apprehension. He had eyes for one man only; Brennan's was the only opinion that mattered.

For his part, Brennan could not tear his eyes away from the picture. Finally, he found words: "We thought you were sitting around all these years pulling yourself. Is this what you've been up to?" The younger brother's face flamed red and he started to retort, but Brennan continued: "I hope to Christ it is." He fell silent again, then began muttering about the picture. "Look at this. Mam's hair, the way she ties it up. He's got that exactly right. And the folds in Pat's jacket, where his arm is raised. If you put your arm up —" he did, and examined the folds in his jacket "— that's just how they go. But it's the life and personality in the faces and in the bodies; how could he capture that in a sketch?" He seemed to have forgotten Francis was there.

Eventually, the artist spoke up. "Listen, could you guys take those home for me? And my knapsack? I want to go somewhere."

"Well, then, why the hell did you call for a lift?" Terry asked.

"I just thought of something. Gotta go." He stood and left the bar with a distracted wave in our direction.

"Where would he have to go, for Jesus' sake?" Terry growled. Brennan shrugged, then gently rolled the pictures up and bound them with the elastic. Terry slung the knapsack over his back, and we left the bar.

Francis didn't have to go anywhere, I knew. The unveiling of the family caricature was too much for him. No doubt he was afraid that if he stayed around, he would blurt out something inappropriate and spoil the moment.

"Imagine having that kind of talent. It's brilliant!" Brennan exclaimed, a man of no little talent himself. I wished Francis had stuck around a minute longer.

Brennan was walking ahead, and I held Terry back for a hasty legal conference. "Sit Francis down right away, tell him what really happened, and get him a good defence lawyer. Not a word to the police or anyone else. Never mind that you think you're exonerating your brother. Just keep it to yourself. Fran has an alibi for the night of the shooting; he was still in Mexico. So counsel will want to gather the supporting evidence: eyewitnesses, plane tickets, what have you. But the police have his prints on the box, so they think he at least imported the rifle. And now there's no Colm Sullivan; he's really Gerard Willman and Declan doesn't want Gerard's name to surface in this. Some good legal manoeuvring should halt this thing for Fran before it goes any further."

✝

Terry, Brennan and I were back at the Burkes' kitchen table when we heard someone coming in the front door.

"Ah," Declan said, taking us all in with his steely gaze. "I suppose young Collins has filled you in on last night's episode."

"He has," Brennan replied.

Declan turned from his sons and looked towards the window. We could almost see his mind working, sorting through the long and complex series of events in his life, events we had only glimpsed in part. What must he have been feeling as he contemplated the brutal death of Gerald Connors, a death that shattered the Connors family and set Gerald's son on a path of revenge that took him nearly forty years to execute? Did his thoughts also turn to the man he had killed in Ireland, the traitor to the cause? And how would he come to terms with the fact that his own sons now knew the awful secrets he had guarded all his life?

Without another word, he turned and headed for the door.

Brennan reached out and grasped his arm. "Declan, for the love of God, explain it to us. Or to one of us. Get it off your chest."

He spoke without raising his voice: "I have nothing to say."

His ferocious blue eyes bored in on his eldest son: "Especially to you, my child." The pain in Brennan's face was that of a young boy who had been publicly slapped by a father he adored. The old man and his son stared at each other for a long time, then Declan put his hand on Brennan's shoulder, leaned down and spoke into his ear, in a voice that was barely audible: "Because you have the power to absolve."

He walked out. Terry and I stared down at our hands.

It was time for me to leave. Terry had offered me a lift to the airport, if I didn't mind being early for my flight. The earlier the better.

283

I had to put the shooting and the murder and the Burke family's pain behind me. I looked at Brennan, who had not moved a muscle since his father's remark. Then he seemed to shake himself and got up from his chair.

"Give me five minutes," was all he said as he left the room and headed upstairs. When he returned he had his suitcase in his hand. "Can you get me on a flight?" he asked Terry.

"Have you a destination in mind?"

"Halifax. But anywhere north of here will do. Let's motor."

Chapter 12

Now here's to old Dublin, and here's to her renown,
In the long generation her fame will go down,
And our children will tell how their forefathers saw
The red blaze of freedom in Erin Go Bragh.
— Peadar Kearney, "Erin Go Bragh"

April 5, 1991

The next day, Friday, I picked up Tommy Douglas and Normie at the address we used to share as a family in downtown Halifax, and brought them out to my place for the night. No objections from their mother, but I hadn't expected any. She knew I'd been missing them, and they had been missing their dad. We arrived at my house on the Northwest Arm, the body of water branching in from the Atlantic Ocean, and bordering the west side of the Halifax peninsula. I liked it there. Not as much as I liked the old family home on Dresden Row, but thinking of that would get me nowhere.

Tom was agreeable to all the regular activities Normie enjoyed in my neighbourhood. We went for a walk in Fleming Park and climbed the Dingle Tower, played hide-and-seek around the house in the dark, made music on my old Fender guitars and keyboard, had cocoa, and watched a goofy movie.

When I tucked Normie in to bed, she looked up at me with her big hazel eyes and said: "Daddy? Is it better to have one little red-haired girl, or four?"

I didn't know where the mines were buried but I knew I had to tread softly. "What do you mean, sweetheart?"

"Well, you just have me. But some other people have four."

"Who has four?"

"Father Burke's sister. She was nicer to you than Mummy is. She kissed you at the wedding. She has four girls. And some boys."

"Normie, I'd rather have you than a whole army of other red-haired girls. I'd rather have you and Tommy than any other kids in the world. If you ever wonder about that, even for a minute, you come and ask me. Or call me. Okay?"

She put her soft little arms around my neck and clung to me. I held her till she fell asleep.

I went to my room, got ready for bed, and brooded on the conversation. How could my daughter ever doubt that she was the only little girl for me? Now that we were all home again, I was sure, the strangeness and the trauma of New York would fade and she'd be back to rights in no time. But New York hadn't yet faded for me. My mind turned once again to the shooting.

We knew who shot Declan Burke, and why. Yet I could not rid myself of the feeling that there was something else going on. What did we know for sure? We knew about the waterfront gun heist in 1952, the senseless killing of Gerald Connors in prison, the alcoholic meltdown of Mr. Desmond and the slaying of Nessie Murphy. We had suspected a Mob connection but, as it turned out, all Declan had done was borrow money from them and work for a few years in one of their nightclubs. He knew the people there, and they helped us unravel much of the story. The fact that he stole guns before the Mob could steal them seemed to be a minor irritation even to Patrizio Corialli.

So, if it wasn't a Mob enforcer Sandra had seen confronting Declan at his house all those years ago, who was it? He had accused Declan of stealing, of slipping an envelope into his pocket. What had the man said? "How could you sink so low?" To me, that suggested Burke had been robbing the blind, stealing from the poor or embezzling money from a charity. I did not see him as a man who would do that.

We were missing something. And it centred on Cathal Murphy,

who was really Charlie Fagan. Whose sister had been murdered and whose papers had been filched from the apartment. Lieutenant O'Brien was convinced Fagan continued to smuggle arms out of the United States and into Ireland. Yet, with the exception of one incident, the police were never able to catch him. O'Brien believed Fagan was using a courier, presumably to deliver money to the arms suppliers. Was Declan the courier? What, then, were we to make of Fagan's clandestine meeting with the man from Washington, DC? Could the fact that O'Brien never caught Fagan running guns again mean he had given it up? That he had turned FBI informant?

If so, and if Declan was his courier, what was Declan passing on? Was he an informer too? Was that even remotely possible? Why not? He had been run out of Ireland on false accusations of being a traitor to the IRA. Was this his revenge against the organization? If so, was Leo Killeen aware of it? Or was this Fagan's revenge on Declan? Declan had stolen the love of his life, Teresa Burke, though more than likely Declan had not even been aware of Fagan pining in the shadows of Stephen's Green. But Fagan's passion continued to burn and it drew him all the way across the Atlantic Ocean. He still followed Teresa around after he immigrated to the States. Could he have set Declan up to take the risk of passing information to the FBI on Irish Republicans operating on American soil? It was beginning to sound plausible, but what evidence did I have?

I got up and grabbed a pencil and paper. I tried to turn my mind to things I had heard but ignored or failed to appreciate until now. What did I know about Murphy/Fagan, aside from what I had heard from Nessie? He lived like a monk, devoted only to Roman Catholicism and Irish Republicanism. He had no friends; he did not go out with co-workers for an end-of-day pint, by the sound of things. His day job was as a maintenance man, no, a shipper in a manufacturing plant. He went to Mass every day. I wondered whether the priest who conducted the funeral knew anything about the man he was burying. Patrick said there was an older priest who spoke. That might be a lead. But what church was it? Patrick didn't say. I would give him a call, but not at this time of night.

Then I remembered Lieutenant O'Brien mentioning a church. The police had followed Fagan to Mass a few times at Saint — Saint

What? This at least was one of the conversations I had taken notes on, and I dug them out. Saint Bridey's. Bridey, as I knew very well, was a nickname for Brigid. Wasn't there also a Saint Bride? I would check tomorrow. But who really cared what church Murphy/Fagan attended if there was no connection with Declan? It seemed I had had a conversation with someone on this very subject. Saint Kieran's of the Crime Scene was the Burke family's church and they had always gone there. Who was telling me? Bridey of course. She had gone to high school at Saint Kieran's and had Brennan as a teacher. So even if there was a Saint Brigid's or Bride's or Bridey's — Bratty's. Somebody had made a joke about Saint Bratty's. But the details had slipped my mind. I was too tired to concentrate. I scribbled a few more notes and climbed into bed.

✝

As I resumed my normal work life and what passed for a normal family life, New York receded from my mind. Until I got a call from Brennan a few days after my return.

"Good evening, Father Burke. What's new in the gentle world of music and prayer?"

"You'll never guess who's coming to town."

"Who?"

"The oul divil himself."

"Not your father! Confession time?"

"I doubt it."

"How long is he staying?"

"Coming Saturday for three or four days."

"What's the story?"

"Didn't say. Just: 'Meet me at the airport and get me a room at the Lord Nelson.' He won't even hear of staying here at the rectory. The Lord Nelson — funny when you think of it, isn't it?" There was a certain irony in a hotel named after a British warrior harbouring a man with Declan's IRA past. "Let's hope me oul da doesn't come with a bag full of Irish play-dough and blow it up."

"That sort of thing is frowned upon here."

"You know they blew up Nelson's Pillar in Dublin in 1966. The 'ra. But I don't imagine that's why he's here."

"Forget the hotel. Bring him here."

"I'll see what he has to say about it."

When I arrived at the office the next morning my secretary, Tina, told me I had just missed a call. "A guy from New York. Said his name was Pat Burke. You don't have to call him back but he faxed this to you."

"Thanks, Tina."

The phone was ringing when I got to my desk, so I put the fax down and picked up the receiver. It was Maura. "I'm taking the kids to Cape Breton tomorrow."

"What for?"

"Funeral back home. It's on Monday but I'm going for the weekend. And I'd like Tom and Normie to see everyone."

"Who died?"

"Old Uncle Joe. You remember him. He was ninety. Smoked and swilled liquor all his life and didn't have a sick moment till he dropped dead last night."

"Who's Uncle Joe?"

"Have you never listened to a word I've said the whole time I've known you? I don't have time to fill you in. Read the obit!"

"There's that word again."

"We're all a little skittish about the obituary page these days, Collins, but read it. I'll call you later and let you know our plans." Click.

Who the hell was Uncle Joe? Her father, Alec, came from a family of eleven, but I didn't remember a Joe. Her mother's family only had five kids; they were regarded with some suspicion by their fellow Catholics in Cape Breton. No Joe there either, I thought. Maybe somebody's husband, though I thought I'd met them all. I placed a call to our receptionist and asked for the waiting room copy of the *Chronicle Herald.* Then I turned to the fax from New York. It was a brief news story dated April 10, 1991. Yesterday. Patrick's name was scribbled at the top.

The FBI is refusing to confirm that it has teamed up with the NYPD in the investigation of the murder of an elderly woman in Williamsburg last month. But sources close to the investigation say the Bureau became involved when it was learned that the victim, Neasa Mary Murphy (formerly Fagan), 74, was the sister of Cathal Murphy, who died late last year. The FBI had "more than one file" on Cathal Murphy, according to the source. Neasa (Nessie) Murphy was found bludgeoned to death in her ground-floor flat Easter Sunday night, after police received an anonymous call. Police say it's likely she had been killed the night before. A department spokesman says it appears that robbery was the motive, but it is possible there was a connection between the woman's death and that of her brother.

So the Feds were involved. And were denying their involvement. No real surprise there if Cathal had been informing to the FBI or some other agency about IRA activity on American soil. I hoped there had not been any agents watching Nessie's house and witnessing my ignominious visit to the scene.

I turned to the obituary page of the *Herald*. Allan James "Uncle Joe" MacKenzie, ninety-one, of Glace Bay. All right, he wasn't a Joe at all. Perhaps not even a relative. Cape Breton was justly famous for its nicknames, though this one would pass unremarked in a province with names like Maggie in the Sky and Father Alec the Devil. "Uncle Joe spent all of his working life underground, first in the Phalen Seam and then in No. 26 Colliery. From the age of 17 he took an active interest in journalism and was a contributor to the *Maritime Labor Herald* until it suspended publication in 1926. Joe was back in print three years later with the *Nova Scotia Miner.*" That, I knew from my study of history, was a staunchly communist publication. Which might explain how the MacNeils knew him so well. The obit said Joe had toured the Soviet Union with a miners' delegation in 1930. Hence his nickname, I supposed, after "Uncle Joe Stalin." I wondered whether he had stayed loyal to the party through the twists, turns, contradictions and purges of the mid-twentieth century. How did he get along with young Alec the Trot(skyite) MacNeil, Maura's father? I put the paper aside; I had done my homework; if she called, I had the facts.

She did indeed call that evening, and I slipped a reference to Uncle Joe into the conversation, hoping to impress her with my memories of her family and friends. If she was impressed she didn't let on, but she filled me in on the plans. She and the kids would be driving to Cape Breton right after school the next day, which was Friday. I got into the car and drove to the house on Dresden Row to say goodbye. Much to my surprise, Maura sat down with me and gabbed about Uncle Joe, his family, the music that would be played at the funeral, the rum-fuelled debates between Joe and Alec the Trot over how best to serve the Revolution; it was almost like old times. Maybe there was hope for us after all. I decided to make a move — not now, but next week after she returned from Cape Breton. I would call and ask her out to dinner. If she said she was busy, I would refrain from making a remark of any kind, and would simply suggest going out on a night of her choosing; she could let me know. I said goodbye to Tom and Normie, and left the house.

I was restless after that so I put some blues on the car stereo and went for a cruise. I headed, as I often did, to Point Pleasant Park, where I sat in the car and watched a gargantuan container ship making its ponderous way into port. I remembered the consternation with which the first containers were greeted in certain quarters on the waterfront. A bit of pilferage from incoming ships had been part of life on the docks; now everything was sealed up in containers the size of box cars. Not so in the days when Cathal Murphy and his accomplices were sending shipments of guns over to Ireland. Why had the police not been able to catch him after that one incident? He must have stopped meeting his suppliers directly. Taken on a courier, according to Lieutenant Shammy O'Brien, to deliver the money. If that courier was Declan, where did they meet? Murphy/Fagan had a limited range of operation. He went to work, he went home, he went to church. He rarely set foot in a pub. O'Brien said they watched the factory and did not see anything amiss. Of course it could have been a co-worker who did the running for Murphy, but then wouldn't the police eventually have cottoned on to this person as an associate of arms smugglers? Maybe not. I made a mental note to find out something about Murphy's place of employment. What was the name? Des Ailes? French for "wings." Desailes Corp. Aviation supplies. Were they still in business? I would give Terry Burke a call and see if he had heard of them. But I could not free myself of the suspicion that Declan was the courier. Old Nessie had left me with the clear impression that there was more to this than Brennan and I had been able to figure out. Surely Declan had not been meeting Murphy/ Fagan at the Williamsburg apartment Fagan had by himself, not after the police searched it. That left me with Murphy's other regular destination, his church. Saint Bridey's or Saint Brigid's, if I was remembering my conversation with O'Brien accurately. But even there, O'Brien had said, nothing was amiss.

Still, there was something that had come to me a while ago. Some play on the saint's name. Saint Bratty's. That's what I remembered. I had asked Brigid about it, and she said the family had always gone to Saint Kieran's. Yet I had seen the words Saint Bratty's scribbled — right, I had it — scribbled in crayon across a Saint Brigid's collection envelope in the Burkes' house. It was in the attic, the day I found the bank records suggesting blackmail. So somebody had been singing from a different hymn book. I went back to the story Patrick had told me about Francis running away as a child, hiding in the family car; he had ended up at Mass. Declan had left the house by himself, driven a long distance, and gone to church, a church where Francis was unable to find the toilets. An unfamiliar church. And when Declan found out Francis was along for the ride, he didn't cuff the little fellow's ears and give him hell; he just agreed that neither of them would mention it. Declan didn't want anyone to know he'd been to . . . Sunday Mass. Did that make any sense? I put my car in gear and drove home. I had some calls to make first thing in the morning.

After clearing my desk of a few tedious matters the following day, I called Terry Burke's number and got Sheila on the phone. Terry would be back from a layover in Frankfurt later in the day and would return my call. I told Sheila I was wondering whether Desailes Corp. was still in business, and whether Terry knew anything about it. I agreed with her that it was unlikely. He flew the planes; he didn't build them. I rang off and called directory assistance in New York for the number of Saint Brigid's Church. It turned out to be in Bay Ridge. My map told me that was in Brooklyn, across from Staten Island, quite a ways from anywhere I had been during my travels in the outer boroughs. I dialled the number, and asked for the parish priest. But what I really wanted was to get through to the older priest, the man in the walker, who had spoken at Cathal Murphy's funeral. It took some effort but I finally had the older man on the phone, in a home for retired priests in Brooklyn. Father Grogan was a little deaf so I adjusted my volume.

"Thanks for speaking to me, Father. My name is Monty Collins and I live in Nova Scotia. I'm doing a bit of genealogy, and you may be able to help me."

"Looking for your roots type thing, would it be?"

"That's right. My mother was a Murphy."

"Aren't they all?" The old man let fly with a guffaw, ending in a racking cough that held up my research for a good two minutes. "I'm sorry, Mr. Collins, sorry. Now, your mother was a Murphy. Go on."

"She had a cousin down your way, and apparently this man did a lot of research on the family tree. Somebody suggested he was a member of your parish, maybe as far back as the 1950s."

"You make that sound like the 1850s, Mr. Collins! It's not far back at all. Not for me. Maybe I can help you."

"Great. Would you happen to remember a Cathal Murphy? I believe he immigrated to the States —"

"Cathal Murphy. Sure, I remember Cathal! Wasn't I just speaking at his funeral the other day? Well, more like a few months ago it was, but, yes, Cathal. He was your uncle, did you say?"

"Not an uncle, but a second cousin, I suppose he'd be. I was upset to hear he died. I had been hoping to get down there and pay him a visit. Just goes to show you, we should never put off things like this."

"No indeed, we should not."

"What can you tell me about Cathal, Father, anything?"

"I didn't see anything of Cathal outside the church, but I saw a great deal of him in my years at Saint Bridey's because the man was at Mass several times a week. Came to the eight o'clock on Sunday mornings, and the noon Mass on weekdays. A very devout man, was Cathal. I was in the parish on and off for over twenty-five years, and Cathal was a regular communicant all that time."

"Did he belong to any church organizations, that sort of thing?"

"No, I approached him to join the Holy Name Society once but he just seemed to want to take part in the sacraments. Not a joiner, I don't think."

"The sacraments including confession?" I said lightly.

"Ha ha. You know I can't speak of that. But now that you mention it, no, Cathal must have had another priest as his confessor."

"Did Cathal attend Mass by himself?"

"Always by himself. He had a sister but I didn't meet her until Cathal died. She apparently went to a church closer to her home. Cathal liked Saint Brigid's so he came to us."

"Was there anyone else in the parish he was close to? Any particular friends?"

"Not that I ever noticed. He was polite and friendly, but I never saw him talking with anyone in particular, no."

"There's another name I want to try on you, Father, because he seemed to be connected to Cathal in some way. He may have been a parishioner. Did you know a Declan Burke?"

"That sounds familiar. I'm getting a picture in my old brain here now, if you'll just give me a second. There's something —" I let him process his memories for a few moments. Then he laughed. "Yes, I knew Mr. Burke. But I knew him, in the beginning anyway, as Donal O'Byrne. I'll explain that to you in a minute. He used to come to the eight o'clock Sunday Mass once a month or so. More like every two months. Now I found this curious because whenever he did show up, he was more than helpful. He always volunteered to take up the collection, sweep leaves or snow off the church steps when the occasion called for it, took his share of church envelopes — in the name of O'Byrne — and gave generously. Yet we wouldn't see him for weeks at a time.

"Then there was an incident, but it turned out to be nothing all that serious really. I didn't see it as —" His voice faded out. I didn't want to lose him now.

"The incident, Father?" He didn't reply. I had better go back under cover. "I'm just wondering whether it had anything to do with my cousin Cathal. I understood he knew this Declan Burke. Were they friendly with each other, as far as you could tell?"

"Far as I could tell, they didn't even know each other. Attended the same Sunday Mass, well, when O'Byrne — *Burke* — attended. I never saw them speak to each other, at least not that I can remember now. And Cathal certainly had nothing to do with the little dust-up that occurred with Burke."

"You've certainly got me curious here, Father. You see, I'm planning to try to track Mr. Burke down. And if there is something serious that I should know beforehand —"

"No, from my point of view, it wasn't all that serious. Though it wasn't exactly kosher. What happened was Burke was taking up the collection as he always did when he came to us. And one of the other men in the parish — Ted Lawlor, God rest him — made an accusation against Burke. That he was stealing money from the collection! Now, I found that difficult to believe. My first thought was that Lawlor's nose was out of joint because he liked to take up the collection himself and Burke always seemed to get to the baskets before he did. But Lawlor bustled over to me on the church steps after Mass one day and told me he saw Burke take an envelope from the basket and slip it into his pocket. Between you and me, I was wishing Burke had managed to drive away before my informant had reached me with the news! I tend to be the type who wants to avoid confrontation! But my parishioner left me no choice. I went down to the basement where the collection was tallied up after Mass, and Burke was just leaving. I was put in the embarrassing position of having to ask if he had taken anything from the basket. He looked at me and seemed to be thinking it over. I must tell you, I was a little intimidated for a moment there. He was a powerful-looking man. But he reached into his pocket, brought out an envelope and showed it to me. It had no name on it, just a check mark or something in ink. He slit it open and invited me to look inside. It wasn't money at all! It was a sheaf of papers with numbers on them. The man was running some kind of numbers racket through the church! Which would explain why he was using a false name. Well, I didn't know what to say. I tried to formulate a response but he spoke first.

"I can't remember his exact words. He apologized. Said it was all just a lark but he knew the temple of Christ was no place for that kind of game. He assured me in no uncertain terms that not one cent had been taken from the church. When he turned to go, he saw Ted Lawlor standing there. You should have seen the look he gave Ted! I later learned that Ted had followed Burke to his house one day, found out his real name and confronted him with the accusations! They had words, as you can imagine, and a bit of a shoving match. Ted told me a young girl was present and caught the whole exchange. Must have been a daughter. Ted felt bad about that part of it. But Burke was telling the truth when he said no money had been taken. We went back over our collections, matched envelopes with amounts collected, compared Sundays. No differences.

"Bit of a mystery about the man, to be sure. We never saw him again after that. Not in person anyway. Saw his picture, though. Years later, long after he stopped coming to Saint Brigid's, I saw a photograph in one of the Catholic publications. A young man by the name of Burke was being ordained. And the man we're speaking of was in the picture. He was the ordinand's — the young lad's — father. So there he was, a good Catholic then as he was when I knew him. Except for a bit of gaming!"

"I'll have to keep in mind that this Burke, if I find him, may be a bit of a character. As for Cathal, you said you spoke at his funeral. Big funeral, was it?"

"Sad to say, it was not. Father McDiarmid said the Mass. There was me, Cathal's sister and her friend. That was it. Well, as I said, Cathal kept himself to himself as far as I could tell."

"So, nobody else on hand to see him off."

"No. Though there was another man in the church. I couldn't shake the impression that he was a — I don't think he was family," Grogan concluded.

"What was it you were going to say, Father? Don't spare my feelings now! Cathal may have been a relative but I never met him, so —"

"He was a policeman. I'd swear to it." He lowered his voice as if, even now, the wrong people might be listening. "And not a city cop either. I knew the police officers in the area; it wasn't one of them. He looked like, well, like a G-man! One of the Feds!"

I had a lot to digest here. Belatedly I remembered my supposed interest in the family tree. "Now you mentioned a sister. I didn't know about her. She likely has some information for me."

"You're out of time again, Mr. — I'm sorry —"

"Collins."

"Yes. Mr. Collins, you are too late. Miss Murphy died very recently. She was —" he cleared his throat as if Nessie's death was not a fit subject for conversation "— she was murdered! This city, I'm telling you."

"Murdered! What happened?"

"Some hooligans broke in. An old woman alone, in mourning for her brother. It doesn't bear thinking about. God rest her soul."

"Robbery?"

"Apparently."

"Father, I appreciate your time. I'll try to find this Declan Burke, to see what he can tell me about Cathal. I just hope Mr. Burke hasn't met an untimely death as well! All my contacts seem to be dying off."

"Oh, I wouldn't worry about Mr. Burke coming to grief at the hands of another. If anyone tried to attack him, he'd be well able for it!"

"Thanks, Father Grogan."

"You're more than welcome, Mr. Collins. God bless you."

A numbers racket. And the man who had confronted Declan at his house when Sandra was there was not a Mob enforcer, but a Saint Brigid's parishioner in high dudgeon!

That afternoon I got a call from Terry Burke. He entertained me with some misadventures during his recent flight back from Europe. Then we turned to his father.

"We're handing him over into your airspace for a while, I hear, Monty."

"So I'm told. Let's hope his stay is pleasant and uneventful. Tell me something. Was he ever into serious gambling that you know of?"

"Gambling? He's enjoyed some success as a poker player, but I don't know of anything beyond that. Why?"

"It's one of the many theories I'm considering. There's no point in filling you in about it until I nail it down. If I do."

"Fair enough. To tell you the truth, I'm not sure I want to know any more about the old renegade; my heart can't take it. I'm still trying to get my mind around the shooting."

"I hear you. I should put it out of my head, but I'm not satisfied with the way things have been left. So. Desailes Company. It's where Cathal Murphy used to work. Ever heard of it?"

"Not till today. But I asked around. It was Desailes Inc. and it ceased operations in the seventies. What's Murphy supposed to have done there?"

"He worked in shipping/receiving. I was wondering whether he might have been running an arms-smuggling operation from the inside. With a co-worker. Raising money, sending some guy out to buy guns. Or having them brought in and shipped out of the warehouse."

"Not much chance of that, from what I heard about the place. This outfit made surveillance equipment for high-altitude reconnaissance aircraft. Top-secret stuff. Nothing was being shipped out of there unless it was going to the Defense Department or to the major aircraft manufacturers. They ran a tight ship. The guy I spoke to knew somebody who worked there. They practically patted them down when they finished their shift. Doesn't sound like the kind of place where a low-level employee could run an operation of his own."

"Right. Well, I'll let you go."

"Have fun with the old man. If he comes back bubbling over with good reports of his trip, I'll hop on a flight some day and take a look for myself."

"You've never been to Halifax?"

"Not beyond the airport. How are the bars?"

"You'll be pleased."

"Great."

I replayed the conversation in my mind. There were two obituaries on my desk and I stared at them for a long moment, then looked at my watch and saw I had twenty minutes before I had to see a client. I picked up the phone, dialled Bridey's number in Philadelphia, engaged in a bit of what I hoped was witty repartee, and asked her again about the man Cathal Murphy had met at the Brooklyn Botanic Garden, the man who shouted but whose words were lost on the two young spies who were watching him.

†

Guinness and Jameson's were on the table, and Declan Burke was in my doorway. It was a cool, breezy Saturday night and Declan had accepted the invitation to be my guest during his surprise visit to Halifax. Brennan had just pulled up with his father in the car. I had some questions for Mr. Burke but hospitality came first.

"What brings you to Halifax, Declan?"

"A man needs a reason to visit his son?"

"I suppose not. What are you going to do?"

"Have tea with him at the parochial house, attend his Masses, listen to his choirs, see his city, drink his whiskey. Anything else you can think of?"

"No, that just about covers it."

"And I know you won't mind at all, Collins, if I move into your neighbourhood and ask all manner of unwelcome questions about your life," he said to me then.

"I would take that as a sign of your interest and friendship, Declan. Thank you. May I help you with your suitcase?"

"I can manage, thanks all the same."

"Come in, then."

"I'll be right back. I left my coat in Bren's car." He headed back outside.

"He won't talk to me," Brennan said as he came up the front step. I followed him to the back of the house, where he stood at the kitchen sink looking out over the waters of the Northwest Arm.

"What do you mean, won't talk?"

"About the shooting, about the gun heist and all the rest of it."

"What else is new? The man's not a talker."

"I just thought — the fact that he's flown all the way up here, after the kick in the nuts he gave me the day I left New York — I thought it must mean he wanted to tell me about it after all."

"Well, he's here, and there can only be one reason for that. He wants to be with you. And it wasn't a kick in the nuts he gave you in New York. He said it plainly: 'Because you have the power to absolve.' He thinks he doesn't deserve your absolution."

"God's absolution."

"Either way, he's the one who's undeserving. Not you."

"Mmm."

"Pour yourself an Irish and have a seat."

We heard Burke Senior coming back in.

"Come on upstairs, Declan. I've given you a room with a view of the water. A calming influence."

"I need calming down, you're thinking?"

You will, I said to myself. But there was something I hoped to clear up first.

"Brennan must be very happy to have his father here."

"He didn't look as if he'd gone mindless with joy, but you can't expect a grown-up son to give you a big sloppy kiss at the airport."

"A grown-up son is never too old to be hurt by a father who means the world to him."

He looked at me sharply. "Is there a point you're about to make here, Montague?"

"That last day in New York, I know Brennan was a little . . ."

"Yes, yes, I know it. I'll have a word with him. Are you hearing me though, Collins? I said 'a word.' I did not say I'm going to make a speech from the dock. I did not say 'Bless me, Father, for I have sinned.' I did not say I would be subjecting myself to an interrogation. I said 'a word.'"

"That sounds clear enough."

It was time to get down to brass tacks. I decided to pop the question without warning.

"Declan." He put his case on the bed and turned to face me. "Did you ever pass information to a Soviet intelligence officer operating in the United States?"

"Did I *what?*"

"Were you spying for the Russians in return for Russian guns for Ireland?"

He stared at me in utter astonishment. I knew beyond a shadow of a doubt that he was innocent of that charge, no matter what else he had done.

"I guess I have my answer."

"How in the hell did you come up with a daft idea like that?"

I had come up with the idea — and it wasn't daft — when I looked at all the evidence from a fresh perspective after rereading the obituary of Uncle Joe MacKenzie.

"Why don't you have a seat, Declan?"

He shook his head, his eyes never leaving my face. He wanted to be on his toes if I got any crazier.

"His loyalty to his Uncle was never in question," I recited from the Cathal Murphy obituary. "Uncle Joe Stalin."

"Have you taken leave of your senses? It was a reference to my uncles, who fought for Irish independence. Along with my father."

"Your uncles, plural. More important to you, your father. If that's what the old lady meant, it would have been worded that way. The FBI is looking into Nessie Murphy's death. You did know that the author of the death notice has been murdered?"

"I know that," he snapped.

"Papers were stolen from her apartment, Cathal's journals." The colour drained from Declan's face. I went on. "Cathal Murphy met secretly — or so he thought — with a man from Washington, who came up to New York to see him in the late 1950s or early 1960s. Probably one in a series of clandestine encounters. I had been thinking of a G-man. An FBI agent." I would spare him the story of his two young children following their mother's admirer all the way to his meeting at the Brooklyn Botanic Garden. I had remembered Bridey saying she couldn't make out what the Washington man said when he shouted at the young boys loitering around his car. He had yelled, but she couldn't understand him. Maybe, I thought, with the Uncle Joe Stalin reference fresh in my mind, the man had a foreign accent. She hesitated only a moment before saying yes when I called her on the phone. That was it: a heavy accent. "It turned out the man was a foreigner," I told Declan. "Cathal Murphy worked —"

"Fagan," Declan interjected. I knew he was poleaxed; he was actually offering me information!

"Did you know Murphy was Fagan when you first read the obituary?"

301

"Certainly not."

"Fagan was working for a defence contractor, Desailes Inc., the manufacturer of top-secret surveillance equipment for spy planes. He couldn't smuggle out photos or papers; security was too tight for that. But he didn't need to. He had a photographic memory, according to his sister. He could memorize the information. Specifications? Details of government orders? He could keep it in his head until he got home. Murphy/Fagan was renting two apartments. How could he have afforded that? Somebody was paying for it. Who? Irish Republicans?" Declan snorted at that. "There were code books in Nessie Murphy's apartment. She lied about where they came from. No doubt his methods, including his code systems, became more refined once he was in regular contact with his Soviet control.

"Obviously you weren't aware of what you were getting when you took up the collection those Sundays at Saint Brigid's and picked up the specially marked church envelopes Fagan put in the basket."

"You're fucking right I wasn't aware of it."

"I know. He probably told you it was coded information about bank accounts, contacts, shipping schedules and other details about the proposed arms shipments to Ireland." Declan was silent but I knew from his expression that I had it right. "In fact, though, Fagan had given up smuggling guns out of the US after being caught and spending time in the clink. He hit upon the idea of trading secrets to the Soviets in return for Russian weaponry, presumably shipped directly from the USSR. You didn't know any of this, but you were the courier." Silence. "Now, I'm sure he didn't have you meeting a Russian. Your contact would have been an American. The man wouldn't even have known your name. Or maybe you didn't meet anyone. You used a letter drop or some other system." Again, no reply.

Declan sat glowering in my direction but it wasn't my face he was seeing; it was Charlie Fagan, who had set him up in a perilous adventure that could, at any time, have been exposed.

"I guess he had his revenge on you after all, Declan."

"What do you mean, his revenge? How many of these goddamn avengers are out there, trying to blow my head off after all these years? What did he have to be vengeful about?"

"You took away the love of his life."

Astonishment gave way to wariness as he contemplated what, or who, I meant. "How could I have done that? I've been married to the same woman for over fifty years."

"He was in love with Teresa. Worshipped her in Dublin, followed her over here."

"What? What are you telling me now?"

"It's true, Declan. He didn't have much in his life: he was saddled with a cranky, resentful, determinedly dependent sister; he loved a woman he could never have; he had his two religions, the Catholic and the Irish. But he took care to ensure that he wouldn't lose that life, such as it was, if his operations were ever discovered. It would be his rival — you — who would face life imprisonment or even execution by the American government if your role as courier were ever revealed. No doubt he told you that one shipment of handguns, as welcome as it must have been back home, would not be enough to return you to the good graces of the IRA. And that he had a way to help you pay for the sins you committed against that unforgiving institution. Old Nessie knew some of this all along. No doubt the rest of it was known to her only after he died and she read his papers. She had it in for you too. For Teresa as well, more likely than not. If it weren't for Teresa, and then you, her brother would have married in Ireland and taken Nessie in. Life would have been much more comfortable with a sister-in-law to cook and clean for her. She hated her life here, and sought revenge of her own."

Declan had sunk down onto the bed. He stared at the wall without speaking.

"Let's call Leo," I said.

"Let's not."

"He told us to drop it."

"Leo's a wise man. What was it about 'drop it' that you didn't understand, Collins?"

"The Russian connection. That's what I didn't understand. I thought he was warning us off for other reasons." *Namely, that your own son had tried to kill you.* "What's his number in Dublin?"

"Leave the poor man alone. He's out of all that now."

Out of it himself but still in the know. "I'm going to find his number."

Declan sighed and drew a scrap of paper from his wallet. "What time is it? Just after seven, so it's midnight there."

"No, it's just a four-hour difference from here."

He grudgingly picked up the phone. "Could I speak to Father Killeen, please. Is he now. Well, I'll hold on then. Tell him it's Declan." He glared in my direction while he waited.

"Dia is Muire duit, Leo!" I did not understand anything he said following the godly greeting, with the exception of something that sounded like *"O Coileáin"* (me) and something else that could have been "Russian." He may have lost much of the Irish he had learned under Leo's tutelage in Mountjoy Prison, but he was able to make himself understood well enough to exclude me from the conversation with his old commander. Then he switched to the language of the oppressor. "Well, he had me gobsmacked here, Leo. I know. I'm sure you did." A reproving look at me. "Here he is. Put the fear of God into him, will you? I'll be in touch. Take care of yourself."

He handed the receiver to me. "Good evening, Leo."

"What did I tell you about this matter, *O Coileáin?"*

"You suggested I drop it, was that it, Father?"

"But you didn't listen, did you?"

"I'm all ears now. When you got back to Ireland, did you mention —"

"I didn't *mention* anything," he snapped. "I asked some questions."

"I have a question for you, Leo. Were there Irishmen in the USA trading secrets to the Soviets in exchange for Russian arms for Ireland?"

"Never say that again. Ever." There was ice in his voice.

But I persisted. "So, when the police solve the murder of Nessie —"

"They're not going to solve it," Killeen said in the same icy voice. "It should never have happened; it was not intended; it was not sanctioned. The poor woman, God rest her soul. But now that it's happened, it will remain unresolved. They will find there is no one to arrest for it."

"So there was an Irish connection after all."

"Not to the attempt on Declan, there wasn't." The words were clipped, followed by silence. This was as close as I would ever come to hearing what I now knew to be the truth. That Irish Republican forces — "not sanctioned," so it was someone acting unofficially — had killed Nessie to protect whatever information was contained in the personal papers of Cathal Murphy/Charlie Fagan. I wondered if the Russian agent was still in place in the United States. The fact that there was "no one to arrest" meant either that the killer had succeeded in getting out of the country, or he had been eliminated after the murder. I would never know.

"Are you still with us, Collins, or have I finally succeeded in shutting your gob?"

"My gob is shut."

"Is your good friend Brennan there?"

"He's downstairs. I'll —"

"Never mind him for now, then. So, Monty, I hope you'll be coming over to see me before I get old and unable to hobble around after you and the Burke brothers. And sisters."

"I thought perhaps I'd just taken a flame-thrower to my bridges with you, Leo."

"Of course not! Young pups have to be brought into line once in a while. I feel quite capable of doing that in my current role, as in my previous one."

"You are capable indeed, Leo."

"I'll look forward to seeing you. God bless you, Monty."

"Thank you, Father. Bye for now." We hung up.

Declan was giving me a fierce look. "If you were my son I'd give you a clout in the head."

"If I were your son I'd take it. Let's go down and join Brennan. Is that the first time you've talked to Leo since he left?"

"No. We exchanged Easter greetings."

"Oh? Easter Sunday?"

"Saturday, it was."

"So, did you call him, or did he call you?"

"I called him, caught him just before he headed out for the Vigil at the Pro-Cathedral. He — You're going to get that clout in the head, Montague, if I hear another fucking word. Or if I even see a look on your face that makes me suspect you're thinking such vicious thoughts again."

We had joined Brennan in the kitchen by that time. He was

looking at us with one quizzical eyebrow raised. "You're going to clout Monty, is that what I heard, Da? Any particular reason?"

"The fecker just interrogated me to check on Leo's alibi!"

"Alibi for what?"

"The murder of the old woman," Declan growled.

"*Íosa Críost,* Collins! How does your mind operate? You didn't honestly think Leo —"

"No, I didn't." I thought it highly unlikely. But it was a relief, nonetheless, to have it confirmed that he was in Ireland at the time Nessie Murphy was killed.

"I'm going to run out and pick up something for us to eat," I said to my guests. "In the meantime I'm sure you gentlemen have things to talk about. Now that I've filled your father in, Brennan." I started for the door, then turned back. "The whole time we were in New York, we thought Declan had all the information we were looking for, and was keeping it from us. Turns out he didn't know the half of it!"

I smiled at Declan and opened my mouth to deliver another remark. I was silenced by a cold blue glare.

The following books proved invaluable in the writing of *Obit*.

Anderson, Brendan. *Joe Cahill: A Life in the IRA* (The O'Brien Press, Dublin, 2002)
Behan, Brendan. *Borstal Boy* (Knopf, New York, 1959)
Behan, Brendan. *Confessions of an Irish Rebel* (Bernard Geis Associates, New York, 1965)
Coogan, Tim Pat. *The I.R.A.* (HarperCollins, London, 2000)

Here's a look at the next book in
Anne Emery's Monty–Collins Mystery series,
Barrington Street Blues

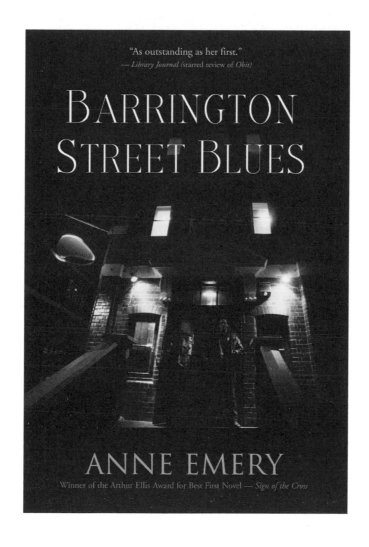

"As outstanding as her first."
— *Library Journal* (starred review of *Obit*)

BARRINGTON
STREET BLUES

ANNE EMERY
Winner of the Arthur Ellis Award for Best First Novel — *Sign of the Cross*

Chapter 1

"Two Dead in Barrington Street Shooting"
— Halifax *Daily News*, January 13, 1991

"It's the end of the road. The dark end, down by the train tracks, where Barrington Street peters out after running its course through downtown Halifax. One man lies face down on the pavement, his canvas field jacket stained with blood, a Rolex watch glimmering on his wrist. The other, dressed in sweatpants and a windbreaker advertising Gatorade, lies on his side, a gun still gripped in his right hand. The first homicides in Halifax in 1991. The city averages eight murders a year. If, as police believe, this was a murder-suicide . . ."

My client looked up from the newspaper clipping. "What's all this about their clothes? How's that news? They make it look like Corey was a bum, and him bein' dead doesn't matter as much as the guy with the watch."

"It's not a news story, it's an opinion piece," I told Amber Dawn Rhyno. "But never mind that. Your husband's death matters to us, so let's talk about him."

"Corey's not — he wasn't my husband."

"Common-law husband. How long did you live together?"

"You mean when he wasn't in jail or the treatment centre? Me and

1

Corey were together on and off for nine years. Ever since I had Zachary."

Zachary was her son. The whole time they had been in my law office, the boy had been sitting on my side table and falling off, sitting and falling. Each time he fell, he took a stack of my files with him to the floor. I tried to ignore him.

"All right, Amber. Tell me what happened when you first heard about Corey's suicide."

"I wasn't surprised at all. Not one bit. He blamed that place. Or, like, he would've if he didn't die. If he came out of it, he woulda said it was all their fault."

I studied Amber Dawn Rhyno, imagining her on the witness stand in a damages suit against the addiction treatment centre where Corey Leaman had been staying before he was found with a bullet in his brain. Amber Dawn was a short, skinny woman in her late twenties. She had a hard-bitten face, and thin brown hair that was straight for about six inches, frizzy at the ends. An acid-green tank top revealed a tattooed left shoulder.

"Who's Troy?" I asked her.

"Troy?"

"The tattoo."

"Oh." She shrugged. "Just this guy."

"Someone you were involved with?"

"We weren't really, like, involved."

I let it go. It was not as if I would allow her anywhere near opposing counsel — never mind a courtroom — in a sleeveless top.

"Zach!"

The child had picked up my radio, and was trying to pull the knobs off it.

"Put that down," I told him. "Now."

"You can't make me!"

"Yeah. I can." I got up and wrenched the radio from his hands. He began to howl.

"It's not his fault," his mother said. "The social worker says he has a problem."

"I'm sorry, Amber, but I have another client coming in. We'll get together again. In the meantime, I'd like you to write up a little history of your relationship with Corey Leaman, including what you recall about the times he was admitted to the Baird Treatment Centre."

"But I already told you everything."

"There's a lot more that you'll remember when you sit down and think about it."

My clients would never sit down and write. But I would worry about that later. Zachary's howling had reached a new, ear-splitting pitch. Time for them to go.

"Call me if you need anything. You have my number."

"Yeah, okay. Thanks, Ross."

"I'm Monty. Ross is the other lawyer working on your case."

"Sorry. Can I have your card? I already got Ross's."

"Here you go."

She read the card: "Montague M. Collins, B.A., LL. B. Right. Okay, bye."

I watched Amber drag her son out the door and thought about her case. Corey Leaman, her common-law husband, and another man, named Graham Scott, were found dead of gunshot wounds at five o'clock in the morning of January 12, 1991, in the parking lot of the Fore-And-Aft. This was a nautically themed strip joint situated across from the Wallace Rennie Baird Addiction Treatment Centre. The two buildings are the last structures at the bottom end of Barrington Street, which runs along the eastern edge of the Halifax Peninsula, from Bedford Basin in the north to the train tracks that traverse the south end of the city. The street had seen better days, and would again, I knew. But that was neither here nor there for the two men who had been found sprawled on the pavement at the end of the road.

The gun was in Leaman's right hand. He had apparently dispatched Scott with two bullets in the back of the head, then put a bullet in his own right temple. Leaman's drug addiction had landed him in the Baird Centre; he had been released shortly before his death. The police were keeping the file open even though the medical examiner had declared the case a probable murder-suicide. Now, three months after the deaths, my firm was representing the families of Leaman and Scott in a lawsuit against the Baird Centre. We claimed the treatment facility had been negligent in releasing Leaman when it knew, or ought to have known, that Leaman presented a danger to others and to himself. It was by no means certain that we could pin the responsibility on the treatment centre, but we would do our best.

†

The following night, Tuesday, I had left the world of drugs and guns and was seated in the choir loft of St. Bernadette's Church. Next to me was another unlikely choirboy, Ed Johnson. Ed and I were more accustomed to wailing the blues in our band, Functus, which we had formed in law school more than twenty years ago; the St. B's gig was something new. A much purer tone of voice was expected here. That wasn't going to be easy, given that Johnson and I had spent the previous night in a succession of bars around the city. But the choirmaster had ordained that we be present, and so we were.

"I hear you've got the Leaman case, Collins," said Johnson. "How much do you expect to rake in?"

"No idea. I've barely looked at the file."

Johnson claimed to hate working as a lawyer but, in reality, the law courts were mother earth to him. He was tall and thin with light brown hair and a bony face; his lips were set in a permanent sneer. Every guy has an old friend that his wife doesn't trust, someone she thinks is going to lead her husband astray in the world of wine, women and song. Or, as we know it today, sex, drugs and rock 'n roll. To all appearances, Ed Johnson filled that role nicely. But in fact, behind the seen-it-all, done-it-all façade, Ed was as tender-hearted as anyone I'd ever met. And, as far as I knew, even his own wife had nothing to worry about.

Ed was still talking about the Leaman case. "Well, I don't imagine you're talking big bucks for lost future income. It wasn't two brain surgeons who shot each other's lights out in the Foreign Daft parking lot."

"No, from what I understand, the families just want —"

"Don't tell me." He put his hand up. "Let me guess. It's not about the money. It's the principle of the thing, right? The families just want justice. So, is it going to be more trouble than it's worth, or what?"

"Could be. But I've got Ross Trevelyan working with me. He's a certifiable workaholic, so I won't be knocking myself out."

"Yeah, I heard. Rowan finally managed to reel him in. Well done."

Rowan was Rowan Stratton, the senior partner at my law firm, Stratton Sommers. Rowan had been trying to woo Ross away from Trevelyan and Associates, his father's firm, for years. Ross was the son of John Trevelyan, one of the city's most eminent barristers, who had recently been appointed a justice of the Nova Scotia Supreme Court. John was considered Supreme Court of Canada material, and the betting was that he would soon be elevated to the Court of Appeal, where he would sit until a place opened up on the country's top court in Ottawa. The Trevelyan name was like gold.

"I thought Ross would be full of shit," I said, "but he isn't. He offered to help me with the Leaman case, among others, and he's doing all the discoveries for Rowan on the Sherman Industries file. So it's worked out well."

"Better him than you. I don't envy you trying to pin those two shootings on Wally Baird's detox. So they released Leaman; they thought he was all right. What else were they going to do, keep him in for the rest of his life? Defence counsel will stop at nothing to keep the floodgates closed on that one. And it definitely won't be about the money for them. Because there won't be much of a claim. They'll just want to avoid setting a precedent for every Tom, Dick, and —"

We heard a whisper hiss its way through the ranks of the boy sopranos on the other side of the choir loft. They straightened up and fell silent as the choirmaster appeared before us.

The Reverend Brennan X. Burke was tall, stern, and immaculate in his clerical suit and Roman collar. He had black eyes, black hair flecked with grey, and an Irish-looking mouth, from which emerged a voice tinged with the accent of the old country whence his family had come when he was but a lad.

"Good evening, gentlemen."

"Good evening, Father!"

"Welcome to the first rehearsal of the St. Bernadette's Choir of Men and Boys. Let us bow our heads and pray. *Exaudi nos, Domine sancte, Pater omnipotens . . .*"

"It's still in Latin?" Ed whispered. "I thought they switched —"

I kicked Ed somewhere between the ankle and the shin to instill in him the proper attitude towards prayer, and he lapsed into silence. Burke communed with God in Latin; that's all there was to it.

St. Bernadette's was a small neo-Gothic church at the corner of Byrne and Morris streets in the southeast part of Halifax, near the harbour. The light of a spring evening shone through the stained-glass windows, giving the church the appearance of a jewel box. More to the point for us, the acoustics were magnificent, which made it the ideal location for the choir school run by Father Burke.

We sight-read our way through a musical history of the Catholic Church, from thousand-year-old Gregorian chant to the multi-layered sound of the Renaissance to the *Ave Verum* of Mozart. The choir director listened to voices and the way they blended, and shuffled people around to get the sound he wanted. I was surprised at how good the younger boys were; their sight-reading and vocal abilities spoke well for the choir school. Johnson and I had the croakiest voices in the loft — no surprise there — and we were the subject of damning looks from the priest as a result.

But all was forgiven when we adjourned for a post-choral pint. Brennan Burke and I had become friends over the past year after I defended him — successfully — on a murder charge. He and Johnson had met the odd time, usually when the priest came to hear our blues band perform. We left the church and got into my car. There was no discussion of where to go; it was a foregone conclusion that we were headed for Grafton Street. The Midtown Tavern & Grill, with its familiar red and green sign and its unpretentious appearance, was an institution in the life of the city. Three draft were on the table before we'd settled in our seats, and the waiter didn't waste our time telling us about himself or about anything with raspberry *coulis* in, on, or around it.

"Can you believe the sound coming out of that little Robertson fellow?" Burke remarked. "He's only nine years old. A little hellion but he's cute as a button."

"You're fond of young boys, are you, Brennan?"

"I am, Ed." Burke took out a pack of cigarettes, lit one, and blew the smoke away from the table. "Young girls, too. And grown women. I tolerate a few obnoxious middle-aged male companions as well. You sounded great, I have to say. A bit rough around the edges, but I may have a solo for you if I can catch you after an early night."

"Could happen."

"How long have you and Monty known each other?"

"Long time," Ed replied. "When I met Collins I wanted his parents to adopt me."

"I can't imagine why they didn't."

"Neither could I at the time. Though it might have had something to do with my debt load in law school."

"Ah."

"Yeah, I was a little out of the adoptable category by the time I met them. I hear they took in a kitten instead."

"So, why Monty's parents?"

"Well, look at him! Did you ever see anybody more placid than this guy?"

"I don't know. I've seen him a little perturbed on occasion."

"Notable because so rare, am I right? His mother was always in pearls, and his father always had his head in a book. 'I dropped in to borrow the car, all right, Dad?' 'Sure, dear, go right ahead.' Dear! To his twenty-two-year-old son."

"He called us all dear. He was a sweetheart."

"See? What did your old man call you, Brennan?"

"'You little gobshite,' most of the time. But he meant well."

"My old man called me 'kumquat.' And he didn't mean well."

"He called you a fruit?"

"No, he called my brother a fruit. He called me 'kumquat' because he's such a dumb fuck he thought it meant something dirty. Probably still does. Ole Vinny ain't never going to be asked to serve on the Greater Halifax Literacy Council."

"Is your father here in town?"

"I hope not. So. Monty's working on a suicide case. Those guys can't be buried in consecrated ground, right?" Father Burke started to reply, but Johnson kept on: "I wonder if you can ratchet up the damage claim because of that. Mental anguish for the family."

"I've met the wife. I can't quite see her wailing and gnashing her teeth over a religious rejection."

"Then you're not doing your job, Collins."

"Moooooo." I looked up the next morning to see Ross Trevelyan standing in the doorway to my office. "Our milch cow just walked in the door."

"Oh?"

"The girlfriend and, unsuspected until now, the wee tiny daughter of Graham Scott. Graham Scott who, his parents insist, was getting off drugs —"

"Scott was on drugs too?"

"*Off* drugs, Monty, *off* drugs. Unlike Leaman, Scott was going clean and was practically on the road to medical school when his untimely death occurred outside the Fore-And-Aft."

"You say he had a daughter? How old?"

"Two."

"Well!"

"And — *and* — any day now, the girlfriend is going to be delivered of a second little calf who'll never know her daddy."

"No!"

"Yes. Dependency claim for millions. Two little girls who lost the guidance and financial support of a father who was almost certainly going to win the Nobel Prize for medicine. So, Monty, do you want to meet them, or would you like me to handle it?"

"You go ahead. Thanks, Ross."

"No problem. And his parents are coming in this afternoon. You may have heard of them. Alastair Scott is a clergyman, but they live well. They're sitting on a pile of old money. I'm going to be in court and may not be back in time for their appointment."

"I'll see the parents."

"Great. Meanwhile, I'll draw up the contingency agreements." We were required to register with the court the agreement between us and our clients to take thirty percent of whatever we recovered in our lawsuit against the treatment centre. Which, as Ross had pointed out, could now be millions.

Ross was in his late thirties. Short, trim, and handsome with thinning dark hair and a winning smile. He was one of those people who look better with eyeglasses than without; his tortoiseshell frames gave him an air of distinction. I had never met anyone who worked harder. He confided to me when he joined Stratton Sommers that he had never felt appreciated when he was toiling away in the middle ranks of his father's prestigious law firm. He was ready when Rowan made his latest offer of a partnership. I walked out to the waiting room and told Darlene, our receptionist, that I would be seeing Mr. and Mrs. Scott when they came in later in the day.

†

I had not even opened the Leaman and Scott suicide file yet, but, as I expected, Graham Scott's parents were not looking for information from me. They were determined to set the record straight about their son, and all I had to do was listen. Canon Alastair Scott and his wife, Muriel, were both tall and slim with blondish hair beginning to turn white. He appeared in a well-tailored business suit, but I could easily picture him in clerical collar and vestments. He was an Anglican priest with a doctorate in divinity. Muriel Scott wore a pale blue dress with a light tweed jacket and a string of pearls. I knew they were friends of my senior partner, Rowan Stratton. I doubted they had even been aware of the Fore-And-Aft before their son was found dead there.

"Our son has been portrayed in the press as a drug addict and a criminal," Canon Scott began as soon as we had introduced ourselves. "In fact, he was not an addict. He was a recreational user of cocaine, not crack cocaine, and he was able to go for long periods of time without it. He had a minor criminal record, for drug possession and common assault. Graham got in with an unfortunate set of companions in high school. I don't put the blame entirely on others of course. Graham was responsible for his own actions, and should have known better. Indeed he did know better. Notwithstanding all this, he got through high school without repeating any grades and, with some interruptions and backsliding, he managed to complete three years of a science degree at Dalhousie U. Graham told us he was planning to go back this September and finish his degree. After that, medical school. It was his dream — to be more accurate, it was his intention — to become a cardiologist. There is no doubt in my mind that eventually he would have achieved that goal."

9

"Graham comes where in the family? You have other children, I know."

"He's — he was the third of four. Boy, girl, boy, boy. None of our other children got into trouble, but Graham was a bit of an adventurer. I always felt he would sink the lowest and, in the end, rise to the greatest heights."

"Canon Scott, Mrs. Scott, where was Graham living just before his death?"

Muriel Scott answered. "He had recently moved back in with us. He had been rooming with some friends, but that arrangement was a trial to him. I think he saw moving home as a way to begin getting his life back in order."

"Did he ever speak to you about Corey Leaman?"

"Never heard of him, until this happened," the canon said.

"So you don't know whether he was acquainted with Leaman before his death." They shook their heads. "Did he talk about his friends, the people he went around with?"

"The only friends he talked about to us were people we knew, youngsters he had been with at the Halifax Grammar School. These other people, he never alluded to them."

"How old was Graham?"

His mother started to speak, cleared her throat and tried again. "Graham died one week before his twenty-second birthday. He had his whole life — I know it's a cliché, but Graham had such a future ahead of him. Despite the trouble he'd been in, and the rough characters he'd taken up with, he never lost his essential goodness. His quality."

"Now, about Graham's girlfriend. And his child."

"Yes?" They both spoke at once.

"Did you know the girl, and your grandchild?"

They exchanged a glance. Eventually, the father replied: "No."

"Had you been aware that he had a child?"

The exchange of glances, the shaking of heads.

"Have you since met the girlfriend and the little girl?"

"At the wake and the funeral for Graham," his mother answered.

"And since then?"

"No."

"Did she tell you, or were you aware, that she is expecting a second child?"

Silence. Not even an exchange of glances.

I would have to check the law on paternity tests, specifically, who could apply to the court to order one. Graham Scott's children would be the key to the damage award. His parents would be entitled to something, as would Corey Leaman's family. But it was Graham's kids who could claim to have lost a lifetime of support from a (hypothetically) high-earning father.

After the Scotts left, I made a pass by Ross Trevelyan's office, but he wasn't there. I saw the file on his side table, picked it up, and took it to my desk, where I dictated a memo on my conversation with the Scotts. I was just finishing up when Ross came in.

"Hi. Court just wound up. Were the parents in?"

"Just left. The long and the short of it is: Graham was going straight to a residency in cardiology." Ross beamed. "He had never mentioned Corey Leaman, but he never talked about any of the other low-lifes he ran around with either. And he never told his parents about the existence of their grandchild. Or of the pregnancy, if he knew of it. The girlfriend was not included in any Sunday dinners with the vicar."

"A respectable family like his, he kept his other life a secret. Having met the girlfriend, I can't say I'm surprised he hid her in the shadows. She's a bit, well, 'not our sort, darling,'" he finished in a posh British accent much like that of Rowan Stratton. Ross looked at my desk. "You've got the file? Good. You may want to read through it before you meet Doctor Swail-Peddle."

"Who?"

"A very favourable witness."

"Oh?"

"Or he will be, if his telephone call is anything to go by."

"You mean he called you?"

"Yes. He heard about the case, and gave me a call."

"What's his interest?"

"He was a psychologist on staff at the Baird Addiction Treatment Centre."

"Was."

"Yeah. I don't know what the story is, except that he's willing to help us out. I've pencilled him in for tomorrow afternoon, late. You may want to sit in if you're still around at six or so."

"Sure."

He waved and went off.

I opened the file and began to read. The first thing that leapt out at me was that the police had initially regarded this not as a suicide, but as a double murder. There was no known connection between the two men, no known motive for Leaman to kill Scott. They each had a history of drug use and trafficking, but Leaman would hardly have executed Scott for a drug deal gone wrong, then killed himself immediately afterwards. Then again, Leaman had a psychiatric history and had occasionally been violent in the past. Who knew what might have provoked him to kill Scott and turn the gun on himself?

That was another thing, the gun. There had been no indication that Leaman had ever used or possessed a gun. The police had not been able to trace it. It was an unusual weapon in this day and age, a German Luger P-08, which was already being replaced by another weapon before the end of World War Two. This one was almost certainly stolen, but no collector had stepped forward to claim it. There were no complete fingerprints on the weapon apart from Leaman's. There were smeared prints, which could have belonged to Leaman or somebody else. This, to me, served to support the suicide theory. Typically, if someone wanted to commit murder and make it look like suicide, they wiped the gun free of prints, then placed it in the victim's hand. Guns used by people like Leaman tended to be passed around; if his had been the only prints on the gun, that would have struck me as suspicious. There was no detectable gunshot residue on Leaman, but there was a handwritten note in the file, probably scribbled by a detective after conversation with an expert: "Recoverable residues generally do not persist on skin for very long . . . residues may be absent for any number of reasons." I knew there had been freezing rain the morning the bodies were found.

In the end, the police had left the file open. With no witnesses and no evidence of a third person at the scene, they could not establish a double murder. The medical examiner's and autopsy reports were meticulous in describing the gunshot wounds; they did not come to a definitive conclusion as to whether or not Leaman's wound was self-inflicted, but the M.E. put it down as a probable suicide. That was good enough for me. And it would remain good enough, as long as we weren't faced with a witness popping up later to say there was somebody else at the Fore-And-Aft that morning.

†

"Collins. Have you forgotten?" It was the Undersigned, the most pompous partner in our firm, who never referred to himself as "I" or "me" but as "the Undersigned" in his correspondence. He had slicked-back fair hair and a perpetually irritated expression on his face. He was vibrating impatiently at my door in his imitation English suit of clothes. Our founding partner raised a condescending eyebrow at the Undersigned's back as he passed by in his real, and threadbare, English tweeds, which he had probably brought over with him when he immigrated in 1945.

I had indeed forgotten. It was Thursday, April 18, the day my firm was taking me to lunch to celebrate what they considered to be my finest achievement. I had just been named a Queen's Counsel. I hadn't even applied for the honour; the Undersigned had. He — his real name was Vance Blake — had taken it upon himself to cobble together my curriculum vitae, and some kind words from references, and submit an application on my behalf after shoving the forms on my desk and having me sign them when I was distracted. I had promptly forgotten all about it. But Blake had not. In his view, the more Queen's Counsels the firm had on its letterhead, the better.

So we all trooped down the hill to the waterfront, to Wiggin-staff's, a self-consciously upmarket bar and dining room favoured by certain members of the Nova Scotia Barristers' Society. We took up all the tables overlooking the harbour and ordered drinks. I watched through the window as a sailboat bobbed along like a toy on the choppy water; it was dwarfed by a massive container ship heading up the harbour to the Ceres terminal. Once the pre-luncheon drinks were in our hands, a toast was raised to me.

"To Montague M. Collins, Q.C."

This was met by the insufferable "hear, hear," which I always associated with mutton-chopped Victorian pomposity. "Speech, speech," they chanted.

I rose to respond: "Our clients come to us because they need a voice. We speak for them in places where they otherwise might fail to be heard or understood. I stand in that proud tradition and I am humbled by the opportunity to do so." I hoped to be even more full of shit when I got wound up. "When the taxman cometh to take his pound of flesh," I declaimed to another round of "hear, hears" from the solicitors in our tax department, "our clients want to be assured —"

"— that they won't have to pay one red cent!" a partner called out.

I continued: "— that their tax dollars are not being squandered on yet more ill-advised attempts by the state to come down on the backs of the citizens and to further grind down —"

"Risk-takers and entrepreneurs who are the engine of the economy in this country, and who are fettered at every turn by —"

I ignored Vance Blake's corporate passion and soldiered on: "— further grind down the poor, the disenfranchised, the marginal and the crazed, those who come before the criminal justice system, propelled there by the misfortune of their birth and their assigned place at the bottom of the heap in our society. Guilty they may be, in the eyes of the law, yet it falls to us, Stratton Sommers, Barristers and Solicitors, to implore the courts for understanding and mercy. Can any one of us, in his or her most private moments, honestly say he has not, at some anguished moment of his life, shared the murderous fury of my recent client who took an axe to the pale and trembling flesh of —"

"We don't want to hear it!"

"Sit down, Collins!"

"I cannot possibly say how much it means to me to have the might and prestige of Stratton Sommers behind me as I go to the wall for these hapless denizens of the criminal courts. To be honoured by you as I am today —"

Rowan Stratton had turned a deaf ear to the protests of certain members of the firm when I was hired to set up a criminal law practice. It was still, evidently, a sore point for some.

"You're an asshole, Collins," Blake hissed as I passed his table at the end of my speech.

"It's an honour and a privilege to be on your enemies list, Vance," I replied, sending a wink in the direction of Monique LeBlanc, who shared my view of the Undersigned.

I sat down beside Monique and picked up my beer. She leaned over and asked: "Who's going to defend you, Monty, the day we find Vance slumped over in the boardroom with a knife in his back?"

"I bear him no ill will."

"I cannot believe the way you let all this run off your back."

"You have distinguished yourself," my very British senior partner muttered from my other side, "as a cad and a blackguard among your partners. For that I salute you."

We finished our celebratory lunch and walked up Salter Street to our office, just around the corner on Barrington. We occupied the seventh floor of a ten-storey glass box recently erected between two old ornate buildings that I much preferred to ours. The firm used to be in one of them, a four-storey Italianate building that I admired; unfortunately the firm had moved to its more modern quarters just before I joined up. The new building struck a jarring note in this block of nineteenth-century structures.

†

I wanted to devote my time to the Leaman case when I got back, but first I had to deal with my other clients. The first in line was Yvette, a hooker and crack addict who was charged with assaulting another woman in a fight over a boyfriend. She was an old client from my Nova Scotia Legal Aid days. She couldn't pay my regular fee, so my partners were never happy when her name came up at the office. We would meet in court the next morning. I went over the statements given by patrons of the Miller's Tale, the bar where the fight had occurred, looking for any indications I could find that Yvette was acting in self-defence when she hit Doris Pickard over the head with a chair.

At nine on Friday morning I was standing with my client outside the provincial courthouse on Spring Garden Road. It was muggy and warm. Grotesque stone faces, fanged and wild, looked out at us from the facade of the Victorian court building. Yvette was wearing purple leggings that might have fit my eight-year-old daughter. A black tube top gave partial cover to her emaciated upper body. Her hair, a startling orangey blonde, was long in back and short in front, the bangs and sides curled away from her lined, olive-skinned face. She took a desperate drag of her cigarette as if, in the unhappy event of a conviction, she might not be able to score any drugs, including nicotine, in jail.

"So, Yvette, before we get in there —"

"Why-vette, not Eve-ette. How many times do I gotta say it for you, Monty?" she asked in a weary voice.

"All right, Why-vette." Why, as in why had her mother chosen the name "Yvette" if she did not even know how to pronounce it? But we were far from Yvette's christening day now.

"Doris's statement says you came at her with the chair because Bo was going to stay with her instead of you when he was released from the Correctional Centre."

"Bullshit! She said Bo got a tat on his arm with her name on it when he was inside. I said she was a lyin' slut, and she held up a bottle of Blue Typhoon and was gonna hit me." She barely got through her story; she seemed ready to fall asleep on her feet. Caution: coming down from this medication may cause drowsiness.

"Don't fade on me, Why-vette. This bottle of — what did you say it was?"

"Blue Typhoon. She was gonna bash me in the head with it, so I hit her in self-defence."

"Right. Let's go inside."

When the trial got under way, one of our witnesses, another hooker named Wanda Pollard, switched loyalties and backed up Doris's allegations. Yvette glared daggers at Wanda and repeatedly gave her the finger. I tried to undo the damage with my next witness, but Yvette had her own ideas of where the case should go. When she took the stand, she told a story completely different from the one she had given me. She decided, on her own, that a defence of drunkenness was her best legal strategy. Yvette did not deny that she swung the chair and smashed Doris in the face with it. But now she claimed she herself had guzzled the bottle of Blue Typhoon. After that, in a drunken rage, exacerbated by a rare medical condition that had not been disclosed until that moment, Yvette had lost it and attacked the other woman. On and on it went, a story I heard for the first time as I stood there poleaxed. Yvette was convicted and remanded into custody; sentencing would follow in a couple of months' time. I had to prepare for a bail hearing, so I clomped down the staircase to the basement cells, pressed the button, and waited for the sheriff to let me in.

I met with my client in a small room. But I didn't stay long. Her conviction, and her need for a hit of crack, had soured her mood. "You're no fuckin' good, Collins. You said you'd get me off. I want another lawyer. You're fired."

"What I said, Eve-ette, was that if the judge believed you and not Doris, your chances were good, but if the other version was more believable, you'd have to pack your jammies. Speaking of your story, Eve-ette, imagine my surprise when I heard it for the first time."

"You fuck off. You're fired. I want Saul Green."

I waved her off and headed for the door. I had planned to get a bite of lunch on Spring Garden Road but I decided to return to my office, grab Yvette's file, and deliver it personally to Green's office before she had time to phone, weeping with remorse, and hire me back. This happened all the time: client changing story or otherwise screwing up case, blaming lawyer, firing lawyer, calling to beg lawyer to represent him or her again. I liked to ship the file out before that pleading phone call, one less thing to worry about. I was known in some circles as the fastest courier service in Halifax.

But not fast enough this time. The message was waiting for me when I walked in. Could I call Yvette? She wanted to apologize and she had something to tell me. Well, she could work on her apology for a while in her cell.

†

I had to pick up an obscure legal text at the Sir James Dunn Law Library, so I drove to the law school on University Avenue. I collected my book, then steeled myself for an encounter with one of the professors at the law school.

"What now, Collins?" Maura MacNeil's brow was furrowed in a scowl.

"Did I catch you at a bad time? Again? Should I come back in, say, the year 2000 when you might be on an upswing?"

"Come back when you've taken the trouble to remember my schedule. I have a class in ten minutes. The way I always do this time on Friday. What are you doing here?"

"I was in the library and I was wondering if you'd had lunch."

"I plan to have lunch after my class. But what's that got to do with you?"

"That's just it. I don't want to have lunch at all. I think I'm eating too much lately and I figured if I stopped by here, two minutes with you would put me off my food. Mission accomplished."

Maura and I had two children together; we'd been separated for nearly five years and shared the kids week on, week off. She still lived in our old family home downtown on Dresden Row. I felt I had made more of an effort than she had to reconcile our many differences. Now, as I hovered unwelcome at the threshold of her office, I wondered for the thousandth time why I didn't just pack it in.

"You're not eating too much," she said. "You're drinking too much. I'm the one who's going overboard with eating. I've gained ten pounds."

Maura was one of those very attractive women somewhat above society's ideal of the perfect size for females. A wide mouth, upturned grey eyes, creamy skin, and shoulder length brown hair. Normally she didn't give a damn about her size so maybe she had gained a few pounds. She looked fine to me. "You look fine to me."

"Thank you."

"What do you mean, I'm drinking too much?"

"I don't know how else I can put it so you can understand, Collins, but let me try. Whenever I've seen you lately, you have a glass in your hand, which you raise to your lips and —" she put her right hand up and mimed someone tipping a glass of liquid down his throat "— guzzle. And that glass always seems to contain, or so I suspect, the chemical compound designated variously as ethanol, ethyl alcohol, or just alcohol, chemical formula: CH_3CH_2OH."

"You rarely see me, so how would you know?"

"I know. The fact of the matter is your drinking has increased ever since you started hanging around with Brennan Burke."

"Am I hearing you right? I must be the only man in the world being castigated by his wife for spending too much time with a priest!"

"I'm just saying you've —"

"Had enough. I'm taking the kids to the Rankins concert. Don't wait up."

"You got tickets?"

"I got tickets."

Silence, as she considered the consequences of being obnoxious to me once again. Then: "How many tickets?"

"Three." She knew I was lying about the number, but I didn't care. I would give the fourth to somebody else.

I retreated from her office but decided that, since I was at the law school, I might as well do a bit of research into the possible liability of the Baird Centre. I went back to the library and gathered some typical medical malpractice cases. Then, with an eye to Graham Scott and the dependency claims of his children, I looked for cases in which people successfully sued institutions for harm done by inmates who were released when they should have been kept inside. I started with a well-known case in which some Borstal boys in England escaped from custody, boarded a yacht, and soon thereafter rammed into another vessel. The question was whether the Home Office and its Borstal officers owed a duty of care to the owners of the damaged boat. Lord Reid considered an American case in which it was held that such a heavy responsibility should not be imposed on the New York State prison system. Distancing himself from the skittish Americans, His Lordship stated that "Her Majesty's servants are made of sterner stuff," and could bear up very well under the duty of care owed to the plaintiffs. I hoped our local courts would feel the same way about the Baird Treatment Centre. But Corey Leaman had not escaped; he had been released. I would hit the books again another day. Before I left, I checked the indexes to see if there were any reported cases in which the Baird Centre was named as a defendant. There was one: a visitor had sprained her ankle when she tripped in a depression in the front walkway, and was awarded two thousand dollars in damages. I went from the library to the Law Courts building, where I looked in the records for any recent litigation in the works. The only case coming up against the Baird Centre was a claim by a contractor who had not been paid for repairs to the building's foundation. Nobody had ever sued the centre for anything resembling malpractice.

†

Before I could go to hear the Rankins, I had to put in an appearance at a house-warming party at Ross Trevelyan's. He had recently moved from a duplex on Lawrence Street to a much grander abode on Beaufort Avenue in the city's south end. The story was that his wife, Elspeth, had put an offer on the place when Ross was out of town, confident that Ross would fall in love with it the way she had. In my experience, men did not fall in love with houses with the same passion women did, especially when those dwellings cost four times as much as the past digs. But Ross must have been impressed by the place, because here they were.

It was big, multi-gabled and vaguely Swiss in style. A nice residence anywhere, a very expensive one on this street. Mrs. Trevelyan greeted me at the door. "I don't believe we've met. I'm Elspeth."

"Monty Collins."

Elspeth was tall and slim with a shoulder-length blonde pageboy. She peered behind me. "Are you alone?"

I followed her gaze then turned back. "Quite alone. We're safe now."

"Ha ha. You're the one who does criminal law, do I have that right?"

"I'm the one."

"No offence, but I'm glad Ross doesn't do that kind of work anymore. He did criminal cases when he articled. That was back before I knew him, but every once in a while we'll be downtown and some really tough character will say hi to him. We go to St. George's Anglican — you know, the round church — and there are a couple of prostitutes who hang around that area. If we go to a function at night, we hear: 'Hey, Ross!' It's embarrassing, let me tell you. Did the firm ever think of phasing out the criminal practice?"

"They're just phasing it in, actually. Or they have been since I arrived a few years ago."

"I see."

"Are you going to phase me out or let me in?"

"Oh! I'm sorry. Come in, come in."

I stepped into the foyer and then the living room, where I spied Ross, red-faced and sweating, working at some sort of gadget by the large stone fireplace.

"What are you doing there, Ross?"

"Oh, hi, Monty. I'm trying to get this fireplace insert to work but I'm not having much luck."

"Just as well. It's too warm for a fire anyway."

"I know, but she wants it. Looks homey. You know how it is." He shrugged and went back to his labours.

"Ross, honey, Daddy said there's an easier way to do that. Don't you remember?"

"No, I don't."

She turned to me. "My father says Ross finds the hardest way to do everything. So, what would you like first, Monty?"

"A beer would be good."

"Oh, right, of course. But I meant would you like a tour of the upstairs, or the main floor? Everyone else is up in the master bedroom."

"Perhaps we shouldn't interrupt."

"No, no, I meant they're just having a look around. Oh, good. Renée. This is Monty Collins. He's one of Ross's partners at Stratton Sommers. This is my sister, Renée. Why don't you take Monty upstairs and show him around?"

Renée seized me by the elbow and led me towards the stairs. We met Rowan Stratton coming down. Stratton was no stranger to fine houses. "The woman whisked me upstairs before I even had a chance to greet young Trevelyan," he said. "And I haven't caught so much as a whiff of Scotch."

Rowan's wife, Sylvia, descended the stairs behind him, looking pained. She whispered in my ear: "I've never seen such an elaborate nursery. One is always astonished at the array of products available for babies these days. Do they have triplets?"

"No kids. One rumoured to be on the way."

The sister was waiting for me on the stairs, so I followed. She took me gently by the hand and drew me towards the sound of other voices. Surely it was only my imagination, but I thought for a moment she made a quick check of my ring finger, which had been bare ever since Maura and I had separated.

By the time a beer found its way into my hand I downed it with what must have looked like unseemly haste, and made my excuses to the host and hostess.

†

When I pulled up at my old house on Dresden Row I could see my daughter, Normie, staring out at me from the living room window. Her real name is Norma, after the heroine of the opera by that name, but don't ever call her that; she answers only to Normie. My son, Tommy Douglas, is more than content with his name. My wife decided to call our son after the leader of the first socialist government elected in North America. I was a fan of Douglas too. He was a great wit and, because of him and his introduction of medicare, I didn't have to pay whopping medical bills for the birth of my children. Tom joined my daughter at the window, and I waved. The grey wooden house had two storeys and an attic with Scottish dormers. Every time I saw the place I felt a pang of regret that I no longer lived there. The kids came out, with their mother at their heels. All three piled into the car for the Rankins concert. I raised a questioning eyebrow, and my wife just smiled. When we arrived at the Metro Centre I handed the kids their tickets, and they bolted ahead.

"And how is it that you are at my side this evening?" I asked her.

"Easy."

Right. She knew that any excursion with our son and daughter would not be shared with another woman, if there was another woman in my life, which my wife always believed there was. So I would have offered the fourth ticket, if there was a fourth ticket, to a friend. First guess would be Brennan Burke.

"Burke just rolled over for you and gave up his ticket?"

"I know every line of every song the Rankins ever did. Brennan Burke doesn't. I promised him another evening of entertainment in return."

"Oh? And what kind of entertainment would that be?"

"There's no need for such an insinuating tone of voice. My usual brand of entertainment, involving me prancing around simpering and naked in a pair of shag-me shoes, is just not on for him, is it? Given that he's a celibate priest."

"How come that brand of entertainment was never on for me?"

"I guess that's because you're not one of the sailors in port with the NATO fleet. So, as I was saying, I'll just have to think up something else for Father Burke. Like dinner at home with the kids. Or lunch at home with the kids. Or a movie and popcorn at home with the —"

"All right, I get it."

The opening band was warmly received, the Rankins were great, and Maura was directing the occasional comment into my ear as if we had never been apart. At intermission I asked what everybody wanted, and I headed out to the canteen to stand in line.

Old Monty wasn't doing too badly at all. Maura couldn't possibly know how I treasured these rare nights when we went out as a family. Well, maybe it was time I laid it on the line. Gave it another try. If we made an effort to get over the mistakes we had both made, the recriminations and resentment we had each generated in the other, and if we were both willing to start all over . . . I would make the first move. Apologizing for things I had done, forgiving her for things she had done. Maybe as early as tonight.

"Monty! How are you doing, babe?" No! Not this, not now. I turned to the voice and found myself grabbed by the belt and pulled towards —

"Bev. Hi."

Bev drew me closer and said: "I've missed you, Monty. In more ways than I can say here in a public place. But I'm willing to ditch the lump I'm with if you'd like to spend intermission out back with your pants around your knees. And that's just for —"

"I hate to be the one to break this to you. Whoever you are." My wife had appeared with appalling timing. She went on: "But the last time Collins stood outside with his pants down, it was thirty below zero, he was too drunk to know the difference and, well, he's just not the man he used to be. Now, if you'll excuse me, I'll escort the poor thing back to his seat."

Bev was a woman I had spent a few raucous nights with, usually following a night of blues with my band, Functus. Due to my stupidity,

Maura had walked in on us one day in my living room. That day, I thought things couldn't get any worse.

Bev released her grip on my belt and melted back into the crowd, leaving me to fall into the abyss and keep falling for all eternity. I had simply ceased to exist, as far as my wife was concerned. She did not speak to me or look in my direction for the rest of the night. Tom and Normie were intent on the show and didn't seem to notice. They gabbed all the way home, covering the frigid silence in the front seat. They got out in a noisy cacophony of "thanks" and "see you soon." MacNeil slipped away without a sound.

†

I was still brooding over my latest marital fiasco when I pulled up outside the Halifax County Correctional Centre on Saturday morning. Yvette had a coy smile on her face when I sat down to speak to her in one of the lawyer–client meeting rooms. "I'll do something for you if you do something for me, Monty."

"I don't bargain with my clients, Eve-ette."

"Why-vette."

"Why-vette. If I came all the way out here, I'm going to do your bail hearing, so there's no need for bargaining. We'll have the hearing on Monday, and you'll be out. Now, should I even ask what you were offering to do for me, or should we move on to discuss your bail application?"

"You don't even want to hear what I got to say?"

"Go ahead." I hoped it would not take long, so I could get home.

"I know somethin' nobody else knows."

Yeah, whether the mayor likes to be the lamb or Little Bo Beep when he —

"I know somebody who was there when that murder happened."

"What murder?"

"At the Fore-And-Aft."

Not a muscle in my body moved. I stared at her.

"You know, when that guy got shot."

"Two guys were shot."

"The Leaman guy."

Leaman? It was Graham Scott who got shot: he took two bullets to the head. Leaman put a bullet in his own brain — I would not have described that as getting shot. "That was a murder and suicide," I said. Did she know I was involved in the case? I doubted it. Ross Trevelyan's was the only name that had been mentioned in the media, as far as I knew.

"Yeah, right." Yvette snickered. "The *suicide*."

"That's the way the medical examiner saw it."

"That's 'cause the medical examiner wasn't down on his knees in the parking lot doing some young dude when Leaman got iced."

Oh, Christ. What was she saying? She sat back, triumphant, arms folded against her scrawny chest. I took a deep breath.

"Tell me."

She made a "maybe I will, maybe I won't" gesture, but I sat tight. It wasn't long in coming.

"That bitch Wanda is gonna be sorry she fucked with me at my trial. She thinks nobody knows she was there. But she didn't count on me doin' my duty as a good citizen, just like she done on the witness stand. Wanda was with this guy —"

"Who was the guy?"

"Beats me. Anyway she was doin' him around the back of the bar. They just finished when they heard voices and then a gunshot. The guy she was with zipped up his pants and took off. She vamoosed in the other direction. She didn't want to see nuthin'. And didn't want nobody seein' her. She was on probation for a whole lot of charges, and she was breachin' her probation just bein' out at that time of night. Let alone bein' high. Eckcetera, eckcetera."

"Let me get this straight. What exactly did she hear?"

"Guys hollerin' and a gunshot."

"A shot or shots?"

"A shot, I think she said."

There was one bullet in Leaman, two in Scott. Did this mean Leaman was shot first and Scott appeared some time later? Or did Wanda hear the first round fired at Scott? If so, what accounted for the gap between the shots?

"And you said guys were shouting?"

"Yeah."

"What were they saying?"

"I don't fucking know. I wasn't there."

"What did Wanda say?"

"Just that they were hollerin' and then blam! End of conversation."

"What time was this?"

"Late. Three, four in the morning." She fixed me with a slightly wall-eyed gaze. "So I figure the killer don't know there was a witness. Witness Wanda. And she sure as hell ain't talkin'. And there's the john, too. Whoever he was."

"How do you know this?"

"She was bombed one night and started blubbering to me about it. Scared the killer knew she was there and would come and get her. Guess she got lucky. 'Cause she's still walkin' around. Let's hope for her sake her luck don't run out."